Wendy Perriam

read History Honours at Oxfor~~d~~ ~~...~~ ~~adver~~
tising and a succession of more unbeat jobs, ranging
from the bizarre to the banal, she now writes full time.

Her novels, which include *Absinthe for Elevenses*, *Born of
Woman*, *Sin City*, *Devils, for a Change*, *Fifty-Minute Hour*,
Bird Inside and *Michael, Michael*, have been acclaimed
for their exuberant style, their provocative mix of the
sacred and the profane, and their extraordinary power
to disturb, amuse and shock.

She has just completed her twelfth novel and is currently
working on some new short stories.

WENDY PERRIAM

Breaking and Entering

Flamingo

An Imprint of HarperCollins*Publishers*

Flamingo
An Imprint of HarperCollins*Publishers*
77–85 Fulham Palace Road,
Hammersmith, London W6 8JB

Published by Flamingo 1995
9 8 7 6 5 4 3 2 1

First published in Great Britain by
HarperCollins*Publishers* 1994

Wendy Perriam asserts the moral right to
be identified as the author of this work

Author photograph by Ed Barber

ISBN 0 00 654671 4

Set in Bembo

Printed in Great Britain by
HarperCollinsManufacturing Glasgow

FOR RUTH AND ROGER HOLDSWORTH
dear and generous friends
and incomparable researchers!

The Angels keep their ancient places,—
Turn but a stone, and start a wing!
'Tis ye, 'tis your estrangèd faces,
That miss the many-splendoured thing.

FRANCIS THOMPSON

To be religious is to know that the facts of the world are not the end of the matter.

WITTGENSTEIN

1

'NO, NO, NO, no, no, no, *no*!'

Daniel was wrenched from sleep, eyes opening to darkness, the taste of fear and curry in his mouth. A last wild 'No!' rumbled from the bedclothes. He raised his head, peered at the alarm clock, its illuminated figures precisely sharp in the soupy gloom of the bedroom. Five past bloody three.

'Stop, Tom, stop! You're hurting. That's not a hedgehog-brush.'

He turned over to the humped shape lying beside him, stroked his fingers slowly down its back. It stirred, but didn't wake.

'Tom, you mustn't do that. It's not the hedgehog-brush.'

His wife talked in her sleep, mostly gibberish. If a nudge didn't stop her, he usually replied. It seemed more polite, companionable. He opened his mouth to answer, but no words came out – nothing but a rasping croak. 'Damn!' he mouthed, instinctively massaging his neck. Last night's sore throat was now full-blown laryngitis.

Slowly, he sat up. His wife's right breast had escaped her low-cut nightdress, a pale, enticing glimmer in the dark. He touched one finger against it, trying not to imagine Tom pawing at the other breast – or something lower down. The fellow was growing clearer in his mind: a hulk still in his thirties, with a head of hair so luxuriantly thick he had to brush it with a hedgehog. His hand fumbled through his own hair, stopping at the thinner patch on top. It was only fractionally thinner, nowhere near balding yet. Penny hadn't said anything, probably hadn't noticed, though it had been that way for months – part of being forty, he supposed. He had hated his last birthday. He had woken with a hangover, and Penny had bought him a sweater in an unflattering shade of purple, a colour he distrusted.

I

'Lamb,' she said. 'Lamb custard.'

Lamb chops, he corrected voicelessly. He could write a thesis on his wife's nocturnal ramblings. 'The hole in the German maid'; 'the price of frogs'; 'red Persil'. Hidden meanings, mumbo-jumbo surrealism. The names were always male: Tom tonight, Mark last week, and a chap called Stewart (Stuart?) had kept cropping up last year. He let his hand close against the breast, insisting on his rights. Jealousy was tiring, and in this case, pretty pointless.

He squinted at the clock again, hoping he'd misread it. Three AM was waking-nightmare time. He had written a poem once called 'Three O'Clock'; scribbled it with a pencil-stub at this same unnatural hour – though no one shared his bed then. He could still remember parts of it, the second verse more or less in full:

> *It is always . . . (something, something)*
> *The few short hours oblivion and bliss*
> *and then awake like this,*
> *as furious midnight*
> *mauls me in its claws*
> *and hell has gaping jaws,*
> *and all the wrath*
> *the world has ever wrought,*
> *from banished Adam*
> *to baffled astronaut,*
> *is concentrated*
> *in this single howling hour,*
> *this holocaust of thought.*

He grimaced at the scansion, the sheer pretentiousness. Good job he'd stopped writing – or at least only innocuous reports now on Third World educational matters. He lay back beside his wife; his soft, inert, still rambling wife. Penelope the faithful, refusing any suitor but her Ulysses. Except she had always been a Penny, despite his objection to the shortening.

If only sleep were infectious, so that he could catch her languid germ; even wake as she did, indulgently and slowly with long, luxurious yawns, instead of erupting into instant fretful consciousness; all the problems fastening on him like a brood of starving

2

leeches. Probably better to get up and make some tea, find something for his throat.

He stumbled to the bathroom, blinking as the light snapped on – a harsh fluorescent glare. The mirror wasn't kind. His skin looked sallow; dark rings beneath his eyes, a dirty rash of stubble on his chin. He inspected his hair again. No different from last night, though follicles must shrivel every day, decaying with one's brain cells. There was so much one could lose: teeth, hair, voice, erections, love. He searched the bathroom cupboard for some pastilles, sorting through his daughter's stuff, feeling oddly touched by her box of heart-shaped soaps, the garish turquoise bubble bath which could only dry her skin.

He drifted into her room, sat down on the empty bed, ran a regretful hand across the flat, unrumpled duvet. She had been away four days now. Had he lost his voice in sympathy with her? Or she lost hers as a rebuke to him? He tried to say her name aloud, irrationally angry when it came out as a grunt. If he thought in terms of punishment, then . . . No, stick to practicalities. It was tea he needed, not pastilles, something to soothe his larynx. He tried to swallow, gagged on broken glass, tiny jagged shards blocking his oesophagus.

He crept down to the kitchen, which still smelt of last night's curry. It seemed alien, unwelcoming, a room which didn't know him. Things looked so different in the middle of the night – the dark panes reflecting nothing; an ordinary cup grotesque. He switched on the portable television, which they kept next to the microwave, so that Penny could watch 'Breakfast News' while he skimmed through the papers. Two forbidding-looking females were conversing on a sofa, conversing with no words. He adjusted the volume, wishing he could bring his own voice back by the mere flick of a switch.

'But surely that's the point, Ruth. I mean, Nietzsche was quite right about the death of God.'

He turned God off, sat waiting for the kettle to whistle out its boil – or had that too lost its voice? Perhaps the non-existent deity had sent a plague on all of them: kettles, daughters, stepfathers.

He took a tea-bag from the container labelled 'SUGAR'. It had worried him at first, the way Penny broke the rules: stored used stamps in the tea-caddy, kept the sugar in its packet. But he was more accustomed now to his wife's chaotic clutter: old letters in the spoon-drawer, piles of ironing on the chairs. He sniffed the milk – tolerably fresh – seized the kettle as it began to pant and splutter, unplugged it in mid-whistle. He dunked the tea-bag, watched the brown stain slowly ripple out, then pale and tremble as he shocked it with cold milk. He shut his eyes and sipped. Still difficult to swallow. It hurt his ear as well. But if he took the day off, there'd be endless complications. He had an important morning meeting with the UN Evaluation Team, followed by an equally important lunch with Juliet. Silent meeting, whispered lunch.

He climbed up on a chair and rummaged for his cigarettes, which he'd put deliberately out of reach on the highest, least accessible shelf. He'd stopped smoking just last week, the day Pippa had departed for her grandma's; made a pact with Whoever might control things: give me back my daughter – and her voice – and I'll give up my Camels. He lit one from the gas, struggled to inhale, relaxing as the pain gave way to an exquisite surge of relief. Starved of nicotine for four whole days, he'd become increasingly uptight. Penny had bought him chewing-gum and some obnoxious herbal cigarettes he had consigned straight to the bin. And he could hardly chew gum at work, not whilst earnestly discussing the desperate lack of funds for teacher-training in Botswana.

He rubbed the misted windowpane, peered out at the garden, which was only void and shadows. He still felt claustrophobic; the house tightening like a noose around his neck. He must get out, get air. He groped his way back upstairs, stripped off his pyjamas and put on a shirt and jeans. He knew Penny wouldn't wake, but he scribbled her a note, in case: 'Walking Rover. He was busting for a pee.' It was a silly joke between them: the phantom dog (like phantom Tom) which needed its night exercise. He called it to heel as he set off down the silent street. He had never had a dog – he found them too exuberant. Penny was his dog: affectionate and loyal, with her wiry hair which needed constant grooming, her deep expressive eyes, the amazing way she trusted – trusted life, and him.

The night was close, oppressive; yesterday's humidity still hanging in the air. It was only the first week of June, yet London had been sweltering in a heatwave. He stood at the front gate, looking back at the house, then up and down the street. Thirty-three Elveley Road was home, though he often needed to remind himself. Some languages possessed no word for home, and he could understand that omission. Wasn't it an arrogance to assume you belonged anywhere?

He lit a second cigarette, then switched his gaze to the sky. The curdled mass of swarthy clouds seemed to be breathing very fast; as overwrought as he was. He couldn't see a moon, but a few stars pricked the darkness. He tried some calculations in his head: this galaxy was only one of some one hundred thousand millions, and each galaxy contained a further hundred thousand million stars, which added up to . . . bewilderment. And, in looking at the stars, he was gazing into the distant past – a distinctly unsettling thought. He exhaled a curl of smoke, wondering what was going on at base. Were the stars which seemed so quiescent to him in fact burning out, collapsing?

He cursed under his breath. He, too, was collapsing, or at least his normal life was. It was no better out of doors: the leeches clamped in place still, and sucking furiously. Yet this was friendly territory: the local shops where people knew his name, where he bought his cigarettes, or popped in for a takeaway. How odd that in a universe of Black Holes and Final Crunches people should still bother with pizzas or kebabs, set up businesses and restaurants, offer 10p off detergent, or four cans of beans for the price of three. If only there were a superstore where he could purchase a new self – an honest, virtuous Daniel who didn't smoke or cheat on his wife; a Daniel with the sort of hair which was faithful unto death.

He trudged on past the greengrocer's, picking up a nectarine discarded in the gutter. Last time he'd seen Juliet, they'd had nectarines for lunch – a picnic in Soho Square, with two tramps sprawled beyond them, and a fret of pigeons squabbling at their feet. He shut his eyes, could see the teethmarks shining in her fruit, juice dripping on her hands – slender hands with varnished nails, not stubby paint-stained fingers like his wife's. He looked down at his own hand, surprised to find the nectarine was mouldy, a huge purple bruise blemishing its flesh. Juliet's flesh was always strangely cool. Even when the temperature was soaring in the eighties, she never seemed to sweat. He felt embarrassed sometimes by his own hot body, sticking to her thighs.

If he walked on to the phone-box, he could leave a message for her: 'I love you, Juliet.' Except that wasn't wise, and it was possibly untrue. If only his mistress and his daughter wouldn't keep on tangling in his mind, each fighting for more space. Pippa wasn't strictly his daughter, but that seemed to make no difference. He had always called her his, avoiding the term 'step' with all its evil connotations. Stepfathers rarely featured in the fairy tales, only wicked stepmothers, but he'd been wicked in his way. It was partly his fault that she never saw her real father, or so her grandma claimed. He hurled the rotten fruit away, then ground his cigarette beneath his heel. So much was his fault.

Start again, he told himself, concentrate on simple things: the solid pavement, divided into squares; the plucky lamp-posts making light of darkness; his own agile, dogged shadow. He longed to speak to someone, if only to prove he still existed; was more than just a shadow. But there was not a soul around – no homeless tramps, no drunken party-goers lurching home. This particular part of Wandsworth was genteel: Victorian houses, rather cramped, admittedly, but adorned with tasteful hanging baskets and self-important burglar alarms; bay trees in rustic wooden tubs flanking the front steps. Maybe he should knock at one and beg to be let in, sleep beside a different wife, soothe a different child. *Was* Pippa still a child? 'It's her age,' their GP said, everybody said. He sympathized. Thirteen and forty had certain things in common.

He was almost at the phone-box. He passed it, then looped back, stood dithering at the door. He needn't say 'I love you'. He could simply make a joke, pretend to be her alarm-call. He pushed the heavy door, recoiling from the smell of pee. The receiver smelt as well, of someone else's sweat; sat clammy in his hand. He dug out a cache of coins, inserted 20p. Juliet's recorded voice sounded imperious and shrill. '. . . Please speak clearly after the bleep.' Boss-pot, he grinned fondly. And what about the mumblers, those who swallowed their words? Would she deign to ring them back, or respond only to the clear-speakers? The bleep sang out three times. He opened his mouth to say 'I love you'.

6

Far from speaking clearly, he had no voice at all. He had totally forgotten, despite the pain in his throat. He coughed into the mouthpiece. Perhaps she'd recognize his cough, realize he was ill. Unlikely. He'd *have* to go to work, to get someone else to phone her and explain the laryngitis. You could hardly ask your wife to ring your mistress. He kicked out at the glass, glad he was wearing canvas shoes which didn't protect his feet. He needed pain, deserved it. He stared at his blurred reflection in the glass, wondering for the umpteenth time what Juliet had seen in him, why she had asked him to that concert. Penny called him dishy, but it was not a word he used. How could you be sure whether you were even passable, let alone appealing, when you were always looking from the inside out?

He stepped into the street again, glancing up as a plane droned overhead. It astonished him that people could actually sleep, hurtling through the stratosphere at four hundred miles an hour, when he couldn't keep his own eyes shut in a securely grounded bed. He checked his watch: ten to four. It would be light in just an hour. June was merciful in that respect, at least. He crossed the road to Gascoigne-Pees and began to read the details of the properties. Estate agents were merciful as well, transforming faults into advantages. Small was 'bijou'; dilapidated 'quaint'. Perhaps he should employ one, to put a more favourable gloss on his own personal deficiencies – faithless revamped as 'sensuous'; forty as 'in his prime'. He started composing their advertisement for insertion in *The Times*: 'Viewing highly recommended for this older-style but still attractive property, beautifully maintained, but requiring modernization and refurbishing. Many interesting features to suit discerning buyer.' Or maybe something snappier: 'Handsome semi-detached man of charm and character . . .'

He wandered two doors on and stopped outside a jeweller's, its glass protected by a latticework of steel. He peered in through the grid, glimpsed a display of wedding rings, each gold band nestling on a tiny blue silk cushion. He began counting in his head again; days, this time, not galaxies. Christ Almighty! It was their wedding anniversary tomorrow – no, today. A shrink would doubtless say he had forgotten it deliberately, but whatever the psychological complexities, it still left him in a sweat. He hadn't bought a present or a card, hadn't ordered flowers. Penny would wake before the shops were open, expect breakfast in bed, with a gift-wrapped package on the tray. He had produced it every year so far, so he could hardly stop at the seventh. Seven was a sacred number, which had always had a marvellous press: seven pillars of wisdom, seven wonders of the world, seven virtues, seventh heaven. On the minus side, however, there were the seven deadly sins. Not to mention the seven-year itch; himself the living proof of it.

He clenched his fist against the glass, tempted to smash through it, filch a pair of earrings or a bracelet. But then he'd spend the day behind bars. It would be imprisonment in any case. He couldn't lunch with Juliet on his wedding anniversary. Thank God for his laryngitis, the perfect foolproof excuse. Though how the hell was he going to let her know, or cancel the reservation at La Barca?

'BUY HER AN ETERNITY RING', a cardboard placard urged. 'DIAMONDS ARE FOREVER', proclaimed another. Important to stress eternity when four in ten marriages broke down, and (according to the statistics) in another twenty years almost every married couple would end up in the divorce courts. Of course, if the jewellers were shrewd businessmen, they could cash in on the trend and design a special range of trinkets for the divorce market – pendants inscribed with slogans such as 'It was great while it lasted', or 'Thanks for the memory – goodbye'. But the pendants in the window seemed unashamedly old-fashioned. They either bore a simple name – Sharon, Michelle, Mum – or gushed with schmaltzy sentiment. 'I love you more each day', a chunky locket confided to him in elaborate Gothic script, and there were several variations on the theme. 'I'll never stop loving you', 'I'll love you more tomorrow than today'. That last one sounded strange: ambiguous, to say the least. Did people really wear such things, take them seriously? Perhaps he ought to buy one for himself, string it round his neck to make its magic work.

He knew which one he'd choose: that eighteen-carat love-heart divided into two; the interlocking edges exactly matching up when you slotted them together. Both halves were engraved: 'Tony' on the left, 'Diana' on the right. 'ENGRAVING FREE' enticed a small card underneath it. Bargains even here. Cut-price love, 10p off fidelity. The only problem was, he needed *three* halves – Daniel, Penny, Juliet.

He shrugged and turned away, heading back for home. He doubted any jeweller could divide one heart three ways.

2

'HAPPY ANNIVERSARY!' croaked Daniel. He had regained a shred of voice now, coaxed back by tea and gargling.

'You're worse,' said Penny. 'Much.'

'No,' he struggled. 'Better.'

She reached up to take the tray from him, her right breast still floating free. 'You're the one who needs breakfast in bed.'

'I've had mine, in the kitchen.' The wretched voice kept cracking, but at least it was holding out.

'What did you have?'

'A quart of tea, with honey, and two fags.'

'Oh, no! You've given up. I mean, you promised, darling, faithfully.'

He winced to hear that word again. 'I know.'

'Oh, Daniel . . .'

'Oh, Penny . . .'

She patted the space beside her; rumpled floral sheets which needed washing. 'Well, get in anyway. I don't fancy breakfast on my own, not on our anniversary. I bought you a new lighter, by the way.'

'Great.'

'It's not great. It's crazy. I bought it a whole month ago, before your Big Decision.' She made the phrase half-jokey, half-sarcastic. •

'Well, you can probably take it back, tell the shop you . . .'

'Wouldn't you like to see it first?'

'Yes, 'course.' He should have warned her after the first occasion not to buy him lighters, but instead he had feigned such gratitude, she kept repeating the performance. It would be unkind to tell her now that the best lighters were the cheapest: matches, Bics, the gas flame on the cooker.

'I'll fetch it in a sec. I wrapped it up and everything, but then you really threw me, giving up like that.'

He unlaced his shoes and got into bed beside her, still in his shirt and jeans. 'So aren't you glad I've weakened, then?'

'No.' She kissed him, seriously. His wife never skimped on kisses, always gave full measure, always took her time.

'You'll catch my germs,' he growled, at last.

'I like your germs. Though I'm afraid they won't at the office. You'd better not go in today, or you'll spread that bug around.'

'I must. I've got a meeting. It'll cause too much aggravation if I miss it.'

'You said that *last* time you were ill, and look what happened – in the end you had to take a whole fortnight off. It's much more sensible to stay at home for a day or two. If you insist on battling on like a martyr, you'll only go down with something worse.'

He leaned over to the tray and passed her the glass of grapefruit juice. 'Aren't you going to eat your breakfast? Your boiled egg's getting cold.'

'I like them cold. And don't change the subject. You look feverish to me.'

'I'm not. I'm fine. I haven't even . . .'

'It's selfish, Daniel, honestly, making everyone else ill, just because you're a workaholic and too stubborn to see sense.'

He lay back against the pillows in a posture of defeat. It was bad enough being deceitful and weak-willed, without adding selfish martyred stubbornness to his catalogue of vices. 'Okay, you win,' he conceded. 'I'll languish on my sick-bed all day, and won't even *think* of work.' Except he'd have to think of Juliet: how on earth he could get in touch with her if he didn't leave his bed?

'Good boy!' said Penny, stroking his hair from his forehead.

She had left her hand against his brow, as if rewarding him for compliance. It felt soothing and arousing both at once. He slid his own hand down towards her breast, savouring its warmth, its weight. 'Penny . . .'

'Mm?'

'I love you.' He prayed God it was true still.

'Love you too.'

'I'll love you more tomorrow than today.'

11

'What?' She pushed him off, took a sip of juice. 'Why more tomorrow? What's happening tomorrow?'

'Nothing. I'll just love you more each day.'

'You're taking the mick.'

'I'm not. And here's your present. D'you want it now, or after your cold egg?'

'Now!' Her full attention was already on the package, squeezing it and shaking it, sniffing at the paper like an eager dog at a fox-hole. He had found some gift-wrap in a drawer (the sheet she'd bought for him, most likely: his lighter and her earrings decked out alike in purple stripes).

She ripped the paper off. Penny never untied knots or unpeeled sticky-tape. It was one of the crazy reasons why he loved her – if he only knew what love was.

She was opening the padded box, exclaiming at its contents, stroking the plush velvet of the lining; her voice high-pitched with excitement. 'Oh, Daniel, they're gorgeous!'

Her whole plump and freckled face expressed unabashed delight; the flax-blue eyes crinkling at the corners, the fair brows lifted and alert, the wide mouth open, displaying gappy teeth. Her skin was fragile-pale beneath the freckles, in contrast to the shock of hair above – shock in every sense: carrot-coloured wire-wool hair, which made people turn their heads. In the early days, he had been embarrassed by the attention it aroused – the way total strangers would stare at him as well, as if examining his credentials as chaperone to such a mop. It would never lie flat, he knew that, and it was impossible to imagine it ever going grey. His wife would reach her hundredth birthday with brittle bones and dicky heart, but hair still that outrageous red.

'In fact, they're almost too good to wear. I'd be scared to death of losing them. They must have cost a bomb.'

They had. More than he had ever spent in any jeweller's shop before; more than he could reasonably afford.

'Are they real stones?'

'Yes. Pearls and amethysts. They're late Victorian.'

She unhooked them from their velvet throne, handling them with reverence, almost awe. 'Wherever did you find them?'

He laughed, a forced and false laugh. 'My secret. Aren't you going to try them on?'

She fumbled at her ear-lobe to locate the tiny hole. He turned away, couldn't bear to watch. It seemed barbaric, piercing ears, like those tribesmen in the bush with bones bored through their noses, sticking out two inches either side.

She leapt from bed to dressing-table, all but toppling the tray; stood close up to the mirror, her full attention first on one ear, then the other.

'Well?' he asked, voice hoarse.

'They're fabulous! The best present you've ever bought me in my life.' She started strutting around the room, tossing her head to make the earrings swing, touching them, admiring them. The transparent nightdress revealed her pubic hair – a tamer red than her head-hair, but still flaming through the washy flesh-pink nylon. He grabbed her almost roughly, steered her back towards the bed, pushing aside the breakfast tray, the torn and crumpled gift-wrap. Guilt twinged again as he noticed the red blotch on her arm, five-fingered from his grip. Her skin bruised terribly easily. The merest touch could mark it. He unbuttoned his shirt, began tugging at his belt.

'Daniel, no, you mustn't! You can't possibly feel well enough to . . .'

He kissed her silent, peeled off her nightie, then pressed his bare chest against her warm and naked flesh. 'You can help out with some first aid,' he whispered. 'Loving ministrations and the laying on of hands.'

She let him overrule her; used her hands obediently: slipping off his shirt and jeans and drawing him towards her on the bed. Her sleep-lapped body smelt of sweat and talc, a smell of rancid honeysuckle he found peculiarly exciting. His mouth moved slowly down towards her thighs. He kissed their flabby plump-ness, though pain was lasering through his throat in vicious spiky jabs. He was angry with his throat, angry with a lot of things, not least his own damned guilt. How could he desire her yet deceive her? It was perverse to crave two women at once, even love them both – though love was such a baffling word, he could only use it now with a sense of dislocation. Penny was right: he shouldn't be making love at all, not with his sore throat and tangled life. Yet, despite the pain and guilt and sheer confusion (or maybe even because of them), he seemed to have spurred

13

himself into a state of wild excitement. And Penny was responding, already whimpering underneath him; her head thrown back, her face screwed up in a provocative grimace. Watching that transformation never failed to fascinate him – the way his bouncy, scatty wife could turn into a vamp: her eyes closing languorously while her mouth drooled slowly open; tongue thrust out, begging to be kissed.

He kissed it, grazed her lips, tasting the sweet sharpness of the grapefruit juice. He was too impatient to continue the caress; burned to be inside her, working off his anger in an act of passionate love. He was aware at some deep level of the paradox involved, but he justified himself because his fury so aroused her. She had started moving with him, picking up his rhythm; her mouth and eyes clamped shut in concentration. She kept crying out, 'I love it, I adore it!' over and over and over, in a sort of breathless snorting gasp; her nails hurting where they dug into his back. The rhythm was so urgent now, the earrings had joined in – shaking, dangling, sparkling in the sunlight – Juliet's earrings, chosen with such scrupulous care for her birthday this weekend.

In an instant he deflated, faltered to a stop. He willed himself to stiffen; did his frantic best to keep his mind off Juliet. He conjured up a different girl – the nymphet in the newsagent's who wore her skirt up round her crotch, and had sultry bee-stung lips. She was no help whatsoever, so he started flicking desperately through the newspapers she sold: page-three bimbos with pneumatic tits but tightly virgin cunts. Even they were useless. He had lost all contact and was actually sliding out; Penny's panting cries dwindling away to nothing.

'I'm sorry,' he muttered, as much to Juliet as to Penny. Pearls were her birthstone, and he had scoured a dozen high-class jewellers' to find something which would suit her perfect taste.

Penny didn't seem to hear. She looked restless and frustrated, as she struggled vainly to coax him back to life. 'Listen,' she whispered, using her fingers as a splint. 'Let's try it with me kneeling and you standing behind me at the foot of the bed. That worked last time, didn't it?'

Yes, the last time I was limp, he thought, shuddering at a memory he had no wish to recall. It had happened a couple of weeks ago, and was also due to Juliet. He had spent the evening in her flat; returned exhausted to a voracious wife.

'I . . . I don't think it's going to work again.'

'Just relax, darling. It will! You'll recover in a moment, if you don't get in such a state.'

'I'm not in a state.'

'You *are*!'

He was becoming tenser still. Penny's efforts to revive him only made things worse. Her eagerness was mortifying; underlined his sense of abject failure. Shamefacedly, he did as she suggested, standing at the end of the bed while she knelt on all fours. He tried to ignore the inner voice warning him it wouldn't work, and braced himself against her, shutting his eyes against the sun.

'That's *it*, darling, that's great!'

Her words misfired, as intrusive as the sun, producing not the desired effect, but its ignominious opposite. The miraculous moment's contact vanished with her praises, and he was reduced again to nothing.

'Look, it's no good, Penny. The longer we go on, the worse it's going to get.' His voice was giving out as well – impotent twice over.

She slipped down from the bed, put an arm around his shoulders. 'Don't worry, darling. It's only because you're ill. We're crazy to be doing it at all.'

He was grateful that she didn't say 'I told you so'. Indeed, she sounded so forgiving and affectionate, he felt even more ashamed. He reached out for his dressing-gown, wrapped it tightly round himself to hide his dangling nakedness, then sagged down on the stool. The sudden silence in the room seemed like a rebuke, but he was terrified of breaking it. In his present flustered state, he might forget his usual caution and blurt out Juliet's name, in an effort to explain the situation. Juliet was definitely to blame. The failures had only happened in the seven weeks since he'd met her – seven weeks of ecstasy and guilt. If only there weren't the parallels: seven weeks, seven years; Pippa's thirteenth birthday the same day as Juliet's forty-first. Weird to have a mistress a decade older than one's wife.

'Are you all right?' asked Penny. Her nipples were erect still – another silent reproof.

'Mm.'

'I only hope it hasn't made you worse. I wouldn't be surprised if you've got a temperature now.'

He shook his head, but she was already moving towards the door. 'I'll go and get the thermometer.'

'Okay.' He dragged himself to his feet, made a half-hearted attempt to straighten out the dishevelled bed, then slumped against the pillows. He was fairly sure his temperature was normal, but he welcomed the chance of a few moments on his own. His skull was splitting from the cacophony inside it – booming condemnations of his betrayal and deceit; cavils from the office about his absence from the meeting today; quieter but still niggling voices, reminding him that he had no present now for Juliet. He couldn't palm her off with the sort of cheap and cheerful jewellery Penny might accept. His mistress was a thoroughbred. 'The type you should have married,' his mother's voice cut in, adding to the babel in his head. His mother had never known his wife. After retiring from her lifetime's work in Africa, she had gone to live in Paris (where he had joined her four years later, still a confirmed bachelor, accepting a job in an educational research unit only a mile or so from her flat). But he knew instinctively that she wouldn't have approved. Penny was too scatterbrained, and not serious enough; more concerned with painting murals on the local shopping-centre walls, or rescuing injured hedgehogs from the bypass, than with improving the lot of suffering humanity.

But would he have married Juliet, he wondered, if he weren't already committed? True, they had a lot in common – worked in the same field, attended the same lectures, enjoyed the same books and plays and music. The first time they'd been out together, she'd had tickets for the Wigmore Hall – Schubert *Lieder*, sung by Wolfgang Holzmair. Penny had never heard of him; preferred Stephen Sondheim to Schubert. And Juliet was something of a wine-buff, even nosed out certain vintages at auctions, whereas Penny had no preferences beyond dryish white and not-too-heavy red.

His eye fell on the wedding photo which shared the dressing-table with Penny's creams and clobber – jars, tubes, bottles, potions, clustering like wedding guests around the bride and groom. If he had his way, he'd consign it to the attic. Most wedding photos seemed a shade absurd, especially seven years on, and theirs was no exception. *He* looked stiff and snooty, while Penny had her hat askew and was turning slightly away from him, as if she'd just spotted someone better and was about to dash off in pursuit. He was appalled to think he had ever dressed so stuffily, bought such boring ties. His flamboyant wife had changed him – but then he had changed her too. If the process carried on, he'd be wearing beads and caftan, and she'd be neat and organized, with a Filofax and filing system.

'Sorry I was so long.' Penny barged in again, still without her clothes. It always disconcerted him the way she wandered around stark naked, apparently blithely unconcerned that people could see her from the street.

'I couldn't find the dratted thing,' she said, brandishing the thermometer. 'I turned the bathroom cupboard inside out, then I remembered I'd left it in Pippa's room.' Her face altered quite perceptibly when she mentioned her daughter's name, becoming older and subdued. 'I suppose I'd better phone again and see how she is today. God! It's awful with you both ill.'

'I'm not ill.' He no longer believed his own denial. His head was throbbing, and every time he swallowed, the pain stabbed to his ear.

'Well, you don't look all that marvellous – sort of grey around the gills. And you must be boiling in that dressing-gown. Here, put these on instead.' She passed him his pyjamas, helped him do them up. 'You'd better stay in bed all day and keep the curtains drawn. I suspect we're in for another dose of flaming June. It's pretty close already, and it's only half past eight.'

Daniel subsided on the bed again, cupping his hand round his throat, as if to comfort it or shield it. The early morning sunlight was glaringly intense, a sign that there would be no let-up in the hot spell. It seemed perverse to be ill in the summer: almost a form of ingratitude to find oneself near-mute when everybody else was waxing lyrical over the bounty of the weather. Or was it really bounty? The office was stifling in a heatwave, and though he couldn't see the front garden from the bed, he was well aware how parched it was – the soil cracking in the flower-beds; the scrap of lawn a faded thirsty-brown.

His mouth felt dry at the thought. He leaned down for Penny's cup of tea, still untouched on the breakfast tray, though tepid now and scummy.

'No!' she ordered, slipping the thermometer deftly under his tongue. He had watched her do the same with Pippa; the child irritable, rebellious, trying to push her mother's hand away. *He* submitted gratefully. It would save him having to speak for a further couple of minutes – longer if she went downstairs. She was putting on her gingham robe, a tatty thing with half its buttons missing. (Juliet wore an immaculate silk kimono.)

She grabbed a slice of toast, the butter glazed and congealing; munched it while she hunted for her slippers. The earrings didn't suit her. They were the wrong colour for her hair, and too long for her chubby, childish face. There had been a booklet at the jeweller's, listing the symbolism of all the different stones. Pearls, it said, were the emblem of fertility, but also of virginity and innocence, which meant they were wrong for Juliet as well – wrong on all three counts.

Penny took a second piece of toast, her fingers slicked with grease. 'Shall I save you some?' she asked.

He shook his head and pointed to his windpipe, indicating that it hurt to eat.

'Well, I'll make you some lemon and honey, nice and hot.'

He grunted his thanks through the thermometer as she departed on her errand. Would she be going out later, he wondered, to Sainsbury's, or to work, or to do her stint for Pippa, so he could phone and cancel lunch? He couldn't leave it too long. Juliet's schedule was always hectically busy, and she hated interruptions once she was closeted in a meeting. Actually, it would be best to catch her before she left for work. Dare he try now? It should be safe enough, with Penny in the kitchen, clattering cups and plates. He removed the thermometer and picked up the phone, glancing nervously around, as if she possessed some magic eye which could see him from downstairs. He dialled Juliet's number slowly; mentally undressing her as he pressed each digit, running his hand across her sinuous haunch; his fingers exploring the inside of her thigh.

He slammed the receiver down again before he reached her bush. Christ! He was incorrigible. His faithful wife was waiting on him, making him hot drinks, yet here he was slavering over his mistress once again. Juliet was dynamite – in all senses – and could blow his marriage to bits. Cancelling the odd lunch with her was neither here nor there – he had to cancel her entirely. That was the harsh truth he had been refusing to confront ever since Pippa had stopped speaking. Finally, reluctantly, he had given up smoking, but he knew deep down that it was only a half-measure, a pathetic sort of substitute. Something more was being asked of him, if he wanted his daughter well again – something which would really cost. Depriving himself of nicotine was nowhere near as painful as ending a relationship with a bewitching woman like Juliet. Not in his wildest fantasies had he imagined such a woman actually approaching him and making the first overtures. And even after he'd admitted he was married and therefore sadly unavailable, she had swept his scruples aside, told him with an intriguing smile that theirs could be a marriage of minds.

He heard Penny coming up the stairs and hastily put the thermometer back in his mouth, closing his eyes and pretending to be dozing.

'Okay?' she asked, easing it from under his tongue. 'You should be good and done now.' She held it up to the light and peered at it, mystified.

'You're way below normal. You didn't take it out, did you?'

He made a noncommittal sound, though Penny wasn't listening; more concerned with his low temperature. 'Maybe low's as bad as high. D'you want me to phone Steadman?'

'Christ, no!' He'd seen quite enough of their GP in the last few anxious weeks. He and Penny had traipsed round to the surgery to discuss their 'problem child' – twice with her, once without. The doctor had been sympathetic, but could he really understand what it was like to live with a child who refused to speak beyond the briefest monosyllables? Her silence put a damper on the house; made his and Penny's conversation seem strained and almost tactless; roused in him a fury at his inability to help. Sometimes he would let fly at her, then immediately regret it because her silence wasn't petulant or sullen, but seemed to spring from an inner wretchedness which left him wretched in his turn.

'Penny . . .'

'What?'

'You know Pippa's lost her watch?'

'Oh no!'

He nodded, listened despondently to her explosion of annoyance. True Pippa seemed to keep losing things just recently, but he didn't feel it was a matter of mere carelessness – rather that she no longer had much interest in material possessions, and was narrowing her world to a bleak and silent emptiness. He picked up the thermometer case, chewed its plastic end: better that than another cigarette. The list of problems was becoming just too onerous – his daughter first and foremost, but also the constant inner turmoil over Juliet, and now another fiasco in bed.

Penny was still fretting about the watch, asking where Pippa had lost it and whether they could claim it on the insurance.

'Maybe,' he said briefly, then stroked a finger down her cheek. 'Let's not talk about Pippa.'

'You started it.'

'I know I did. I'm sorry. I suppose she's on my mind a lot. But I suggest we have one day's moratorium, for our anniversary.'

'Some anniversary!'

'What d'you mean?'

'Well, you at death's door and her so bloody miserable.'

He winced. Penny rarely swore. She was probably still resentful, though she had shown no trace of it. It wasn't her nature to sulk. 'Look, I'll take you out to lunch,' he offered, suddenly realizing how lucky he was to have a good-natured cheerful wife. He wanted to repay her; make some restitution for his own infernal grouchiness; lavish her with gifts.

'But you can't go out to lunch darling, if you're not well enough to go to work.'

'That's the sort of priggish thing *I'm* supposed to say.'

'I know it is. Well, can you?'

His 'yes' was so emphatic, it came out like a growl. 'To hell with "shoulds" and "buts"!' he rasped. 'I'm going to be a hedonist for once. I'll loll around all morning and rest this scratchy voice, then we'll amble down to Freddie's and celebrate in style – and just pray we don't meet anyone who'll tell on us!'

She sat down on his feet, her forlorn expression changing to delight. 'No, a French restaurant, not Freddie's. It's got to be a French restaurant.'

'Yes, of course, a French one!'

They laughed. His laugh was real this time. She was crushing his feet, but who cared? He felt close to her again, truly thankful he'd married her. To hell with his mother. Concerts didn't matter, and wine snobs could be boring, not to mention ruinous.

'We'll order P . . . P . . . Pernod.'

'And P . . . P . . . *Pineau de Charentes*.'

'With pâté for our first course.'

'And *palette de porc* to follow.'

'And profiteroles for pudding.'

'And Perrier-Jouet, to wash the whole lot down.'

'*All* the Ps.'

'Yes, all the Ps.'

'Oh, Daniel, darling wonder-man, I'll never forget that lunch.'

'Nor will I.' He drew her down towards him, kissed every missing button on her robe.

3

'BONJOUR, MONSIEUR HUGHSON.'

'*Bonjour, Pierre.*'

'*Comme d'habitude, m'sieur?*'

'*Oui, s'il vous plaît.*' Daniel slumped back in his chair, unfolded his *Figaro*, tried to concentrate on the headlines. There'd been an earthquake in Armenia (three hundred feared dead), yet his own concern was focused on his mother. She had phoned him late last evening and he had rushed to her apartment in a taxi, driven her on to the hospital, waited there two hours. It proved to be a false alarm – they hadn't taken her in – but he had stayed with her all night, watching by her bedside while she dozed. Then she'd confounded him by sitting up in bed at dawn and declaring she was starving.

He had lost all appetite for his own breakfast, though Pierre had just set down his customary *café complet*: the silver jugs of coffee and hot milk, the two warm croissants embracing one another in their small snug wicker bed, the unsalted butter and apricot preserve. He poured a cup of coffee, strong, and lit a cigarette. Should he be sitting with his mother now, instead of on his way to work? She had rarely been ill before, never been a trouble to him – nor he to her, for that matter. He had hardly known her, actually, until she'd reached old age. In fact, he sometimes suspected he had only taken this Paris job to have his Mummy near – a luxury, a rarity. And it was a venture they'd approve of – his mother *and* his father. His father had died five years ago, but his approval was essential still. Both his parents had always opposed mere money-making, or selfishly advancing one's career. Service to others was the all-important criterion, commitment to a cause. He had never let them down: had slogged away at school (five thousand miles away from them), stayed on at Cambridge to do his PhD, then worked in educational research, even choosing a field which was related to their own, if not perhaps as worthy and demanding.

He broke off a knob of croissant, crumbled it to flakes. Yes, he had made the right decision. His mother wouldn't want him skiving off work, or paying more attention to some minor malfunction of her lungs than to the major problem of the illiterates in Africa. Anyway, he could call in at lunchtime, spend all evening with her – would welcome the chance, in fact. They were still strangers to each other, still far too stiff and formal; needed time for the relationship to thaw. After all, they were making up for twenty years of absence.

'*Tout va bien, m'sieur?*' The waiter hovered, glancing at his untouched plate with a just perceptible air of reproof.

Daniel picked up his knife, spread butter slowly, thinly, on his croissant; regretting, as usual, the lack of English marmalade – the classic bitter chunky stuff, glistening with rough peel. Still, he liked the Parisian habit of breakfasting in cafés, instead of in one's flat. It made one feel less alone, more connected to the human race – or at least half a dozen members of it. He did a speedy head-count. Yes, seven fellow humans were sitting at the tables, mostly men on their own. A few he knew by sight, after eight months of daily breakfasts, though people rarely spoke to each other beyond a polite '*Bonjour*'. He had first chosen this particular café not only because it was a stone's throw from his office, but because it was quiet and well-behaved. No music, no invasive chatter, no roar of rush-hour traffic, no hordes of tourists or squabbling raucous kids.

No kids? He looked up from his paper to see a small obstreperous girl suddenly dart in from the street, a child in fuchsia-pink shorts and emerald top, with an aureole of flaming orange hair – colours far too crude for this hour of the morning.

'Pippa, come back here this minute!'

He was jolted by the voice – an English voice, female, young, and desperate, all but fraying into tears. He turned round to see a second shock of hair, exactly the same shade, but wilder and more wiry; the girl beneath it pale and drawn (though pretty); her eyes inflamed, as if she had been crying for some time.

The child began to cry as well, an ugly wailing sound, and he watched in horror as a stream of urine trickled down her legs and pooled on the brown lino.

'Pippa, stop it! *Don't!* Not here.' The girl seized her daughter's hand, tried to drag her back towards the door. The child pulled away, wriggling like a frantic fish determined to escape the hook. She dashed straight past her mother and veered sharply to the right, cannoning into a waiter who was loaded down with a tray of plates and cups. Daniel closed his eyes, heard the crash of breaking crockery; bewildered shrieks and sobs; a volley of remonstrations from the waiter. Then, above all the commotion, the indignant female voice rose in equal fury just behind him.

'I don't understand a single word you're saying, so you might as well save your bloody breath!'

The waiter shouted back in French, and the two continued lambasting one another in mutual incomprehension, while the child howled its eyes out on the floor.

'It was your fault anyway,' the girl insisted angrily, breaking off a moment to pick up her daughter and start wiping her wet legs and face. 'You weren't even looking where you were going.'

Daniel took a deep drag on his Gauloise. Did they *have* to be English, for heaven's sake, so that he was more or less duty bound to help? If they were Japanese or Polish, he could simply sit there as a mystified spectator. But, as it was, he found himself following every word – which was more than could be said for Jules, who was dim-witted, defiantly Anglophobe, and on trial in his first job. Two other waiters had joined him, and the cacophony was becoming quite intolerable; even some of the customers chipping in on one side or the other, in a mêlée of excited Franglais.

He rose to his feet, explained the situation to the waiters in a tone of what he hoped was quiet authority, translating what the girl said, but minus the hysteria. The child had a bladder infection, which meant she had to relieve herself every half an hour or so, and hadn't much control. They'd been looking for a public toilet, but had got themselves completely lost, and were strangers to Paris anyway, with not a word of French. And probably very little cash, he added to himself, noting the girl's cheap handbag and scuffed shoes, down at heel. She was wearing a creased denim skirt which stopped well short of her knees, and a tee-shirt blazoned 'MUSCLE'. There was flesh beneath the tee-shirt, not

24

muscle: plump curvaceous breasts. The outline of the nipples was showing through the fabric, two alluring little studs. He forced his eyes away, fumbled for his wallet, turning his back so she wouldn't see the fifty-franc note he was passing surreptitiously to Jules. That should cover the damage, restore the shattered peace. He also settled his own bill, aware that it was getting late and he should be in the office.

But he had reckoned without the females, who were now closing in, preventing him from leaving, the child staring with huge whipped-dog eyes, while her mother trapped him in a lasso of grateful words.

'Gosh! Thanks. You're an angel. You deserve a medal, honestly. You're the first decent human being we've met since we arrived here. Say thank you to the man, Pip.' She pushed her daughter towards him, but the child shrank away, abashed. 'It's really not her fault,' the girl continued confidingly, moving even nearer herself, so that he could smell her hair, which she must have washed with some strawberry-scented shampoo. How odd, he thought distractedly, that carrot-coloured hair should smell of strawberries. He tried to put a word in, explain he couldn't hang about, but the lasso was pulling tighter.

'She gets cystitis quite a lot, you see, and when she has to go, she has to go. I've had it myself, so I understand the problem. Beyond a certain point you can't hang on. There's this stuff you can get from the chemist – I've forgotten what they call it, and maybe they don't sell it over here. Hey, I couldn't possibly ask you one more favour, could I? I mean, even if I found a chemist I wouldn't know what to ask for, but if you came with us and acted as interpreter . . . Oh, I realize it's a cheek, when I don't even know your name. Mine's Penny, by the way. And this is Pippa.'

'Yes, I gathered that.' Did he have to sound so insufferably scathing? He was embarrassed, for God's sake – all that talk of bladders, 'hanging on' – and he'd never been much good with children, never knew what the hell to say to them.

'We shouldn't be here at all,' the girl was now admitting. 'In Paris, I mean. Pippa's missing nursery school, and we had quite a job persuading them to take her in the first place. But I . . . I'm looking for my husband.'

'Looking for . . . ?'

She nodded. The blue eyes filled with tears. He watched her struggle to control them, blinking hard, biting her top lip. He was struggling himself between sympathy and selfishness, pity and annoyance. So it wasn't merely a matter of tracking down some nameless English medicine, but of locating a lost spouse.

'Look, let's get out of here.' People were still staring, not just the child, whose grey-green eyes had never left his face, but several of the customers and waiters, who were obviously intrigued as to what might happen next between *les Anglais*.

He mumbled a farewell to Pierre, doubling back to leave a tip beside his untouched breakfast. He heard a step behind him, smelt a whiff of strawberry.

'Do you mind if I have those?'

'Have what?' he asked, perplexed.

'The croissants. Our hotel doesn't lay on breakfast – or any meals at all. It hasn't got a restaurant, and the bathroom's a disgrace. In fact, it's the crummiest hotel I've ever seen.'

He wasn't listening, just watching in incredulity as she sat down on his chair, split the croissants open, larded them with butter and then jam, wrapped them in a paper napkin, and transferred them to her bag. Next, she up-ended the sugar bowl, tipped out all the little cubes and crammed them in on top.

'Pippa likes them, and they help to fill her up. We're trying to manage on just one meal a day. You see . . .' She glanced over her shoulder, to make sure the child was safely out of earshot. 'My husband's left, walked out on us, so money's very tight.'

Daniel sank down on the other chair, lit a cigarette. He had just stubbed out the last one, but this was clearly a crisis. He offered the packet to Penny, but she shook her head, pulled her chair towards his, speaking in an undertone so Pippa couldn't hear.

'I know it sounds stupid, but I'd no idea Paris would be so big. I thought I'd find Phil fairly easily – *and* his rotten woman. Well, I didn't think, to tell the truth, I just went raving mad. I mean, I never knew there *was* another woman, not until three days ago, and then it all came out. An Arab girl, of all things, with a cosy little pied-à-terre in Paris, and a husband and three children of her own – though *they* live somewhere else. Why does it have to be so complicated?'

26

Yes, why? Daniel echoed silently, picking up his knife and drawing neat straight lines with it, up and down the tablecloth. If she took him for a marriage guidance counsellor, then she had chosen the wrong man. He'd had no experience of marriage, had always felt it safer to avoid solemn ensnaring vows. And anyway, this was hardly the right setting for a therapeutic session. He'd be back here in the morning, and shuddered at the thought of a cross-examination from the inquisitive Pierre. What had happened with *les jeunes rousses*? Were they acquaintances of his? Had they come to look for him?

No, he mouthed to no one. They're strangers, total strangers. Yet how could he say that when the girl seemed so damned trusting, and even the child was sidling up to his chair, as if she too was relying on him to be a sort of instant Santa Claus?

He put the knife down, kept his own voice low. 'Have you no idea at all where your husband might be staying?' He ought to take some interest, show he was concerned. 'I mean, this pied-à-terre you mentioned – did he give you any clue as to where it was?'

'Not the faintest, no.' Penny retrieved one of the sugar-lumps and crunched it in her teeth. 'Look!' she said to Pippa, who was now pulling at her sleeve. 'There's something shiny on the floor, under that big table by the window. Go and see what it is.' The child scurried off obediently, and Penny used the respite to blurt out another rush of words, keeping one eye on her daughter all the time.

'He just said Paris – and Khadisha. What a name! I ask you. I mean, it would be bad enough if she was common-or-garden English, and working in his firm or something, but at least he wouldn't have rushed off across the Channel. Well, I expect he flew – it's quicker – but it also costs a bomb. *We* came the cheapest way – overnight coach and ferry – which is probably why Pippa caught cystitis. The ferry was delayed, you see, and she was sitting on the deck for half the night – I mean, right on the wet wood. All the seats were taken, and every time we went inside, she started to feel sick.'

He swivelled on his chair to appraise the child again. She had just crawled from under the table with a gold foil wrapper in her hand, which she rushed to show her mother. Despite her pleasure in the find, she did look ill, and fragile – sparrow-boned, with pale translucent skin, eyes too big for her face. 'Well, we'd better get her medicine,' he said. Best to deal with the matter in hand and leave Phil to the divorce lawyers. It was too difficult, in any case, trying to talk frankly without her overhearing, and it was beginning to make him edgy, concerned on her behalf.

He pushed his chair back, checked his watch. There was a pharmacy three streets away, which opened early and was on his route to work. Penny didn't seem to realize he was pressed for time. She was still rattling on (though now about the Channel ferries), and had both legs hooked around her chair-leg, as if she was entrenched there for the morning. He cleared his throat, suggested that they move, then tried to steer his protégées in the direction of the door. Never, in eight months, had he roused such lively interest; all eyes in the café following his progress. He couldn't even make a hasty exit, since Pippa held them up by peering under every table in search of further treasure.

Once they reached the street, Penny stopped to take her shoe off, balancing on the other foot while she examined it with a frown. 'Damn! The heel's coming loose. I only hope it lasts.'

Daniel glanced from mother to daughter. Neither of them seemed adequately shod. The child wore flimsy sneakers, and one of her white laces was half-undone and trailing. 'Won't she trip?' he asked.

Penny knelt to do the lace up, her skirt straining over her thighs. She wasn't overweight, but her clothes seemed skimpy on her, as if they had shrunk in a hot wash. She gave her daughter an affectionate kiss on the nose, then pretended to bite the nose off. The child didn't smile, just pulled miserably at her clothes.

'Mummy, my shorts is wet.'

'Yes, I know, pet, it must feel really horrid. We'll go back and change them in a sec, but we're going to get your medicine first.'

'I don't want any medicine.'

'Yes, you do. It's only like a drink – a glass of fizzy stuff.'

Daniel tried to slow his usual rapid stride. They were walking three abreast, though the child kept lagging behind, still tugging at her shorts. Thank God the sun was shining – it would help to dry her clothes, prevent her going down with something worse. She seemed worryingly vulnerable, too small and frail for such a hectic city. They had reached the crossroads and a van was rattling past; someone else's hooter blaring out a warning; buses blowing hot breath on their legs. They waited for the pedestrian signal to change from red to green.

He raised his voice above the din: 'There's a pharmacy just past the next lights. We'll be there in a few minutes.'

'Thanks,' she said, smiling. It was the first time he had seen her smile, and it brightened her whole face. He suddenly longed to be Canute, to step out and halt the traffic for her, push back the pounding waves of motor-bikes and cars.

They crossed at last, and continued down the street through the tide of stone-faced office-workers; the delivery-men with their trays of downy peaches, crates of knobbly cauliflowers. Shop-keepers were cranking back their shutters, arranging wares in windows; an overweight *pâtissier* washing down his narrow strip of pavement with steaming soapy water. A waiter in a long white apron ambled from his restaurant to pin up the day's menu, nodding to the customers who were breakfasting outside. It was the last week of September, but warm and almost summery; the striped umbrellas still in place on the wrought-iron pavement tables; a few men in their shirtsleeves sipping *café crème*. Daniel glanced down at his own grey suit and sober dark-toned tie. They must look a strange trio: one formal, two in deshabille. The carrot-heads were already attracting notice, people's eyes lingering, the odd surreptitious smile. Did they imagine he belonged with them, his wife and little daughter? He quickened his pace, as if to distance himself from both the thought and the dependants. Penny trotted to keep up, but the child was dragging at her hand, and finally shuffled to a stop.

'I'm tired, Mummy. My legs hurt.'

'We're almost there now, darling. It's just a skip and a jump. Okay, okay, I'll carry you, but you're not to cry, you promise? Here, have a sugar-lump.' She unwrapped one from its paper, popped it in the open mouth, then picked up the fretful child.

Daniel tensed, uncertain of the drill. Should he offer to carry the kid himself? The idea wasn't exactly appealing. Suppose she made a scene, saw him as a bogeyman? Though she didn't seem too happy as it was, drumming her feet against Penny's rucked-up skirt, dribbling sugar-spittle on her neck. But he couldn't turn up at the office with his shirt stained (or worse, smelling of stale pee) when he was due to give his quarterly report to the agency which was funding his research. He knew from past experience that its director, Jean-Claude Benoît, was often highly critical, and had to be handled with diplomacy. Yet it seemed uncharitable and churlish to let Penny soldier on, encumbered as she was not only with the squirming child, but with a bulky carrier-bag.

'Shall I . . . er . . . ?' He opened his arms, indicating his willingness to do what was required. Duty again. His mother would have carried the entire unlettered Tonga tribe in her staunchly zealous arms – probably had done in her youth.

'I'm not sure that she'll go to you,' Penny murmured dubiously. 'And I'm afraid she's rather damp.'

'That's okay,' he lied. He was more concerned about frightening the child. Absurd to fear rejection from a mite of three or four, but it somehow seemed important that Pippa didn't shrink from him. That unnerving grey-green gaze was fixed on him again as he transferred her to his arms. He was doing it all wrong. He could feel the child's discomfort – her unease and apprehension added to his own. He tried to settle her less awkwardly, even dared a word or two. 'Is that all right? You comfy?'

Pippa nodded timidly. She hadn't made a sound, hadn't screamed or struggled. Wasn't that a sort of triumph in itself? He walked on slowly, with a crazy sense of achievement. He was carrying a child, the first time in all his thirty-one years; experiencing the same relief as if an unknown and risky-looking dog had licked his hand and wagged its tail, instead of biting him. There were so many things he had never done, or deliberately avoided. He had no siblings or even cousins, so had never been confronted with nephews, nieces, other people's offspring. His friends and colleagues were mostly fellow bachelors, and the married ones with children rarely invited him to their homes.

He let go of his frown, only now aware of how he had been tensing all his muscles. He must get things in proportion. It was hardly a big deal to carry one small child for five minutes of his lifetime. All the same, he tried to do it well, move as carefully as possible, without jolting her unduly. The poor kid had lost her father, needed no more shaking up. Damn, he thought, I'm already getting involved; must extricate myself. I'll see them to the pharmacy, sort them out some medicine, then put them in a taxi straight back to their hotel.

The second set of lights were green. He strode across, feeling a new confidence as Pippa put both arms around his neck. He was irrationally elated by the gesture, its combination of trust and tenderness. Or was she simply clinging on for dear life? He realized that he'd unconsciously speeded up again; had never really noticed till this morning how rushed his normal pace was, as if he were permanently late for something – perhaps for life itself. In fact he was a punctual man: obsessively punctual, so some of his friends complained.

'See that big green cross?' he said to Pippa, pointing out the pharmacy, which was now only two doors down. 'That's where we get your medicine.'

'Come on then, Miss Lazybones,' said Penny, reaching up to take the child, who was staring at the neon cross in anxious fascination, as if she expected some green medicine to come bubbling out of it. 'You can stand on your own two feet now and give this poor man a break. What *is* your name?' she asked him. 'You haven't told us yet.'

He was surprised and disconcerted. Could he really have been so secretive? Yet, even now, he was reluctant to reply. Names were very intimate, invited other questions, and he might never get away. His report this morning was vital, the culmination of three months' solid slog.

'Daniel,' he said tersely.

'Oh, nice! I used to know a Dan once, and he was a really super guy.'

'I'm Daniel, not Dan.' The remark was a slap in the face, he realized, when he saw her hurt expression. He backtracked hastily. 'It's just that I don't like shortenings – not for any name.'

'Well, you won't approve of ours, then: Penny, Pippa, Phil.'

'All Ps.'

'All Ps,' she repeated. 'And pee-pees! Are you okay, Pippa, or d'you need to go again?'

The child shook her head, her face pressed close against the window of the pharmacy, absorbed by a display inside: two cardboard children rocking back and forth as they sucked the juice from gigantic oranges.

Penny gave him another grateful smile. 'Perhaps you've worked a miracle,' she joked. 'And we won't even need the medicine!'

'Best get it anyway.' Daniel ushered them inside, relieved to see there were only two customers waiting to be served. With any luck, he would be sitting in his office by 9.30. The fellow here was good, didn't waste your time. He'd used him before, when he'd gone down with some strange bug, and had followed the French habit of consulting a *pharmacien*, rather than a doctor.

He waited his turn, then explained the child's symptoms, breaking off now and then to ask Penny for more details, or translate the questions for her. It was all a bit of a rigmarole – switching from one language to the other, repeating the instructions and advice – but it was finally sorted out, and the medicine entrusted to him. He felt a nudge from Penny and looked round to see her handing him a battered scarlet purse.

'The money's double Dutch to me, but just help yourself from here.'

'Don't worry, I'll take care of it.'

'No, really, that's not fair. You've already given up your time, so I can't possibly expect you to pay, on top of everything else.'

He laughed to hide his embarrassment, loathed discussing money. 'My good deed for the day.'

'But you've already done one good deed.'

'Well, my good deed for tomorrow, then.' He picked up a jar of vitamin C, the brand on display in the window, asked the man to take for that as well. If the kid was existing on sugar-lumps, then she could do with what they were advertising as a *tonique anti-infections*.

He passed the package to Penny, pocketed his change. 'I'm afraid I'll have to leave you – I'm late for work as it is. But I'll put you in a taxi, so you don't get lost again. What's the name of your hotel?'

Extraordinary how her face could change. There was panic in it now, not just disappointment, and he could see her mouth trembling; the eyes beginning to brim again. Oh God, he thought, don't cry.

'It's . . . it's called the . . . the Manchester,' she said, her voice dangerously unsteady. 'I can't think why, in Paris. But that's where Phil comes from – Manchester, I mean. I thought it was a good omen and that it might help to bring him back.'

'Well, let's hope it does,' he smiled. He must harden his heart, find an empty cab. His mother had always taught him to put the general good before the individual. His report concerned the fate of several thousand illiterates, not two feckless females.

'Taxi!' he shouted, flagging down a white Mercedes, and handing Penny a clutch of twenty-franc notes. The morning was proving expensive, and jobs like his didn't pay that well. Still, money was so relative, and these two were truly skint.

He asked the driver if he knew the Hotel Manchester, received a surly nod in reply. Pippa at least seemed thrilled by the prospect of a taxi–ride: she climbed in with alacrity, and started bouncing on the seat. Penny followed slowly, still trying to detain him. Did he work round here? How would she repay him?

'There's nothing to repay.'

'But . . .'

He blessed the discourteous driver, who was already pulling away, cutting off her words. He stood waving from the pavement, watching the cab manoeuvre through the traffic. Framed in the back window, two pale faces gazed at him, the larger one dabbing at her eyes.

Oh hell, he thought, she *is* crying. He fumbled for his cigarettes, lit one angrily, then turned on his heel and strode towards the office.

4

DANIEL CLOSED HIS OFFICE DOOR and walked briskly down the stairs. His report had been extremely well received. Even the pernickety Jean-Claude was clearly impressed, and had actually lingered afterwards to offer his personal congratulations on all the time and effort he'd put in. And his mother was much better: up and dressed, and working herself, or at least catching up on her post. All her work was voluntary now: beavering away for charities, sitting on innumerable committees. He'd phoned twice to see how she was, warning her not to overdo it, and saying he'd be round there in the lunch-hour. The weather was still glorious; the sun throwing golden swathes across the stair-carpet, burnishing the yellow leaves outside. He paused a moment to look out of the window, admire the row of chestnut trees at the far end of the square. He was lucky to have an office which overlooked a green oasis, in contrast to the rackety roads on two sides of the building. His mother was less fortunate. The only view from her poky flat was of other bricks and mortar. But she did have a minuscule balcony, which she had enlivened with some flowering plants and a primitive wooden sculpture she had brought back from Lusaka. Perhaps it would be warm enough to sit out there at lunchtime – pretend it was July, forget the sombre fact that the days were drawing in.

'Hey, Daniel, it's us again!'

Abruptly he swung round, returning from July to late September. There, in the foyer, not a dozen feet away from him, stood the two English carrot-heads. He stared in disbelief. How in God's name had they traced him to his office? Nervously he carried on downstairs, stopping three steps from the bottom, as if afraid to come too near.

'I've brought your change back,' Penny said, diving towards

him with a wad of grubby notes. 'You gave us far too much, and I shouldn't have taken it anyway, when you'd already been so decent.'

He ignored the money, confounded by a flash of cleavage. She had changed her clothes and was now wearing tight blue jeans and a low-cut top in a violent shade of cyclamen which quarrelled with her hair.

'I hope I'm not being a pain, but I felt I had to come and thank you. I mean, not many men would have taken all that trouble. Pippa! Blow, don't sniff.' She rummaged for a hankie, wiped her daughter's nose, then planted herself at the bottom of the stairs, effectively blocking his getaway.

'We watched you as the cab drove off,' she told him. 'But then you disappeared – turned the corner out of sight, and I felt so . . . well, just terrible. I suppose it suddenly dawned on me that the only person we knew in the whole of Paris had just vanished into thin air. So I shouted to the driver to turn round and catch you up. He didn't understand at first, and by the time he'd done a U-turn and crawled through all the traffic, I'd resigned myself to losing you again.' She paused for breath, sounded puffed and flustered, as if still dashing in pursuit of him.

'Then clever Pippa spotted you, running up the steps and through this door. I banged on the taxi window, but you didn't seem to hear, and though we scooted across the road and straight into this building, there was no sign of you at all. I knew you'd told us you were late, so I didn't like to ask if they could find you.' She inclined her head to indicate the receptionist, sitting in her cubbyhole further down the foyer. 'That lady there speaks almost perfect English, and when I said a tall good-looking Englishman called Daniel, with brown eyes and dark straight hair, she said oh yes, Daniel Hughson, and you'd just that minute gone into a meeting, which would probably last till lunchtime. We were back here on the dot of twelve – and didn't even get lost. Well, I bought a map this time, and made a special effort to notice all the places we were passing, and actually it's not that far, so Pippa had a sleep first, and she's already taken two lots of her medicine . . .'

'It was yuk,' the child put in, screwing up her face. She was sprawling on the floor beside her mother, a gap of naked flesh

35

around her midriff. She too wore different clothes: scarlet leggings with a blue and purple jersey. These two seemed to go in for colours as eccentric as their lives.

'Yuk maybe, but it did the trick. You're much better, aren't you, pet?'

'Good,' said Daniel lamely. He was still reeling from the flood of words and from the shock of seeing them again. He had assumed it was a one-off meeting, and had dutifully removed them from his mind, so as to devote his full attention to educational pro- grammes in Kakuma. But now he was confused – on his guard, self-conscious, yet experiencing a peculiar excitement. 'A tall good-looking Englishman,' she'd said. Had she really meant good-looking, and why should she notice his looks at all when she was so preoccupied with her husband?

He fought an urge to retreat back up the stairs. Her body was disturbingly close, and it was more or less impossible not to look down between her breasts when he was standing directly above her. The tiny buttons on the hot-pink top were straining at their fastenings, the top two undone, unnerving.

She ran an anxious hand through her hair, then slumped against the banisters. 'I know it sounds awfully sort of pushy, but I won- dered if you could spare us any time? I mean, if you're free for lunch, perhaps you'd let me buy you a sandwich. You see, I've made a list of things I need to say in French, and if you could possibly write them down for me, then all I'll have to do is pass the piece of paper across and point to the right one.'

He was taken aback, unused to women inviting him out and invariably disconcerted when he had to change his plans. He stalled and played for time. 'But . . . but how will you understand when people reply?'

'Oh, shit! I hadn't thought of that.'

And anyway I've got a prior engagement with my mother. Somehow he couldn't say it. She looked too crestfallen as it was.

'Well, all right,' he offered hesitantly. 'I suppose we could have lunch . . . I'll have to make a phone-call first, but I can do that from the restaurant.' He didn't want to leave them with the recep- tionist. If they'd arrived here on the dot of twelve, then they'd already been waiting an hour for him, and Penny had probably regaled Marie-Thérèse with the whole elaborate saga, Arab girl and all. He dismissed thoughts of errant husbands and turned his mind to lunch instead; running through the names of nearby restaurants and trying to come up with one where he wouldn't meet his colleagues and where the food would suit a four-year-old, yet still impress her mother. Though why the hell should he care about impressing her? Earlier that morning, on their way to the pharmacy, she had spotted a branch of McDonald's, and her spontaneous whoop of delight had revealed her as a Big Mac fan. No, he drew the line at burgers, eaten with their fingers out of a polystyrene coffin, amidst the smell of grease and onions. After the exertion of his meeting and the paean from Jean-Claude, he deserved to lunch in style. He'd had nothing for breakfast beyond a gulp or two of coffee, and it would be a snack meal this evening with his mother.

'Gosh, thanks,' the girl was saying. 'You are an absolute angel!' She suddenly lunged forward and gave him a brief impulsive hug. It threw him totally. Her private smells of breath and sweat were jangling at his senses, clashing with the whiff of strawberry hair; his whole body stirred by this contact with her own. She pulled away, rubbed her nose, made some odd remark to Pippa in a casual tone of voice. How the devil could she sound so cool? He glanced down at his suit, amazed that it looked no different. Those two startling seconds pressed against her breasts should have left some imprint, surely?

'And please do take this money,' she urged, brandishing the notes again.

His embarrassment was doubled now. He mumbled something fatuous, and managed to squeeze past her to the doorway, where he pretended to be checking on the weather. 'The . . . the sun's so bright, we ought to make the most of it. Let's get out of this dark hall and find somewhere to eat.'

They followed with no further prompting, Pippa gambolling down the chipped stone steps, then racing to the top again, so she could jump off the last two.

'It's left here,' he informed them as they turned into the street. Gradually he was recovering his composure; his flushed cheeks sallow-pale again, his voice less agitated. And he'd just had a brainwave. There was a Café Pénélope which had opened only recently in the square behind his office. The food was good, by

37

all accounts, and Penny would be tickled by the name, yet it was not the sort of place to attract either Georges or André – too offbeat, too lively.

He slowed for Pippa, who was collecting fallen leaves. 'There's a new restaurant round the corner which might be worth a try.'

'Oh, we don't want a full-scale meal,' said Penny. 'I'm afraid I can only run to a sandwich, and it's not fair for you to pay again.'

He saw her reaching for her purse. She had just put those wretched notes away, but any minute he would be refusing them a third time. 'No, please, that's quite okay,' he said, forestalling any argument by adding, 'You can always buy me a drink, if you insist. And then let's call it quits.'

'Can *I* have a drink?' asked Pippa, discarding her leaves and pulling at her mother's hand.

'Yes, 'course you can,' said Penny. 'I'm so rich you can have two!'

'Something fizzy?'

'Yes.'

Let's all have something fizzy, Daniel thought, as he turned the corner and Penny's arm brushed his. He couldn't explain it in the slightest, but instead of being irritated that his lunch-hour was disrupted, he was almost willing to celebrate the fact.

'Another P,' said Penny, lolling back in her chair and surveying the crowded café. Every table was full; the pink walls barely visible beneath posters, pictures, playbills; the steamed-up windows mobbed by climbing plants.

'What is?' Daniel asked.

'That blonde girl at the bar. I just heard the waiter call her Pascale. D'you think there's a real Penelope as well?'

'Bound to be – a fat Madame, oozing cream and garlic, who bosses all the staff about.'

'I want my drink,' wailed Pippa.

'Well, you'll have to wait, they're busy.' Penny watched the waiters charging to and fro; other frustrated customers trying to catch their eye with no success. 'What d'you fancy – orange?'

'No, Pepsi.'

'P for Pepsi!' Penny opened the menu, exclaiming at its length – a list of fifty-odd dishes scrawled by hand in purple ink. '*I* know!' she said suddenly, leaning forward and raising her voice above a snort from the espresso machine. 'Let's have all Ps. I mean, everything we eat and drink has got to start with a P, okay?'

'Why, Mummy?'

'Because today is P-Day, isn't it, Dan?'

Daniel nodded, hardly objecting to the shortening. Her previous Dan had been 'a really super guy', and yes, it *was* a P-day: peculiar, preposterous, and really rather puzzling. He couldn't understand why he was actually enjoying being in a restaurant where the service was deplorable, the noise level horrendous, and the menu looked both pricey and pretentious. Two more Ps, he noted wryly, scanning the wine list for a drink which fitted Penny's rule.

'Well, I'd better have a Pernod, I suppose.' He hated the stuff, especially before a meal. But the alternative was Perrier, and he needed something stronger than mere water. He was nowhere near relaxed yet; felt overdressed among this casual crowd, and aware that they were still attracting glances. There was no doubt about it: neither he, nor most of the people here, had ever seen hair quite so flagrant.

'I'm having *Pineau de Charentes*,' Penny said, pronouncing it all wrong. 'I don't know what it is, but it's a different P from yours and Pip's, and that's one of the rules. We've all got to have different Ps, right on through the menu.'

Daniel found to his surprise that he was willing to obey. He usually made the rules himself, at least on matters of food. 'Ps in French or Ps in English?' he asked. Whoever made them, rules always needed clarifying.

'Ps in French,' said Penny, 'since the menu's all in French. But you'll have to do the translating.'

'Well, we could all start with *potage*,' he suggested. 'But each have a different kind.'

'What's *potage*?'

'Soup. And as it happens there are three soups on today – fish soup, vegetable, and leek.'

'No, that's cheating,' Penny said. 'They're still all soup. I want pâté anyway, and Pip won't have a starter. She'll never manage three courses.'

'I will!'

'I'll give you some of my pâté, then.'

'What is it?' Pippa up-ended the pepper-pot, showering pepper over her hands.

'Sort of liver-sausage stuff.'

She made a face. 'I hate liver.'

'It's not liver. It's cold, not hot, and squidgy.'

'Can I have chips with it?'

'No, they don't begin with P.'

'Yes they do,' said Daniel. '*Pommes frites*. And you can have peas as well – *petits pois*. And do you like fish?'

Pippa shook her head, still nervous when he spoke to her.

'That's a pity. Because fish begins with P.'

'No it doesn't,' she corrected him. 'It begins with F.'

'Yes, F for fish. But P for *poisson*. When you want to order fish in France, you ask for p- p- poisson.' He stressed the initial Ps, remembering how he'd been taught himself, at his nursery school in Lusaka – well, hardly a real nursery school, just a group of other children's mothers, who'd had less to do than his.

'P- p- poisson,' Pippa repeated solemnly.

'That's right! You've got a really good French accent. Now say chips.'

'Chips.'

'No, in French. *P- p- pommes frites*.'

'*P- p- pommes frites*.'

Daniel lit a cigarette, reached out for the ashtray. The child was a natural, or at least a skilful mimic. What other talents might she have, he wondered, and would they ever reach fruition? It was like his Africans again: potential going to waste. 'You ought to get someone to teach her, Penny. She'd pick it up in no time.'

'Someone *is* teaching her,' Penny retorted with a grin. 'And perhaps you could teach me, while you're about it. It's so frustrating being in France and not understanding a word.'

'Right. Jump in at the deep end and have a go at ordering the drinks – *un Pepsi, un pastis, et un Pineau de Charentes, s'il vous plaît*.'

'Hold it! You're going far too fast! I'll never remember that lot.'

40

'*I* want to do it,' Pippa shouted. 'Let me, let me!'

'Okay.' He slowed his voice. '*Un P- P- Pepsi, s'il vous plaît.*'

Pippa's brow was creased in concentration, the pepper-pot forgotten, her whole attention focused on his lips. '*Un P- P- Pepsi, s'il vous plaît.*'

'Perfect. Now all we have to do is find a waiter.' He waved his arm, annoyed when no one noticed. He preferred the sort of place where his drink arrived without him even asking.

'*I'll* wave!' Pippa clambered up on her seat and started semaphoring wildly with both arms. She seemed to have lost her initial shyness, though she subsided pretty quickly when a swarthy man strode up to her and bowed in mock-servility.

'*Oui, mademoiselle?*' he drawled.

'*P- p- poisson,*' struggled Pippa.

Daniel and Penny laughed. 'No, that's fish,' said Daniel. He noticed how the child's face was as expressive as her mother's. She looked totally deflated, her triumph turned to shame. 'Don't worry,' he assured her. 'You were very clever to remember the word at all. Now start again, okay? *Un P- P- Pepsi, s'il vous plaît.*'

'*Un P- P- Pepsi, s'il vous plaît.*'

Penny sat fidgeting with her bracelets, cheap plastic bangles in shades of pink and mauve. 'They'll go mad at her nursery school if she keeps repeating all her Ps like that. They'll think she's started to stutter.'

Daniel didn't answer. He had stuttered himself as a child, though not until the age of seven, when he'd been sent away to boarding-school. He banished the dark memory, ordered his and Penny's drinks, then began rehearsing conversations in his head. He ought to be making an effort to entertain this girl, but was unsure where to start. It wasn't easy to embark on idle chit-chat, with the shadow of her husband's desertion looming over them both. And anyway he'd never had the gift of the gab, nor André's knack for polished opening gambits. He could ask about her life, perhaps, but questions might sound nosy – a form of inquisition – and they'd probably all lead back to Phil, and cause her more distress. He often felt uptight himself when people started closing in with their 'Where do you live's?' and 'What do you do's?'; usually felt his answers were inadequate. But why should he assume that Penny was like him, when she was patently a different type entirely: much more free and forthright, more inclined to open up. She might jump at the chance to talk about herself, especially now, when she had no other adult company.

'Er . . . do you work at all?' he enquired. Jobs were fairly safe, and she'd just mentioned Pippa's nursery school, so she might well work, with her daughter off her hands.

'Actually, that's rather a sore point. You see I've been doing really dreary things like dishing out the pizzas in a takeaway, and cleaning my sister's house for her, then feeling sort of restive and frustrated. I'm not qualified for anything much, so I suppose I shouldn't complain. But I can't help wishing I could find a job that's – you know – more inspiring. I've always wanted to go to art school, but Phil says it's too late.'

'Too late?' he echoed. She looked about eighteen, though with a child of four, that wasn't very likely.

'Most people go straight from school, so I suppose he's got a point. The maddening thing is, I was accepted myself when I was only sixteen and a half – offered a place on the foundation course at Wimbledon School of Art. I was over the moon about it. I'd spent all my spare time drawing, filling loads of sketchbooks to impress them at the interview, but . . .' She shrugged, slipped one bangle off her wrist and started twisting it round and round between her fingers. 'I'm afraid the interview was as far as it ever got. The course itself never happened – like a lot of other things. I mean, you probably won't believe this, but I've never been abroad before.'

He did find it hard to believe. Surely everyone went abroad these days, if only on package tours? He'd spent half his childhood traipsing from pillar to post, and still travelled for his job: long-haul trips to Kenya at least three times a year.

Penny removed a second bangle, laid one on top of the other on the table. 'My mother was widowed in her thirties – left with four small girls, but not much else. So we never really went away, except to stay with relatives, or odd trips to the seaside. Then I married very early, and Phil had this thing about the Norfolk Broads. He'd stayed there in his childhood, you see, so it had very happy memories for him, and he liked playing at being a ten-year-old again. He also bought a share in a boat, which tied us down, in a way, prevented us ever going anywhere new. I wonder if Khadisha likes boats,' she added, with an unconvincing laugh.

'*I* like boats,' said Pippa, grabbing the two bracelets and slipping them on her own wrist.

'Yes, I know you do, pet. Remember that day you fell into the river and ruined your new shoes?'

'I'm hungry,' the child said fractiously, dismissing boats and shoes.

Daniel opened the menu again, reminded of his duties. They hadn't even ordered yet and he'd been remiss about the translating. 'Well,' he said, flicking swiftly through the *entrées*. 'There seem to be a lot of Ps to choose from for the main course. *Poulet* – chicken. *Pot-au-feu* – that's a sort of casserole with beef and vegetables. *Porc, pigeons, pieds de cochon.*'

'What's that last one?' Penny asked.

'Pig's feet.'

'You can't eat feet,' said Pippa.

'You can,' said Daniel. 'People do in France.'

'With shoes and socks on?' Pippa asked, her eyes opening even wider.

'Well, I'm not sure about the shoes. *We* couldn't have them anyway, because they don't begin with P.'

'Pigs are my favourite animals.' Pippa had regained her confidence and was almost flirting with him now, head tipped to one side, pink tongue-tip poised between her lips.

'Well, in that case,' Daniel said, 'perhaps you shouldn't eat them.'

'I'm having chips, not pigs.'

'Yes, that's right – *pommes frites*. But you can have something else as well.'

'Ice-cream!' she yelled, eyeing the exotic-looking contents of a tall glass sundae dish, which had just been whisked past on a tray.

'I'm afraid that begins with G – *la glace*. But if you wouldn't mind a peach with it, and some delicious raspberry sauce, then you could have a *P- P- Pêche Melba.*'

'What's a P- P- . . . ?'

'Look, pipe down, you two,' Penny ordered, raising her eyes

43

to heaven in a pretence of irritation. 'Here come the drinks – at last!'

Daniel subsided, astonished at himself. He was talking to a child and actually enjoying it; teaching her, diverting her, had even made her laugh. And all without a drink. He sipped his Pernod, which tasted almost tolerable, consulted the wine list again. They'd be limited to P-wines: Pouilly Fuissé, Pomerol . . . No, wait a minute, he'd promised something fizzy – well, not exactly promised, but it would still be rather fun. He ran his finger down the list of sparkling wines, dismayed to see there wasn't a single one of them beginning with a P – only champagne, and that would break the bank. Perhaps the whole idea was over the top, and they should stick to fizzy water. After all, these girls had nothing to celebrate. Even apart from the crisis in her marriage, Penny's life seemed sad and rather constrained: the cloistered childhood, the talent unfulfilled. He presumed her widowed mother had insisted that she earn her living the minute she left school, rather than 'waste her time' on art. How different their two backgrounds were: five females in her household, and a dearth of education, whereas he'd been pitchforked into prep school with no women but the butch and brutish matron, and had still been knee-deep in his studies at the age of twenty-four.

Almost absent-mindedly he took a large swig of his drink, instantly recoiling at its kick. He had forgotten quite how power-ful Pernod was. It might be wiser to lay off the wine, with a busy afternoon ahead, or he'd be floundering through the rest of the day in an alcoholic haze.

He cursed himself for remembering work, aware now of the fact that they'd been sitting here a good twenty minutes and hadn't even got as far as ordering their food. He was normally back in the office by two – if he left at all. On busy days, lunch was just a coffee at his desk. Thank God he'd told his colleagues he was calling on his mother, having already filled them in on last night's little crisis. If he was still shovelling in peach Melba at half past three or four, they'd assume poor Madame Hughson had taken a turn for the worse.

Pippa looked up from her Pepsi which she was gulping through two straws. 'Where's Daddy?' she asked suddenly.

Despite the surrounding hubbub, the silence was disquieting.

Penny hadn't answered, but her face had changed again – defensive now and bleak.

'You said we were going to see him,' the child insisted, crumpling one of her straws.

'Yes, we . . . are. Quite soon.'

'Where is he, then?'

'I told you, darling, he's having a little holiday.'

'But why didn't we go with him?'

'He . . . he had to leave earlier than us. But we've come to Paris to find him.'

Daniel watched the child's expression – confusion and anxiety. The green eyes met his own again, appeared to be trying to make sense of him.

'Does *he* know where my Daddy is?' she whispered to her mother.

Penny chewed her lemon-slice, then sat studying her glass.

This second silence was longer. Images from the earthquake in Armenia started seeping slowly into it from some corner of his mind. He and Georges and André had been discussing the disaster before they left for lunch, but only now did its full impact really hit him – the demolished homes and devastated families. One of the child-victims had been photographed in close-up; a kid of roughly Pippa's age, sobbing for its parents.

He straightened the straw, replaced it in her glass. 'Have you ever had champagne, Pippa?'

She shook her head, subdued still.

'It's a fizzy wine which goes pop when you open it. P- P- POP! And it comes in a big bottle with gold stuff on the top. It's really a special drink for grown-ups, but I wondered if you'd like a tiny bit?'

She stared at him, unsure.

'Well, look, why don't I order some, so you can try a sip or two?'

'Does it begin with a P- P- P?'

'Well, one brand does – Perrier-Jouet, and that's half a P- P- P.' It was also worryingly expensive. Yet he had to lighten the mood, banish P for Papa, rebuild the shattered villages.

'Champagne costs a bomb!' Penny demurred. 'And I feel guilty as it is, with you coughing up for all this . . .'

'It's much cheaper over here,' he lied, registering the fact that not only had he misinformed her, he had also interrupted her – two violations of his parents' stringent code (*three*, if he included unwarranted extravagance). But he somehow wanted to spoil this pair, to change their diet of filched croissants to something P for princely; even change their lives – conjure up instant trips to exotic foreign capitals, cruises down the Nile, French lessons and art tutors, rich Daddies, faithful husbands . . .

He signalled to their waiter and ordered the champagne, then tried to get some decisions on the food. Pippa refused anything beyond chips and ice-cream, but Penny plumped for *pigeon aux petits pois*, which gave her three Ps on the trot. He upstaged her totally by choosing *petit pâté de Pézenas* and then the *plat du jour* (an extra P in itself) which happened to be *palette de porc* with *purée de pommes de terre* and *poireaux à la Picarde*. Then he wished he hadn't – he wanted *her* to win – began suggesting more P-vegetables to accompany her pigeon.

'I'll burst!' she protested, though eventually agreeing to both the *petites pommes persillées* and the *salade panachée*.

'You'll go p- p- pop!' said Pippa. 'Like the drink.'

'Yes, and here it is,' said Daniel, watching the waiter zigzag between the tables with their champagne held aloft.

Pippa observed the whole palaver with fascinated eyes: ice-bucket, white napkin, and finally the POP. She jumped back in surprise, gazing at the whoosh of bubbles exploding into her glass.

'Well, aren't you going to try it?' Daniel prompted, once all three glasses were filled.

The child took a cautious sip, and sneezed, flinching away distrustfully. 'It tickles my nose,' she complained.

'But do you like it?' Daniel pressed.

She dipped her finger in the glass and licked it, sat considering the taste. 'It's not as nice as Pepsi,' she concluded.

'Would you prefer another Pepsi, then, instead?'

'No, I want another P- P- POP.'

'Pippa!' Penny remonstrated. 'You'll bankrupt this nice man.'

'What's "bankrupt"?'

Daniel wondered how to explain the term, though he was more concerned with 'this nice man'. 'Nice' was rather a bland word, nothing like as flattering as 'good-looking', but she had said it

46

very warmly. She had also moved her hand towards his on the table: not touching – nowhere near – but still a gesture of affection and acknowledgement. He fumbled for his glass, perplexed to see a cigarette expiring in the ashtray: a long cylindrical tube of grey. He couldn't even remember lighting it. 'Why don't we drink a toast?' he said. 'A P-toast. How about "to Paris"?'

'No,' said Penny. 'To Phil. We've got to drink to finding him.'

Daniel put his glass down. He was damned if he'd drink to some heartless philanderer who could abandon his wife and daughter, waltz off without a backward glance and leave them penniless.

'You *eat* toast, you don't drink it.'

Pippa's interruption punctured his annoyance. Crazy to be angry with a man he'd never met. And, after all, he had only heard one side of the story. Phil might be sitting with his Arab girl, not a million miles from here, telling her how impossible his wife was.

He glanced across at Penny, trying to imagine her as a nagging shrew or cruel vindictive mother. She was chattering away to her daughter, giving a demonstration of the liquid sort of toast. 'You raise your glass like this,' she explained. 'And then you say "To Daniel", or "To Mummy", or "Good health", or . . .'

'Or "Happy birthday, Pippa",' he chimed in.

'But it's not my birthday,' she informed him. 'Not for ages and ages.'

'We could always pr- pr- pretend it is,' he joked, wishing they could all lay claim to birthdays, which might justify a long and boozy lunch. He had started his champagne already, without waiting for the toast, gulping it like water, hardly knowing why.

'But birthday doesn't begin with P.'

'No, you're right. It doesn't.'

'Pigs begin with P,' the child remarked authoritatively.

'Yes . . . So shall we drink a toast to pigs?'

She nodded, raised her glass.

'Or how about to polar bears, or porcupines, or porpoises?' Hell! He must be pissed already – P for pissed. Hadn't he just told himself that Pernod was a treacherous drink, especially when augmented by champagne, not to mention lack of food and sleep? He had been up all night with his mother, had found nothing in her store-cupboard beyond Complan and dried prunes, and had survived a tough morning on three small cups of coffee. He made a half-hearted attempt to stop the waiter refilling his glass; secretly relieved when his ineffectual hand-flapping was ignored or misinterpreted.

'You're cheating,' Penny objected. 'They're all English Ps.'

'Porcupines are French – *porcs-épics*. And maybe platypuses, I can't remember the word for them. And how about a praying mantis? I wonder what the hell they are in French.'

'I don't know what the hell they are in English!'

Daniel felt shocked. Surely Penny had heard of them? He'd been familiar with the word himself as long as he could remember. Admittedly they were as common in Africa as spiders were in England, so he'd had an unfair advantage. All the same, he couldn't help wondering what other areas of ignorance Penny might reveal, and had to hide his disapproval of her cheerful unconcern. He gripped the stem of his glass, suddenly seeing in his mind again that intimidating scene he had witnessed as a lad of barely seven: the female mantis blithely gobbling up the male, immediately after mating. It had probably contributed to his first misgivings about sex, his first vague unspoken fears of being swallowed.

He dismissed the gruesome image, resumed his jokey tone. 'They're big green insects – rather vicious chaps, I'm afraid, which feed on other insects, and sometimes gulp down their own young.'

Pippa was all eyes. 'Where do they live – in the zoo? Or can you keep them as pets?'

'Oh, yes. I've got a couple in my flat – very hot and bothered ones, with bubbles streaming out of their heads.' He was describing himself, he realized: a drunken preying mantis who was talking arrant nonsense and feeling quite okay about it.

'You're a fibber!' Pippa accused.

He nodded in agreement. A fibber and an absconder. He had suddenly decided not to return to work that afternoon. Dammit, they owed him a day off after all his hours of overtime. He'd make a second phone-call from the restaurant, tell them his mother couldn't be left alone (having just told *her* that a crisis had occurred at work). Yes, a fibber, he reflected with an uneasy twinge of conscience. And a souse, he added, downing more champagne to dilute his sense of guilt.

Penny clinked her glass to his. 'Well, *I'm* drinking to my pâté,' she announced. 'Because if it doesn't come soon, I'll start chewing up the tablecloth. I'm absolutely ravenous!'

'I'll see if I can hurry them up.' Daniel craned his neck, searching vainly for a waiter among the sea of heads. But there *was* no rush, he reminded himself, not now. They had all afternoon to eat, or to do anything they pleased. 'Look, I've got a suggestion,' he ventured. 'When we've had our lunch, let's . . .'

'*If* we ever have it,' Penny interjected.

'Actually, I think it's coming now. Yes, that's our waiter, isn't it?'

Penny sat back in relief as the stocky fellow served her with her pâté – a generous portion, studded with black olives. The toast was cut in triangles and swathed in a napkin to keep it hot. She unwrapped a piece, daubed it with pâté, then passed it to her daughter. 'So what were you saying about after lunch?' she asked, sniffing Daniel's soup appreciatively as it was ladled from the tureen.

Daniel didn't answer till the waiter had withdrawn. He never liked to talk in front of strangers. 'I . . . I thought I'd show you Paris. I mean, we'll look for Phil, of course. That's the whole point of the exercise.' Another lie, he noted, spreading his napkin on his lap. 'But we could still continue the P-theme. Paris is positively bursting with Ps. There's the Panthéon, the Picasso Museum, the Pompidou Centre, the Petit Palais, the Pyramide. And Pippa would probably like the planetarium. And if you fancy a little wander round the shops, Printemps sells everything but the kitchen sink – and probably that as well. Or we could always . . .'

'Hang on, hang on! We'll never manage that lot in one afternoon, and anyway I haven't brought a pushchair, and I doubt if Pippa's legs will last the course.'

'Well, let's fit in just a couple of things, and then stop for tea in Pons. Or we could find a bench in a P for *parc*. Or sit and rest by the Seine.'

'That's an S, not a P.'

'Ah, but the bridges are all P, though – P for *pont* – and there are some wonderful old bridges here. The Pont Neuf is my favourite. You can see right along the . . .'

'Mummy!'

'What?'

Pippa slid down from her chair and started jigging. 'I want to go pee-pee.'

'Oh, strewth, Pippa darling, you do pick your moments, don't you!' Penny jumped up to her feet, hastily cramming in a piece of toast and pâté before grabbing her daughter's hand. 'Mind you, you've done jolly well to last this long. That's thanks to Daniel's medicine.' She smiled and squeezed his arm. 'It'll probably take us an age to fight our way to the loo and back, so don't let your soup get cold.'

'Don't worry,' he murmured, having no intention of starting his meal without them. He watched them skitter off, then pushed his plate away and sat holding his arm just above the elbow – the exact spot she herself had touched. It had only been a light and fleeting touch, yet his whole left side was tingling.

He gave the arm a slap. He was behaving like some mawkish adolescent, going completely over the top. This girl meant nothing to him – she wasn't even his type. She also happened to be married, and if he really had her welfare in mind, he would call a halt to all this P-tomfoolery and help her find her husband, instead of embarking on some drunken spree round the tourist spots of Paris.

'Hypocrite!' a voice chipped in, the voice of the champagne. 'You know you haven't a dog's chance of tracking down a man with no address in a city of eight million people. And, anyway, you don't want to find him, do you?'

'No,' he admitted silently. 'I don't.'

He reached out for his glass. He had still not drunk his P-toast. 'To Penelope,' he mouthed. 'Who is personable, and pretty – not to mention prolix – but who may well prove a problem, unless I change my mind and head straight back to work the minute we've had lunch.'

5

'JUST LOOK AT THAT FANTASTIC SKY!' Penny shaded her eyes from the glare, then switched her gaze to the rippling, shimmering surface of the Seine, its drab olive-green ablaze. 'Did you lay it on for us specially, Dan?'

Daniel laughed, uncomfortably aware of all the clichés – the Technicolor sunset, the picture-postcard view, even the lovers on the next bench along: mouths meeting, arms entwined. All the scene required was the statutory Parisian artist with beret and wild beard, slapping crimson lake and vermilion on his canvas, to compete with fiery nature. He stretched his legs indulgently, leaned back against the bench. Today *he* was the artist, composing sonnets in his head, setting street-names to music, working Penny's flaming hair into his own romantic riverscape. Could he still be drunk, he wondered? Surely not, when they had spent all afternoon walking off the lunch, then sobered down with English tea, and had now stopped for a breather in the most historic part of Paris, with the Pont Neuf just behind them and Notre Dame a pigeon's flap away.

'I want to go on a boat,' Pippa clamoured. She was standing by the railings, inspecting a large motor-cruiser tied up just below. It was moored so close that they could see the smallest details in its cabin, even without moving from their bench: a plastic Virgin Mary staring with distaste at a plaster Venus de Milo; a photo of the owner's wife and family smiling shyly from the wall; a single long-stemmed plastic rose too gangling for its vase.

'No,' said Penny. 'We've done quite enough for today, and if you're not tired, I jolly well am!'

'We're on a boat already,' Daniel remarked, with a sidelong glance at Penny. He hoped that she was joking. His aim had been to divert her and entrance her, not to wear her out.

'We're *not*!' The child rounded on him indignantly and smacked the back of his hand. She had grown bolder with him throughout the afternoon – trying to grab his lighter, pleading for ice-creams.

'Well, we're on an island which is shaped like a boat, and we're sitting in the very front, where the captain always sits. Wait! I'll draw it for you.' He picked up a horse-chestnut twig, stripped off its remaining leaves and used it as his pencil. The ground was dry and dusty, perfect for a sketch. He scrawled the outline of the Ile de la Cité, with pointed prow and rounded stern, added a few choppy waves to indicate the river, and finally three matchstick figures, poised on the boat's sharp nose.

He looked up from his drawing, to check he'd got the angle right, admiring the gnarled willow tree, which seemed to be stooping over the water to wash its long green hair; the heavy-shouldered chestnuts spitting conkers at their feet. He had always loved this small secluded triangle (which he sometimes shared with no one but the sparrows, when the larger Paris parks were packed to overflowing); liked the fact there was water on both sides, so that you could indeed imagine you were chugging down the river on a pleasure-craft. The traffic noise was muted here, and although the thrustful city pulsed and throbbed all round you, you were more aware of dappled leaves, or the play of sun on water.

Or more aware of lovers, he reflected, his eyes stealing back to the couple on the bench. How could they be such advanced adventurous kissers, when they were little more than kids? They seemed to be devouring one another, tongue consuming tongue, oblivious of anything beyond each other's mouths. French kissing, he thought wryly; a million miles away from his own restrained and timid English style.

'Is it a P-boat?' Pippa asked, pulling at his arm.

'What? Oh, yes . . . of course.' He returned to the task in hand, added a few more ripples to his earthbound River Seine. 'It's called the Princess Pippa. Shall I write the name on the side?'

Pippa nodded, crouched on the ground beside him, their heads almost touching. She watched him critically, making sure he spelled the 'Pippa' right. 'I've got three Ps in my name,' she observed, as he gave the final 'a' a Gothic flourish.

'Yes, so you have.'

'Have *you* got any in your name?'

'Well, none in Daniel, I'm afraid, but my middle name begins with P – Paul – and also I live above a bookshop called Peyrefitte. D'you think that counts?'

'No,' said Pippa, unimpressed.

Daniel rubbed his palm across the rough surface of the stick. He was opening up, he realized, actually volunteering information. Earlier on, over tea and almond gâteau, he had given Penny a brief outline of his work: the impact of the new government education programme on illiteracy in Kenya, and the variations in literacy levels according to family size. She had shown a touching interest, though clearly had no grasp at all of the politics or even geography of Africa. (She had thought Nairobi was in Nigeria.)

He glanced at her again. She had kicked off her shoes and was half-lying on the bench, with her head down on the arm-rest and her hips skewed at an angle. He found her body mesmerizing, especially in that position – the way the denim stretched so tautly, outlining her thighs; the bracelet of bare flesh around the top of each brief sock, the tantalizing glimpse of her tongue as she chewed her little finger. He hoped she was truly resting, not slumped there in dejection. She had been fine all afternoon, chattering and sparkling as if fuelled by the champagne, but in the last half-hour she had gradually subsided, seemed to have turned in on herself. It was probably his fault. He'd done absolutely nothing to find Phil; had abandoned any pretence of trying once they'd reached the Pompidou Centre and become engulfed in jugglers, buskers and a throng of American tourists who'd provided quite an entertainment in themselves. Or perhaps he'd bored her by his talk of work. He had discovered long ago that illiteracy was a turn-off for most people. Starvation, famine, terminal disease – *those* were the headline-grabbers, but who cared a jot that more than a hundred million children had never laid eyes on a reading-book?

'Give *me* the stick! I want to write your name.' Pippa wrested it from his hand, traced a large and bulbous D beneath his drawing of the boat.

Daniel Paul, he mused, as she continued with a lopsided 'A' – safe and rather dull. He wished he had a dashing nickname like

Daniel *Vert Galant*. This tiny park was called the *Vert Galant*, in honour of the sixteenth-century king, Henri IV, whose statue reared behind it. He'd tried to explain the name to Penny, but it was difficult to translate. *Vert* meant green, in the sense of lusty, vigorous – sap rising, juices flowing – and *galant* was the old-fashioned word for playboy, ladies' man. He had always envied that type of man, who could sweep women off their feet, break hearts right and left. Sometimes he'd even imagined himself as Henri, strolling in the palace gardens with his string of voluptuous mistresses, his brood of bastard children, or riding his black stallion up and down the corridors of the Louvre. If he changed places with him now, discarded his boring business suit in favour of regal frills and furbelows, then Penny could be his paramour; Pippa his favourite love-child, even at this moment tugging at his embroidered ruffled sleeve.

'Wake up, Dan!' she ordered. 'You're not to go to sleep.'

He opened his eyes. Yes, he echoed, wake up, Dan – and grow up too, while you're about it. These were the sort of fantasies he had harboured as a shy and tongue-tied schoolboy (then run a mile if a girl so much as looked at him).

'Pippa! Do stop hassling the poor man.' Penny watched him rub his eyes. 'He's probably dead beat.'

'No, I'm fine.' He picked up a conker, traced the matt white cuticle on its highly-polished brown. He was still humming from the excitement and anxiety of negotiating Paris with two females in his care, and determined that they saw it at its best. Every coil of dog-shit on the pavement, every decrepit tramp snoring on damp cardboard, he'd regarded as a personal affront, and had laboured to distract his charges by pointing out instead the inscription on a statue, or the wide majestic vista up a boulevard, or some incredible confection in a *pâtisserie*, fashioned like a lovers' knot or a swan. It had been strain as much as pleasure, especially having to talk so much; make casual conversation more or less non-stop. Yet he was still eager for more: more inscriptions, statues, vistas, pastries, chat. Why limit themselves to the Ps, when they could work through the whole alphabet? – A for Arc de Triomphe, B for Bois de Boulogne, L for Louvre, which he could see if he stood up.

He looked in its direction, dazzled by the water, the sweep of

54

gilded façades on the elegant right bank. He was tempted to haul the sun back like a kite, to prevent it ever setting; longed to keep this radiance all year, keep things green and vigorous, refuse to allow autumn to creep up on him before he'd had his spring. But the trees were already yellowing, he noticed; dead leaves frail and wrinkled on the path, the last roses in the flowerbeds dropping petals like small bloodstains.

'Well, I'm whacked myself,' Penny announced, sitting up and stretching. 'And Pippa must be asleep on her feet. I really ought to take her back to bed.'

'I don't want to go to bed, Mum. I want to stay with Dan.'

He felt himself blushing the way he had as a boy; lit a cigarette to cover his confusion.

'Grandma says it's silly to smoke,' Pippa said reprovingly.

'Yes, it is – extremely silly.' God, the power of four-year-olds! He had resisted months of nagging from clean-living, clean-air Georges, dire warnings about cancer from his mother; yet here he was stubbing out his Gauloise because a babe in arms had flattered him. Yet he had to admit he liked doing what she wanted, enjoyed her adulation.

'We could ride back on a bus,' he suggested. 'And then you wouldn't be in bed for ages. The buses take for ever in the rush hour.'

'No, I want to go on a boat.'

'I'm afraid none of the boats go in that direction. But we could catch a number twenty-one, and sit at the back and watch all the lights come on.'

An emphatic answering nod, then a sharp tweak at his hand, as if to haul him to the bus stop there and then.

'Don't wait for *me*,' Penny said sarcastically. She eased her shoes back on, began collecting up the P-things he had bought her: *pain d'épice*, *pâte de fruits*, and a large bunch of delphiniums – *pieds d'alouette*.

Of course he'd wait for her – all night, all week, if need be. That was the whole object of the exercise. He had only suggested the bus because it took longer than the metro, and would spin out his last hour with her. But then back to stern reality. He must dust himself down, in all senses, take the quickest, most direct route to his mother's, and serve her up a rather different version of the day. He began sifting through a long list of excuses – rambling explanations for his lateness.

Extraordinary, he thought, with a double prick of conscience, as he dismissed them all as unworthy, not to say dishonest. His mother's very existence had gone clean out of his head since that moment in the restaurant when Penny fed him a mouthful of her p- p- profiteroles, and her chocolate-coated fingers touched his lips.

'This is us,' said Penny, stopping outside a tall and dingy building squeezed between a furniture shop and a fleapit of a cinema. Its neon sign was flickering uncertainly, and some of the letters had failed to light up at all, so that instead of HOTEL MANCHESTER, it proclaimed itself in lurid purple as the H TEL MA CHE TE. Yes, a machete wouldn't go amiss, Daniel reflected grimly, as he surveyed the narrow street, appalled that Penny had landed up in such a sleazy area, a notorious haunt of prostitutes and drug-pushers.

'Will you be all right?' he asked, transferring Pippa into her arms. The child had flaked out on the long trek from the bus stop, so he had done his chivalrous bit again and carried her up the hill.

'Yeah, fine.'

Was she trying to get rid of him? The neon sign above them cast an eerie mauvish light on her face, making her look ill. Perhaps she was so exhausted herself, she couldn't wait to collapse into bed. 'Shall I help you up with the stuff?' he offered, wishing he could carry her as well.

'It's okay, there's a lift.'

He felt snubbed by her brusque tone. Surely she should be asking about tomorrow, scribbling down his phone number, suggesting that they meet again? She had seemed so keen before, as if she couldn't bear to let him out of her sight, yet here she was more or less giving him his marching orders.

'Well, goodbye then,' he said flatly.

'Goodbye, and thanks for everything. It really was sweet of you.'

Yes, sweet, he brooded bitterly. That was the whole damned trouble. Henri IV would never have been called sweet – nor Henry

56

VIII for that matter. It was the bastards who always got the girls, not the sweetie-pies. He said goodbye again, to detain her a few moments longer, but he could hardly keep repeating it like a record stuck in a groove. In any case, she had turned her back and was halfway through the door.

'Goodbye,' he said one final time, though only the door could hear him, and even that was shuddering shut. He forced himself to move, trudged halfheartedly down the street, riled by all the litter, the crude graffiti daubed on vandalized shops. Was Paris really so wonderful? All afternoon he'd been singing its praises, enthusing about its treasures and its culture, but had forgotten how unfriendly it seemed when he had first arrived as a foreigner. He'd known the language all right, but not the social nuances, the nitty-gritty of day-to-day survival. But then he would always be a foreigner in one sense, wherever he fetched up. He had no proper roots. Born in Lusaka, then dispatched to school in Wales – so far from his home and parents that he spent most of the school holidays with odd relatives in England – then a spell in Tanzania (after Cambridge), and now this job in Paris, with trips to Kenya several times a year. Whereas Penny had lived in the same house all her childhood, and never ventured further than Great Yarmouth.

He mooched back to the cinema, its garish posters advertising a film called *Sexorama*. He was tired of sex – its enticements and its lies, the way it flaunted everywhere yet nowhere. It had always caused him problems, especially in his boyhood when the whole mysterious subject was hedged around with dangers and restrictions: warnings from his mother, diatribes at school; vague threats and hints of retribution if one ever dared indulge. His contemporaries at Greystone Court, brought up just as strictly, had laughed their mentors to scorn once they reached maturity, shrugging off the admonitions as so much stupid claptrap. He alone was retarded, somehow believing that his mother (or the masters in that creepy school) still kept up a Black Book, in which every sexual transgression, however brief or petty, was recorded as a defilement.

Angrily he lit a cigarette, exhaled a spurt of smoke in the face of the nymphet who was smirking from the poster, displaying her half-naked breasts, as if to show him what he'd missed. The furniture shop was equally obsessed – a double bed in the window, with a black lace negligée draped suggestively across it. What the hell was he doing hanging round here anyway? He should be heading for his mother's — who slept in winceyette pyjamas buttoned to the neck.

'Dan!'

He wheeled round at the voice, flung his cigarette away.

'Thank heavens you're still here! I'm at my wits' end. The dratted lift's conked out and I didn't know how on earth I was going to manage carrying a screaming child up seven flights of stairs.'

The screaming was audible even before they stepped into the foyer — though foyer was hardly an appropriate word for the low-ceilinged scrap of hallway which boasted nothing but a reception desk, a single vinyl chair, and the abandoned broken lift. Pippa was huddled at the bottom of the stairs, surrounded by the packages, her face puffy and distorted as she sat howling in frustration.

'She's overtired,' said Penny. 'She gets like this if I keep her up too long. The only answer is to shove her into bed. Gosh! I just can't tell you how pleased I am to find you. I hope you're feeling strong, though! I'm afraid we're right up at the top.'

Daniel stooped to pick the child up — easier said than done. She was evidently determined to resist him, holding her body rigid and pushing with her hands against his chest, all the while yelling at full volume. He felt a churning mixture of guilt, exasperation and resentment. It was petty of him maybe, unworthy of a rational adult, yet he was secretly aggrieved that she should repay him in this way, when he had indulged her every whim for the last six or seven hours.

Penny was on edge as well: pitching into Pippa, pouring out apologies to him, scattering parcels on the stairs in her haste to find the key, though she would hardly need it yet — they were still nowhere near the top. He stopped on the third-floor landing to rest his aching legs. The stairs were steep and narrow, meant only for emergencies, and carpeted with nothing but fag-ends. A door slammed in the passage to his right. He turned to see a bare-chested man emerging from the bathroom, clad in dirty corduroys, with a towel slung round his neck. Penny's fellow-guests did little to reassure him. Two floors below, a couple of

58

well-oiled lads had lurched past him to their room, tattoos of naked women on their arms.

He dared not stop for long. Pippa's shrieks were still resounding through the stairwell, and any moment some outraged resident would start protesting at the noise. She was also flailing with her feet and fists, battling to get down, snail-trails from her runny nose smeared against his suit.

'Pippa, *stop* it!' Penny snapped. 'You really are a little beast.'

He winced at her sharp tone, as if the rebuke were directed at him. All three of them were angry now, he realized with a twinge of fear, as he tramped on up the stairs. The gleaming magical afternoon had shattered like a fragile toy.

'Almost there – thank God!' Penny pounded on ahead to open the door.

He caught her up, stared appalled at the tiny shabby room, which was completely filled by its meagre-sized twin beds. There was no space for anything else: no chest of drawers or wardrobe, not even a small chair. And as for refinements such as bedside lamps or a mirror on the wall, this hotel had clearly vetoed them as an unwarranted expense. Penny's battered suitcase lay open on the floor, disgorging clothes and clutter (including some scanty undergarments he felt embarrassed to have seen). The room was dim and shadowy, lit by an unshaded bulb dangling over one bed. The apology of a window looked out on a flat concrete roof which, like the stairs, had been used as a spare ashtray.

'Can you put her on the bed?' said Penny, moving a sweater and a furry frog to make more room for Pippa. 'She usually has a bath, but there's no way I'm going to give her one tonight. She seems to have quietened down at last, and I can't face another bout of screaming.'

He laid the child on the flimsy cotton coverlet, astonished at the change in her. She had switched from hysteria to torpor in a matter of two minutes.

'Where's my book?' she asked, groping out a sleepy hand.

'Down there by the case. Be an angel, Dan, and throw it over, will you? I can skip her bath, but not her precious story. However tired she is, we still have to plough through *Peter Rabbit* – right on to the camomile tea!'

Daniel passed her the book, then stood awkwardly at the foot of the bed. It was time for him to leave. This was a private ritual between mother and child, and he'd only be in the way; already felt uneasy about seeing the child undressed. Penny had removed her top and was now pulling off the leggings and the white pants underneath. 'Goodbye, Pippa,' he called, averting his eyes from her body.

She didn't answer, just swivelled her head on the pillow and looked at him in silence, a long and searching look, then turned back to her mother. 'Is he going to find my Daddy now?'

Penny blundered out of the room, pushing past him almost rudely. He realized she was crying, but trying to hide the fact. She ran on down the passage, dived into the bathroom and banged the door.

'Where's Mummy gone?' Pippa sat up, instantly alarmed.

'Just to the . . . er . . . toilet.' He didn't know what word they used. 'You know – to have a pee-pee.'

The child appeared suspicious, while he himself was fretting about what he ought to do. Surely he should go and comfort Penny, yet how could he leave Pippa on her own? Besides, wouldn't she get cold lying naked on the bed like that? 'Have you got some pyjamas?' he asked her.

She shook her head.

Stalemate.

'Well, why don't you get into bed? You'll be warmer under the covers.'

Another shake of the head.

In desperation, he picked up *Peter Rabbit*. 'Would you like me to read you your story?'

'No. I want Mummy to read it.'

'She will in just a second. But I could start it, couldn't I? And look – tuck these blankets round you. You must be freezing cold!' He was terrified she'd shriek again, so he scooped the covers over her, perched on the edge of the bed and opened the book before she had time to object.

'"Once upon a time,"' he read, feeling slightly ridiculous in this unfamiliar role, '"there were four little rabbits and their names were Flopsy, Mopsy, Cottontail and . . ."'

'No, you don't say it like that.'

'Like what?'

'You say it like *this*.' She plucked the book from his hand, repeated the passage by heart in a slow and singsong voice, pausing on each name, and ending with a triumphant cadence for 'PE-TER!' as her mother slipped back into the room.

'Sorry,' Penny murmured, avoiding his eyes. Her own eyes were inflamed.

'Ssh, Mummy, I'm reading.'

Daniel stood up, started edging towards the door. 'Look, I . . . I really must get back. I don't want to be a nuisance.'

'You're not a nuisance at all.' Penny sounded agitated, still not that far from tears. 'Please stay. I'd like you to. Just let me get Pippa settled, then we can sit and talk.'

He subsided on the bed again, watched her rummage under the pillow, pull out a crumpled tee-shirt – adult size.

'We left in such a rush, I forgot to pack half our things, so the poor kid's been sleeping in this.' She pulled it over Pippa's head, tucked the blankets round her again, then retrieved the book and began to read. He listened to the opening words – third time. Penny's intonation was identical to Pippa's: rhythmic, lulling, strangely comforting.

'"Now, my dears," said old Mrs Rabbit one morning . . ."' (Mrs Rabbit's voice was different – fusspotty and clucking.) '"You may go into the fields or down the lane, but don't go into Mr McGregor's garden.""'

He found himself utterly absorbed, hanging on to every word. He had never heard the story before. In fact, it occurred to him that he'd probably missed out on all the classic children's books: he certainly couldn't remember his own mother ever reading to him. All he could recall was his black nanny: a bolster of a woman with polished shiny skin, whose white teeth seemed to split her face every time she laughed. She had laughed a lot, a huge happy wobbling laugh, and would sometimes hug him close to her, so he'd become part of the wobble himself.

'"Then old Mrs Rabbit took a basket and her umbrella, and went through the wood to the baker's. She bought a loaf of brown bread and five currant buns . . ."'

Listening to the homely words, he felt unaccountably moved; felt himself changing into Penny's second child – a normal English child who hadn't grown up in a warm indulgent land, then been

61

banished to another country; a cold and punitive place, where he'd never so much as glimpsed a currant bun.

'"Peter gave himself up for lost, and shed big tears . . ."'

Daniel glanced at Penny as her voice became a sob, but saw with relief that the tears were only in the text this time. The child was enacting them too, wiping her eyes on the sheet. The pair were accomplished performers, milking every ounce of emotion from the tale, Pippa mouthing the words in time with her mother's voice. That voice continued hypnotically as Penny turned each page. He was reluctant for the story to end, wished he could demand 'More, more!', the way Pippa had when he'd pushed her on the swings. Though the child said nothing as her mother closed the book. Her eyes were shut already, and she gave only a brief murmur in reply to Penny's 'Goodnight, pet.' He watched the goodnight kiss, irrationally jealous.

'She's dead to the world,' Penny whispered, moving from Pippa's bed to her own, and patting its tattered counterpane. 'Come and sit down here, Dan. I'm sorry I can't offer you a drink or anything. Even the water in the bathroom comes out brown and murky!'

'That's all right. I've drunk quite enough for one day.' He found he was also speaking in a whisper, constrained not just by the sleeping child, but by the strangeness of the situation. He would have felt less nervous sitting in a proper chair, or ensconced in another restaurant, protected by the noise and bustle, the general bonhomie. The bed was hard and lumpy, and he was so close to Penny now, he could see the pattern of the freckles on her skin. If anyone had asked him, he'd have said that he disliked freckles, but hers were somehow attractive, gave her face a certain childlike charm.

'Actually I don't know why we're whispering. Once Pippa's asleep, I doubt even a bomb would wake her. I'm much the same myself. I set three alarm clocks last month, when Phil was away and I had to go to a wedding at the other end of England, and I slept through the whole damned lot!'

He suppressed a stab of envy. Sleep wasn't his strong point. He cleared his throat to tell her how he'd never needed an alarm clock in his life, not even when he'd been working in Tanzania and had to be up at five AM. But she was speaking again herself,

62

and in a very different tone from the jokey one she'd used for the alarm clocks.

'Look, I . . . I'm sorry I got upset, but I keep thinking about Phil, and what will happen to Pippa if he doesn't' – she swallowed – 'come back. It's been weighing on my mind, especially this last hour or so. In fact, the longer I was with you, the worse it seemed to get. I eventually decided I shouldn't see you any more, just say goodbye and thank you, and leave it at that. I'm sorry,' she repeated, pulling at a strand of hair, which sprang back to its wiry curl the minute she let go of it. 'You must have thought me really grouchy, but I was feeling so screwed up, you see, and though we'd had a super day, that only made things . . .'

The sentence petered out, leaving Daniel grappling with new guilt, though he wasn't sure exactly what he'd done. He tried to steer the conversation from himself to Phil again, having a hunch it would be safer. 'Was your husband very fond of Pippa?' he asked, cursing himself for using the past tense, which sounded as if he'd already written Phil off. It was a stupid question anyway. Penny was obviously upset about the breaking of the closest kind of bond.

'Well, no, he's actually rather cool. He puts up with her, but not much more than that. You certainly couldn't call him the proud and doting father. Mind you, I don't think Phil is very fond of anyone – except himself, of course.' She gave a bitter laugh, which jolted Daniel as much as her words.

'Don't get me wrong – I'm not saying he's all bad. And to be fair to him, he never wanted a kid at all. That was the whole trouble. You see, we only got married because I . . . I discovered I was pregnant, and I panicked.' She reached out for the furry frog and sat it on her lap, began twiddling its limp legs. 'Lots of girls would have . . . you know . . . got rid of the baby, or maybe had it and stayed single. But I didn't have the guts to do either. It was crazy, in a way. I was only just eighteen and about to start at art school, but I chucked up everything and got hitched to a man who'd planned to sail round the world on a trimaran, not settle down with a wife and kid. We were both resentful, naturally. We'd both lost out on our dreams, and got landed instead with a load of dirty nappies and a whopping great down-payment on a Hoover Keymatic.'

She laughed again, unconvincingly. 'I'm afraid it's not a very original story. It must happen to hundreds of couples, and maybe some of them are lucky and live happily ever after. I was even stupid enough to imagine that Phil and I were happy in our way. I mean, he's got a reasonable job now, so money's not so tight, and though he's away a hell of a lot, and not exactly the world's best father, I've got masses of my own friends, and my sisters all live near, and . . .' She broke off, turned the frog the wrong way up and stroked its green-striped stomach. 'I don't know why I'm telling you all this, except I feel so . . . muddled. All afternoon I've been watching you with Pippa, and you're absolutely brilliant with her. It sort of churned me up, made me realize how Phil never gets involved with her like that, yet he's her father, for God's sake.'

Daniel said nothing. Absolutely brilliant? Penny must be joking. He was only too aware that what he shared with Phil was the fact he'd never wanted children either. The relationship between parent and child was too dangerous, too precarious. Supposing your own flesh and blood hated or resented you? And was it fair to pass on genes which might land the kid with problems – not illness necessarily, but fears, inadequacies?

Penny's hands seemed unable to keep still. She had abandoned the frog, but was now fiddling with the bedcover, poking her finger through one of the small rips and pulling the loose threads. 'I sometimes used to think he had doubts about *being* her father. He hinted at that once, though there's not a shred of truth in it. But he's the suspicious type – maybe because he was having affairs himself – ones I never knew about, long before this Arab girl. And I suppose part of the trouble is that Pippa looks nothing like him at all. I mean, she's not just got my hair, but my eyes, my type of skin, even the same shaped nose. Phil's entirely different – he's dark with brown eyes, and much brawnier altogether. Wait a sec – I'll show you!'

She scrabbled in the suitcase, finally came up with a snapshot wrapped in clingfilm, pressed it into his hand. 'That's him! My other half.'

He could hardly bring himself to look, and when he did he felt still more confused. He had somehow been imagining a crude and hardened man, but Phil looked harmless, even sensitive, and quite astonishingly young – not a man, a boy. He was smiling in the photograph, a shy apologetic smile, and his big brown spaniel-eyes seemed to plead for kindness, not invite contempt.

'You know, there *is* a resemblance to Pippa,' he managed to say at last. 'Something about the eyes. They may be a different colour, but the expression's rather the same, and their mouths are similar too. See the shape of that top lip?'

Penny wasn't looking. Her head was in her hands, her shoulders shaking silently. 'Don't cry,' he muttered desperately. 'Look, tomorrow I'll ring the embassy and see if there's anything they can suggest, any way of tracking him down.' Even as he said it, he knew that it was hopeless; tried another tack. 'He can't simply walk out on you, Penny, not if you're married. You have rights in law, and . . .'

'I . . . I don't want him back,' she blurted out, with another burst of tears. 'That's why I'm so upset. It's only just dawned on me, this minute – I've been kidding myself all through our so-called marriage. I've always made excuses for him – to myself, I suppose, as much as other people. When I got fed up because he was away again, or out, I'd fill the house with my sisters' kids or invite my friends and neighbours round. But all I was really doing was running away from the fact that he and I had nothing much in common and couldn't even communicate. Actually, it's you who've made me see it. You've got this way of listening – really listening seriously, as if what I say's important. Phil's always inter-rupting. Sometimes he even wanders out of the room when I'm in the middle of a sentence. I hadn't realized till now that it makes me feel like shit. I'm not worth five seconds of his time – and nor is Pippa.'

Daniel sat in silence, indignant at Phil's rudeness, yet wary of getting too involved himself, or being seen as something he wasn't. He didn't want Penny putting him on a pedestal, or trying to come too close – not until he'd made some sense of his own contradictory feelings. He was already conscious at some level that she'd been acting on him all afternoon like a powerful sort of magnet, making him behave completely out of character.

Again, he used his cigarettes as a convenient excuse, fumbling for the packet, edging down the bed. It would be dangerous to light one until he'd shifted a safe distance from the tinderbox of her hair.

'Please don't smoke so much, Dan. I'm beginning to worry about your lungs.' She leaned over and removed the cigarette, so teasingly and graciously, he couldn't bring himself to object.

'And I do care about your lungs, you know. In fact, I care about all of you. You're such a lovely person. Phil's friends are only interested in making money, or buying themselves new office toys, but you're different altogether – someone with ideals. I could see that when you talked about your work – the way you're so concerned about those African kids, and get all steamed up about the unfairness in the world, when most people couldn't give a damn. And I love the way you treat Pippa like an equal, instead of talking down to her.' He wanted to break in, cut short this tide of adulation, but the thought of Phil and his constant interruptions made him hesitate. And, anyway, such praise was rather gratifying. Jean-Claude might compliment his work (occasionally, untypically), but no one had ever told him before that they cared about the whole of him.

'Put your arms round me, Dan. I'm feeling really down tonight, and horribly alone. If I've got to accept that it's all over between me and Phil, then it means I've got to start again from scratch, and frankly I'm scared stiff.'

He was terrified himself, thrown by her request. He placed one tentative arm on her shoulders, noticing his hand was sweating. She responded instantly, turning towards him as if hungry for some comfort, and looping both her arms around his neck. He allowed her to cling on to him, hoping he was soothing away her problems, making her forget the squalid ill-lit room: the dark shadows in the corners, the damp-stains on the wall. It was comfort for him, too, in fact: the warmth of her, the softness, the way she was nuzzling against him with an eager childlike trust. She had called Phil 'her other half' (and the term had stuck in his gorge), but wasn't *he* in that position now as their two bodies seemed to merge?

'That's nice,' she whispered. 'Cosy.'

No, he thought with alarm – cosy was no longer the right word. Her breasts were pressed so close he was becoming sexually aroused, overwhelmed by their solidity and fullness. He longed to see them naked, to cup them in his hands and feel their marvellous weight. He tried to imagine the nipples – small and pink like those little cone-shaped sweets he had eaten as a child, or maybe longer, darker, already standing up. It was all he could do not to move his hands from the safety of her waist and let them creep inside her top, touch her bare warm flesh.

'Relax, Dan, you're so tense. Isn't it nice to cuddle up, and just let go of all the hassles for a while?'

He daren't let go – not of anything. She was still using words like 'cuddle', affectionate and childish words, while his obstreperous erection was growing more and more insistent. He must control himself, for Christ's sake! She had asked for help and comfort, not some sordid grope. He removed his jacket and placed it on the bed, ran a nervous finger round the collar of his shirt. He needed more than just a collar – something tight, relentless, which would cover his whole body, keep everything in check. She was looking at him anxiously, so he put his arms round her again; let her rest her head against his own.

Her cheek felt wonderfully soft, and he could smell almonds on her breath – a faint relic of their tea. He remembered how she'd licked cream from his thumb, once they'd both abandoned their cake-forks; the way she'd scavenged crumbs from her plate with one greedy moistened finger. Her mouth had been distracting him all day: that deft pink tongue flicking out at lunchtime, to retrieve a swirl of sauce, or to first-aid Pippa's hand when she'd grazed it in the park. Would it really hurt to kiss her? – just one brief and gentle kiss, a child's kiss on the cheek.

There was a muffled grunt from Pippa, turning over in her sleep. He sprang away from Penny as if her cheek were blistering hot. He had forgotten all about the child – deliberately, perhaps. 'I doubt even a bomb would wake her,' Penny had assured him, but could he really take the risk? A kid of four might be terribly disturbed if she woke to see her mother in a clinch. He glanced at her with something close to fury, tempted to haul her out of bed and deposit her on Phil's doorstep, let the bloody man look after her himself.

'What's the matter?' Penny asked. 'You keep bobbing around like a jack-in-the-box.'

'I . . . think I've got something in my eye.' He started rubbing it and blinking, to convince himself it was true. He was utterly confused: ashamed of his spiteful reaction towards an innocent child, yet still struggling with both anger and frustration.

'Here, let me have a look.' She gently pulled the eyelid down and peered into his pupil; he sitting on the bed, she standing over him, with that enticing, troubling cleavage displayed to him again.

'I can't see anything,' she said, stooping even closer. 'But I'll palm it for a moment.'

'Do what?'

'Just hold my palm across the eye, so you can't see out of it. That often helps to soothe tired eyes, and I suspect yours *are* simply tired. You told me yourself you've been working all hours, and didn't get much sleep last night.'

He made a heroic effort to relax, expelled his breath in a protracted sigh. Her palm was hot and moist, and pressed so firmly over his eye that his lashes fluttered against it every time he blinked, which he was doing far too often – nervousness again.

After a few moments, she took her hand away. 'How's that?'

'Fine,' he mumbled, more concerned about concealing his erection. He crossed his legs, studied a burn-hole in the carpet.

'Or shall I kiss it better now?' She laughed, made a *moue* with her lips, kissing the empty air. 'I always do that for Pippa, and d'you know, our doctor said it works. I mean, it's not just psychological, apparently, but has an actual physical effect on the nerve-endings or something.'

Yes, he was experiencing that effect – the most intense exquisite pleasure, sensuous and slow – surely no mere medical procedure? He had never had his eye kissed; wouldn't have believed that the sensations could be so powerful. Did Penny know what she was doing to him, or was she simply playing, treating him as her child? She was using her tongue as well, now: running it along his lashes, then across his eyebrow. It seemed to thrill each individual hair, each smallest pore and follicle, spark off miniature explosions which shocked through every fibre of his body, as if his eye were a lightning-conductor channelling a violent force. It was torment not to touch her, not to reach his hands out and trace the slow curve of her hip, or ease that provoking zip down and . . .

He jerked abruptly back. The harsh wail of a siren was ripping

68

through the room, shattering the silence. It shrilled to a crescendo, then faded just as quickly; a second siren taking over with the same nerve-racking urgency. He yanked at his tie, loosening its constricting knot. 'What the devil's going on?'

'Don't worry,' Penny said. 'We had the same last night, but it died down pretty quickly. I think it's the police out on a drugs raid.'

He was amazed by her sang-froid. She seemed as unperturbed as Pippa, who hadn't moved a muscle. The child was sleeping on her stomach, her breathing slow and rhythmic, despite the pandemonium below – slamming doors and pounding feet, voices raised in fear.

Suddenly, on impulse, he pushed Penny back on the bed, using the cover of the noise outside to commit his own small crime. If Pippa could sleep through such a racket, it wasn't very likely she'd be woken by one brief and gentle kiss.

It wasn't brief – or gentle. He had no idea what the hell was happening to him, except he was no longer English Daniel, shy of English Penny, but had become that shameless French kid on the bench, devouring his Parisian girl with lips and teeth and tongue. And the girl was equally hungry, opening her mouth and revelling in the kiss, making tiny breathless gasps through it, while her hands clutched at his back.

Then, unbearably, he felt her grip relax, her wild lips pull away. 'Oh, Dan,' she whispered. 'We really shouldn't . . .'

'Call me *Daniel*,' he said. It was imperative that she used his proper name; took him absolutely seriously. This was a serious moment. Without knowing how or why, he was aware that he had broken through some barrier, crossed some boundary.

'Call me Daniel *always*,' he insisted, then moved his mouth lower, to her breasts.

6

DANIEL CREPT DOWNSTAIRS, praying the concierge wasn't up and about yet. Usually he sneaked out in the early hours when the foyer was deserted, but today his watch said nearly ten to seven. It was a miracle he had slept at all (let alone so long) in that narrow, lumpy, creaking bed, with sirens blaring through his dreams – another proof of Penny's magical powers. He had spent the whole weekend with her, the best weekend of his life, and they'd fallen asleep exhausted, last night, with her still underneath him; had woken only ten minutes ago in delight and consternation. It was far too risky with Pippa there for him to stay so late, and he was still blessing his good fortune that she hadn't woken first, or heard him as he scrambled into his clothes. They would have to be more careful. She was showing signs of jealousy, and continually fretting about her father: when was he coming back from his holiday, and why couldn't she talk to him on the phone?

He smoothed his uncombed hair, ran a hand across his stubbly chin. He really ought to be behaving more responsibly, feeling more concern about the kid, but it was difficult to worry after such an enchanted week. His character seemed to be changing. He was becoming less obsessional, an almost carefree hedonist who could saunter past the concierge (just emerging from his lair), smile at the stout cleaner, and feel only a faint frisson of embarrassment.

He stepped into the street, gulping fresh cold air – a contrast to the stale fug of the bedroom. A smudge of moon still lingered in the sky, and the light was blurred and grudging, no match yet for the garish yellow street-lamps, the frenetic neon flashing red and purple. He had come to like this area; preferred the Hotel Manchester to all the hotels in Paris, including the fabled Ritz. Penny hadn't made love to him in the Ritz.

He broke into a run as he turned the corner into the main thoroughfare, dodging the jet of water from a fiercely gushing hose. The street-cleaners were out, swooshing down the gutters from their automated vans. '*Bonjour,*' he nodded to the man behind the hose, tempted to peel off his clothes and enjoy an instant shower, waltz along the pavement in the buff. He felt a bond with everyone this morning: the delivery boy with his orange plastic crates, the mangy dog sniffing round the lamp-posts, the cyclist in his waterproofs wobbling down the road. He hadn't even noticed it was drizzling. The sun had shone all week, and everything had seemed brighter and more spring-like – especially at the weekend when he was free to be with Penny all day, as well as half the night.

He was relieved to see a cruising cab, waved it to a stop. He had already blued a fortune on cabs, returning to his flat in the middle of each night, but he would never get to work on time if he hung around for a bus. He still had to shave and change, grab a bite of breakfast. Penny had said she liked him dressed more casually, but a polo neck and cords weren't quite the thing for the office, and anyway his clothes were creased – had spent their startled night spreadeagled on the floor of the hotel room.

He climbed into the cab, grinning to himself, surprised he didn't feel more tired after a run of such late nights. But he was wired up to a drip-feed labelled 'Penny', which pumped adrenalin and elation into his veins. If he were to leap out of the taxi and gallop alongside, he knew he'd overtake it easily – a Hermes with winged feet. He contented himself with leaning forward and peering out of the window, gobbling bricks and mortar for his breakfast, washing them down with water from a fountain, admiring its stone nymph who was caressing a smug dolphin with a fervour very similar to Penny's.

Paris looked bewitching at this hour; its buildings throwing off the heavy blue-black duvet which had covered them all night, and emerging wet and naked; the murky sky dissolving into grey and glinting daylight. The plane trees lining the boulevard were reaching out their branches to each other, almost touching in a green tangle overhead. Every other street they passed reminded him of Penny: an ancient church he'd shown her, or a gallery they'd visited; the seedy little bar where they'd drunk *Kir à la*

Mûre; the *confiserie* where he'd bought her hand-made chocolates. If only he could keep her here for ever. Each time she mentioned going home, it was as if the tubes and respirators which kept him alive and kicking were in danger of being suddenly wrenched out. But she was worried about Phil's reaction if he returned home himself and found she'd disappeared; even more disturbed by Pippa's increasingly frequent tantrums. He kept wondering if he should invite them to move in with him, but that would unsettle the child still further; anyway, did he really want a four-year-old creating mayhem in his flat? They had come to lunch on Saturday and Pippa had broken a vase – a present from his father, which was precious not in cash terms, but because presents from his parents were a rarity.

He was so engrossed in his thoughts, the cabby had to raise his voice: if Monsieur would be so kind, that would be forty francs – unless of course he had changed his mind and wanted to go further?

'*Oh, excusez-moi!*' Daniel flurried, realizing with a jolt that they had pulled up at his door, a bookshop in the rue St Jacques with a *crêperie* on one side, a hairdresser on the other, and three apartments above. He jumped out of the cab, overtipped the driver, to wipe the disgruntled scowl off his face. He wanted everyone to smile today, even the gargoyles on the churches and the statues in the squares.

He unlocked the door to the tiny stone-flagged courtyard – 'picturesque' in Penny's eyes, though actually it smelt of cats, and the dour stone walls were clammy-cold even in the summer. One of the offending cats was prowling on the stairs. He stroked its ears, and was rewarded by an affectionate miaou. It was more friendly than its owner, whose usual form of greeting was a brief condescending nod. With such stand-offish neighbours, how could he ask Penny to stay, let alone a screaming child? He had already received old-fashioned looks from Madame Morisseau, who happened to be passing at ten o'clock on Saturday night as he emerged from his flat with a fractious little girl in his arms and a miniskirted female in tow. No, the more he thought about it, the more impossible it would be for him to exchange his quiet respectable bachelor image for that of harassed family man.

And yet the flat was full of Penny, not just her bits and pieces scattered messily about, but her presence and her voice – her expressions of delight as she'd stood admiring his possessions: his prints of eighteenth-century Paris, his jam-packed shelves of books, his African masks on the wall above the sofa. He had always regarded the place as rather small and shabby, but she had pronounced it 'fabulous'; had loved the old oak beams (woodworm and all), the brass bedstead with its sadly sagging mattress, even the cupboard of a kitchen tucked between the bedroom and the antiquated shower.

He made straight for the kitchen now, closing the door on the still effusive Minou, who had followed him up the stairs. If black cats brought good luck, then maybe Penny would stay another week in Paris – or stay a month, six months. He swilled out the cafetière and spooned fresh coffee in, hacked off a chunk of staling bread, then dashed to check the hot water tank. He was trying to do everything at once – shower, shave, snatch breakfast on the hoof, and tidy up as he went. The place was certainly a mess; its usual harmonious order totally disrupted, and not just by the child. But it had seemed absurd to waste time washing shirts or taking out the rubbish, when Penny was counting the hours till their next meeting.

He switched on the radio, tuned it to the news. He ought to know what was happening in the outside world, instead of focusing his whole attention on the new world between his legs.

'. . . et maintenant, de notre envoyé spécial en Grande-Bretagne: hier soir une explosion a complètement détruit une maison inoccupée à Streatham, dans la banlieue sud-ouest de Londres . . .'

Strange how everything led back to Penny. She and Pippa lived in Streatham, with one sister round the corner, another half a mile away, and the third in Twickenham. He could hardly believe how much he'd learned about her in just under a week. Everything she'd told him had made him more aware of the differences between them, but somehow it didn't matter. What they had in common was so much more important: their tastes in sex, in bed.

He lathered his face in the bathroom, shaving with great concentration. It wouldn't do to be bristly when he kissed her again tonight. He rinsed his razor, traced a P on the tiny steamed-up mirror. He was reluctant to wash her off – her stickiness and heat, her lush and private smells – or to allow his stern mint toothpaste to douse the taste of her mouth. He glanced down at his body as he stepped into the shower, inspecting himself with a new compulsive interest. 'P- p- for penis,' she'd teased, the first time they'd stripped naked; then, kneeling at his feet, she had taken it in her mouth. He'd been absolutely electrified; still marvelled at her lack of inhibition – the way she made sex fun, removed all the sin and guilt. He couldn't imagine ever being so abandoned himself, but he rejoiced in the fact that for once in his life making love meant love, and not a perfunctory screw.

He gave his prick a cold blast from the shower. He had to get to work, wrest his mind from Penny. He wandered dripping from the bathroom, rubbing his hair on a towel. There wasn't a single clean shirt, so he chose the best of the grubby ones and hunted for a tie. Once dressed, he gulped his coffee, then riffled through the papers on his desk, sorting those he needed for the office. Beneath the pile of photocopies from *Education in Austerity: Challenges, Dilemmas* were half a dozen messy sheets scribbled in felt-tip. His poem! He'd composed it late on Tuesday night when he'd come bounding back from the hotel, far too high to sleep. Except 'composed' was the wrong word. The lines had simply poured themselves on the page, with very little effort on his part. It was the first poem he'd produced in years – a sort of resurrection, his potency restored. And what had sparked it off was that phrase he had used to Penny: 'Call me Daniel always'. Why the devil had he said that, when 'always' was a word he didn't trust, and Penny was a virtual stranger? There had never been an 'always' in his childhood; everything he'd cherished had ended prematurely, including childhood itself. Yet the word ran through the poem like a sort of leitmotif. His hand groped for his cigarettes; returned empty to the desk. He had promised Penny he'd cut down, though his natural inclination was to chain-smoke the whole packet, to give him courage to re-read the thing. Up till now, he had purposely avoided even glancing at it again, for fear his *tour de force* would be revealed as limping doggerel.

He sat down at the desk, steeled himself to skim through the scrawled sheets, his apprehension giving way to a new burst of excitement. It was the best thing he'd ever written. All it needed was a few small changes here and there to lick it into shape – he must cut that clotted metaphor, for instance, keep the whole thing

74

taut. He seized a pen and started crossing words out, jotting down replacements; his mind and hand working at top speed. Once he'd given it a final polish, he'd make a fair copy and present it to its dedicatee, or, better still, read it out loud to her in bed. She might not realize it was a love-poem, with its deliberate understatement, its ironic mocking tone, and she certainly wouldn't pick up all his references to other poems. But what the hell? She'd still be thrilled; see him as a cross between Byron and Bob Dylan. Perhaps he'd write her a new poem every day, collect them in a book, even get it published so the whole English-speaking world would know how . . .

The phone shrilled through his reverie – Penny ringing from the call-box in the hotel. She often phoned just before he left for work, to tell him how fantastic he'd been, or to check the lunch arrangements, or simply to say that she was missing him already. He picked up the receiver, pen still in his other hand.

'Penny, listen! I've written you this poem! What? Oh, I'm so sorry.' He switched to French, though his voice had shrunk to a hoarse and tortured whisper. He kept repeating, '*Je suis désolé* . . .' He was sorry, very sorry, but, yes, he *had* been out all night . . . A wave of sickness juddered through his stomach. This was retribution. If he hadn't been with Penny, his mother wouldn't have landed up in hospital – or at least wouldn't have gone there all alone. She must have been shovelled into an ambulance by cold impassive strangers, while her only son was wallowing in bed. He could hear that heartless phone, ringing, ringing, ringing in his dark deserted flat, while he was in a hotel room, clamped against a naked female body, oblivious to everything but its choked ecstatic cries.

He assured the nurse he would come at once, panicked by her urgent tone. Yet he still clung to the receiver, unwilling to let go, bracing himself to ask that one dark question. '*Elle . . . elle n'est pas . . . ?*' No, he couldn't say it – dared not even think it. Yet the unspoken word hung in the air, numbing his whole body. All his recent sleep-starved nights seemed to have caught up with him remorselessly. His eyes were sore and smarting, his legs as weak as straw. The scrap of bread he had eaten was bloating and fermenting in his gut. And he wasn't even clean – about to visit

75

his mother in a soiled and sweaty shirt, with his body probably smelling of a woman's.

The nurse had said '*Au revoir,*' but he seemed physically unable to put down the receiver, as if replacing it would cut the umbilical cord, kill son as well as mother.

He stared blindly at his poem. The words he had thought so brilliant were nothing but black stains. Suddenly, he slammed the phone down, tore the paper into shreds, dumped it in the garbage-bin, then grabbed his mac and hurtled out. The street was jammed with traffic; windscreen-wipers frantic; impatient drivers leaning on their horns. Not an empty cab to be seen. The metro would be quicker, but he couldn't face the crowds – the thought of those packed coffins, joined nose to tail and shuttling underground. How could they put his mother underground? They hadn't had the time yet to get to know each other, become proper mother and son.

He blundered through a puddle, spattering his shoes. He'd probably find a taxi in the boulevard du Montparnasse, but it would take a miracle to reach it. The narrow pavements were clogged not only with pedestrians but with displays of fruit and vegetables, deliveries of fish. His mother was fighting for her life and these crass moronic stallholders were polishing red apples, or slapping skate on slabs. The damned rain didn't help – early morning shoppers entangling their umbrellas, then wasting time apologizing; cars spraying him with water as they all but grazed the kerb.

At last he reached the crossroads, almost sobbing with relief as he saw a girl just paying off a taxi. '*Attendez, attendez!*' he shouted, wrenching open the door and promising the driver double if he could make the hospital in ten minutes.

He swallowed his fury at the negative response. He could hardly blame the fellow for the rush hour or the rain, or the fact that every light turned red at their approach, or a lorry started backing out in lumbering slow motion, forcing them to yet another halt. He unclenched his fists, willed his foot to stop its nervous tapping. He must calm down or he'd be no help to his mother. Let her be all right, he implored, and I'll never see Penny in my life again.

He realized he was praying, to the God who wasn't there; pleading, making bargains – the hardest, cruellest bargain it was possible to make.

'Get on, get *on*!' he muttered, seething at a new delay – a cleaning van, like the one he'd seen an hour ago, blocking half the road. The green-clad men were still sluicing all the pavements down, their relentless hoses attacking secret dirt. If only they could purge him too, wash his rutting night away, so that when he saw his mother he wouldn't feel such shame, wouldn't have to weave a web of lies. Perhaps there'd be no need for words, and they could just clasp hands in silence, while he imbued her with his own health and strength. Surely she wasn't as ill as they'd implied? They were probably exaggerating, frightening him on purpose as a punishment for staying out all night. After all, he had phoned her several times last week (rushed, impatient calls, he realized now, with a shudder of remorse), and she'd seemed absolutely fine; said he mustn't worry about making time to see her – she understood the pressures of work better than anyone. The pressures of work . . . He had never worked less in his life: sloping off at four, spinning out his lunch-hours, and so obsessed with Penny that the figure sitting at his desk was a mere set of empty clothes; the real Daniel having floated back to the Hotel Paradise.

Perhaps this crisis was a warning to him, a salutary shock to bring him to his senses while he still had time to put things right. Once his mother was discharged, he'd devote his evenings and weekends to her – work at fostering a relationship he'd so culpably neglected. He began running through the things they'd do as soon as she was well enough: gentle strolls in her favourite park, visits to museums, meals together, even excursions to the countryside.

The cab was speeding up, thank God, and they must be nearly there. He recognized that spiky modern sculpture they had passed a week ago, when he'd accompanied his mother on her first dash to the hospital. Could it only be a week ago? It seemed like another lifetime – his existence now divided into before and after Penny. Except he mustn't think of Penny, must banish her from his mind, focus every shred of energy on his mother.

He was already poised to leap out – a clutch of banknotes in one hand and the other on the door-handle. He didn't wait for change or thanks, but sprinted towards the elegant grey building, resenting the opulence of its façade. Behind those marble columns, those carved swags of fruit and flowers, people's mothers were fighting for their lives. It was like a mausoleum – grandeur shrouding bones.

Inside, the twentieth century was more in evidence. Stark white corridors led off from a reception area, with glaring fluorescent lights and padded vinyl benches, and, to the right, a row of high-speed lifts. The middle lift stood open, though already crammed with bodies. Noiselessly, the doors began to close. He dived forward and squeezed in. He was pressed against a woman who smelt of cheap carnation scent; could see the fillings in her teeth as her red zipped mouth burst open in a laugh.

The lift glided from floor to floor, people elbowing in and out, delaying him still further as they manoeuvred bulky pushchairs, or dithered over which button to press. Every time the doors closed, *he* jabbed number seven – seven floors, like the treacherous Hotel Manchester. They should be going down, not up: down to fear and darkness, the furthest pole from paradise.

He pushed out first, unsure which way to go, then saw the name of his mother's ward, with an arrow pointing to the right. He followed the directions, overtaking a porter wheeling a trolley; averted his eyes from the ashen-faced woman lying on it, swaddled in a sheet. 'Let her be all right,' he prayed, determinedly picturing the future: himself and his mother walking in the park together, or admiring the Veroneses in the Louvre.

A young nurse touched his arm, pointed to a notice: *Défense de fumer*. He removed his cigarette, irrationally annoyed. He *had* to smoke – at least until he had seen his mother and knew that she was safe.

His steps began to falter as he approached the wide swing-doors. Unthinkingly, he straightened his tie, smoothed his ruffled hair. Then he took a deep breath in, slipped through the doors and went straight up to the desk; identified himself as Madame Hughson's son.

This nurse was older, plainer, with a sallow coarse-grained skin. She asked him to come into the office and sit down. He sat stiffly, with his hands clasped, noticing tiny irrelevant details: a scuff-mark on the lino, the ridged sole of her shoe. A clock was ticking through the silence. He liked that safe white silence. So long as no one spoke, his mother was alive.

The nurse cleared her throat, shifted on her chair. '*Monsieur . . .*' she began. Her voice was all compassion and respect, the alabaster voice of death. '*Je suis navrée de vous informer que votre mère est . . .*'

'*Non! Non!*' He cut her short, excised the hideous word. 'No,' he repeated, breaking into English. 'It isn't true. You're wrong!'

He stumbled to the window, looked out at the skyline. The view was very fine from here. You could see the Eiffel Tower, and the graceful spire of the church of . . .

No, you could see nothing but the rain – rotting the grey stonework, weeping down the panes – and death, everywhere. A dead bird on the roof below, dead leaves on the trees, and that path down there was only a dead end. He pressed his forehead against the glass. Dead end.

'*Monsieur Hughson, je comprends bien votre émotion. Vous avez subi un grand choc, mais je vous assure . . .*'

The marble voice was dirging on behind him, but he was hearing different words – a child's book, read aloud.

'*I'm sorry to say that Peter was not very well. His mother put him to bed and made him some camomile tea.*'

He repeated the words to himself, still not moving from the window. '*His mother put him to bed and . . .*'

'No,' he said, shaking his head and watching in bewilderment as someone's tears fell scalding on his hands. 'You see, she never had the time.'

7

DANIEL WAS BURSTING for a pee. But he could hardly stop the car and risk losing track of the vehicle ahead – the small white private ambulance which contained his mother's coffin. He had tried as far as possible not to be parted from her body. He had taken leave from work, so as to devote every waking moment to her: sorting out her things; checking through her address-book for all the friends he should contact; arranging her funeral in England via a series of long-distance phone-calls. Then, just this morning, he had accompanied her on the plane from Paris, resentful that he'd had to sit beside a young canoodling couple who'd spent the entire journey exchanging kisses and sweet nothings, while she lay in the cargo-hold, alone.

The English undertakers had met him at Heathrow – a pair of sombre-suited men with plaster-lily expressions and fulsome voices to match – and they were now on their way, in convoy, to the small decaying south coast town where his father was already buried. The grave would be opened and the second coffin laid on top, reuniting his parents in death after their forty years of life together. Secretly, he had balked at the instructions in the will – all that paraphernalia and unwarranted expense – but, as obedient son, he could do nothing but comply.

He changed down for the bend, then accelerated up the hill, anxious to keep the ambulance in sight. It felt strange to be behind the wheel again after eight months without a car. He had sold his Renault 5 before he moved to Paris, and this Astra was a hire-car he had collected from the airport. He'd particularly asked for a black one when he'd originally made the booking, but the model which materialized was red. He hadn't made a fuss. The flaunting scarlet seemed a fitting symbol of his guilt. A dozen different guilts were churning in his mind at present – the long delay perhaps the worst of all. It was nearly three weeks since his mother's death, and the funeral was still four days away. He had all but foundered in red tape: footling regulations entrapping him on every side; officials to placate; endless documents to sign; to say nothing of the decisions about coffin, service, wording of the death notice. His mother never dithered or procrastinated; she would have abhorred the waste of time, the indignity of remaining so long unburied.

He braked sharply to avoid running into the back of the ambulance. Unwittingly he had come up right behind, as if he couldn't bear any distance between his mother and himself. Yet *was* it still his mother shut up in that monstrous box? They had shrouded it in hessian to disguise it on the plane. Businessmen and lovers couldn't be expected to have their pleasant journey spoilt by any glimpse of death. He had learned already how everyone denied death. In fact, his mother hadn't died at all: she'd passed over to the other side; gone to her eternal rest. And those dexterous French embalmers had contrived to restore her to the pink of health. Another source of guilt – the phoney titivation of a woman who preferred the natural look: rouge and powder larded on a face unused to any make-up; straight hair coiffed in curls. He had broken down and wept when he'd seen her primped like that; had been crying on and off since his first outburst at the hospital. Yet his parents and his school had both taught him the importance of concealing one's emotions behind the traditional stiff upper lip. It was a wonder he wasn't crying now, with that horrendous vehicle in front: its blacked-out windows signalling death, its raw red cross for danger. But the control he needed for his bladder seemed to have extended to his eyes; both tightly held in check.

He reached down for a cigarette, fumbled with the lighter on the dashboard. These last few weeks he had been smoking more than ever; felt so desolate some days he craved a stronger drug, something to numb his mind, drown the harsh regrets. He glanced out at the bare late-autumn countryside. It looked tired and apathetic: hedges battered, dowdy trees half-naked, the clouds lying very low, as if the sky had suffered an injury and was falling on the fields. The light was muted, a dingy sallow-grey; the sun too lethargic to break through.

He slowed to check a signpost – only two and a half miles to go now. The journey had been swift and uneventful: little traffic on the roads; no hold-ups or diversions; the only log-jams those in his own head. He felt increasingly uneasy about this whole palaver, the unnecessary upheaval, the distances involved. His mother should have been buried in some gracious Parisian cemetery, where her son could visit every week and her friends attend the funeral. As it was, she'd be lucky if half a dozen mourners turned up in this backwater.

A sprawl of stagnant shops and a garage strung with plastic flags heralded the outskirts of the town. The ambulance continued straight on, heading for the funeral directors' office in the High Street. He dithered at the crossroads, unable to decide whether to accompany his mother on the last lap of the journey, or make a short detour to visit her old home – his dead and living mothers tugging him two ways.

The living mother won. He swung left, then left again, surprised that he remembered the way when he had visited so rarely. His parents had returned to England after a lifetime spent in Africa, only a month before he himself left for Tanzania, so that they were making the same journey but in opposite directions. But then wasn't that the story of his life?

The pebble-dash semis were beginning to thin out, replaced by dumpy bungalows set decorously apart. He continued down a rutted road, pulled up outside 'Seaview'. The new owners hadn't changed its name, despite the blatant lie. (The coast was a good three miles away; the only water in sight a small ornamental pond in the rockery next door.) It was still a mystery to him why his parents should have retired here in the first place, when they had no connections with the area, no friends or contacts to provide a base for their new life. He suspected they had idealized the delights of rural England; let themselves be sold on the notion of a country cottage with roses round the door and an idyllic sandy beach just a stone's throw from the garden.

That garden had changed utterly, he noted with dismay as he got out of the car and walked towards the fence. His father's well-staked dahlias and crazy-paving path had given place to muddy grass littered with broken toys. Three young children were playing in the front, muffled up in coats, while their scruffy dog raced round and round in circles. He watched the trio hungrily – a normal traditional family with brothers, sisters, pets; five people sitting round a table sharing boisterous meals, instead of a lone boy eating in the kitchen while his black nanny ironed the sheets. This house had never seemed like home to him on his three or four brief visits here, especially after his father died. The memories of that first death came suddenly choking back: the grim hearse at the door; the stilted funeral tea; his mother's mask-like face as she played the stoical hostess, mouthed the correct urbanities.

The role of full-time widow had proved even more constricting, so she had jumped at the chance of upping sticks to Paris with an old and trusted friend who had worked with her in Lusaka – a woman called, improbably, Marigold Ross-Pilkington. He had tried to share her pleasure at the move, hiding his disappointment that the nearest he had ever had to a proper English home was about to be abandoned. He doubted that his mother ever thought of the place again. The two women had enjoyed a brief but busy time together, involving themselves in a whole host of activities which, after Marigold's early death, his mother then continued on her own. And today her final obligation was to rejoin her husband in the country of their birth.

Though not *his* birth, he reflected, as he edged closer to the gate and tried to peer in through the windows. He half-expected to see his parents still sitting in the alcove reading some report, or earnestly discussing the problems of recruiting teachers in the poorer African countries. But he couldn't see a thing through the grubby white net curtains, and the eldest child was watching him suspiciously, so he carried on along the road, now desperate to relieve himself.

Once he'd turned the corner, he dived behind a bush, peering round him warily as he unzipped his flies. The steaming jet of piss seemed to belong to someone else – someone vigorous, dynamic, without his weight of grief. It shocked him, in a way, that his body should still function in such a crassly normal manner when his mother was lying dead. His stomach was even rumbling, reminding him he'd eaten nothing except a handful of peanuts on the plane.

Well, he'd better stop his mooning around and make his way to the undertakers' office. They'd probably give him a cup of tea, and, with any luck, a biscuit. He set off towards the car again, his loping stride gradually slowing down. Could he really face another dose of euphemism, another pile of that infernal paperwork? They would be heaving out the coffin now, stripping off the hessian wraps and giving it a last spit and polish, before depositing it in the Chapel of Rest. And if this English chapel was anything like the French one, it would be oppressively theatrical: spotlights on the body, heavy velvet curtains shutting out all natural light, bogus religious trappings like candles on an altar, even a solemn churchy smell. Anyway, a Chapel of Rest was really quite incongruous, since his mother had never believed in rest (nor even in retirement), and would certainly not be happy lying idle there when there were problems left to solve in the world, or injustices to right.

He got back in the car, turned the key in the ignition. He'd phone the funeral office from a call-box; say he'd changed his mind and had decided to check in to his hotel first, and would it be convenient if he called round later on? What he needed was not a cup of unctuous tea, sweetened with obsequiousness, but a straight Scotch on the rocks.

He drained his whisky, slunk out of the empty bar and trailed upstairs to his room. The whole place seemed deserted, the barman taciturn, apparently resentful at having to serve this solitary lunchtime customer. There were no sandwiches available, nothing but more peanuts and a few bags of staling crisps. Yet the hotel was neat and clean, the essence of gentility, and they'd given him a pleasant room overlooking the garden at the back.

He unlocked his door, the sight of the twin beds instantly conjuring up fiercely painful memories of another small hotel. The night after his mother had died he had lain awake for hours, but when at last sleep came, he had dreamed of Penny, naked, beckoning him to join her in that narrow lumpy bed. He had woken with a hard on, forgetting for one glorious second the horror of the day before.

He was still torn between the two of them: missing Penny, aching for her, yet feeling in some irrational way that his mother's death was a punishment for that ecstatic magical week. Their final night together he had lasted a whole hour – shy and prudish

Daniel who usually came in seconds. Penny had transformed him, worked such wonders on him that he could scarcely recognize himself.

Christ! He mustn't think of sex – not now, not here – with his mother's corpse lying half a mile away. He should be sitting with her, or at least signing funeral papers, choosing funeral flowers.

He paced across the room. For the last eighteen days it had been incessant and relentless death, which had left him completely drained. He was crying out for a respite – one longer than the time it took to down a double Scotch. He'd unpack his things and run a bath, ease his stiff shoulder muscles with a long relaxing soak. He hauled the case up on the bed, tossed his sponge-bag in the basin, put away his socks and shirts in the dressing-table drawers. At the bottom of the case was his mother's old brown purse, mended in neat cross-stitch where it had split along one side. She would never dream of buying a new one; had always considered it wrong to spend money on herself when two-thirds of the world was starving. He had found it in her handbag and now took it with him everywhere – that ancient battered plastic purse with less than thirty francs inside and a few steamed-off African stamps.

As a boy, he had never touched her handbag. It was something intimate and sacrosanct, almost like a body-part, which was out of bounds to any child, particularly a male one. After her death, he'd had to embolden himself (with another double Scotch) before he'd dared to open it, perhaps scared of what he'd find. But all it contained were a few pathetic relics: metro tickets, plastic comb, a tube of indigestion tablets, and some bright misshapen conkers she must have picked up in the street. No letters, photos, trinkets – nothing personal at all. He had stowed it in his flat, along with her clothes. Impossible to dump them, yet equally impossible to keep them there for ever, reminding him, reminding him . . .

He tucked the purse in his pocket, mooched over to the window. A woman was working in the garden, raking fallen leaves. She glanced up at him a moment with a blank unsmiling face, as if looking right through him. He had a sudden frightening feeling that he didn't actually exist, or that he'd been transported to a different world, where he was essentially an exile. Since he'd been on leave, he seemed to have been dealing only with strangers:

strangers at the hospital, strangers in the coroner's office, strangers at the undertakers' (first in Paris, then in England), strangers in this strange hotel. The word 'orphan' drifted through his mind — a self-pitying, Dickensian word, but one which now applied to him. If only he had family: sisters or brothers to share his grief, or some kindly cosy auntie who could have shouldered some of the burden, invited him to stay.

He groped in his back pocket for two crumpled well-thumbed letters. *Penny* had invited him to stay, poured out every comfort and support. And he'd utterly rejected her: turned down all her offers of help the week his mother died; refused even to see her before she returned to England. She had gone back almost straight away, as if, deprived of his help and company, she couldn't survive in alien Paris. He traced the outline of the smudgy Streatham postmark, recalling all she'd told him about her life — more snippets of news in these letters, which he hadn't even answered. He'd *wanted* to reply, but somehow couldn't trust himself to pen her a single word. He scanned the untidy sheets, scrawled in her exuberant hand, each page ending with a lopsided row of kisses. She was begging him to keep in touch, saying she thought of him each day, and that even Pippa had been asking where he was.

Would it really hurt to ring her? There was a pay-phone in the hall. He could at least apologize, make her understand that he hadn't intended to be cruel. Of course he wouldn't sleep with her — they didn't even have to meet — but it seemed heartless to ignore her altogether; leave her thinking he was an ungrateful callous sod.

He took the stairs two at a time, dialled her number, and stood waiting with a clutch of coins. He'd explain his state of shock, the overwhelming need he'd felt to be totally alone. '*Answer!*' he implored her, as the ringing tone shrilled vainly on and on. Was she merely out at work, or had she dashed off somewhere else — to Kuwait this time, in pursuit of Phil and his Arab girl? Or worse: were she and Phil lying on some bed together indulging in a second lecherous honeymoon, the mistress abandoned in favour of the wife?

He slammed down the receiver, stomped back to his room. This was idiotic — he was overreacting to everything. He flopped down on the bed and closed his eyes, no longer seeing rosesprigged wallpaper, but peeling paint and burn-holes. Even the smell of the Hotel Manchester was insinuating itself beneath the door: the whiff of musty bedclothes; the dank smell in the bathroom. His hand moved to his flies. His erection was un-comfortable, needed Penny to take care of it. He could feel his penis sliding into her mouth, her warm lips clamping tight; her tongue making frantic little forays, flicking up and down and round.

Suddenly another mouth irrupted into his mind: his mother's greasy crimsoned lips as she lay in the embalmers' parlour – lips parted in an unnatural smirk.

He dragged himself up from the bed, now completely limp. It was not a long indulgent soak he needed, but a short sharp walk in the raw October air. He would go on foot to the undertakers', instead of taking the car; try to clear his head.

He banged the hotel door behind him, turned out of the residen-tial avenue into the first straggle of the town. More strangers on all sides – unreal and wooden people doing extraordinarily ordinary things: buying food or clothes, queuing at the post office, stopping to chat in the street. He kept his own pace brisk, only slowing down to glance in a shop window at a display of expensive leather goods: briefcases and handbags, purses, wallets, belts. He was about to hurry on, then changed his mind and stepped into the shop.

'May I help you, sir?'

Politely, he declined. The assistant wouldn't know what he was looking for. She was completely the wrong type – too chic, too overdressed. He hunted through the shelves himself, searching for something restrained and serviceable, but still luxurious enough to compensate for those years and years of thrift. He ignored the price tags, concerned only with the size and shape, the softness of the leather, its suppleness and grain. Many of the styles on show he dismissed out of hand. She wouldn't want glittery gold fastenings, or fancy decorations on the front, just a simple sturdy handbag which would last a lifetime, never need first-aiding with her cross-stitch.

At last, he found a classic style in an attractive chestnut brown, and a matching zippered purse; took them to the assistant, watched while they were lovingly wrapped in layers and layers of tissue.

He wandered on along the street with the bag beneath his arm. He shouldn't really give it to her empty – it would only end up stuffed with conkers again. He stopped at the next large chemist, touring the whole shop, selecting various items from the shelves: a tortoiseshell comb, a jar of nourishing cream, a twist-up stick of eau de Cologne. He examined a small red manicure set, wondering whether his mother would regard it as a frippery. He had never bought her anything personal before. It was nearly always books, high-minded tomes related to her work. The last time he'd bought presents, they'd been P-things. Should he pick something out for Penny too – a p- p- powder puff?

Hell! He could no more escape his mistress than his mother. The two women were like different counters in a store – one selling frivolous fancy-goods, the other basic durables. He walked determinedly past the powder puffs, paid for his other purchases and left the shop with his loose change in his hand. There was a phone-box directly opposite, which he had noticed earlier. He crossed the road, and dialled Penny's number again, jingling the coins impatiently. He hung on a full five minutes, watching luckier couples conversing with each other as they strolled past him arm in arm. Still no reply. Was this another sort of punishment? Because he had snubbed her and neglected her, she had decided to have Phil back, and was sitting over lunch with him – a luxurious, expensive lunch, which would linger on till bedtime.

He was only yards now from the undertakers'. He trailed down to their door, scrutinized the window display: a miniature marble headstone, tastefully engraved, with a vase of artificial lilacs standing stiffly to attention at the back. What flowers should he choose for his mother? Lilacs were out of season, and he had always hated lilies. All he could come up with were Penny's *pieds d'alouette*. She'd been charmed by the name – lark's feet – and had poked a gentle finger into each of the blue flower-heads, expressing her surprise that you could buy them on a market stall. Actually, delphiniums would be right for his mother, if he could only lay his hands on some. D for Dorothy. He had written that name so many times on all those black-edged forms: Dorothy Alice Hughson. It always sounded odd, though – impersonal and cold. Her important name was Mother.

He pushed the heavy door, running through all the other

flowers beginning with a D: daffodils, daisies, dahlias, dianthus
. . . None of them would do. They all suggested spring and hope,
or at least a warmer season.

'D for death,' he murmured, as he stepped into death's lair.

8

'GOODBYE THEN, DANIEL. It was a great pleasure to meet you.'

Daniel shook the pale plump hand, wishing he could return the vicar's compliment. Hell! He couldn't even bring himself to use the fellow's name. '*Do* call me Basil,' he had been urged at their first meeting, but 'Basil' sounded faintly comic, and anyway Christian names suggested a degree of intimacy which was entirely spurious. At the service half an hour ago, it had been Dorothy this, Dorothy that, as if the vicar was her bosom friend. In fact, they'd never met.

'Are you going straight back to Paris, or staying over here a while?'

'I'm booked to leave tomorrow – one-thirty from Heathrow.'

'Well, have a good flight.' The vicar pumped his hand again, then strode along the path to his canary-coloured Beetle.

Daniel turned away. It would hardly be a good flight with the memories of the outward journey still chafing in his mind. He had taken an instant dislike to breezy Basil, but the minister his parents had known had recently retired, so the undertakers had come up with this substitute. As far as he could fathom, the choice of vicar for a non-churchgoer's burial was very much a random thing: whoever happened to be available was roped in to officiate, and some ministers could notch up four a day. Was Basil dashing off to preside at one more matey send-off, Daniel wondered resentfully as the car snorted into raucous yellow life.

Everyone else had left already, save for an old schoolfriend of his mother's who was standing by the open grave, leaning on her stick. She was the only one he knew by name – the score of other people who had turned up for the funeral must have all been close to Dorothy, yet were total strangers to him. It made his mother's life seem still more of a closed book, more cut off from his own.

They didn't even look alike. He had inherited neither her steel-blue eyes nor her tall and angular figure, so that no one ever said, 'Oh yes, I see a likeness,' or 'He's the image of his mother.'

He approached the white-haired lady at the graveside, offered her a lift. She looked far too frail to cope with unreliable trains or long bus journeys in the dark. Dusk was already falling, a dank and clammy mist beginning to shroud the graves.

'It's kind of you, my dear, but my son brought me in the car. He's over there, waiting to take me home.'

Lucky man, thought Daniel, to possess a real live mother – not to have just consigned her to the ground. The service had been a travesty, conducted in a hideous modern chapel with taped music and purple nylon drapes. The cemetery was modern, too – no ancient spreading yew trees or weeping marble angels, but stark and ugly gravestones in regimented rows. Even the sad plants in the geometric flowerbeds were graded by size and height, and the severely pruned rose bushes looked little more than stumps.

He escorted Mrs Clifford up the path, spoke briefly to her son, feeling a new surge of guilt that he hadn't organized any funeral tea. Some of the guests had travelled miles, and must have judged him most inhospitable not to have offered them so much as a sandwich. But he couldn't face prolonging the ordeal, playing dutiful host to a crowd of elderly strangers. And anyway, he could hardly invite them to tea in his hotel room.

He waved off mother and son, then unlocked his car, took the package from the passenger seat and walked back to the grave with it. He surveyed the mass of flowers: huge bouquets more suited to a prima donna; solid cushions of decapitated flower-heads which his mother would have loathed. His own red roses seemed equally inappropriate; that hateful rustling cellophane choking life and colour from the blooms – an ugly see-through coffin in itself.

He shifted several wreaths, so that he could slip his second offering underneath. He unwrapped the layers of tissue first, then slowly ran his fingers across the supple calfskin, sniffing its rich leather smell. Along with the bits and pieces from the chemist, he had wanted to include something of himself, so he had written a long letter; tried to put on paper the things he'd never had the time or courage to say to her in person. He had placed it in the bag with a photo of himself (taken at the age of four on his father's ancient Kodak), but it still hadn't seemed enough. He'd been tempted to add a lock of his hair, but that would be too mawkish, and more fitting for a lover than a son. Yet if there'd only been a way to squeeze his soul into one of the zip compartments of the handbag, he would have done so willingly.

He knelt on the wet turf, lowered the bag deep into the hole, then rearranged the flowers on top. He remained on his knees, unhappy at the thought that he had somehow short-changed his mother in failing to provide the proper ritual. If this were an African funeral, he could wail and shriek and tear his clothes, even throw himself on the coffin, beating on it with his hands to wake her from sleep, as mourners did in Zambia. But in undemonstrative England you contained your grief in one flimsy cotton handkerchief.

He yanked out a clump of dandelions which had sprouted on the path, removed a trampled paper bag. He wished he had a remit to clear every speck of litter from this place; to landscape the whole cemetery – replant it with majestic trees, add statues, bronzes, shaded walks. As it was, the plot looked raw and crude, bereft even of its headstone. The polished slab of granite would not be replaced for another six months, to allow time for the ground to settle. Would *he* have 'settled' by then, he wondered, or still be prey to this despair? What upset him most was that once again his parents were together, while he himself was left out in the cold. There was no room for a third coffin, nor even for another grave – the cemetery was full. In another forty years or so, where would he land up? Miles from them, as usual, he supposed.

He got up from his knees, glanced along the rows of tombs, his mother's silent neighbours. Only the dead in sight now – no one living left; even the birds flying home to roost. The mist was getting thicker, obscuring all the landmarks, blanking out the graves. Yet still he hung on, reluctant to leave his parents, unsure when he'd return. With nobody to tend it, weeds would choke the grave; stray dogs even shit on it. When they'd been processing from the chapel, he had noticed a scruffy mongrel squatting near a tombstone, its body trembling with the strain, its entire attention focused on its bowels. 'Get *out*!' he'd shouted wordlessly as he followed the four pall-bearers, resenting them as well. He would have preferred to carry his mother on his own.

He stretched out his hands, as if to push away the darkness. The trees were semi-bare, the year dying into winter. It was almost November, the furthest point from spring. He paced up and down, up and down, remembering last spring. He'd been in Paris with his mother, yet had hardly managed to see her – so absorbed in his incessant work he'd allowed it to encroach even on his evenings and weekends.

A firework suddenly exploded through the silence: someone celebrating Guy Fawkes in advance. A few more bangs reverberated, like warning shots driving him away. It was time he left, in any case – the grave-diggers must be waiting for him to go. They still had work to do: filling in that hole, tucking up his mother for the night. He had a sudden choking vision of wet and heavy earth falling on her open eyes, damming up her mouth.

He broke into a run towards his car, wrenched it into gear and drove too fast out of the cemetery gates and along the road that led back to his hotel. He approached the crossroads, juddered to a stop. The signpost pointing to the right said 'Dover, 13 miles'. He was barely any distance from the Channel ferries; could be back in his own flat tonight if he went by boat instead of air. He'd been dreading the thought of the plane journey; the prospect of another night in that anonymous hotel. Yesterday had been bad enough – killing time in the deserted bar, ordering drinks he didn't want; then driving aimlessly round the side-streets to escape his gloomy thoughts. If he left this evening, he could be back at work tomorrow, sitting in the refuge of his office, catching up on everything he'd missed. And his mother would most certainly approve. He'd spent far too long wallowing in self-pity, fixating almost morbidly on his loss.

He lit a cigarette – the first since lunchtime – inhaled luxuriously, gulping down a lungful of relief. His ordeal was almost over: a brief trip to the hotel to pack his things and pay the bill, a short drive to the coast, and then a strong restorative sea-wind to blast away his grief.

He stood on the top deck, leaning on the rail, waiting for the ferry to pull out. The fog had changed to rain: a cleansing, healing rain which spattered against his face, relieved his deep fatigue.

Everything had gone without a hitch: the hotel had waived all charges for tonight; Hertz had agreed to collect the car from Dover, and he'd arrived to find a ferry due to leave in half an hour. An express from Calais would whisk him into the Gare du Nord just before eleven. A taxi to his flat, a nightcap to relax him, and with any luck he'd be in bed by midnight.

A hooter sounded through the darkness, signalling the boat's departure. Most of the passengers were sheltering from the rain, relaxing in the restaurant or the bars. But he was quite content to commune with the night sky; the brooding clouds above more in keeping with his mood than the noise and glare below. He picked up his case and moved towards the prow of the boat, dodging the large puddles on the deck. He could suddenly see Pippa squatting on that deck – carrot hair and fuchsia-pink shorts – as Penny's voice came back to him. 'That's how she got cystitis. The ferry was delayed, you see, and all the seats were taken, so she spent half the night sitting on the wet wood.'

He stood stock-still a moment, then wheeled abruptly round and dashed back the way he'd come, searching for an exit sign. He had to say goodbye, couldn't leave for France without knowing how she was. He'd phone her from the terminal, tell her that he'd tried before, hadn't simply forgotten her existence. He could always catch the next boat – they went every couple of hours.

He dived towards a flight of steps, half-ran, half-stumbled down them, clunking his case awkwardly behind him. He strode on along the deck and through the door into the lounge, taken aback by the noisy scrum of drinkers jostling round the bar. He tried to squeeze between them, zigzagging his way through the obstacle course of baggage; his own bulky case banging at his side.

'Watch it, mate!' snapped a student with a rucksack, trying to protect his overflowing beer-glass.

Daniel cursed him under his breath, shaking lager off his sleeve as he blundered on past another group of students clustered round their camping gear: bedrolls, backpacks, sleeping bags, piled up on the floor. He reached the other side at last, and emerged into a corridor. He sprinted down it, but came to a dead end – a locked door marked 'NO ENTRY'. He swung back the other way and out on to the deck again, flinching at the shock of cold after the stifling heat inside. How the hell did he get off this boat? It was departing any moment and he'd completely lost his bearings. He peered over the rail to orientate himself – saw the gangplank just below, but already roped off and about to be winched up.

'Wait!' he shouted desperately. 'I've changed my mind – I'm not sailing after all. Hold it just one second – *please*!'

A score of startled heads looked up – crewmen, other passengers – some relishing the prospect of a drama. He hadn't time to be embarrassed, but hurtled down the stairs and along the final stretch of deck. The gangplank was still in place, thank God, though a burly man in uniform was trying to bar his way, barking some reproof. He ducked under the rope, shouting an apology, then clattered down the gangplank and on across the quay, almost tripping on the wet and slippery surface.

He arrived breathless in the waiting-room and made straight for the nearest phone booth. He dialled the Streatham number, praying Penny was alone. He was longing to tell her how he'd missed her; how even during the funeral service he'd been thinking of her body, remembering how they'd . . .

'Shit!' he muttered furiously, raging not at Penny but at her bloody stupid phone. Why did no one answer it? He slammed down the receiver, slumped against the wall. He must be out of his mind: he'd missed his crossing and she wasn't even there. She was obviously away from home – and probably with Phil. He had tried a dozen times already in the last four frustrating days, and never once got a reply. In the end he'd given up; telling himself it wasn't fair to contact her again. If she and Phil were back together, any overture from him would only be impolitic. So why in God's name had he changed his mind, or assumed so glibly that *this* time he'd get through? All he'd done was waste two hours, when the whole point of going by boat had been to avoid these futile stretches of dead time.

He found an empty seat, rammed a cigarette in his mouth, and sat there snapping matches in half, their broken bodies falling on his lap. Two hours was an eternity in this hell-hole. There wasn't even a drinks machine, let alone a proper bar. He glanced irritably at the people sitting round him – an old gaffer with a cold, constantly honking into his handkerchief, and three frumpy-looking matrons talking with their mouths full as they shared gossip and cheese rolls.

Snatches of their conversation drifted past his ears, continually revolving round the subject of their husbands, children, grandchildren. It must be daunting to be part of such a tribe, bonded so inviolably by ties of blood, of steel. And yet how much worse to be alone, to have spent four days in England and not spoken to a single friend. But that was his own fault. He could have rung a dozen friends if he hadn't been so apathetic, moping around each evening feeling sorry for himself.

He got up from his seat, too restless to sit still. He could always ring them now. It would be a relief to talk to someone he knew, and would help to pass the time. He stubbed out his cigarette, mooched back to the phone. He'd try Anthony in Cambridge first, catch up with his news. He dialled the number, thinking back to the years they'd spent together: drinking, smoking, discussing books and politics. He'd been out of touch too long; had neglected all his English friends once he'd moved to Paris.

He jumped. An unknown female had answered, breaking into his thoughts; informed him in her drawly voice that Anthony was out.

'D'you know when he'll be back?'

'Sorry – no idea.'

The sense of unreality he'd felt in the hotel began to take a grip again. Was he really standing in this claustrophobic phone-box with a receiver in his hand, or dreaming the whole thing? Perhaps he'd never actually left Paris, and his mother was alive still, waiting for his rat-tat on the door.

He snatched up his address book, began flicking through the pages to find Roberto's number. His Italian friend was a natural clown, someone who might make him laugh, banter him back to normality.

He inserted another coin and dialled 01 for London, but instead of Roberto's Kensington exchange, he found he was dialling Streatham – hardly surprising when he'd been programmed in the last four days to follow up 01 with Penny's number. It was a total waste of time. Why should she answer now, when she'd been out ten minutes ago? He might as well sit down again, do the crossword, read a book. Knowing his luck, Roberto would be out as well – all his friends busy with their lives.

'Yes, hello?'

He all but dropped the phone. It wasn't Penny, but another girl who sounded very like her. 'Er . . . is . . . is Penny there?' he asked.

'I'm not too sure. Hang on – I'll go and see.'

He could feel his heart hammering in his chest, cold beads of sweat snailing down his back. Had that been Penny's sister, or a relative of Phil's? Even if Penny *was* in, there was nothing he could say. He rehearsed his lines while waiting in a fever of impatience: he was catching the next ferry and was just ringing to say goodbye; he'd been hoping they could meet, but it wasn't really possible; he was due back in the office and . . .

'Hello?'

Her voice was an electric shock jolting his whole body. How could two brief syllables affect him so profoundly?

'Hello?' she said again. The tone was flat, expressionless, with none of her usual verve. 'Who is it?' she asked tersely, after a third and increasingly irritable 'Hello'.

He tried to answer. Failed. She could slay him with one word. If he told her who was speaking, she might say a curt goodbye and slam the phone down. He must get in first, make her understand that he wasn't being cruel, but they had no choice but to go their separate ways.

Seconds passed as he tried to find his voice. If he didn't take this chance, he would never dare to ring again. She was beginning to sound quite hostile, threatening to hang up.

'It's . . . Daniel!' he blurted out, noticing with horror that he was running short of coins. He raked frantically through his pockets for more change. 'For Christ's sake don't ring off, Penny. I've got to talk to you.' He slammed in several tens, drumming his fingers impatiently on the cold impassive metal as he waited for each one to rattle down.

'Are you there? *Penny!*' His voice rose in a howl. She had cut him off, vanished, refused to say so much as . . .

'Yes, Daniel, I'm here.'

He struggled to control his voice. It was essential that he sounded calm – not overwrought, hysterical. 'Penny,' he said, closing his eyes, to focus his entire attention on the most important question of his life.

'Penny, will you marry me?'

9

'HAPPY ANNIVERSARY!' said Daniel, clinking his brandy glass to Penny's.

'Happy anniversary – six times!'

'No, five.'

'Six,' insisted Penny. 'We drank a toast with the sherry, two each with the Perrier and the wine, and now this one with the brandy.'

'Okay, happy anniversary to my darling gorgeous wife.'

'That's seven times – perfect! One for each year.'

He leaned forward, took her hand. 'You don't regret them, do you?'

'Regret what? All the drinks?'

'No, all the years.'

She smiled and sipped her brandy, her pale cheeks unnaturally flushed from the sultry heat, the wine.

'Shall we go for a walk?' he suggested, slightly disconcerted that she hadn't answered his question. 'Cool down by the river?'

'Sober down, don't you mean?'

'*I'm* not pissed.'

'You must be.'

'No.' He shook his head. 'It was probably all that throat stuff I forced down. Perhaps it diluted the alcohol, or coated my stomach, like milk's supposed to do.'

Penny spooned half-melted sugar from her empty coffee-cup. 'Well, something's worked anyway. Your voice is almost back to normal.'

'Maybe it's the country air.'

She glanced out of the window at the jammed and noisy road. 'Hampton Court's hardly the country.'

'It was in Henry VIII's time. I remember reading once that

Wolsey fixed on Hampton for his palace because all his physicians assured him it was the most healthy spot within twenty miles of London. Though I'm afraid they wouldn't think so now,' he added wryly, grimacing at the traffic. The restaurant was right opposite the palace, and coachloads of tourists were being disgorged at its gates; more coaches lumbering over the bridge towards the congested roundabout.

'Well, let's get out anyway and walk off all that food. Come on – finish your coffee.'

Daniel drained his cup, took a last long swig of brandy. 'I'll just ask them for the bill.'

'And I'll go and have a p- p- pee.'

He grinned and watched her bounce across the room; sat wondering what she did regret. Every anniversary he found himself reflecting on his marriage, always secretly astonished that he had managed to propose at all. He'd had no idea when he'd made that fateful phone call how much turmoil and complication would ensue, and today the memories were surging back unchecked, perhaps because they'd repeated their P-lunch. He could remember really vividly that sense of guilty frustration he'd battled with nine years ago, when he'd wanted Penny as his wife, but was opposed at every turn. Divorce had been just a word to him, and he was pathetically unprepared for the toll it took on Penny, the brute emotions it unleashed in her and Phil, the bitter legal wrangles which hammered on interminably. Even without Phil and both the lawyers, there'd been so many other obstacles – Pippa and her nightmares, his Paris job, his way of life, Penny's intrusive retinue: the sisters, squatters, nomads, who dropped in and out of the house. Once they were finally married (a minor miracle in itself), he'd insisted that they found a place of their own, and then barred access to the oddballs. He'd also taken a strong line on the dogs and cats and other assorted animals previously allowed the freedom of her sitting-room. Now they had one hamster (in a cage) and a house more or less to themselves.

Of course, he'd had to make his own concessions, some of them quite painful. It had been a wrench to give up Paris and his flat; a total shock to the system exchanging bachelor existence for the roller-coaster of family life. And the work he did now – an admin job in a Third World development agency – was nothing like as challenging as his previous work on illiteracy. But then he couldn't keep beetling off to Africa with a wife and child in tow, and Penny had hated the thought of him going on his own, or working in a field where there was any element of danger.

'Your bill, sir.'

He hadn't seen the waiter stealing up; changed his face from frown to smile as he rummaged for his credit card, suddenly realizing how far he'd come since he'd paid the bill for that first P-lunch in Paris. Many of the problems, which he'd regarded as insuperable, had simply faded into oblivion, or actually been solved.

He added a fat tip, handed over bill and card, then relaxed back in his chair. He was definitely feeling better. The wine had helped, of course, and an indulgent morning lying around in bed; and another heartening thing was that Juliet had receded, temporarily at least, as if she'd had the natural tact and grace to absent herself on his wedding anniversary. From the moment he'd phoned her to cancel lunch (grabbing his chance while Penny was listening to 'Midweek' in the bath), he'd experienced a huge relief. Up till then, his mind had been stretched to breaking point by his mistress, daughter, wife – each fighting for more space in it. Juliet had sounded cool. He'd been vaguely hurt by her businesslike response; would have liked a little sympathy, some concern about his croaky shred of voice. But then he'd received that from his wife. Penny had been up and down the stairs all morning, bringing him antiseptic gargles and hot drinks.

He watched her returning from the ladies' room, the outline of her figure seductively revealed through the flimsy fabric of her dress. He was seized by a strong urge to have her, there and then; strip off the skimpy sundress and roll her over and over on the restaurant's plush pink carpet. They could always skip the walk, go straight home to bed. But dare he risk another failure? Juliet's damned earrings had put paid to his attempt this morning. Thank God he'd persuaded Penny to take them off – they were too dressy for the daytime, he'd told her with (spurious) sartorial authority, and didn't match her outfit. Lunch would have been intolerable with those traitorous pearls and amethysts dangling just in front of him. The thought alone was enough to kill his desire stone dead. And anyway, he'd drunk too much. All that wine and the remnants of a throat infection might put him off his stroke.

Penny picked up the last chocolate mint, offered him a bite. 'Why don't we walk in the palace grounds? I'd love to see the flowers. I bet they're quite fantastic at the moment.'

He crumpled up his napkin. He had no objection to the flowers – it was the prospect of the trippers which depressed him. He could see them from where he was sitting: trooping in across the bridge, armed with radios and camcorders, manoeuvring their way between the ice-cream vans and hot-dog stands which had sprouted on the pavement; the tacky souvenir stalls selling policemen's helmets, Union Jacks.

'It'll be cooler by the river,' he said, pushing back his chair.

'Not so special, though. We've got the river any old day, but we haven't been to Hampton Court in ages.'

'Okay.' He ushered her through the door, recoiling from the heat outside, as if from a physical blow. It was her day, after all, and at least the trees would provide some welcome shade.

They crossed the road and walked into the palace grounds through the elaborate wrought-iron gates. There was a queue at the main Gatehouse, so they turned into the rose garden. Daniel caught his breath. He had never seen such a magnificent display. It seemed almost a sin of indulgence to stand neck-deep in roses, feasting on their colours, drinking in their smell. Intoxicated bees were lurching from flower to flower, dazzled, as he was himself, by the fiery reds, vermilions, deep yellows, vibrant pinks. Some bushes were so laden they appeared to be spawning as he watched – each lush bloom bringing forth another.

Penny thrust her nose into a brilliant scarlet tea-rose. 'We should have brought the empty wine bottle and filled it up with all this gorgeous scent!' They wandered down the path, examining the tags, reading the names aloud. 'Mischief, Sensation, *Cuisse de Nymphe*. That's French, isn't it? What does it mean?'

'Nymph's thigh.' He touched the shell-pink petals. Strange how all the names were related to seduction.

'Have you found a Penelope?'

'Not yet.' Nor a Juliet, he thought. Perhaps he should take up rose-growing – a new hobby which would anchor him to home. His modest fifteenth of an acre couldn't rival this extravaganza, but even a few bushes would make a decent show. 'Oh, look! Here's one called Guiding Spirit, and another with . . .'

He was interrupted by a shout – someone calling Penny's name. They turned to see a tall blonde figure dashing excitedly towards them: a girl in skin-tight jeans and a striped sailor-top.

'Alison!'

'Penny!'

The girls hugged each other in delight and some surprise. 'What are you doing playing truant?' Penny asked. 'I thought you had some super-duper job in a swanky office in Mayfair.'

'Yeah, that's right. I'm here for work. We're designing a new brochure on all the London palaces, and I've been asked to do the illustrations.'

'Lucky thing! I never get commissions like that – only deadly boring stuff. You'll never guess what I'm doing at the moment – drawing men's Y-fronts for a mail-order catalogue!'

Daniel crushed a rose petal in his hand. Why did Penny always put herself down? Last month she had designed a book jacket for a major publishing house, who'd declared themselves extremely impressed. He was proud of the fact that she was working as an illustrator, and had completed her degree course, notwithstanding all the turmoil of divorce, remarriage, moving house. It was he who had suggested that she re-apply to art school, fulfil her childhood dream.

'Remember when we came here in the first year?' Alison was saying. 'To do that project for the photography course?'

'Yes, and you brought Matthew in a baby-sling, and he spent the whole day yelling. How is he, by the way?'

'Still yelling, but no longer in a baby-sling – thank God! How's Pippa?'

'Okay.'

Daniel heard the change in Penny's voice, though Alison was rattling on regardless, relaying news of other students: a successful exhibition, a new baby, a plum job. She had ignored him altogether, but then they'd never really hit it off. He was annoyed that they had run into her at all. Her presence reawakened those unpleasant memories he hoped he'd left behind him in the restaurant. In the first months of their marriage, soon after they'd moved house, Alison had dropped in fairly frequently – always, it seemed, at some inappropriate moment, when Pippa was in the middle of a particularly violent tantrum, or Penny bristling over the latest skirmish with Phil. (Her ex had been living only a mile or two away from them, and continually making trouble. His affair with Khadisha had proved stormy and chaotic, and he was clearly venting his spleen on the world.)

Alison looked much smarter than the scruffy girl he remembered; the once-tousled hair now sleekly groomed; the long limbs shown off to their best by casual but expensive clothes. He had never really understood what Penny saw in her. They'd been thrown together, more or less, as the only two mature students, the only ones with children, in their year. All the rest had come straight from school, and were more concerned with their sex-lives or the latest fashion-craze than with playgroups or the price of children's shoes.

'Why don't we have a cup of tea?' Alison suggested. 'Catch up on all our news?'

'Oh yes!' said Penny eagerly, turning to Daniel to ask him if he'd mind. How could he object when the two friends hadn't seen each other in years? After graduation, Alison had gone to work abroad, and had returned to London only a few months ago.

'That's fine by me,' he lied. 'It'll give me the chance to have a quick look round the palace. You go and have your tea and I'll join you in the café in half an hour or so.'

Penny kissed him gratefully, then linked her arm through Alison's. They had resumed their duologue before he could so much as say goodbye.

He meandered back the way he'd come, noticing couples everywhere – intimate, companionable couples, sauntering along with their arms around each other, or sprawled on benches, kissing. Now he was parted from Penny, his thoughts kept returning to Juliet. Was she missing him, he wondered, or regretting their cancelled lunch? It would have been an entirely different experience with *her* – different food, different wine, different conversation. And yet he'd enjoyed the meal with Penny: her non-stop lively chatter; the way she'd tucked in with such gusto to all the most fattening items on the menu; polishing off the remnants of his pudding on top of her own gâteau and ice-cream. (Juliet would have opted for melon and grilled fish; refused even to look at the dessert trolley.)

He walked across the Moat Bridge into the first courtyard of the palace, squeezing his way past a gang of adolescent schoolgirls clustered round their teacher. He couldn't shake them off. They were on his heels as he strolled across the next court; hemming him in under Anne Boleyn's Gateway, where their teacher instructed them to look up at the carved stone roof and note the fine example of fan-vaulting. She pointed out the Tudor roses, and the initials H and A, intertwined on small stone squares – Henry and Anne Boleyn. He found that he was eavesdropping as she explained to the group that Henry had resolved to remove all traces of ill-fated Anne when he married his next wife, but that these monograms had somehow escaped his notice.

He peered up at the initials himself, watching them change in his imagination to D and J, entwined. He closed his eyes – to no avail. They still taunted him indelibly in stone. He tried to conjure up a chisel, hack them from his mind. He must take a leaf from Henry's book and erase all traces of Juliet: burn her letters, give away her presents, stop carrying round the ticket-stubs from that first momentous concert. He patted his pocket instinctively (as he did twenty times a day). He had also kept the programme – *all* the programmes, actually, of every play and concert they'd attended, and foolish things like book-matches from their favourite bars and restaurants. His Juliet collection, which he knew he must destroy.

But why was it so difficult? Christ Almighty! Henry VIII could jettison his women without the slightest qualm, yet he himself was agonizing about disposing of a few mementoes. How could you behead two wives, divorce another two, and still carry on as normal – feasting, dancing, jousting? The mere thought of ditching Juliet, let alone his wife, brought him out in a cold sweat.

He followed the school party as they continued into Clock Court, taking advantage of a guided tour for free. The teacher was now expounding on the astronomical clock: it had been made in 1540, she said, and so showed the sun going round the earth. Some of her baffled charges started asking questions, apparently believing that they still inhabited a geocentric universe. He wished to God they were right. It would provide a stable base, more sense of man's importance in the cosmos. Modern physics and Chaos Theory didn't make for much security in life.

He gazed up at the elaborate painted dial, which showed the hours, the days, the months, the year and the phases of the moon. How could he survive that eternity of hours and days without Juliet to gild them? He fumbled in his pocket for his Camels, brought his hand back empty. Cigarettes were banned as well. Over lunch, he had solemnly reiterated his promise to give up. He and Penny had even drunk a toast to it – to the new healthy virtuous Daniel.

'Alexandra!' The teacher's angry shout cut through his thoughts. 'I've warned you twice already. If you persist in misbehaving, I'll have to report you to Miss Jackson.'

He turned his back on the miscreant and walked off on his own. He'd become uneasy in the midst of all those girls, surrounded by their whispers, their secret jokes and giggles. They reminded him of Pippa and the private life she led at school. So much of her existence was totally shut off from him, whereas once they'd been so close. And it worried him that she was missing school at present, ill with some condition he couldn't begin to comprehend. What ghastly hidden trauma could make a child stop speaking? *Was* she still a child, though? She would be thirteen in three days – the beginning of her teens. He thought back to last weekend, when she had gone to stay with Penny's mother. He had taken her to Lewisham himself; tried throughout the journey to lighten the grim silence, but his voice had sounded intrusively fake as it met with no response. Driving away, he'd glanced back in his mirror at the small pale figure standing on Kay's front step; her shoulders hunched, her face forlorn and closed. And yet in previous years a week with Grandma Kay had been a source of genuine pleasure; Pippa noisily regaling him with a preview of the treats in store, then waving him off with unrestrained excitement.

He traipsed into the next court, still preoccupied with the distressing change in his daughter and baffled by the reasons for it. He stopped short in astonishment at the sight of a mysterious figure dressed in a full-length velvet gown, with her hair in a jewelled snood – a lady from some bygone age, looking utterly incongruous amidst the tee-shirts and blue jeans. He felt the blood drain from his face as he recalled the disturbing rumours about the palace being haunted by the ghost of Catherine Howard. But he didn't believe in ghosts. He blinked to disperse the mirage, but, far from disappearing, the figure continued to glide hypnotically towards him. He must be hallucinating – his mind so beset with problems, so fraught from lack of sleep, he was in danger of losing his wits. He stood his ground, determined to dispel his fear at the soft-footed but inexorable approach. Yet his heart was beating uncomfortably fast as the woman drew level with him, raised her hand in greeting. Now that she was closer, he saw she looked too sensuous for a ghost: the square-necked bodice of her dress cut provocatively low; more teasing flesh revealed through the slashings in her sleeves. Their eyes met for a moment, unnerving him completely. Those were Juliet's eyes – the same amused expression, the same shade of bluish-grey. Could this be some symbolic ghost, warning him that there was no escape from Juliet, that she would haunt him all his life?

'Good afternoon, sir,' the woman smiled.

'Er . . . good afternoon.' His voice felt strained and rusty. He was still unsure whether this was delirium or dream. Impossible to converse with spectres in normal waking life.

'Are you enjoying your visit?'

'Yes . . . yes, thanks.' He was foundering in her smile – a Mona Lisa smile, unsettling, irresistible. Her intense grey gaze seemed to pierce right through his skull.

'Look, who the devil are you?' he asked suddenly, aware that he was flushing – and not only from the heat. Of course she wasn't a ghost. The tiny details proved it: the mascara on her lashes, the twentieth-century hairgrip escaping from her snood. He felt well and truly duped, yet still bewitched, in a different sense.

She laughed at his discomfiture. 'I'm a lutenist,' she explained. 'We play music of the Tudor period to entertain the visitors. Why don't you come and hear us? The next performance's just about to start.'

'I'm afraid I . . .' The sentence petered out. Juliet had a passion for Elizabethan music. And Juliet was tall like that – enigmatic, maddeningly seductive. He could almost smell her perfume: that heady musk he'd had to beg her not to wear, for fear he'd carry it home with him in the crannies of his skin. He'd been congratulating himself at lunch on having expelled her from his mind, but now he'd met her shadow and was thrown into confusion again. He could even visualize her body beneath that voluminous dress – cool, despite the heavy velvet; open to him, naked . . .

'Well, goodbye then,' she was saying, gathering up her skirts. 'I must away to the Great Hall, or I'll be late for the performance. I'm sorry you can't make it, but we're playing again at five, so perhaps you can come then.'

'Er, yes,' he murmured, 'I'll do my best.' He was due back in the café in ten minutes, to rejoin his lawful wedded wife, yet he realized he was being drawn into a further round of danger and delusion.

He set off in the opposite direction, to avoid any more temptation; escaped into the Fountain Garden, screwing up his eyes against the glare. The sun was so strong it had enamelled all the colours in the flowerbeds; hung deep dramatic shadows from the trees. The yews were clipped remorselessly: not a hair out of place; not the smallest sprig or shoot breaking their crisp lines. He must prune himself like that: strip off all desire, cut down any rising curves of lust. And to prove his new resolve, he would go instantly and claim his wife. He knew that he belonged with her – the rest was chimera.

He skirted round a family party: a babe in arms, a toddler in a pushchair and several older offspring whining at their parents. The heat was fraying tempers, melting ice-cream cornets. One bedraggled infant sat howling on the ground, refusing to budge an inch. Daniel gave the father a sympathetic smile. Since his marriage, he felt a natural bond with parents; they were no longer an alien species, but valiant fellow-sufferers.

He strode along the Broad Walk, through the wooden gate and along the path which led back to the café. He scanned the tables set outside – no carrot-head, no sailor-top. He was about to go and look inside when he spotted the two girls lying on the grass together, their bodies almost touching.

'Penny!' he called, running over to join them. She scrambled to her feet, her whole face lighting up. He held her close and kissed her, a long proprietorial kiss.

'Wow!' said Alison, raising a quizzical eyebrow. 'Is this your second honeymoon or something?'

'Yes,' said Daniel. 'It is.'

'Well, perhaps I'd better scat then, and leave you lovebirds on your own.'

'Don't be silly. Daniel's only joking.' Penny sounded anxious, well aware of the unspoken animosity between her husband and her old art-school friend. She picked up their empty tea-cups, placed them on a bench. 'Alison's got to do some drawings of the maze, and she suggested we come too.'

'Okay.' He wasn't particularly keen about having to play goose-berry to Penny and her bosom friend, but it wasn't often he had a chance to please his wife – not these days, anyway. She complained that he was always out, and often strangely moody. Well, that was going to stop. He offered an arm to each of the girls, steered them towards the maze.

'Hey, let's split up,' said Penny, as they filed in through the narrow gate. 'And there'll be a prize for the one who gets to the centre first.'

'What's the prize?' asked Daniel.

'A kiss!'

'Well, I'd better not win *that*!' Alison said caustically.

No, you hadn't, Daniel cautioned under his breath.

'Okay, I'm off!' said Penny, overtaking a group of Japanese.

Daniel took his time, struggling to recall something he'd read about the maze; some trick or secret which led you to the centre. Didn't you take the left-hand path each time? Yes, that was it – he remembered now – it was called the hand-on-hedge method. You kept your left hand on the left hedge, following all the twists and turns (including the dead ends), but always bearing left at any junction.

He watched Alison take the right-hand fork; set off himself the other way with just a hint of smugness in his step. He couldn't actually keep his hand on the hedge with so many people crowding the paths, but so long as he didn't get disoriented, he should be at the centre well before the other two. He felt a childish glee as he negotiated the first dead end, accepting it as a step on the way rather than a time-wasting frustration. If mazes symbolized the Path of Life, then for once he was on the right path, and going in the right direction.

Snatches of conversation, some in unknown languages, rose above the hedges from invisible fellow-travellers; the occasional raucous laugh or wail of bemused defeat. A small boy in a baseball cap barged rudely past, followed by an elderly man with a bald and sunburned head. All ages on the Path of Life, all races, classes, types, and many of them destined to go wrong. He forged ahead himself, again compelled to double back, but aware that he was making progress, despite the constant zigzags.

He passed a huddle of French children, arguing vociferously about which fork they should take. He didn't offer to enlighten them – nor Alison for that matter. She had just swept by, flinging him a supercilious smirk. The design of the maze was ingenious. Several times the paths skirted tantalizingly near the centre, giving the impression that the goal was almost in reach, only to meander away from it again.

He could hear the tramp of confident feet echoing behind him, then the sound of muttered curses as the footsteps shuffled to a halt. He, too, was forced to stop. A rumbustious family group was bearing down towards him from the opposite direction, threatening to engulf him in their sticky-fingered tide. He let them pass, then set off once again, feeling momentarily nonplussed as he realized he was weaving back the way he'd come already. This particular path was empty, so he placed his left hand on the hedge, niggled by the suspicion that perhaps he'd made a fundamental error and it was the right-hand fork he should have taken all along. That would mean going back to the beginning and starting from square one. No – he'd better trust to his left-hand method for just a little longer, and *keep* his hand on the hedge this time, however difficult it was.

He strode doggedly along, turned a blind corner, then stood staring in surprise at the two tall chestnut trees which marked the centre of the maze – right there in front of him. He walked over to one tree and touched its slender trunk, to confirm he'd reached the finishing-post. He'd made it, won the prize – which meant more than just a kiss. The fact that he had solved the puzzle was important on another level: it seemed a propitious sign; a prediction that he would unravel his own problems and put his life to rights. He already felt much lighter, as if he had dumped his guilt and conflict in the dead ends of the maze; shaken off the spirit of that taunting lutenist. He wasn't one for superstition, but he had a strong instinctive feeling that if Penny reached the centre before Alison, then everything would turn out doubly well.

He felt he deserved a cigarette, but resisted the temptation; kept his hands occupied by picking up a spray of leaves and using it as a fan. Actually, there was plenty to distract him. He'd pictured the centre of the maze as a sort of sacred empty space, but there was barely room to move. It was very small, in any case, and a tribe of oversized Americans had already planted the flag, and were complaining to the world at large about the heat, the crowds, the midges, while their enterprising children were busy carving graffiti on the tree-trunks, adding their crude hieroglyphics to the hundreds defacing the bark. He flattened himself against the hedge, as far away from their barbarity as possible, keeping an anxious look-out for Penny's beacon-head. Strange he hadn't passed her once in his progress through the maze, when he'd seen Alison three times. He suspected Alison had abandoned the whole venture and started on her sketches. After all, she'd come here to work, not to compete for the dubious prize of a kiss from one of the Hughsons.

There was a sudden yelp of laughter from the bench beneath the left-hand tree. A group of young Italian lads were jumping up on it, striking affected poses, then pushing each other off. One had removed his tee-shirt, exposing a tanned and hairy chest. Daniel's eyes were immediately drawn to that expanse of naked flesh. Penny liked hirsute men. Only last month she had been admiring a photo in a woman's magazine of some film star dressed in nothing but his chest-hair and his swimming trunks, and her exaggerated praises had made him absurdly jealous. He imagined her now, crushed against a macho young Italian; huge hairy hands fondling her bare breasts, the brute's iron-stiff erection never going down. He ripped a leaf to pieces. His wife could actually be deceiving him and he wouldn't even know. After all, he was always telling lies himself, to excuse his absences; saying he'd been kept at work when he was really meeting Juliet. So when Penny told him airily she was going to a yoga class, or off to see a friend, that too might be a cover-up. The trouble with lying was that it made you, in turn, start suspecting other people; deception breeding mistrust. But then Penny had slept with *him* on the very first day they met, so might she not repeat the performance with another willing bachelor?

He dropped his shreds of leaf. It was hardly fair to blame her when he had seduced her, more or less, then betrayed her nine years later. He wasn't just a hypocrite – he was also deceiving himself: full of good intentions, but never taking any action.

He groped in his back pocket for the grubby, precious ticket-stubs which had become his talisman. He glanced down at their numbers: H9 and 10. Nine was a magical number, but magic didn't last, and though H might stand for heaven, it could swiftly change to hell. He took a last regretful look at them, then crumpled them to nothing and stuffed them into the thickest part of the yew-hedge. When he withdrew his hand, he noticed it was scratched; tiny beads of blood gleaming on the back like out-of-season yew berries. He wiped it roughly on his handkerchief. No sacrifice without some pain. He unbuttoned his other pocket, removed his packet of Camels and rammed them into the hedge as well. They were further proof of his hypocrisy. You didn't carry cigarettes when you had vowed to give up smoking.

He sank down on the bench, which he now had to himself. The Italians had trooped off; in fact everyone had vanished, leaving him alone. He had wanted peace and quiet, but instead of revelling in his solitude, he found it strangely threatening. He could see the clock dial in his mind, the little golden orb of the sun travelling steadfastly round the earth. Those Tudor astronomers had got it totally wrong, and perhaps their twentieth-century counterparts were equally wide of the mark. Man knew next to nothing; simply needed to persuade himself that he was making sense of a senseless universe. He stared down at his hand: a tracery of fine pink scratches, encrusted with congealing blood. He thrust both hands in his pockets, started pacing round and round the cramped deserted space. He almost wished those schoolgirls had caught up with him; rebellious Alexandra answering her teacher back. Anything to connect him to humanity.

He swung round at the sound of his name – Penny's voice, rising in excitement as she ran towards him, launching into a garbled explanation of why she'd been so long. Someone had been taken ill – nothing serious, just a touch of heat-stroke – but she'd stopped to help and . . .

'Penny, listen!' he implored, cutting her off in mid-sentence. 'You'll never leave me, will you? I want you to promise – now, this instant – say you'll . . .'

'Daniel, whatever's wrong? You sound quite hysterical.'

'Nothing's wrong. Just promise you won't leave me.'

'Well, of course I won't. Why should I?'

'You'll never go off with anyone else, or lie to me, or deceive me?'

'Darling, what *is* all this, for heaven's sake?' She stepped back in bewilderment, eyed him with concern. 'You've been so strange these last few weeks, and I was hoping things were better. Don't spoil our lovely day. It *was* good, wasn't it – I mean, the lunch and everything?'

He nodded, gripped her hand.

'By the way, what about the prize?' She tilted her face towards him, suddenly coquettish as she pursed her lips, mimed a kiss. 'Aren't you going to claim it?'

He seized her by the shoulders, repeated the first kiss he'd ever given her – that violent, frenzied, greedy kiss in the Hotel Manchester. He sensed her trying to pull away; heard voices, muffled giggles. Reluctantly he opened his eyes to see half a dozen cameras pointed at them. A party of Japanese had burst into the heart of the maze and were recording the kiss for posterity on their Nikons and Yashicas. He didn't care – he wanted it recorded. These were his witnesses, bearing testimony to the fact that he and Penny were committed to each other for the next seven times seventy years.

10

'FANTASTIC CAKE!' said Sonia. 'One of Penny's creations, I take it?'

Daniel nodded. His wife's designer birthday cakes were nothing if not original. This one was in the shape of a frog squatting on a lily-leaf, its mouth agape, and a gold and purple butterfly alighting on its tongue. 'HAPPY BIRTHDAY PIPPA!' was written on the frog's green back, and thirteen candles circled the base. The only problem was who would blow them out? Pippa was upstairs, had refused even to come down to greet her guests.

Sonia touched an admiring finger to a bulging marzipan eye. 'I don't know where she gets her ideas. It's all I can do to produce a plain round Victoria sponge!'

Daniel murmured some inanity. He always found it difficult to talk to Phil's mother. Phil himself had been working in the Middle East for the last five years or so, having finally married Khadisha, who had obtained her own divorce only after a mammoth battle involving her whole extended family. Since arriving in Bahrain, he had broken off all contact with his daughter and ex-wife, perhaps exhausted by contention, or simply trying to avoid the strain of divided loyalties. But Sonia, for her part, was determined not to lose touch with her grandchild. Daniel tried to be relaxed with her, but the guilt he felt about stepping into Phil's shoes invariably affected his behaviour; made him tense and tongue-tied. Not that Sonia ever blamed him, or hinted at regrets of her own. On the contrary, it was more likely to be Penny's mother who would voice her worries openly, or make sly digs about his snobbishness or his smoking.

He swallowed his sliver of Polo, replaced it with another. He was doing jolly well: four packets of Polos a day was far less reprehensible than two packets of cigarettes. He glanced swiftly round the room – red hair in preponderance, even a red setter. Penny's sisters were there in force, with their respective children, husbands, dogs, plus a few good friends and neighbours. Pippa's birthday bash had become an established event, and although this year she had made it clear that she didn't want a party in any shape or form, Penny had hoped (vainly) that if the usual crowd showed up, it might bring about a cure; coax the deaf-mute back to life.

'I did once go to cookery classes,' Sonia was saying, as she settled herself back on the sofa after admiring the frog-cake. 'But I'm afraid it was very basic stuff and I didn't actually learn much.'

'They're a waste of time, those classes,' Penny's mother remarked, squeezing up to make more room for Sonia. 'Either you *can* cook or you can't.'

'Well, I'm not so sure,' said Daniel diplomatically, perching on the sofa arm. 'Penny's managed to teach me quite a lot.' It needed tact to juggle both the grandmas, who couldn't be more different, not only in their views, but their appearance. Sonia was grey – grey hair, grey face, grey frock – whereas Kay loved daring colours, like her daughter, and though her hair had faded, it was still the famous Hethrington red.

'How's your job, dear?' Sonia asked Daniel, pointedly changing the subject.

'It's going pretty well, thanks.' He knew the question was just a social formality rather than an expression of genuine interest, yet he was still tempted to enlarge on it. The conversation so far hadn't moved beyond the drought, the recent tube strikes and Sonia's arthritis, whereas his work was one of the topics he could discuss with real enthusiasm. But he'd probably only bore them if he started sounding off about the soul-searching his job involved: the constant daily struggle reconciling high ideals with a chronic shortage of funds. Funny things, families: supposedly your nearest and dearest, who were meant to understand and empathize, yet you were often more aware of a yawning gulf between you; a sense of inhabiting different worlds.

Penny didn't have his hang-ups. She and her sisters were kindred souls, chiselled from a single block. She was sitting with them now – Ros, the eldest (who had the bluest eyes, the wiriest hair, and four freckled gingery sons), deep in discussion with his personal favourite, Jo (married, rather surprisingly, to the platitudinous Fergus), while the youngest sister, Lindsay, was sponging trifle off her daughter's dress and trying to restrain her squirming baby. All their faces were animated as they chattered excitedly away, exchanging jokes and news, their talk punctuated by frequent bursts of laughter. He was astonished Penny could laugh like that when her only child was moping on her own upstairs, and had shown not the slightest interest in her presents or the cake. As far as he was concerned, Pippa's silent absence was a source of grief, of shame. He kept wondering what she was doing – reading, crying, staring into space? Or maybe she resented all the rumpus, and couldn't wait for the invasion to be over.

Kay's chirpy voice broke into his thoughts. 'Did I tell you that I'm going up to Edinburgh? It's one of those Bargain Break things, with all your meals thrown in, and the coach fare there and back.'

'Lovely,' he said vaguely. 'When are you off?'

'The weekend after next. We're leaving at the crack of dawn on Friday, but they pick you up at your door, thank heavens, and then drop you back at midnight on the Sunday.'

'Sounds good.' He racked his brains without success for something more inspiring to say. 'Have you been to Scotland before?'

'No, never. You know me, Daniel. I'm a real old stay-at-home.'

'Well, make sure you see the castle. It really is impressive.' His eyes strayed back to Penny. She and her sisters had been joined by two bohemian types – her old next-door neighbours from Streatham. They were all huddled on the floor amidst a tide of boisterous offspring. Lindsay's baby was now crawling around half-naked, while another tot (he wasn't sure whose) was dismantling a plate of sandwiches, licking out the cream-cheese filling and smearing the residue on its face. The chaotic scene stirred uneasy memories of the months before his marriage, when he'd felt swamped by Penny's family and friends – unknown and daunting people from what he called her 'former life' – with no one of his own to redress the balance. Even Alison was here, with her obstreperous six-year-old. He had promised to be nice to her, though he was secretly alarmed that she seemed set to become a permanent encumbrance since their Hampton Court encounter. Not only were she and Matthew staying the whole weekend, but Penny had agreed to spend next Saturday helping her move house.

'I suppose you miss all your trips to Africa,' Sonia was saying. 'Didn't you use to go there several times a year?'

He suddenly felt claustrophobic closeted indoors; changed the scene to Kenya – the Masai Mara national park. He was driving north to south; no one sharing the terrain with him save a herd of wildebeest browsing in the distance, or a flock of crested hoopoes flapping up into the limitless horizon. He could even smell African smells: wood smoke, bush fires, heat and dust and dung.

'I keep hoping to take Penny there,' he said, aware that Sonia was still awaiting some reply. 'And Pippa too, of course – show them where I was born, and where I used to work. But somehow we always seem too busy, and anyway I'm afraid three air fares would probably break the bank!'

Kay bit into her sausage roll, spraying pastry flakes on her lap. 'The nearest I've got to Africa is watching that new series on the box. Have you seen it, Daniel? There's this doctor-chappie who's trying to build a clinic in the wilds of . . .'

Her words were cut short by a dramatic squall of rain, slamming at the windows, putting paid to all conversation. A flash of lightning lasered through the sky, followed almost instantaneously by a deafening crack of thunder.

'Wow!' exclaimed Ros. 'We were saying only yesterday how desperately we needed rain, and someone's answered our prayers with a vengeance. Arthur, *sit*!'

The lunatic red setter was plunging about the room, excited by the violence of the storm. His windscreen-wiper tail swept a tumbler from the coffee-table, cascading orange squash all over the rug.

Daniel swore under his breath. Penny had her hands full trying to calm the frightened children, so he dashed out to the kitchen for a cloth. He couldn't see one anywhere, and there was so much mess and clutter they would need a veritable army to restore the place to order. Every available surface had been used for sandwich-making and still bore its jumbled cargo of fillings, chutneys, spreads. The sink was chock-a-block with baking trays and cake tins, and the setter's muddy paw-prints patterned the pale floor. He jammed the fanlight shut, to stop the rain coming in. It was sheeting down outside, battering his geraniums, turning the lawn into a swamp. He stared out at the overflowing gutters, recalling last year's barbecue – the sun shining serenely and a normal, happy Pippa larking with her friends. They usually held the party in the garden, but today's early morning forecast had warned of a break in the weather, so they'd had to change their plans. He should have taken a much stronger stance and cancelled the whole thing. It was farcical to celebrate a birthday when Pippa was so miserable and had refused point-blank to invite any of her classmates, even her best friend.

He rubbed the misted window, though it was difficult to see beyond the rain-lashed patio. A year ago, he had been out there in his bush-hat, grilling sausages and spare ribs, while the girls played some ear-splitting pop music. He remembered complaining about the din, yet now he would give anything to hear that raucous noise again, or see his daughter cavorting around doing her Michael Jackson take-off.

He rummaged in the cupboard for a cloth, but found only dirty dusters, caked with polish. He was tempted to give up; leave not just the puddle on the rug, but escape from the whole shambles. If he slipped out the back way, nobody would notice he had gone. He could tramp across the common in the rain and let the drenching downpour flush away his gloom.

He closed the cupboard door, forced himself to go back to the sitting-room, his host's smile firmly in place. Ros's husband, Brian, was mopping up the spillage with his handkerchief; his two youngest sons floating cheese-straw boats on what remained of the orange lake.

Brian squeezed out his hankie, then used it to wipe both sticky faces. 'The usual peaceful family gathering!' he joked. 'Sorry about our pooch! They say owners take after their dogs, but I hope I never get as neurotic as dear Arthur.'

Daniel smiled apologetically, fearing Brian could read his thoughts, suss out his aversion to uncontrollable dogs. He stole a glance at his brother-in-law – a broad and burly type, exactly the same age as himself, but who had viewed his fortieth birthday as a milestone, not a trauma. Of course, Brian had more to show for it – those four strapping sons, to start with – and had better things to do than worry about soggy rugs or a few scratches on the furniture. Nor did he fret about his bald patch; merely laughed it off, instead of wasting time and money on bogus lotions and potions which promised miraculous regrowth. Secretly, he envied Brian his easy-going attitude, his total lack of vanity or angst, but the two of them were poles apart and there seemed very little prospect of their ever closing the gap. In fact, no one in this room really shared his interests and ideals – or his wretched self-absorption, come to that – and he suspected all his brothers-in-law regarded him as a bore, if not a prig.

'So the birthday girl's sticking to her guns then, and refusing to honour us with her presence?'

'She'll . . . come down a bit later, I expect.' Daniel excused himself to Brian, grabbed a plate of cakes and started passing them round. Whatever happened, they must avoid the subject of Pippa. There had been quite enough fuss as it was: rumblings of disapproval, cluckings of concern, whispered speculations about how and where she was.

Alison took an almond slice, patted the arm of her chair. 'Slow down, Daniel, for heaven's sake! You've been charging round like a steam engine the whole afternoon. Come and sit beside me and tell me something riveting!'

Okay, he almost said, it's my mistress's birthday too, today, but the only present she's received from me is a short and business-like note informing her that the affair is over.

He could just picture Alison's face – its prurient excitement, or malicious curiosity, or perhaps simple disbelief that stolid worthy Daniel could ever have got involved in an affair. What *he* was finding incredible was that he had absolutely no regrets about sending that curt note, though it did require a huge effort on his part to keep his mind off Juliet entirely. Wounds could easily bleed again if you started picking at the scabs.

'So I take it nothing very enthralling's been happening in your life?' Alison prised an almond from her cake, nibbled it fastidiously.

'No, not really – unless you count renegotiating the house insurance! But how about you? How are the drawings coming on?'

'Oh, they're going fantastically well. I only wish I had a bit more space. But we're doing just the one brochure, you see, for several different palaces, so a lot of what I sketched on Wednesday had to be left out. By the way, what's all this with Pippa? Penny told me she's more or less stopped speaking. I must say I find it hard to imagine any child clamming up like that, but don't you think it's wrong to let her get away with it, and just sulk upstairs in her room? If she was my daughter, I'd insist she showed her face, if only out of common courtesy.'

She's *not* your daughter, Daniel stopped himself from saying, recalling his promise to be on his best behaviour. 'She hasn't been too well,' he explained, in what he hoped was a conciliatory tone.

'Yes – so Penny said. Has she seen the doctor?'

Daniel nodded. 'Several times.'

'And what did he have to say?'

'Oh, something about her age, and maybe a depressive reaction following her illness. Apparently these viral things can leave you feeling really low, mentally and physically.'

'Yeah, but refusing to speak's a pretty extreme reaction, I'd have thought – I mean, more than just the normal adolescent glooms. Didn't he suggest that she ought to see a psychiatrist or someone?'

'No,' said Daniel tersely.

'Well, what about school? Aren't her teachers bothered?'

'Yes, of course they are, but they think it's best to play the whole thing down. It may be just a phase, you see. Though I must admit I'm concerned myself about all the work she's missing.'

Alison laughed sardonically. 'You would be, you old clever clogs! I suppose you're worried that she won't get her PhD until she's fourteen and a half!'

Daniel bit back a retort, mumbled something about going to fetch a knife to cut the cake. In fact, he was going straight up to see Pippa. How could they cut the cake or light the candles, carry on this fatuous charade that everything was fine and dandy, when the most important person was missing from the ceremony?

His steps began to falter as he approached her room. He would only be intruding, and what was the use of continuing the argument (one-sided and therefore futile) they'd already had this morning? He stood uncertain on the landing, listening to the voices rising from downstairs. He could also hear a noise in their bedroom – a muffled sort of crooning sound. Mystified, he peered in through the open door; immediately ducked back out of sight when he saw Penny in the wicker chair holding Lindsay's baby, humming softly while she rocked him in her arms.

He retreated to the bathroom, assailed by bitter memories of an earlier conflict he hoped he'd left behind. Penny had always wanted another child – *his* child, their child, a new life to complete them. He had dredged up every possible reason to dissuade her; had no desire himself to enlarge their perfect family of three. He still felt guilty about his obstinate refusal, knowing it was totally unfair, but how could he explain the tangled skein of jealousies and fears which engulfed him when he thought about the subject? He didn't want to share his wife with a demanding helpless baby, though that was purely selfish and not worthy of him anyway. There were other reasons – less shaming ones – which he could hardly put into words.

He caught sight of his reflection in the mirror, noting how his frown-lines were becoming a permanent feature; mentally comparing Brian's relaxed and cheerful grin. Great to be a parent like Brian – approachable, affectionate – but what if he turned out more like his own father? His parents had conceived him late, almost as an afterthought, and he had always felt daunted by their high ideals and philanthropic work. His father had been frequently away, travelling the length and breadth of Zambia in his capacity as an education officer. As a boy, even as a teenager, he'd been frightened of that aloof and distant figure. His own life had seemed so puny – a timid, greedy, shallow life – compared with a man who was half despot and half saint. He couldn't bear the thought of any child of his feeling the same way, or accusing him (with good reason) of being too involved in his job.

He unlocked the bathroom door, walked slowly back to the bedroom, resolving to tell Penny how sorry and ashamed he was; swamp her in apologies, as he had eight years ago. Now, as then, he marshalled all his arguments, determined to convince her that he wasn't just a selfish brute, but had considered her daughter too. Pippa might well be jealous of a sibling, especially one who was more his child than she was, so surely he'd been right in thinking that the only reasonable compromise was to accept her as his own?

And I've *done* that, he pleaded silently to Penny. She's Pippa Hughson now, not Pippa Clarke. And you know I've made a will, for no other reason than to ensure that she'll inherit in exactly the same way as any natural child of ours.

His hand groped for his cigarettes, then realized they weren't there. He hadn't said a word yet, but was standing in defensive silence watching Penny rock the baby; her cheek against its face, its pudgy hand clasping at her pendant. He felt utterly superfluous, an intruder, a voyeur.

Penny raised her head and saw him, put a warning finger to her lips. 'Have you escaped too?' she whispered, her doting gaze returning to the child. 'I came up to change Simon, but then he went all sleepy on me and I hadn't the heart to disturb him. But I'm getting really desperate for a pee. Here, hold him for a moment, darling. I'll be back in two ticks.'

His first instinct was to resist, but before he could say anything, she had motioned him to the chair and handed him the bundle. He sat stiffly with the dead weight on his lap. He had never learned the knack of handling babies, and they never failed to rouse in him a whole set of different fears: fear they'd scream, reject him; fear of their vulnerability, their terrifying smallness; fear that he was freakish for not wanting one of his own. He stared down at the fuzz of reddish hair. In fact, this could be their child, the son they'd never had. Weren't men supposed to crave sons – to carry on their line, or to complete them or fulfil them or extend their individual lives? Anne Boleyn had been put to death for failing to produce one. So what was wrong with *him*?

'That's better!' Penny said, returning from the bathroom, still straightening her skirt. 'And now I'm about it, I think I'll change my shoes. These sandals of Ros's are pinching at the toes.'

He watched her balance on one foot, wrestle with the buckle, then kick the sandal off. At first he had found it distasteful that she and her sisters should swap their clothes so readily, wear each other's cast-offs, as he put it, but now he almost envied them that special sort of intimacy. You could only really share your clothes with people who were close; whose sweat and stains and body-smells you accepted as freely as your own. Perhaps he'd been wrong about Pippa's reaction to a sibling. Instead of being jealous, she might have welcomed another child, someone she could have turned to as an ally or a soul-mate, a support against the grown-ups.

'By the way,' said Penny, rubbing her cramped toes, 'Ros is pregnant again. Her doctor's just confirmed it.'

Daniel shifted the baby, which seemed to be slipping from his knee. Penny's tone had been studiously casual, but he could guess the depth of feeling she was struggling to conceal. He had never realized till this moment how acutely she must suffer every time she was presented with a newborn niece or nephew, without ever producing a new infant of her own. He stroked a tentative finger across Simon's downy hair, trying to imagine it erupting into Pippa's wiry mop. There was still time to change his mind. Penny was only thirty-one, three years younger than Ros. If he could somehow overcome his fears, they could actually conceive a child tonight. Penny would be ecstatic at the thought, and it would set the seal on his new start, his renunciation of the past – and Juliet.

Simon began whimpering and threshing about in his arms. Was he clutching him too tightly, or had he hurt him in some way? That was the whole problem – the way you could damage a helpless child and not have the faintest notion that you were doing anything wrong.

No, he *couldn't* change his mind. The risk was too great, and forty far too old for a nervous first-time father. 'Look, I . . . I'm sorry,' he said bleakly.

'Whatever for? You should be glad, you chump! Brian and Ros are over the moon! You know how they're always joking about wanting their full rugger team!'

'No, I meant I . . .' Why bother to go on? There was no point in dragging up the past, repeating the same arguments, re-living the same fears.

'You do say funny things,' Penny murmured, pulling on her moccasins. 'There, that's better. Now hand me over Dozy-Drawers and I'll take him back to Lindsay. Aren't you coming down, darling? It must seem a bit peculiar – us both sneaking off upstairs.'

'I'll just look in on Pippa, see if she's all right.'

'Okay, don't be long. You know what we agreed – we'd get the party over first, then try to talk to her afterwards.'

He nodded. It wasn't a question of talking: he simply felt he ought to show her that she hadn't been forgotten. He stood outside her room again, as hesitant as before. If only he could get through to her, resume their usual dialogue. They had always been so close, had struck up a rapport almost from the start, reacting to each other at some deep unconscious level, so that he'd sometimes felt she was more his child than Penny's. But now he hadn't the remotest idea of what was going on in her mind. Had she sussed out his affair, and was responding with silent disgust, or did she hold him responsible for ousting her real father? Or perhaps it was less to do with him than with the fact that she'd reached puberty – the age of disillusion, when children no longer saw the world as a cosy, rosy place, or their parents as infallible. He remembered himself at thirteen, becoming more judgemental of the adult world in general; regarding his friends' parents with prissy disapproval on account of their various trifling misdemeanours. Maybe Pippa despised him for smoking (and had scant faith in his promise to give up), or found him introspective and bad-tempered. Once, she had thought the world of him – continually drawing pictures of him in her art lessons at school, or making 'cakes' for him at home from greyish scraps of pastry, or presenting him with treasures such as a lop-sided desk-tidy, lovingly constructed from half a dozen toilet rolls and rather too much glue. But now she shut him out – literally as well as metaphorically.

He tapped lightly on her door, then opened it a crack, knowing that she wouldn't say 'come in'. She was sitting on the bed, picking at her thumbnail, her pale face listless; her eyes fixed on the floor. He felt a rush of conflicting emotions: pity and protectiveness, annoyance and resentment, even self-reproach because he had failed in his resolve never to let his eyes stray to the vicinity of her breasts. Those newly developed breasts were an embarrassment to both of them. She did her best to hide them by wearing baggy tee-shirts, but they were both self-consciously aware that she was no longer Daddy's little girl. And yet her face was still so childlike, with its rounded cheeks and translucent fragile skin – no adolescent spots amidst the galaxy of freckles. She seemed a mass of contradictions: the stridently red hair at odds with her diffident expression; her coltish legs and bare and grubby feet contrasting with the womanly curves above.

He forced his eyes away; had to make a constant effort not to look at the changes in her body, but the fact that he should want to look worried and confused him.

'D'you mind if I come in?' he asked, pitching his gaze somewhere between her ankles and the carpet.

She made the slightest inclination of her head; holding her hand in front of her face, as if even that must be protected from his scrutiny.

He positioned himself just inside the door. If he kept his distance, he'd seem less of a threat. 'Do you want another cup of tea? There's plenty in the pot.' He noticed that she hadn't drunk the first one, and that the plate of sandwiches he had brought up earlier on had been left untouched on her desk.

'No, thanks.'

Her voice was so low it was practically inaudible, but at least she had actually spoken. Some days she would say nothing at all, turning meals into endurance tests as he and Penny tried to keep the conversation going across her mutely miserable form. Weekends were still worse – their once gregarious daughter sitting silent in her room, utterly indifferent to what was going on in the house; refusing to join him in the garden or go shopping with her mother; apathetic even when her friends phoned.

Encouraged by her two whispered words, he enquired about the birthday cake – was there any chance she'd changed her mind and would come down after all? It would be such a shame if she didn't blow the candles out, and besides, what about the wish? She only got one wish a year, so she ought to make the most of it.

Not a flicker of response. He was probably taking the wrong line, treating her like a baby. When *he* was thirteen, he'd been precocious for his age – at least in terms of his intellectual interests – and Pippa was very similar. Ironically enough, it was largely he who had made her so. He'd introduced her to Keats and Dickens when other children were still reading picture-books; taught her French and chess; accompanied her on the piano when she played her guitar, and encouraged her to try her hand at more challenging types of music than those provided at school. Yet now he was resorting to wishes – childish magic to make things sweet and simple again, and banish the bad fairies.

He cleared his throat, tried a different tack. 'Wouldn't you like to come down and see the dogs? You know how Arthur adores you. And there's another little terrier thing, sleeping on a blanket in my study. He's a bit raggedy round the ears, I'm afraid. Apparently he got involved in a dog-fight, and Auntie Jo rescued him . . .'

It was useless going on. She wasn't even listening, just staring out of the window, watching a plane plough a deepening furrow through the sky. The rain had stopped, giving way to an eerie, brooding stillness, as if time had been suspended, summer swallowed up. This morning's vivid colours were engulfed in a grey gloom; the once cloudless sky now overcast and scummy.

Suddenly he felt weary; drifted to the window and sat down at her desk. A bird flew past – a magpie – a flash of metallic blue highlighting its gleaming black and white. One for sorrow, he mused, instantly dismissing the thought with a twinge of irritation. He was for ever telling himself he wasn't superstitious, yet he had noticed in these last few weeks that he seemed increasingly susceptible to irrational ideas.

He fidgeted with the books on her desk, noticing the *Pierre Lapin* – Peter Rabbit in French – which he'd bought her years ago and read to her each night, alongside the English version. In only a few months, she had learned to recite it with him, stumbling over words like *parapluie* and *épouvantail*, which he patiently corrected. Perhaps he'd worked her too hard, expected too much of her too soon. Yet she appeared to enjoy the nightly ritual, and would rush up to him eagerly with the book open at page one, chanting: '*Flopsaut, Trotsaut, Queue-de-Coton et PIERRE!*'

That exuberant child had died, to be replaced by one who froze him off, ignored her favourite books, lost her prized possessions, rebuffed her former friends.

'What's Emma doing today?' he asked, glancing surreptitiously over his shoulder to check on her reaction. Emma Hayes was her best friend – or had been for the past eight years. The two had met at primary school, and had soon become inseparable.

Pippa shrugged, scuffed her foot against the edge of the divan.

'Why not invite her round tomorrow? We could save the cake till then, if you like, and have another party – just you and her and us.'

She might have been stone deaf for all the acknowledgement he received. He snatched up a pencil and started doodling on her scribble-pad. On *his* thirteenth birthday, he'd been stuck in bloody boarding school, where no one gave a toss whether he was happy or not, hungry or not, and there was more chance of a caning than a cake. Pippa's school was paradise compared with the barbarities of his. He didn't believe in private education (partly on principle and partly because of his own grim experience), so when they'd moved house, they'd deliberately picked this area on account of one particular state school. Northfield had an oustanding reputation, due largely to its head – the formidable Miss Whittaker, who had transformed a previously run-of-the-mill establishment through a combination of idealism and sheer bloody-minded obstinacy.

But perhaps he'd been misguided, after all. Penny had voiced doubts herself when they were still at the decision stage; feared Northfield was too big. They had been to see a much smaller school, but this time *he'd* objected on the grounds it was girls-only. He was well aware at an intellectual level that single-sex schools were often preferable for girls, who achieved better academic results without pressure from the boys. But emotionally he distrusted them. His own segregation amongst three hundred macho males had left him shy and callow, so that when he had finally escaped at the age of eighteen and a half, he'd blushed to the ears every time he'd been forced to meet a member of that strange species known as females. He didn't want his daughter similarly ill at ease, or emerging into adult life with an impressive string of A-levels but no basic social confidence.

The choice of school had proved quite a problem, one way and another. They had tried to keep their options open, and even considered a Church of England school with the unlikely name of St Willehad's. It was smaller again, and said to have high standards, but the thought of endorsing a religion he didn't actually believe in made him feel uneasy. It had been bad enough at Greystone Court – kneeling in a cold chapel every morning, begging an unresponsive God to please let the place burn down, so that he could be shipped back to his parents in Lusaka.

Now he was beginning to wonder if he had allowed his personal history to influence him unduly; whether in trying to save Pippa from what he himself had suffered, he had overlooked more subtle sorts of problems.

Dammit! He was frowning again. He ironed his forehead with

126

his fingers as he turned to face his daughter. 'How d'you feel about going back to school on Monday, darling? I could take you in the car, if you like, and you can always leave at lunchtime if you've had enough by then.' It was probably best to take things fairly slowly at first, give the child a chance to find her feet. On the other hand, he certainly didn't want her to miss any more of her school work, or fall seriously behind. She was no longer strictly ill. Dr Steadman had given her the all-clear, confiding to him and Penny that the sooner she got back to normal, the better she would feel. It wasn't good for adolescent girls to moon around doing nothing in particular, or cut themselves off from their friends.

He coughed, to fill the silence. Pippa's expression was so forlorn he couldn't bear to look at her. Instead, he looked around the room, trying to derive some comfort from his surroundings. This small untidy lair contained a potted history of his marriage: their wedding photo with Pippa as a scowling bridesmaid; the bear they'd bought her to keep her company when they went away on honeymoon; Penny's graduation photograph tacked up on the noticeboard beside snapshots of their holidays abroad. It also expressed the dichotomy between Pippa as a child and Pippa as a woman. Her cuddly toys were still lined up on the bed, yet there was an assortment of new make-up on the dressing-table, and a slinky black silk skirt lay crumpled on the floor.

There was another sort of conflict – between the Pippa he knew and the one her schoolfriends saw. It was *de rigueur* in her crowd to rave about pop music and be interested in boys, and she gave a convincing performance on both counts. But he was well aware of the strain involved in concealing one's true self for the sake of conformity. He had done the same at her age: avoided at all costs the stigma of being different from his peers. He found it rather strange that she was growing to resemble him in temperament – becoming highly strung, withdrawn and over-sensitive. Whatever had happened to Phil's and Penny's genes, which should have made her extrovert and bouncy? Or perhaps he had simply influenced her by a sort of slow osmosis.

He glanced at her again. She was still sitting in grim silence, one foot jigging nervously, as if his very presence frightened her. Alison had mentioned consulting a psychiatrist, but he recoiled from the idea of his daughter being turned into a 'case'; so-called experts sinking probes into her skull, dredging up a rich haul of neuroses which would only alarm her more. Then they'd turn their microscope on *him*, no doubt; ferret out his affair, blame him for her condition. They were bound to suggest that he too needed therapy – or radical restructuring, more likely.

Suddenly, he caught her eye. She looked away, confused, and he too felt uncomfortable; made a show of studying her noticeboard. One of the faded snapshots had, in fact, attracted his attention: the three of them in Venice – Penny in a crazy hat, and Pippa in his arms. The child was smiling up at him, offering him a lick of her ice-cream; their faces almost touching. It had been so easy then to please her, in those uncomplicated days when she was still a non-stop chatterbox, and long before she'd developed breasts or started insisting on strict privacy, barricading the bathroom door if she so much as washed her hands. All he'd had to do was buy her little treats, read her bedtime stories, give her piggybacks.

He pushed his chair back, overcome by a simple longing to feel her arms looped round his neck again, her warm body on his lap. That was out of the question, but surely some small affectionate gesture wouldn't hurt? He stepped towards the bed, made a move to sit beside her, reaching out his hand.

She flinched as if he'd struck her, retreated to the far end of the bed. 'Look, I'd rather you left me alone – okay? I've told you loads of times.' The words were quite distinct this time, and quite unequivocal. He blundered to the door, angry with himself as much as Pippa. All his good intentions of keeping his distance had been blown apart by one spontaneous move. It was impossible to win. Whatever procedure he adopted, he was met with blank rejection.

He trudged downstairs again, paused outside the sitting-room, dismayed to hear a babble of voices discussing Pippa and her problems – was she malingering, or sulking, or genuinely disturbed, and wouldn't it be wiser to take a stronger line with her and insist that she came down? It was only his presence which had stopped them prattling earlier, for the minute he walked in, the conversation died away and several of the faces looked shifty or embarrassed.

Katie broke the awkward silence by standing on the pouffe and yelling, 'Can *I* blow Pippa's candles out? It's my birthday in July, so I'm the next birthday-girl.'

'Well, it doesn't seem quite fair,' Penny said reluctantly, clearly opposed to the idea. 'It's Pippa's special cake, you see, and anyway you'll only be eight, so you shouldn't really blow out thirteen candles.'

'Oh, go on, Pen!' urged Lindsay, championing her daughter's cause. 'Tell you what – let Beth and Katie do it together. Beth will be five in August, and eight and five make thirteen, which is just exactly right.'

'Good thinking!' said her husband, and some of the others nodded their approval, obviously relieved to have been offered a solution.

'Okay then, Sis?' asked Lindsay.

'I'm still not sure. I mean, Pippa may object, or think we're trying to exclude her.'

'But if she won't blow the candles out herself, she can hardly make a fuss if another child wants to do it for her. That's just dog in the manger, Pen.'

Daniel stood in tetchy silence as Penny gave a final grudging assent. The hostess had been overruled; the host not even consulted. Though if Lindsay had used her wiles on him instead, he would have given her short shrift. This was *Pippa's* cake, made in honour of her oldest toy – the furry frog which had accompanied her to Paris. She had always shown an interest in frogs, and now owned a whole collection: frogs in felt and porcelain, paper frogs and bronze frogs. So why should Lindsay's daughter or that spoilt-rotten little Beth oust her from her position centre-stage?

Yet the two girls were already hovering by the cake; the other children crowding round excitedly; Lindsay rushing off to fetch matches and a cake-knife, while Brian restrained an ever-frantic Arthur.

Daniel eased the knife from Lindsay's hand with as much grace as he could muster. She might have won her point, but he'd be damned if he'd allow her to usurp his role as host – or his brother-in-law Fergus, come to that. Fergus was lighting the candles, but had managed only three so far, burning his fingers in the process and dripping hot wax on the cake. Daniel took over, asking Kay to draw the curtains, to provide a more dramatic atmosphere. At least this little ritual would bring the party to a close, after which (with any luck) the guests might trickle off. So it was clearly in his interest to conduct it with some ceremony, so that everyone could leave feeling something had been salvaged from an otherwise abortive afternoon. He composed his face into a smile, moved the cake a little nearer to the children, and instructed Beth and Katie to give the biggest puff they could.

There was a spontaneous burst of applause as every small flame died, then one uncertain voice struck up 'Happy Birthday'. Other voices gradually joined in, increasing in both confidence and volume until they reached what should have been 'dear Pippa'. There were various permutations – 'dear Beth', 'dear Katie', 'dear everyone' – though both the grandmas and Penny stuck loyally to 'dear Pippa'. Daniel wasn't singing at all. 'Dear Juliet,' he was thinking with a surge of hungry remorse, transforming the thirteen candles into forty-one tall gold ones: bewitching, tasteful candles, always strangely cool, despite the passionate heat of their flames. He could feel those flames scorching his bare body, shrivelling his marriage vows, his more recent vow to stay away from fire.

He drew in his breath as deeply and emphatically as he had directed the two girls to do, then snuffed out all forty-one candles in a single violent blast.

11

DANIEL SAT AT THE DESK in his study, eyeing his last Polo. He was uncomfortably aware that there was something faintly comical about a rational and intelligent man being mesmerized by a peppermint. He was wasting vital energies on the life-and-death decision as to whether to consume it now, or save it for the night. It was too late to venture out to the shops and buy a whole crate of mints, plus a ton or so of chewing-gum. The shops were shut, their owners fast asleep. He envied them their beds; would be lying in his own if only Kay and Fergus and Alison weren't still nattering in the kitchen with an apparently tireless Penny. Fergus had left hours ago, in fact – driven Jo home with the baby and the dog, but he'd breezed in again at ten o'clock to take Kay back to Lewisham. Penny had offered him a coffee and a snack, and they had evidently embarked on a second, smaller party, before the debris of the first was cleared away.

He made a move to get up. If he'd had his way, he would have tidied up the sitting-room, washed the dirty dishes and restored the house to some semblance of order. But Penny had objected, saying it was rude to start fuss-potting about before the guests had gone. But would they *ever* go, he wondered, subsiding in his chair again and sorting through the papers on his desk. At least his study was unscathed – his own private sanctum where no one had intruded save the puppy. He looked with satisfaction at the sparsely furnished room, uncluttered and well-organized. It was here he kept his African mementoes: masks on the wall, his mother's wooden sculpture on a low shelf in the corner, photos of his Kenyan children grinning from their frames. And he tried to contain his memories of Africa within these four white walls, unwilling to reveal to Penny how much he missed his trips there;

missed the spaciousness, the solitude, the huge dramatic skyscapes and fiercely brilliant light.

He chewed the end of his paper-knife, realizing with a certain shock that he had turned the room into a bachelor domain. There were no photos of his wife around, no souvenirs of family holidays, and even Pippa's desk-tidy had landed up in the kitchen, rather than its intended destination. Yet for the last few weeks his daughter had been constantly on his mind, so that whenever he tried to settle down to work, his anxiety about her would distract him from statistics or accounts.

He had been up to see her ten minutes ago, and she appeared to be asleep, though he feared it was only pretence; her closed lids another barrier against him. Last night, when he was lying awake, craving both a cigarette and Juliet, he had heard her moving around in her room. If she started missing sleep as well as school, then things would get really serious. Perhaps he should go up again; check on both the children. Alison's obnoxious son was sleeping in the spare room with a scaly orange dinosaur as his bed-mate.

He stepped into the hall, colliding with Penny, who was on her way to prise him from his study.

'What on earth are you doing, Daniel? Mum says you're as bad as Pippa, shutting yourself away like this. And Fergus has been complaining that he's hardly exchanged two words with you the whole of the afternoon.'

'I was . . . just finishing something for work tomorrow.'

'Tomorrow's Sunday.'

'Oh, is it? It feels like Sunday now.'

'You're hopeless, darling, honestly. Come and have a glass of wine. It'll help you relax.'

'I'd rather have a coffee, to stop me nodding off.'

'Shh! They'll hear you. And whatever you do, don't mention work to Fergus. He's been threatened with redundancy. He's only just come out with it, and he's obviously quite shaken.'

'Okay,' said Daniel glumly. He felt sorry for his brother-in-law – a well-meaning, inoffensive sort of chap, who believed in Christian charity and wouldn't hear an unkind word against his wife, his friends, the MCC, or God. Which didn't make for incisive conversation. In fact, all they normally talked about was their respective jobs and holidays, so now half their conversational fodder had disappeared at a stroke.

'If you ask me,' Kay remarked, giving Daniel a withering look as he followed Penny into the kitchen, 'Pippa's only started this recluse business because of the example of her stepfather.'

He winced at the word. He had once looked up 'step' in the dictionary and found it was related to the Old English word for bereaved. The definition pained him by its poignancy. Pippa was bereaved in the sense of her real father being absent, if not strictly dead. She no longer even used his surname. Perhaps it had been insensitive to change her name to Hughson, though he had done it with the best of intentions.

He was suddenly aware of the silence in the room; realized Kay was still looking at him accusingly. 'Oh, come on, mother-in-law,' he said, adopting a jokey tone. 'I've been a paragon today – the life and soul of the party. I've almost lost my voice again from chattering so much.'

'I can't say I've noticed.'

'More coffee, anyone?' Penny filled the kettle – his tactful wife, endeavouring, as always, to keep the peace.

'Yes please,' said Fergus, passing her his mug. He was small and rather wispy, with an over-eager smile and eyes which seemed uncertain whether they were grey or smudgy blue.

Daniel sat down between him and Alison, having first removed a lump of soft green squidgy icing from the chair – the last remnants of the birthday cake. He had never got a piece himself. By the time he'd saved the head for Pippa and then served all the guests, there was nothing left but crumbs.

'Jo tells me you've given up smoking,' Fergus beamed. 'Well *done*! I really do admire your . . .'

Whatever quality he admired was eclipsed by Kay's rejoinder. 'And about time too!' she barked. 'I've always said it was a dreadful habit. Are you sure you didn't sneak off just now for a quick puff on your own?'

'That's defamation of character!' Daniel objected, still in bantering style. 'Hell, I even managed to resist a Polo. I'm down to my last one.'

'Here, have these,' said Alison, scrabbling in her bag. She produced a mini-pack of peppermint creams, which she slipped into his hand. 'I nicked them from a restaurant. We were having a long working lunch at the Grosvenor Hotel, and I was far too full to eat them with my coffee, so I took them home instead.'

'Talking of hotels,' said Fergus, turning back to Daniel, 'where are you off to this year? Prague, Athens, Oslo, Lisbon – or are you willing to settle for a week in Broadstairs, like the rest of us poor mortals?'

Penny laughed, started refilling all the mugs. It had become a standing joke that Daniel swept her off each summer to some famous foreign capital, to compensate for her previous lack of travel.

'Well, actually,' said Daniel, 'we haven't got round to booking anything yet. We had hoped to go to Rome, but what with Pippa being unwell . . .' He could hardly add that his reluctance to go abroad this year had more to do with Juliet than Pippa. Until two days ago, he had refused even to contemplate being parted from his mistress, especially for as long as three weeks. And it seemed wrong to go to Rome with Penny, when Juliet would appreciate it on a deeper level altogether, be *au fait* with all the galleries and churches, whisk him off to concerts and museums.

'The child needs a proper rest,' said Kay. 'She still looks awfully peaky. Why not take her to the seaside?'

'Or a farm,' suggested Fergus. 'We stayed on one last year and had a whale of a time. And you know how Pip loves animals.'

'She also likes going abroad,' Daniel countered irritably, suppressing the image of a whale floundering along amidst a herd of dairy cattle, spurting water through its blow-hole. 'And she's keen to learn Italian.'

'Come off it,' Alison said. 'It's meant to be a break for her, not another dose of school. And Rome's not exactly restful. I was there last year and the traffic was appalling. You risk life and limb every time you cross the road. And the heat was overpowering – a hundred in the shade at times.'

Daniel took a biscuit, rammed it in his mouth. If only Penny's friends and family wouldn't interfere. It was a good six weeks before they'd need to leave for any holiday, and Pippa would be better by then. After all, the doctor had said she was merely going through a phase, and though the easy cliché had annoyed him at the time, perhaps he had been too critical. GPs saw scores of adolescent girls, so they must know something about them – more than he did, anyway. Steadman had also told them that a change might do her good, and Rome would certainly be a change. In fact, the more he thought about it, the more he felt that Rome would suit them all. If he concentrated on teaching Pippa Italian, it would encourage her to speak, as well as creating a new bond between them. It would also put nine hundred miles between him and Juliet. And he owed it to Penny, after his recent bad behaviour, to introduce her to another capital city; try to make the holiday as special as he could.

'Hey!' said Alison, banging down her coffee-mug excitedly. '*I* know where you ought to go. There's this healer chap in Wales, a sort of modern miracle-worker – or so the locals say. I've only just remembered him. I was in Wales myself at Easter, working on a commission for the Landmark Trust, and I stayed on for the weekend with some friends. We drove out to the wilds and . . .'

'We are *not* going to Wales,' said Daniel, voice rising on the 'not'. His boarding-school had been in Wales and he'd vowed never to return there – hadn't weakened yet in twenty years.

'Hold on a minute, Daniel, this might actually help Pippa. I know it sounds way-out, but you said your doctor was useless.'

'I didn't say any such thing.'

'Yes you did!'

'Stop bickering, you two,' said Penny. 'At least let Alison finish, darling. The guy sounds rather intriguing.'

'Where was I?' Alison asked, mopping up her spilt coffee with a piece of kitchen towel.

'In the wilds of Wales,' grinned Kay.

'You can say that again! It was bloody miles from anywhere.'

'In North Wales, was it?' Fergus asked, shaking back his limp toffee-coloured hair.

'No, the bit right in the middle – it's like a no-man's-land. There were all these abandoned mines and rather creepy ghost-towns. Anyway, we stopped for a drink once we reached civilization – well, hardly civilization, just a village with a decent pub. We got chatting to the landlord, who was a friendly sort of chap, not one of those sour Taffies who hate the English on sight. We stayed for simply ages, buying him drinks and generally putting the world to rights, and eventually he told us about this strange man

135

in the next valley who says he's descended from Merlin . . .'

'Come off it, Alison,' Daniel interrupted. 'You don't expect us to believe that, do you?'

'I expect you to shut up and do me the courtesy of listening. Why pour scorn on something when you haven't even heard the facts?'

'Miracles aren't facts.'

'We haven't got to the miracles yet,' Kay observed tartly. 'And we're not likely to, at this rate, if you keep on putting your oar in. Go on, Alison, tell us more.'

'Yes, it sounds really fascinating,' Fergus enthused, placing his palms together as if he were about to say a prayer. 'Is it like another Lourdes or something?'

'No, I don't think the guy's religious. And the landlord didn't mention any sightings of the Blessed Virgin.'

'What a pity,' Daniel jeered. 'Naturally, we'd change our plans if we could be assured of a few visions on top of all the miracles.'

'Darling, what's got into you?' Penny tried to catch his eye, but he looked obstinately down at the table. Okay, so he was overreacting, but Wales was no-man's-land for him in a quite different sense from Alison's. He'd be damned if he'd spend his precious summer holiday in a place tainted by dark memories. His school had been in central Wales, and, as far as he was concerned, it had cast a far greater blight on the countryside than any number of derelict mines.

'All the fellow claims,' said Alison, 'is that he's got some special gift which has been handed on through generations, and ultimately from Merlin.'

'That's just plain ridiculous! If you're as gullible as that, then . . .'

'Will you kindly stop insulting me, and also stop interrupting. Maybe the others would like to hear about him, even if you're determined not to.'

'Yes,' said Kay. 'Quite right. Anyway, I'd rather see my granddaughter enjoying the peace and quiet of Wales than trailing around museums in the heat.'

'You've got a point,' said Fergus, with his maddeningly placatory smile. 'In fact, you could forget about the miracle-worker and just go to Wales for a gentle little potter around the countryside. I mean, you wouldn't have the hassle of a flight, then. You know what airports are like in the middle of the summer – packed to the gunwales and absolute chaos! And if Pippa needs a rest, I must admit I tend to agree with Alison – most big foreign cities are pretty hellish in August, and you often come home again more frazzled than when you left.'

'And wasn't it Rome they had those bombings?' Kay put in anxiously.

'No, Milan,' said Penny. 'And you can stop fretting about Rome, Mum, because we're not going there in any case.'

'Who said?' Daniel snapped.

'*You* did, darling – about two weeks ago.'

'That's not true. I merely mentioned that we ought to keep our options open, in case Pippa was still unwell.'

'You ought to keep your mind open,' Alison retorted. 'Pippa *is* still unwell. And this man might have the skills to make her better, if only you weren't too prejudiced to consider the idea. Okay, I can understand your attitude. He *does* sound like a crank, and I pooh-poohed it all myself at first, until the other people in the pub started chiming in as well. Without exception, they all backed up the story, and some of them even trotted out the details of amazing things he's done.'

'Like changing water into wine, I suppose? Or feeding the five thousand with two fishes and five loaves.'

'No, like curing a girl with anorexia who'd more or less been given up for dead.'

'So why haven't we all heard about him? Shouldn't he be on Wogan, or have a flourishing practice in Harley Street?'

'Don't be such a smart-arse, Daniel! The fellow doesn't operate like that. Besides, he's only been there a few months, and these things take time to filter back.' She paused to drain her coffee, then wiped her lips delicately on her paper serviette. 'Though it sounds as if the news *is* getting round. According to what I heard, people are already trickling in to see him – more than trickling sometimes. Apparently there was quite a little crowd there over Easter.'

'But you just said the place was deserted. You can't have it both ways.'

'It *is* deserted – practically a wilderness. But they camp out in

137

the ruined buildings, or bring tents and sleeping-bags, or even build rough shacks. And anyway, no one stays that long.'

'Oh, I suppose the cures are so instantaneous that the halt and the lame stagger in on Monday and bound home again on Tuesday, leaving their discarded crutches and stretchers behind?'

'I'm sorry, Daniel, but if you're going to take that tone, there's no point in my carrying on. Let's change the subject, shall we, and talk about the weather. The rain appears to have stopped.'

'No, wait a minute,' Fergus interjected, gesturing with his tea-spoon. 'Have you actually thought of camping, Daniel? It might well be the answer. I don't mean in Wales necessarily, but just as a relaxing sort of holiday – not to mention dirt cheap! We went camping in the Lake District the summer before last, and after ten days communing with nature we came back feeling totally restored.'

You *would*, thought Daniel sourly. Fergus would probably return restored after ten days in Alcatraz. 'It's not exactly my idea of fun,' was all he said aloud.

'But we've never tried it,' Penny pointed out.

'I've camped in the bush, frequently.'

'Wales is not the bush, though.'

'No, you're right. It's wetter, colder, and more unpleasant altogether.'

'Okay, point taken. My husband doesn't want to camp.'

'I'd say your husband doesn't want a holiday at all.' Alison pushed her mug away, as if she'd like to do the same with Daniel.

'Look,' he said, with an attempt at weary patience. 'Most of the people I know – normal, reasonable people – would draw the line at visiting some witch-doctor in the back of beyond and living in a ruined shack, and even if they were forced at gunpoint, I hardly think they'd describe it as a rest cure.'

'I have to say,' Kay murmured, 'I'm not too keen myself on the idea of Pippa getting mixed up with a faith-healer or hypnotist, or whatever he's supposed to be. It sounds a bit dodgy to me, and could be downright dangerous.'

'But what about that girl with anorexia – didn't you say she was genuinely cured?'

'Who can possibly tell, Penny? Anorexia's a long-term thing, and for all I know she may have had a relapse. I'm not vouching

138

for any miracles myself, simply reporting what I heard. But I'll tell you something you can't deny – lots of things which are initially laughed to scorn often turn out to be true in the end. And look at how many folk remedies or so-called old wives' tales are now being proved effective in scientific tests.'

'Well, it's a pity your healer chap can't be subjected to a scientific test.'

'He's *not* "mine", for heaven's sake! And I wish to God I'd never mentioned him in the first place. I just thought it might be helpful, considering the fact that we've all been at a party where the birthday-girl wouldn't even show her face. If you don't think she needs help, Daniel, then all I can say is you're a pretty crummy parent.'

Daniel jerked up to his feet, mumbled something about needing a pee, and shut himself in the cloakroom, banging the door behind him. He stood with his back to the cistern, staring bleakly at the walls. There was no avoiding Pippa. One of her primary-school drawings was tacked up even here: a sketch of two sad zebras, which Penny had judged promising. He ran his finger along one drooping stripy neck. Alison might rouse him to a fury, but he had to admit her accusations contained a hint of truth. He *was* thinking of himself rather than his daughter; allowing a whole flood of fears arising from his boyhood (which any halfway sensible man would have long ago forgotten) to blind him to her welfare. Since no one knew about the horror of his schooldays, they wouldn't understand his extreme reaction, let alone extend him any sympathy. He hadn't even told Penny more than the barest details of his 'prison years', and as they had never considered a holiday in Wales before, there'd been no reason to explain his abhorrence for the place. And if he did explain, wouldn't it sound utterly pathetic – a man of forty condemning an entire country because he had wept into his pillow there as a sissy of a kid? If only he had voiced his objections in a more gracious or conciliatory way, instead of snapping everyone's head off.

He was too ashamed now to rejoin them in the kitchen, so he slunk back to his study and began pacing up and down, watched by the wooden faces of his grinning African masks. He *did* miss his trips to Kenya; missed his former job, when he hadn't been so desk-bound, and had enjoyed much greater freedom and a constant sense of challenge. And, however paradoxical it sounded, it was actually less of a burden to worry about several million illiterates than about one disturbed and moody daughter.

'Daniel?' Penny was calling. He heard her stop outside the door, as if she feared he'd round on her again if she ventured any further.

Grudgingly, he opened the door. 'Yes, what?'

'Mum's just leaving. You'd better come and say goodbye.'

He motioned her inside, then put his arms around her. 'Look, I'm sorry darling, honestly. I know I've been a pain. It's just that I'd more or less decided we'd go to Rome after all, and it upsets me when your family start trying to live our lives for us.'

She pulled away, clearly resenting his embrace. 'Alison's not my family. And anyway, what d'you mean you'd more or less decided? How about consulting *me*? Or Pippa?'

There was a peevish summons from the hall. 'Penny! Wherever have you got to now? I've never known a house like this for people disappearing.'

'Coming, Mum!'

Penny ran to the front door, squeezed Fergus and her mother in a bear-hug, then stood back to let Daniel say his more restrained goodbyes. He closed the door behind them with an audible sigh of relief.

'Well, can we go to bed now?'

'As soon as Alison's finished her drink.'

'Another drink? Surely you haven't started on the booze again?'

'No. It's only hot milk and honey. Do you fancy some yourself? It might help you sleep. I heard you prowling around last night at some ungodly hour.'

'I wish I shared your touching faith in hot milk.'

'The trouble with you, my darling, is that you have no touching faith in anything. You're always so suspicious.'

'If we're back to discussing that quack again . . .'

'We're not. You've made it perfectly clear that "discuss" is not a word you're very fond of at the moment.' She kissed his cheek, to anaesthetize the barb. 'Look, you go on to bed and I'll join you in a moment.'

Daniel took himself upstairs. Despite the kiss, his wife's sharp tone had wounded him; forced him to face the truth. He *had* been autocratic in the way he made the decisions on their holidays, fostering the myth that he was making up for Penny's past privations, but always choosing places which he was keen to see himself, and certainly not allowing her much say. Perhaps both she and Pippa did need a different type of holiday this year – a quiet break in the country, instead of their usual strenuous sight-seeing. But supposing Pippa still refused to speak? It would be much harder to ignore the problem in the silence of the country-side than amidst all the welcome distractions of a busy foreign town.

He undressed and put his clothes away, picked up Penny's things from the floor, then went to the bathroom to wash and clean his teeth. He hoped the mint-flavoured toothpaste might quell his desperate craving for a smoke, but it had no effect at all. Sticking to one's resolutions always seemed more difficult at night, especially this particular night, when he was not only worn out, but guilty and dispirited as well. He grabbed his dressing-gown, extracted a small envelope from its hiding-place in the wardrobe, and crept down to the study. He had locked his last remaining packets of cigarettes in the bottom drawer of his desk, feeling they'd be safer under lock and key than on the high shelf in the kitchen, especially if he kept the key in a sealed envelope upstairs. Penny had urged him to stop messing about with such nonsensical precautions, and eliminate temptation altogether by dumping them straight in the bin. But that would be throwing money away, so he'd told her he was saving them for some inveterate smoker who didn't have his willpower. Willpower! He'd lasted three pathetic days.

Feeling like a criminal, he opened the window to dispel the smell of smoke, then took his first luxurious puff, savouring the familiar sensation of being calmed and comforted, plugged in to a lifeline. He inhaled so deeply it made him cough; instantly clamped his hand over his mouth, to stifle any noise. The last thing he wanted was Penny coming in, with a contemptuous Alison in tow, sneering at his lack of self-control. Though he was probably fairly safe. Once those two got talking, they soon became oblivious to trivial things like time or sleep. He remembered one famous occasion when Alison had 'popped in for a quick coffee' halfway through the evening, and still been there at dawn.

Well, tonight he wouldn't stand for it. As soon as he had finished his furtive cigarette, he would slip into the kitchen and claim Penny for himself. He was feeling unexpectedly randy. He hadn't dared approach her again since the débâcle on their anniversary, but he might just take a chance tonight. If things didn't quite work out, he could always blame the lateness of the hour or the stresses of the day, then turn over and feign sleep.

He used his last Polo to disguise his smoky breath, sucking on it vigorously to extract all the flavour possible. Then he locked the drawer again and padded along the passage to the kitchen; stopping dead in his tracks as Alison's bossy voice echoed from the half-open door.

'You know, the more I think about it, the more I feel you ought to give that healer chap a try. I mean, I'd no idea Pippa was so bad. When you said "not speaking", I assumed you meant just sulking – being bolshie – but this sounds more like some full-blown neurosis, and as you say, who else is going to . . . ?'

Daniel sidestepped into the sitting-room and stood fuming at the window. God Almighty! Couldn't they leave the subject alone? It was all he could do not to burst into the kitchen and eject Alison from the house, hurl her child and suitcase after her, and forbid her to return. Instead, he wrenched open the french windows and emerged into the garden, gulping down huge lungfuls of night air. He must try to get a grip on himself, stop behaving like a savage. At least the garden was peaceful – no sound except the occasional drop of rain plopping on to the path from an overhanging branch. The light from the kitchen was shining on the flower-bed, showing up his storm-wrecked plants, but the lawn was dark and shadowy, the beech hedge just a blur. No stars were visible at all, and last night's moon was engulfed in heavy clouds. The air smelt damp and faintly perfumed – a combination of wet grass and scented stocks.

He leaned against the plum tree, already feeling calmer. The immensity of the sky helped to put things into proportion; reminding him he was nothing more than a pinprick in the universe. How absurd that pinpricks should take themselves so seriously, indulge in childish outbursts. He walked slowly down the path, resolving yet again to be a loving, faithful husband, finish with all anger and deceit.

He looked over his shoulder, haunted by a sudden sense of someone being there with him, an unseen presence infiltrating his mind. It was as if he'd received a flash of insight, been shown a strangely fitting means of making reparation – the most painful means imaginable. He had set his face against going to Wales because it was the place he dreaded most, and because the suggestion had originated from a girl he'd always loathed. But maybe those were precisely the reasons why he should agree to go, in fact. There was a kind of poetic justice in it; what he might call nemesis. He had hoped he could cheat fate, get away with the puniest of sacrifices, but all this time he had been avoiding the bleak truth: until he himself was willing to suffer, his daughter's suffering would never be alleviated.

He strode back to the tree, slammed his hand against the trunk. What arrant superstition! No one was speaking to him, except the voice of guilt, delusion. He was overtired, overstressed, and suffering from nothing more momentous than nicotine withdrawal. All he needed was a good night's sleep, then, in the morning, he could sit down with Penny and discuss (yes, discuss) the whole business of the holiday; reach a reasonable compromise – one which didn't involve some crackpot of a miracle man.

'But wait a moment,' the patient voice persisted. 'If there's the remotest chance of someone helping Pippa, isn't it irresponsible to dismiss it out of hand?'

Yes, he thought despairingly. How could he deny that, when he'd criticized Penny for not taking Pippa's symptoms seriously enough? Now he was being equally offhand, deluding himself that the child would be better in a matter of six weeks or less, so he wouldn't have to miss his precious holiday abroad. If she actually got worse, instead of better, Penny might well blame him for turning down their one hope of a cure, and he'd certainly never forgive himself.

A few drops of rain spattered on his forehead. He glanced up at the threatening clouds now choking the dark sky. If there was going to be another downpour, he'd better get back inside. Yet he was reluctant to return to an empty, silent bedroom. He could see Alison and Penny still chatting in the kitchen, all set for another marathon, by the looks of it. They had forgotten him entirely, or perhaps assumed he was asleep. He plucked a leaf from the tree, flicked it irritably against his face. Fat chance of ever sleeping, with rain drumming at the windows half the night. It was already getting stronger, and suddenly started pelting down full force. He made a frantic dash for the house, but slipped on the wet grass and crashed down on his knees, hands flung out in front of him to break the impact of his fall.

'Shit!' he muttered under his breath, struggling to sit up and wincing at the pain in his knees. He was worse than just a pinprick in the universe – he was a clumsy, bungling idiot. If Alison could see him with mud all over his dressing-gown and a rip in one pyjama-knee, she would laugh in sheer derision, and not without some cause. He deserved to be cut down to size: a pretentious ass who indulged in high-flown converse with Unseen Presences.

Yet the voices were still there, chivvying and hassling – not just one, but several; all offering him conflicting advice, and all inducing guilt. And while he struggled to make sense of them, the rain continued to hammer down, soaking him to the skin; his saturated pyjamas clinging to his body, his mind a quagmire like the lawn.

Look here! he shouted silently to Nemesis, or Fate, or whoever, as he limped towards the shelter of the house, I'll really give up smoking this time, and I promise not to weaken over Juliet. I'll abandon any hope of Rome – museums, churches, galleries – I'll ditch the whole damned lot. I'll go serenely to the seaside, or plod through rustic lanes in a horse-drawn caravan. I'll even camp, or build a shack, but I will not, repeat *not*, ever set foot in Wales.

12

'WELCOME TO WALES!'

'See the red dragon, Pippa?' Penny said, pointing to the sign. 'That's the Welsh emblem.'

Pippa didn't answer, but her face looked animated instead of listless and morose. She even opened her window and peered up at the dragon as Daniel slowed the car.

'Let's get out,' he said impulsively. 'Stop for a drink, to celebrate the crossing of the border.'

'Celebrate?' Penny echoed. 'I thought the whole of Wales was anathema for you.'

Daniel laughed. 'Perhaps I'm ready for a truce, at last.' He pulled off the road on to a narrow rutted cart-track which led into an open field. He got out and stretched his legs a moment, then rummaged in the picnic box for the fizzy lemonade; poured three toasts in plastic cups.

'To the land of bards and dragons,' he proclaimed, holding his cup aloft. 'And a new start for us all.'

'Wow!' said Penny. 'You do sound high-falutin'. I feel we should be standing to attention.'

Instead, she sprawled out on the ground, her crumpled sundress riding up her thighs; her face framed by feathery grasses. Daniel squatted beside her, gazing at the landscape, which stretched away, away, until it blurred into a heat haze on the shimmering horizon. It *was* a new beginning – he was confident of that. He had watched the change in Pippa as they left the fumes and grime behind, and clogged roads gave way to free untrammelled countryside. When they'd set out in the morning, she had been huddled in the corner with her arms clamped tight across her chest (as if to force her breasts back inside her body, or at least prevent them growing any further), but now she was relaxing on the grass: stretched right out, with both her arms flung wide. True, she had hardly spoken on the journey, but once they had left the motorway in favour of a more scenic route, she had begun to follow the map and take an interest in her surroundings. And he too had felt the tension ease with each mile out of London; responding to the larger sky, the sense of prodigality. Everything was lush: the unstinting sun pouring down its munificence on to rippled fields of wheat; tangled hedgerows bursting with green life, the hills curving like voluptuous breasts. In the adjoining field, greedy lambs were suckling still, although they were now sturdy adolescents, pushing at their mothers' flanks with arrogant impatience. And beneath his feet was a luxuriance of tiny flowers: blue speedwell, yellow trefoil, fat pink honeyed clover. He picked a stem, sat chewing it reflectively. No one was about, no snorting tractors or sweaty farmhands labouring in the fields, just an air of peace and plenty, as if Nature's bounty made all such toil superfluous. He lay back and closed his eyes; let himself become part of the profusion – a carefree loafer ripening in the sun.

'You won't believe this,' Penny said, reaching for her lemonade. 'But I'm feeling rather peckish again, despite that whopping great lunch.'

'It's the air,' he said, breathing in dramatically and imagining his lungs no longer blackened and polluted, but lovingly restored like some long-forgotten treasure salvaged from the rubbish heap. He hadn't had a cigarette for six weeks and a day; no longer even bothered to suck sweets. 'Do you want some fruit?' he offered. 'There's a good two ton of apples in the back.'

'Yes, to last us the whole month,' grinned Penny. 'Though at this rate we'll be running short on supplies before we even pitch the tents. D'you realize, Daniel, I've never pitched a tent in my life? I'm a complete novice at this camping lark!'

'It'll take me back to my youth,' said Daniel, nibbling on the clover-head. 'Except there won't be any hyenas prowling round the campsite, like we had in Lupande.'

'Hyenas?' Pippa exclaimed.

He and Penny both looked at her incredulously. She had reacted with genuine interest, spoken almost eagerly for the first time in weeks. He willingly recounted his hyena story, adding a giraffe or two, a wildebeest – anything to extend this marvellous moment: his once indifferent daughter listening and involved. She had even taken off her funereal black sweatshirt, revealing a sleeveless top in an upbeat shade of blue. He refilled her cup, wanting to rival Nature and heap her with largesse. He contented himself with passing her a harebell, a frail and faded specimen he'd found trembling in the hedge, and was gratified when she stuck it in her hair.

'Let's push on,' said Penny. 'We've still got quite a way to go.'

Daniel got up reluctantly. For once he was the layabout, content to sit and stare. Hyenas notwithstanding, the problems of suffering Africa had mercifully receded, now he was away from the pressures of work. He tightened the straps on the roof rack; rearranged some of the bulging boxes in the boot. When they went on holidays abroad, they usually restricted themselves to one small suitcase each, but for this trip they seemed to have accumulated trunkloads. Camping sounded marvellously simple – just a matter of a tent, some bedding and a few rudimentary utensils – but he and Penny had kept envisaging new contingencies which made it absolutely vital to pack a hacksaw or a double-boiler or his entire collection of nature books. Yet he had to admit he was secretly excited at the thought of camping again, returning to his early boyhood – sleeping under the stars, perhaps, if this kind-hearted weather held.

'Are you sure you've got enough room, Pippa?' He watched his daughter clamber into the back and squeeze herself between the various bags and cartons on the seat. Despite the obvious improvement in her spirits, she was still looking pale and drawn, but then he knew she had her period. It had been something of a shock to him to discover just last night that she had actually started menstruating way back in April – the same month he'd met Juliet. What a fool he must have seemed, sitting in the surgery with Penny, playing the role of caring parent, yet ignorant of such a crucial fact. Penny had explained to him that Pippa had sworn her to secrecy, so upset by her first painful monthly bleed that she couldn't bear anyone discussing it. He was hurt at being excluded: he wasn't 'anyone', for heaven's sake, but the second closest person in her life. And if only he'd known earlier, it would have spared him all those weeks of racking guilt. Her introverted silence was not, as he'd feared, the result of his affair, but due simply to her own resistance to becoming officially a woman. He wasn't exactly an expert on the female reproductive process, but he had heard it was not uncommon for girls to find their periods distasteful, and to want to retreat into a state of perpetual childhood.

He glanced in the rear mirror at his newly adult daughter with something approaching awe. Being female seemed a daunting responsibility – nurturing life for nine demanding months, then giving birth, giving suck. He looked out at the sheep again, their uncomplaining patience as they were butted in the stomach by dirty strapping offspring, jostling for the teats. His eyes strayed back to Pippa. Only a blurred strip of her face was visible in the mirror, but he was picturing her body, and particularly her breasts – more conspicuous than usual beneath the lightweight cotton top. He imagined himself a grandfather – some tiny, helpless infant latched on to those breasts; a child he'd be involved with and who would look to him for love. He felt the old familiar terror clutch briefly at his gut. He sympathized with Pippa. If *he'd* been born a girl, he was sure he would have panicked at the onset of his periods, and would have loathed the whole idea of giving birth.

'Gosh! Look at those fields of rape,' said Penny, grimacing at the expanse of strident yellow which greeted them as they turned the corner. 'It's such an acrid colour it sets my teeth on edge.'

And an acrid word, thought Daniel. If his daughter were raped, she would be capable of conceiving, bearing some vile yobbo's child. He felt an urge to protect her, to build a powerful barrier around her, an electric fence like the one enclosing the sheep.

He accelerated up the hill, leaving his dark thoughts behind. This was his long-awaited summer break, not a time to brood on rapists, or indulge in his own idiotic fears. He must look outwards, not inwards; make the most of the month that lay ahead. It was just as well they hadn't gone to Rome. They were all in need of an undemanding holiday, after the last few pressured weeks. He'd been sweating in his office up to eleven hours a day, trying to catch up with the backlog and also cover for a colleague in the throes of a divorce. And Penny too had been working all out, tackling a spate of commissions for a new mail-order catalogue.

He gazed at the play of light and shadow on a cornfield; the sudden jolting scarlet of ripe berries on a bush; the contrast of black rooks against white clouds. He had forgotten the simple pleasures of the countryside, the sense of things being firmly rooted and beyond mere human time-scales, like the ancient oak they were passing, or the squat stone church which grew like a natural outcrop from the hillside. The peace was like a tranquillizing drug, which had calmed them all already, even Pippa. Admittedly she wasn't saying very much, but the change was still impressive, and she would probably return to her old self again once she'd got more used to having periods, and had accepted them as an inevitable fact of life. It was a definite advance that she'd allowed Penny to confide in him, though he did feel rather awkward knowing how she felt, and he had found himself reacting with the same embarrassed shyness. But now even that was subsiding, as if the nature-drug was taking effect, flowing through their bloodstreams and removing the constraints.

'Anyone object to Brahms?' he asked, rooting for the First Piano Concerto and slotting it into the tape-player. The first movement in particular was wonderfully exhilarating, and he wanted the sound to soar across the countryside, to match his exuberant mood.

'No, fine,' said Penny, 'but not too loud. You know what you're like with your music. You expect me and Pippa to put up with it full blast, and then get huffy when we listen to our own stuff at anything above the merest whisper.'

'I *don't*!'

'You *do*!' Penny and Pippa chanted in one breath.

'Okay, I do,' he admitted. He'd gladly be accused of anything and everything for the sheer joy of having Pippa chiming in like that, following the conversation, rather than locking herself away in a mute world of her own. He switched on the cassette and savoured the titanic opening: a thunderous roll from the tympani, answered by impassioned strings. The heady combination of the music and the open road had affected his usually cautious style of driving, and he noticed that his speed was creeping up. He longed to swap his overloaded Vauxhall for a powerful Maserati, so he could really put his foot down and let rip; make the most of the intoxicating sense of space after the stop-start-stop of congested London streets. Everything seemed larger – the sky expanding to

infinity, the horizon reeling back, the hills rising more majestic-
ally, and a giant pylon stretching strong steel arms across the
widening shining landscape.

Penny was humming to the music – a habit he normally
detested, though in his present genial humour it didn't bother him
at all. He used one hand to conduct, urging on the woodwind,
restraining the fierce brass. He'd love to be in charge of a huge
orchestra, sweeping on to the podium to a tumult of applause.
He and Juliet had often argued about this particular recording: she
preferring the Ashkenazy version, while he championed Arrau for
his well-nigh perfect balance of lyricism and bravura. No! He
jabbed the stop button; the vigorous crescendo skidding abruptly
to a halt.

'Hey!' protested Penny. 'I was just enjoying that.'

He mumbled some excuse about the tape being scratchy, then
changed Brahms for Richard Strauss – the *Symphonia Domestica*.
Juliet detested Strauss, but Juliet was history. He had received two
letters from her in reply to his own, one blistering, one hurt, and
though their astringent prose was etched into his brain, he had
refused to write again.

'Daniel, watch the road! You're driving like a maniac! What on
earth's got into you?'

He slowed reluctantly, making a conscious effort to leave Juliet
in London and focus on the scenery in Powys. He admired a
clump of newly-planted conifers, their soft, young, springy green
contrasting with the darker green of an ivy-clotted wall. There
was no trace of brown or yellow in any of the trees. Summer was
at its height – prolific, overflowing, blithely unconcerned with
autumn's bleak decay, which seemed light years off, almost
inconceivable. He felt rejuvenated himself; instinctively put his
hand to his head, imagining his thin patch sprouting like ripe corn.

'I wouldn't fancy living here!' Penny was saying with an exaggerated shudder. 'These farms are so remote.'

He glanced at the grey-stone farmhouse they were approaching
on the right. Its roof was furred with moss, and dilapidated
outbuildings clustered closely round it, like nervous hangers-on
seeking reassurance. It seemed quite untouched by the frenetic
twentieth century; a self-sufficient bastion constructed in an earlier
age which stressed hardiness, endurance.

'Oh, look!' Pippa shouted. 'A Shetland pony! The smallest one I've ever seen.'

'Where?' Penny swivelled round in her seat.

'In that field beside the farm. And there's a goat as well – no, two! Stop, Daddy, quick! Can I go and see them?'

Daniel stopped, so amazed by Pippa's eager shout that he scrambled out of the car with as much alacrity as she did. They all three stood by the fence, he and Penny exchanging delighted glances over Pippa's head, while she sweet-talked the animals, trying to cajole them to move nearer. The goats only looked up briefly and gave a baleful stare, but the pony seemed more friendly, trotted over inquisitively and blew warm velvet breath on Pippa's outstretched hand. They marvelled at its size. It was hardly bigger than a large Alsatian, yet perfectly in proportion, with a flowing mane and tail. Its piebald coat looked polished, its belly tautly swollen, like a stuffed toy stitched too tight; its ears flicking back and forth as if responding to the endearments.

'Oh, isn't he gorgeous! Can we give him an apple?'

'I don't see why not.' Daniel found it difficult to keep his own voice nonchalant, so immense was his relief. This was the old Pippa – enthusiastic, spirited. She had dashed back to raid the fruit box, and was now holding out an apple on her palm. The pony crunched it greedily, showing well-worn yellow teeth.

'He's getting on a bit,' said Daniel. 'A fair old age, I'd guess.'

'But he looks so tiny – just a foal.'

'No, he's fully grown all right. They've got one like that as a mascot in the Horse Guards – Toby, I think he's called. Funnily enough, I saw his photo in the *Guardian* just a week or two ago. He was standing beside the biggest horse in the troop, and the pair of them looked like completely different species. Talk about Little and Large!'

'I wonder what this one's called?' Pippa glanced around her, as if searching for the owner. She looked galvanized, dynamic: released at last from her straitjacket of sullen, brooding silence.

'There's a sign over there saying "Bed and Breakfast",' Daniel pointed out. 'Which probably means they do teas as well. How about stopping for a bun or something, then you could find out.'

'Oh, yes!'

Penny looked more dubious. 'Well, we mustn't be long. That

guy I spoke to on the phone said we could have trouble finding the camp. There aren't any signposts – not even the name of a village. We don't want to arrive too late. I don't fancy struggling with guy-ropes in the middle of the night.'

'But it's only four o'clock, Mum, and it doesn't get dark for ages. Come on, you two.' She took her parents by the arm and steered them towards the farmhouse. '*I'll* pay for tea, so long as you don't eat too much!'

Daniel and Penny caught each other's eyes again. This was resurrection on a grand scale.

The door was opened by a short and stocky woman in an apron. Her eyes were washy blue; her ruddy face crinkled into tiny lines, as if it had cracked in the firing and was hot and brittle still. She greeted them with an anxious smile, which deepened the pattern of cracks, revealed china-smooth false teeth. 'If you've come to buy eggs,' she flurried, 'I'm afraid the hens aren't laying.'

'No,' Penny interrupted. 'We were just wondering if we could have some tea.'

'Oh, that's no trouble. Come on in. When I heard the bell, I thought it was the vet. Or the man come to mend the boiler. I don't get much trade, to tell the truth. I'm rather off the beaten track. But I'm sure I can rustle up a pot of tea and something to go with it.'

They followed her into a gloomy hallway which smelt of old wet dog, and along into a parlour overstuffed with heavy dark-oak furniture. Photographs were everywhere – brightly coloured snapshots of family groups, or children riding ponies, interspersed with faded sepia studies of stiff Victorian couples, or men with waxed moustaches posing with their gun-dogs. Nothing was too clean; a film of dust veneered the dresser, and a large irregular stain obscured some of the red squiggles on the carpet.

'Make yourselves at home in here, and I'll go and put the kettle on.'

'Excuse me,' Pippa asked before she could depart, 'but is that your Shetland pony in the field?'

The woman's face brightened at the prospect of a chat. 'Yes, Hannibal. He's twenty-three years old. We rescued him from a circus when he was barely more than a foal. My children used to ride him, but . . .'

They were treated to the saga, which encompassed three more ponies (two decrepit and one dead); two daughters and a son (all married and moved north); a husband (passed away last year); a pair of Nubian goats (kept for milk and cheese); half a dozen cats (to exterminate the mice); and the whole protracted chronicle finally trundled up to the present with the collie's seven puppies, born a fortnight ago.

'Puppies!' Pippa exclaimed, breaking into the monologue. 'Could I see them, d'you think?'

''Course you can.' She swept out to the kitchen, ushering Pippa in front of her and still prattling as she went.

Penny raised her eyes to heaven. 'Gosh! She does go on. D'you think her husband died of ear-strain?'

'No – overwork, more likely. I can't say I envy the poor chap. Even cleaning out our one disgusting hamster seems to take for ever.'

'I doubt if they do much cleaning here. It looks as if . . .'

'Shh!' he warned. 'She's coming back.'

'I've brought you some Welsh currant cake – bara brith, we call it.'

The woman set down a chunk of leathery-looking cake, badly burnt on top. 'I'll just go and make the tea. You try the cake and tell me if you like it.'

'Well,' said Daniel, once she'd disappeared again, 'Fergus said we ought to take Pippa to a farm, and here we are knee-deep in goats and ponies.' He helped himself to a slice of cake, discarded the burnt currants, then sat back with it contentedly.

'Yes, but Fergus's farm would have roses round the door and hot scones dripping butter. This stuff's terribly stale. It's probably as old as Hannibal!'

Daniel laughed. 'Okay, the cake's not up to much, but I must admit I like the place. At least it's genuine. Those chocolate-box cottages are usually horribly bogus, full of horse brasses and pot-pourri.'

'They'd need more than pot-pourri to douse the smell of dog. D'you think she notices?'

'I doubt it. People never think their dogs smell.'

Penny flicked a crumb from her mouth. 'Well, I only hope

Pippa doesn't catch something. Those cats are probably covered in fleas.'

'You're beginning to sound worse than me.'

'I suppose we're growing like each other. I always had loads of animals before I married you, but now I'm getting all worked up about a few common or garden cat-fleas.'

He leaned forward and kissed her neck. 'Don't grow *too* like me, darling. I rather like the differences.' He slipped his hand inside her dress, cupped her heavy breast. He had been tantalizingly aware of those breasts during a good part of the journey, especially as she wasn't wearing a bra. If Pippa hadn't been around, he would have touched them long ago. The sun had been working on him like a powerful aphrodisiac, rousing all his senses, so that now he was aching to make love to her. He knew she would respond. He could feel her nipples already taut as he gently kneaded them with his thumb.

They sprang away from each other at the sound of footsteps tap-tapping down the passage, the chink of cups and saucers on a tray.

'I've made it nice and strong.' The woman put the tray down, unloaded a brown teapot muffled in a cosy, and some unpretentious crockery, plain white and rather thick. 'Your daughter didn't want tea – she's too busy with the dogs. She's not a great talker, is she – I could see that straight away. I managed to coax her name out of her, but not much more than that. Still, she's happy enough with the puppies. I said she could feed the two smallest. They have to be bottle-fed, you see – their mother isn't producing enough milk. It's a help for me, to tell the truth, to have another pair of willing hands. I'm up to my eyes at the moment, trying to cope on my own. In fact, I told her if she stayed till six, she could help me milk the goats.'

'Six!' Penny clattered a cup on to its saucer. 'I'm afraid that really is too late.'

'Well, she'll be ever so disappointed. She's got a way with animals – believe me, I can tell. My granddaughter's the same. And they're alike in others ways, you know – both pale and on the skinny side – though Rhiannon's hair is nothing like as red, more a darkish auburn. Look at me! I'm rattling on, and I've clean forgotten the sugar.'

'I have to say,' said Daniel, once the door had closed behind her, 'I like the thought of Pippa as a goat-girl. D'you really think it's not on?'

'I don't see how we can fit it in. I mean, if we stay that long, we'll never make the camp in time. It's an awfully narrow road, so we can't go very fast. And we haven't even got directions – or only very vague ones.'

'We could always go tomorrow, though. After all, nobody's expecting us, so there isn't any rush. And it does seem rather unfair to drag the poor child away when she's obviously in her element.' Daniel fiddled with the crumbs on his plate, arranging them in a circle. He was uncomfortably aware that he wasn't acting solely out of paternal solicitude. Of course he wanted Pippa to be happy, but he also relished the prospect of retiring early and making love to Penny in a decent double bed, rather than flogging on for miles and miles into the wildest part of Wales, and then fumbling around exhausted in a tent.

'You mean, stay the night here and set off in the morning?'

'Why not? The sign said Bed and Breakfast, and it's bound to be dirt cheap.'

'I can hardly wait. Porridge with sour goat's milk, and a few fleas thrown in for free!'

'No, seriously, would you object?'

Penny put her cup down, tried another morsel of the cake. 'I don't see how I *can* object when you and Pippa are obviously so keen.'

'So you'll let me go and tell her we can stay?'

'Okay, if you insist.' Her smile changed to a grimace as she sipped her sugarless tea. 'Be an angel and bring the sugar back with you. I've got a strong suspicion Mrs Whatsit's forgotten it again. I expect she's either communing with her goats or doing a King Alfred and burning another cake!'

He got up from his chair, leaned down and kissed her on the mouth, let his lips glide slowly towards her throat. 'You never know,' he whispered. 'Fleas or no, we might even enjoy ourselves tonight!'

13

'WINNIPEG,' said Penny.

'What?'

'Winnipeg rebound.'

Daniel smiled and shrugged. Penny's sleep-talking often became more abstruse when they were away on holiday. He kissed her, in the hope that she'd wake up, but she only murmured something indecipherable and turned over on her back. He had been awake at least an hour himself, savouring the unaccustomed luxury of having nothing else to do but watch the shy unhurried dawn filter through the curtains. The bed, though ancient, had proved supremely comfortable, and they hadn't had to share it with a single flea or bed-bug. He lay with his arms behind his head, listening to the country sounds: the bleat of lambs, the clanking of a milk-churn, the passionate soprano of a thrush. He was getting more like Fergus by the minute – contented in his rosy cot, with no grudge against the world.

Of course he was aware of the real reason for his euphoria: he had surpassed himself last night – surprised himself as well, to tell the truth. Since the fiasco on their wedding anniversary, every attempt at love-making had been embarrassingly brief. He was so nervous about losing his erection that he hadn't dared spin things out, but simply come in a matter of minutes, reverting to his gauche bachelor days in Paris. That bungling greenhorn should never have emerged again after seven years of marriage, but in the last frustrating weeks he appeared to have taken over from the more controlled proficient husband.

But last night had broken the spell. It was like a second honeymoon – no, better: there hadn't been the stresses of a wedding, coupled with jet-lag and a cold. (Did other men go down with heavy head-colds on their wedding day?) They had retired at an absurdly early hour, after ploughing dutifully through Mrs Gwynfryn Evans's rissoles and rice pudding, and had spent from nine o'clock to midnight christening the astonished bed. Penny had suggested a new fantasy: they were staying at the Paris Ritz, in the most palatial suite; two jet-setters in matching sealskin coats who had just flown in from Hollywood for a première, followed by a ball. And – miraculously – he had lasted, right on to the last waltz. He felt enormously relieved, not only because he had gratified her, but because it proved there was nothing physically amiss. He had been beginning to suspect that he was suffering from some debility which might gradually get worse, and had even viewed it as a punishment for his affair. It would be an ironical but appropriate form of justice to lose one's sexual powers as a penalty for abusing them. Yet all he'd needed, in fact, was to escape from the pressures of work, and from his constant trepidation about bumping into Juliet. The risk was actually quite small: she lived in Hampstead and worked in Camden Town, whereas both his home and his office were safely south of the river. But he still dreaded a chance meeting in some cinema or restaurant, and deliberately kept his distance from the whole area of the London Library (where they'd met originally, both in search of the same book).

'Juliet,' said Penny.

He looked at her in horror. No, he was imagining things. His guilt was still so sharp that he was turning vague grunts into accusing names, to lacerate himself. He sometimes suspected that the reason he was a poor sleeper was his fear of going down too deep into that mysterious and dangerous world where all control was lost. If he slept too long and soundly, the padlock on his tongue might be released, so that he too might start babbling in the night, revealing intimate secrets. His wife had no such qualms. She was breathing deeply, rhythmically, muttering odd phrases – no more Juliets, thank God, but vague, nonsensical words.

'I'm sorry, Penny,' he whispered, saying things he could only say when there was no chance of her hearing. 'I can't think how it happened. It was like a sort of madness.'

'Belloc,' she replied.

He lay musing on the word. Gobbledegook most probably, though it could be an allusion to Hilaire Belloc, or even the name of a new French wine. Language had always fascinated him, especially the myriad African languages of his boyhood, which had baffled him and challenged him, since he had mastered only two. Yet languages were dying, becoming threatened species like white rhinos or giant pandas. Every year some thirty or forty died out. He deplored their loss, the impoverishment it caused. Each one was a freedom, another individual way of looking at the world, even a kind of luxury.

There was a light tap on the door – Mrs Gwynfryn Evans with their early morning tea. She had arranged to bring it at eight o'clock, though actually it was only twenty to.

'Just a minute!' He reached out for his pyjama top, scrambled swiftly into it. 'Yes, come in,' he called, fastening the last button. He didn't want to shock her by his nakedness.

'Daddy!' Pippa burst in, fully dressed. 'Can I have my breakfast early? Then I can help milk the goats. And after that I'm allowed to groom the ponies. And the puppies have to be fed again and . . .'

She was hopping from one leg to the other, unable to keep still, reminding him of long-past Christmas mornings when she was forced to endure the torture of a protracted breakfast before they opened their presents.

'Yes, that's fine,' he said, again concealing his elation by adopting a casual tone. 'We'll see you later, darling. Your mother's still asleep.'

'No, I'm not.' Penny opened her eyes and peered uncertainly around, finally focusing on Pippa's yellow tee-shirt.

'Mum, I've got to go – okay? I'm late already.' The door slammed shut; eager footsteps clattering down the uncarpeted wooden stairs.

Penny sat up slowly, one hand groping out to Daniel. 'What's she late for, darling?'

'Goats, ponies, puppies, hens.' He cocked an ear, heard the whinny of a pony in the yard. Mrs Gwynfryn Evans must be thrilled with her new unpaid but willing farmhand. What were routine chores for her would be supreme delights for Pippa. He was beginning to see how unreasonable he'd been in vetoing all pets except a hamster. If his daughter had an inborn knack with animals, as Mrs Gwynfryn Evans had insisted, then he ought really to encourage it. He must take a leaf out of Fergus's book and invest more time and faith in simple pleasures, rather than concentrating solely on Pippa's academic progress, and her skills in art and music. Maybe they should stay here a few days. In fact, there was no real need to press on to that outlandish camp at all. She was so much better already, thanks to nothing more miraculous than a change of scene and a few assorted quadrupeds. They could still camp if she wanted, but find somewhere more accessible. Or, alternatively, they could stay at other farms, where she could enjoy a range of animals from pigs to Jacob sheep. And he must resist the temptation to start teaching himself Welsh, or wading through the entire Mabinogion so that he could brush up on his folklore. For once, they'd vegetate.

'Any tea?' asked Penny, though her voice was indistinct, and she looked as if she were drifting back to sleep.

'I'll go and fetch it,' he said. 'Make sure we get the sugar this time!' Tea would keep his wife awake, and he wanted her awake; wanted to lie beside her and enjoy her full attentions, the way he'd done last night. Pippa would be busy for the best part of two hours, so he could have a relaxed and naked Penny to himself.

He collided with Mrs Gwynfryn Evans in the passage, relieved her of the tea-tray and asked if it would be all right if they had their breakfast late.

'It would suit me very well – give me a chance to feed the animals first.'

'Right, we'll see you about ten.'

He was not to get away so easily. She had already embarked on an epic about the boiler and the boiler-man, with a long involved digression on the new European regulations governing the sale of eggs.

The tea was cold by the time he returned to Penny, who lay dozing on her back. He roused her with a kiss, in the fashion of a fairy-tale prince who had swum a moat and felled a briar hedge to claim his spell-entranced princess. He did feel as if he had strayed into a fairy tale – the house in the middle of nowhere, the dark forest on the hill.

He leaned over Penny's shuttered face, chanting in a singsong tone:

> *'There was an old woman who lived in a shoe*
> *Who had so many puppies she didn't know what to do . . .'*

Penny laughed, drew him down towards her.

'Don't you want your tea?' he asked.

'In a minute. I'll have you first. Ouch! Your bristles hurt.'

'I'm afraid I haven't shaved yet.'

'Well, you'd better go and do it – I'm still sore from last night. I'll sit here drinking tea like Lady Muck, and keep the bed warm for when you get back all nice and smooth.'

He dragged himself away, wondering how many hours he had devoted in the course of his whole adult life to that tedious daily ritual with the razor. He collected up his shaving gear and slipped along the passage to the bathroom. The drab walls and cracking lino contrasted with the majestic view enticing through the window. The sun had painted its own decor on the sky – glints of gold, swathes of rose and amethyst against hazy preening blue; the colours on the fields below brilliant and new-washed. How could he have imagined that Wales was such a hostile country? He had simply built up all the horrors through years and years of prejudice; blanked out its unspoilt beauty, its air of sequestered peace. He shifted his gaze from the horizon and the distant hills to the cluttered yard below. Mrs Gwynfryn Evans was waddling to the hen-house with a bucket in each hand, accompanied by an enthusiastic Pippa.

He returned happy to the basin, surprised to find the water hot after the mishaps with the boiler. He lathered his face, deciding to enjoy his shave for once; derive real satisfaction from making his chin so sensuously smooth that wherever he kissed Penny it couldn't hurt or chafe again.

Suddenly he heard her voice, peremptory outside the bathroom door.

'Quick, let me in! I've just got to have a pee!'

She dashed over to the toilet and sat down. He looked away tactfully, even ran both taps to camouflage the noise. She was far more free and easy than he could ever be. Nothing would induce him to use the lavatory in front of her. She wiped herself and pulled the chain, which was actually a piece of string dangling from an ancient rusting cistern. The bath looked equally venerable – a huge metal tub on four claw feet, with a dark stain beneath each tap and an old-fashioned wooden bath-tray to hold the soap and sponges.

'I think I'll have a bath,' she yawned, 'now I've made the effort to haul myself out of bed.' She peeled off the sundress she was using as a dressing-gown. They had unpacked the barest minimum – just toilet things and clean underwear.

He leaned towards her, daubed her wiry ginger thatch with a blob of shaving soap. 'You were wonderful last night, you know.'

'No, *you* were. I always think it's a bit like ballroom dancing. Despite all the spiel about equal rights, it's still the man who leads.'

He retreated to the basin. Wasn't that a criticism – veiled perhaps, but still an indictment of his recent dire performance? Until his recovery last night, his wife had been unable to indulge in fancy footwork because he had failed her as a dancing partner.

'Blast!' he muttered, wiping off a drop of blood beading on his upper lip. He started to make some comment about his clumsiness, but his voice was lost in the fury of the taps. Penny was running her bath – the water spurting out in short spasmodic bursts, like a peevish sergeant-major barking orders.

'It's a jolly peculiar colour,' she said, raising her voice above the roar. 'All brown, as if it's rusted. I'll go and fetch my sponge-bag. I think I brought some bubble bath and it might cheer it up a bit.'

She bounded out, still naked, returning with the towels and a shiny plastic udder of some virulent-looking bath-stuff which frothed beneath the spluttering taps into a cloud of candyfloss.

'Penny, you really ought to put something on. What if you bump into someone?'

'What d'you mean, "someone"? There isn't anyone around. Except perhaps the ghost of Mr Gwynfryn Evans. I wouldn't be surprised to stumble on a few ghosts here – nice-natured friendly ones.'

She stepped into the bath, looking anything but ghostly herself; her flesh solidly voluptuous; her hair a bright reproof to any spectre. She lay back beneath the bubbles, only her nipples showing, pink against the deeper pink.

161

He finished shaving, watching her in the mirror, the expression on her face sensuous and languid, as it was when they made love – eyes closed, lips parted, head tipped languorously back. He had always envied her lack of inhibition; the way she didn't care how abandoned or even grotesque she looked in bed. When she was about to come, her face would contort into an almost-snarl of pleasure, and her enthusiastic cries were enough to wake half Wandsworth. He, in contrast, maintained a strenuous silence; seemed to need to concentrate, conserve his energies. Or perhaps, if he were honest, he was simply scared of showing his feelings, or making a fool of himself. It was the same thing as with sleep – he could never quite let go. Even last night, in the throes of his euphoria, some part of him still held aloof, alarmed and slightly shocked by the other, rampant Daniel.

Yet just recalling it excited him again; his erection pushing up through his thin pyjama bottoms. Maybe they could make love on the duvet on the floor, imagine they were camping already – not in Wales, but in the bush; the hot sun beating down, and various exotic beasts copulating around them with full-throated yowls of ecstasy.

He mopped the perspiration off his chest. He was sweating in the Zambian sun. 'I think I'll have a bath as well, but no rush – when you've finished.' His eyes were drawn to her nipples again. Were they stiff already, or was he just imagining it?

She scooped up a handful of pink foam, began sculpting it in shapes. 'Why don't you get in with me, then you can share these lovely bubbles. There's miles of room. My feet don't even reach the end!'

He rinsed his razor, dried it carefully. They never had baths together. Usually he insisted on his privacy, locked the bathroom door, to keep wife and daughter out. It was a reaction to his schooldays, he supposed. He had dreaded the morning ablutions at Greystone Court, performed in public in a spartan white-tiled washroom, where any moment some pint-sized tyrant might douse him with cold water, nick his toothpaste, or jeer at his anatomy. But here on holiday, he was determined to break the rules; leave the grim past behind.

He removed his pyjama bottoms, put a foot into the water. 'Ouch! It's fearfully hot.'

'No, it's not – it's perfect! You always have your baths too cold, then you can't relax.'

He wondered how she knew, though it was all too true, in fact – part of his eternal rush and hurry. He preferred showers to baths, in any case, on the grounds that they were quicker and more efficient. But today he planned to wallow.

Penny pulled up her knees to make more room for him; jabbed him with a teasing foot as he lowered himself in. He sat facing her, trying to get comfortable with two knobbly taps sticking into his back; one dripping icy water, the other scalding hot. He was sitting over the plug – another source of discomfort – but, bit by bit, the benison of the hot water worked its minor miracle and he let himself relax. He liked the feel of her body lapping his, one plump foot lodged gently in his groin, the blurred red of her pubic hair barely showing through the foam. Perhaps he'd initiate a fantasy himself, not keep it a dark secret (like his couplings in the bush), but actually suggest a scenario to Penny, instead of her invariably allotting them their roles. No way would it be jet-setters in Hollywood – more likely him a stripling of fifteen, with Penny as the Older Woman, dominant, alluring, maybe even cruel.

He felt instantly ashamed, without understanding why; busied himself with washing. He picked up the bath-brush – another Victorian relic, with a long pitted wooden handle and half its bristles missing. 'Look at this weird object! It's almost a museum piece.' He tried it on his leg, rasping it from thigh to knee. 'Actually, the bristles are still quite hard – those that haven't fallen out. Would you like me to scrub your back?'

'Mm.'

'Turn round, then.'

'I can't. I'm too comfortable like this.'

He knelt over her instead, rubbed the brush lightly across her breasts. 'Does that feel nice?'

She nodded.

'Shall I do it a bit harder?'

'Mm.'

'Harder still?'

'Okay.'

'Doesn't it hurt?'

163

'Yes, it does a bit, but I like it.'

He laughed. 'You'd complain if it was *my* bristles.'

'I wouldn't.'

Encouraged, he used his chin, chafing it back and forth across her nipples, then traced a wider circle, keeping it lingeringly slow. But he was perilously close to swallowing a mouthful of water, so he shifted his position and used his thumbs instead, gliding them from the underside up along her cleavage. Then he fished out the bar of soap (which had fallen into the bath and was melting into slime), and began to soap her breasts.

'That's lovely,' Penny murmured. 'Squeeze them both together, the way you did last night.' She gave a low grunt of approval, then opened an eye. 'Oh, look! You're sticking up through the foam!'

He followed her gaze, immediately covering his erection with his hand, embarrassed by its blatancy; feeling as he often did, absurdly, that it had no right to assert itself, not even with his wife.

'I'll wash *you*.' Penny grabbed the soap; the water seesawing dangerously and almost sloshing over the sides. She worked up a rich lather, then slicked her soapy hands around his penis. Mrs Gwynfryn Evans had provided unerotic coal-tar, but that didn't diminish his pleasure in the slightest – the luxurious sensation of her warm and slippery fingers sliding slowly up and down. Next she ran them teasingly along the inside of each thigh, going right down to the knees, before allowing them to creep ingeniously back. Then she cupped his balls, first lathering the soap again, to coat them in a spume of yellow froth. She knew exactly how to touch him, never squeezing too tight or hurting with her nails, but maintaining just the perfect pressure, so that it was all he could do not to forget his usual shyness and cry out in abandon.

Now she had found a loofah and was fretting its rough surface gently along his penis, even across the tip, which made him shudder with an exquisite sort of pain.

'Do that again!' he urged. 'It feels amazing.'

She took the loofah on a tour of all his curves and crannies, which ended by circling both his buttocks, grazing down between them.

164

'Darling, you're driving me mad! Let's go back to the bedroom.'

'No, I want to do it in the bath.'

'We *can't!*'

'We can. I'll kneel up on all fours, and you come behind me doggy fashion.'

'But we'll splash water all over the place.'

'Not if we let some out – not too much, though. I like the thought of doing it in water. I'm surprised the bubbles have lasted this long. They usually go flat.'

Like me, he thought, hastily suppressing the comparison before it could affect him. There was no more need to worry. He was cured now, like his daughter; could even make triumphant love in a constricting metal bathtub.

He released the plug and watched the water gurgling rudely out, then rammed it back before Penny lost her bubbles. They bumped into one another as he stood up and she knelt down, and he banged his elbow on the wall in trying to position himself.

But Penny was encouraging him, telling him it was fantastic before he'd even begun. Her wild words egged him on; the sight of her pale rump curving up in front of him; the caress of the warm water on his thighs. He disregarded the pain in his knees (which were pressing into the hard unyielding surface of the bath) and concentrated instead on the soft cushion of her flanks, the tingling of the bubbles as they fizzed against his skin. The angle was an awkward one, and his movements were restricted, but the restriction somehow added to his pleasure, made him feel adventurous, audacious.

'Daniel stop! It's hurting.' She all but threw him off, cascading water over the floor. 'You were right, I'm afraid. It isn't going to work.'

There were red ridged patches on her knees, and she was rubbing them and biting her lip; easing her cramped legs. Her hands also looked inflamed where she had gripped the taps too tightly. She stepped out on to the bath-mat, helped him out in turn. 'Let's go back to bed.'

They dried each other on Mrs Gwynfryn Evans's stiff and skimpy towels, then Daniel folded them neatly; started mopping up the puddles on the lino.

'Leave that, darling. We can always do it later. Listen, I dare you to run naked to our room!'

His initial consternation changed into a laugh. 'Okay, you're on!'

He sprinted ahead, collapsed on to the bedroom chair. Fondly, he surveyed their palatial Paris suite – the shabby walls, the shrunken curtains (which didn't reach the sill), the not-quite-fitted carpet with odd-shaped gaps revealing strips of floorboard. The morning sun had transformed the room, brightening the faded poppies on the curtains, gilding the white duvet. He especially liked that duvet. Although it had long since lost its original snowy freshness, it was still a bridal colour, affirming the idea of honeymoon, even of virginity, in the sense of a new start.

Penny followed, stretched out on the bed, her legs spread wide and one hand fondling her bush, as if she was too impatient to wait for him to do it. Her whole body was flushed pink from the heat and steam and the friction of the towels; a wisp of foam still clinging to her hair. He crept towards her and kissed it off, but she arched her back imperiously, using her body to tell him where she wanted him – inside.

He did as she demanded, and she immediately began to move – avidly, explosively, like a starving woman making up for months of deprivation. The bed was moving with her, creaking on its springs, emitting breathless moans of pleasure. She let out a muffled giggle. 'D'you think we'll wake the goats?'

'We'll certainly shock them,' he grunted, suddenly aware of the sounds beyond the bed – not a goat, but the crowing of a cock – an exultant doodle-doodle-do which matched his own elation. He grabbed the headboard to give himself more leverage; started lunging backwards and forwards, riding Penny, spurring her. She was making a low rumbling noise, like a lioness or tiger, growling her approval. It excited him to imagine her an animal, because *he* could be one too, then; return to the bush and play the part of the rutting king of the beasts. Why be a puny human, when you could turn yourself into the wildest of wild animals; mate twenty, thirty times a day; drive your worshipping females into transports of delight?

He made himself slow down. If he wanted to repeat last night, then he mustn't come too soon, but relish the sensation of being in control; the leader of the pack who had all the time in the world to pleasure his sleek mates, one by rapturous one.

'Don't stop!' said Penny urgently.

'I'm not.' He was merely drawing breath, holding back a moment so he could rub his mane across her swanskin breasts. Through the open window he could hear the lazy morning igniting into life: a van pulling up outside; feet tramping to the door, the pealing of the bell. It was probably a delivery – a parcel, or some groceries, or perhaps the boiler-man or the vet. He pitied those poor drones, with their schedules and their daily grind, their obeisance to the clock, while his only arduous task was to disport himself in bed.

Penny suddenly pushed him off. 'I want to come on top.'

He rolled across the duvet and stood up. His easy-going wife changed character in bed; often taking the initiative, and issuing her orders with a certain brusque imperiousness which never failed to turn him on.

'Hey, look!' she said, pointing to the wall, 'you've got two pricks!'

The sun was flooding through the half-drawn curtains, casting strong dramatic shadows, giving him a second body, and a second – longer – penis. She darted over to the wall, stroked the shadow-phallus from insubstantial root to evanescent tip. 'It's growing even bigger,' she said, teasingly.

'Quick!' he urged, pushing her back towards the bed before the real version could droop and disappoint her. That exaggerated shadow seemed to mock his flesh-and-blood dimensions, demonstrate an unobtainable ideal. The mere thought of it unnerved him, and he could feel himself already going softer, but Penny climbed astride him and started reviving him – thank God. Her breasts looked more voluptuous from that angle; shimmying with her rhythm, all but swamping him in flesh. Her excitement kindled his, as he kissed the breasts, buffed them with his chin; felt them jouncing wildly in his hands.

'Don't come yet!' she commanded.

'I won't,' he reassured her, though he wished she hadn't spoken, or made it quite so clear that she wanted more – and more. Not only had the shadow undermined him, but he had lost his strutting confidence now he'd changed back from lion to man. The sun

167

was in his eyes, and as he moved out of the glare, he was suddenly reminded of that intrusive sun the morning of his wedding anniversary; Juliet's earrings glinting in its merciless light.

In seconds he was limp – totally, demeaningly – already slithering out. He blundered off the bed before Penny could start commenting or offering him first aid. Her frantic (hopeless) efforts to revive him would only make things worse, underline his failure. He kept his voice determinedly cool as he slunk towards the door. 'I . . . think I need a pee, that's all.'

He stumbled to the bathroom, where the moist air reeked of bubble-bath – carnation mixed with pear-drops, a sickly, mocking smell. He sat hunched on the edge of the bath, jabbing at the wet towels with his foot. The taunting sun had pursued him even here, and was striping his bare body like the swaggering wild animal he had so patently failed to be. He jumped up and drew the curtain, swathed himself in the towels. He knew he was overreacting. He had lasted very well, in fact, far longer than in recent weeks; far longer than the average man, if you could believe those endless sex-surveys. But he'd still lost his erection, suddenly and groundlessly, which meant he had a problem, and one which could only get worse. He couldn't take his potency for granted; would always be on edge in case he deflated prematurely, and the fear alone was enough to make it happen. Even now, Penny was waiting eagerly, expecting him to frolic back and continue where he'd left off. He simply couldn't face her – neither her passion nor her pity. Once she realized he felt wretched, he knew exactly what she'd say: that they couldn't expect to rival last night's marathon, and that it had all been marvellous anyway.

But she didn't understand what was going through his mind. This was more than just a physical problem, though it was well nigh impossible to put the notion into words – it would sound utterly absurd. But he knew at some deep level that because he'd tried to delude himself that both he and Pippa had recovered from their different forms of disablement, he was being shown how wrong he was; reminded of his promise to make proper expiation for her sickness and his own. The voices in the garden the night of Pippa's birthday party had first tried to point the way, but he had refused to give them credence. They had warned a second time, when she had returned to school and her condition had got worse, so he had finally capitulated and agreed to visit the Welsh healer.

Well, he had agreed up to this morning, at which point he'd changed his mind again, tortuously convincing himself that there was nothing wrong with Pippa except the business of her periods and too much pressured school-work, and that both could be alleviated by a spell of pastoral bliss. But was it really likely that three months' silence could be cancelled out so easily, or had no more complex cause? Supposing she had a relapse and returned to her mute world? If he refused to meet the healer or even visit the camp at all, then his only chance of . . .

Suddenly he tensed, hands gripping the edge of the bath. He could hear noises from the bedroom, intruding even here – loud orgasmic noises. Penny had obviously given up all hope of his returning and was bringing herself off. He sprang up in a fury. Did she have to be so blatant, trumpet to half Wales that she didn't need him anyway and could climax on her own?

He darted to the basin, grabbed his toothbrush and started scrubbing and swilling, then gulped a glass of water to douse his irrational rage. He was being totally unfair. If he'd left her high and dry, why shouldn't she take over and finish the job herself? If anyone was angry, it should be her, not him. He ought to go and tell her he was sorry, instead of skulking in the bathroom indulging in a fit of pique.

The 'sorry' came out gruffly. He was embarrassed by her body, spreadeagled on the bed; the nipples still erect, the skin sheened with perspiration and flushed from her exertions.

She sat up slowly, looking sated, almost drugged. 'There's nothing to be sorry about. It was absolutely great.'

He shrugged. Hadn't he known that was what she'd say? Her voice sounded husky – what he called her bedroom voice. It always deepened after they'd made love.

'I've been thinking,' she continued, one hand laid across her breasts, as if savouring a last flicker of gratification. 'Why don't we stay here for a few days? Pippa would adore it, and it would do you good as well.'

He filled in the sub-text: do my erections good, you mean. But she was wrong, in fact, quite wrong; adopting the same false reasoning as he had. He mumbled something inaudible, reluctant to upset her, or embark on an irrelevant discussion about what might be best for Pippa.

She patted the rumpled bed. 'Come and have a cuddle, darling. You're looking really miserable.'

'No,' he said, reaching for his shirt. 'It's time we were up and dressed.'

'What's the rush?'

'I want my breakfast. I'm starving!' Actually, he had lost all appetite, but he hoped it might be easier to talk to her over breakfast. It was essential to convince her that they must leave immediately, press on to the camp without any further delays. But he seemed lost for words at present, and Penny looked crestfallen before he had even spoken, as if she had picked up on his own mood.

They dressed in gloomy silence. One part of him was tempted to tear off all his clothes again and burrow back beneath the covers; to accept that promised cuddle and dally here all week in a cosy farmhouse fantasy. Yet he knew it was impossible.

He glanced out of the window at the narrow road leading past the farm. It coiled and switchbacked up the hill, then lost itself in woodland. The drive would be long and difficult, but there was no alternative. He had to honour the solemn commitment he'd made to seek healing for his daughter.

14

'WE MUST BE NEARLY THERE,' said Penny. 'We've been driving half the day.'

'Well, we're not,' said Daniel tersely. 'In fact, we're well and truly lost. I've got a strong suspicion we've been going round and round in circles for an hour or more. These roads all look the same.'

'Wouldn't it be better to go back to the last village, and sort of start again from there?'

'Well, it might be if I knew the way. But there isn't a signpost to be seen. And look, the sun's beginning to set. Once it's dark, we'll really be in trouble.'

'Still,' said Penny, leaning out of her window, 'you must admit it's beautiful.'

He grunted noncommittally. It was the sort of majestic beauty he found threatening; man dwarfed to insignificance by the grandeur of the landscape. The brooding conifer forests were dark stains on the hills; bloated purple clouds crouched loweringly above them. There was a sense of being on the outskirts of the world, as if they had driven off the map into no-man's-land, or some realm of ancient myth. A few deformed thorn trees cowered in supplication to the wind; a wind which stalked tyrannically from the high and lonely peaks. A while ago, they had seen wild ponies grazing; white sheep clotted on vibrantly green grass; silken-trunked beeches dappled by the sun; spires of yellow ragwort. But here everything was bleak: clumps of rough serrated ferns in place of summer flowers; deep ravines ripped into the hillsides; harsh grey rock protruding through the turf.

'Look!' said Penny suddenly. 'There's an old man with a sheepdog. Let's stop and ask him where we are.'

'I'll go,' said Daniel, braking sharply. All the people she had asked so far had been dour and uncommunicative, and without exception had expressed total ignorance of any camp or healer in the vicinity. He didn't want her snubbed again, or stared at disapprovingly on account of her skimpy dress.

'Are we there?' asked Pippa, her voice poised between petulance and hope. She had been trying to snatch some sleep – not easy with the bumpy road and frequent stops.

'I'm afraid not, darling. We're just trying to get directions.'

'What, again?' she groaned, returning to the refuge of her Walkman.

Daniel got out and approached the gnarled old man, but couldn't make him understand at all. He might as well have been speaking to a foreigner. The man gazed blankly back at him, his bloodshot eyes watering in the wind; his bald head shaking in bemusement as he repeated no, he didn't know, he couldn't help. The dog was making a low growling noise, its hackles raised in warning.

Daniel strode back to the car, his frustration overlaid by fear. This was the foreign country of his childhood. At the age of seven he'd been plucked from the warm safe womb of Africa and deposited here in the barren wastes of Wales. Nobody had understood him then. He couldn't express his longing to go home – so intense it was a pain – nor explain his utter bewilderment at things like snow, or syrup of figs, or dormitory inspections (when Matron examined your hair and nails and tongue, as well as the contents of your cupboard and how you'd made your bed). He had spoken a different language himself when he'd first arrived from Zambia – a brightly-coloured cheerful language, with words for hope and play – but the new compulsory 'school-speak' encompassed only rules and punishments.

'Well?' asked Penny. 'Any luck?'

His response was deliberately jokey: alas, he hadn't been successful in getting through to the 'native', either in English, French or Swahili, and perhaps he should have asked the dog instead. He owed it to Penny and Pippa to keep his spirits up. They both looked pale and tired, and it was his damned fault they'd got lost in the first place. It was crazy to have set out without a definite address, though he had spent ages on the phone, trying every conceivable source – first Alison, then her Welsh friends, and finally the actual pub where she had heard about the healer. But everyone he'd rung had been maddeningly imprecise, unable to supply a detailed map reference, so in the end he'd bought a large-scale Ordnance Survey, ringed the few vague landmarks mentioned by the landlord, and assumed that they would find it with a little kindly assistance from the locals.

Now he cursed himself for his naïvety, and also for giving in to his wife and daughter's pleadings and agreeing they could stay for lunch at Mrs Gwynfryn Evans's. If they had set off after breakfast, as he'd wished, they wouldn't be faced with the grim prospect of darkness falling before they found the camp.

He put the car in gear once more, steeled himself for another stint of motoring. The road meandered on interminably, up hills and then down, zigzagging its benighted way across the countryside. They skirted a lake, its dark forbidding water ringed by sentinel firs, and then traversed a stretch of heather, the sky above them black with rooks wheeling home to roost. The road swooped down again, snaking past a secret stream, closed in by reeds and bulrushes, and suddenly they found themselves at a crossroads with a signpost.

'Hooray!' cried Penny, winding down her window and reading out the place-names.

Daniel consulted his map. Not one of the names was on it, nor had been mentioned by the landlord in his long spiel on the phone. 'Well, your guess is as good as mine,' he shrugged. 'Which way now, d'you think?'

'Left,' said Penny. 'It looks a marginally better road.'

You wouldn't say that if you were driving, Daniel thought morosely, as he manoeuvred the car round ruts and potholes, and negotiated blind corners. Penny had never learned to drive, but he'd give anything to change places with her and rest his aching back. He checked on Pippa in the mirror. Her eyes were closed again, but she was still hooked up to her Walkman, doubtless trying to drug herself on the latest unmelodious offering from some pop group. It was getting near her bedtime, and she would be completely flaked out by the time they reached their destination – *if* they ever reached it.

'Hey – a village!' Penny exclaimed, pointing to a cluster of grey roofs ahead.

'Thank God!' said Daniel, relieved to see signs of civilization after mile upon mile of wilderness. There must be someone around with a tongue in his head, and with any luck there might be a pub or a guest-house where they could put up for the night. 'Look, it might make sense to stay here, Penny, rather than push on any further and still be driving round in circles at midnight.'

'Oh, let's not give up now, when we've driven all this way. We must be more or less on top of the place. It's only ten past nine, for heaven's sake, and not even dark.'

'Yes, but I don't like the look of those clouds. What if the weather breaks?'

'Don't be such a pessimist. Why should it break when the forecast was so good?'

'Hell!' he muttered, jolting to a stop. 'We can't stay here in any case. It's completely derelict.' He got out and slammed the door, trudged up to the nearest house; its splintered windows gaping, its door hanging on one hinge. The other houses were similarly deserted; glass shattered, paintwork peeling, gardens overgrown. Further up the street, there *was* a pub – the Pen-y-Gwryd – but the sight of its empty shell dashed all hopes of bed and breakfast. The shuttered general stores next door looked equally unwelcoming, unlikely to stock anything but rats and rusted cans.

Penny and Pippa joined him by the ruined shop. Neither said a word. Penny shivered, rubbed the gooseflesh on her arms. Daniel kicked at a heap of broken roof-tiles. In the leaden silence he seemed to hear the murmurings of dead shopkeepers and publicans; the complaints of ghostly villagers who had long ago crumbled into dust. If man had seemed insignificant before, here he was redundant. The land had no more use for him; had wrecked his buildings, disfigured his brave monuments.

'Well,' said Penny with unconvincing brightness. 'This must be one of those abandoned villages Alison was telling us about. Which is actually a hopeful sign because it means at least we're in the right area.'

Daniel didn't answer, just traipsed gloomily past more ramshackle homes. He came to a small church, set back from the road; its roof open to the sky, its gravestones cracked or fallen. He wandered up the path, pausing a moment to touch a headless angel; manacles of ivy shackling its stained arms. The ancient

174

yew in the graveyard was nothing but a mockery – a symbol of immortality presiding over death and decay.

Penny and Pippa caught up with him and started examining the tombstones. 'The inscriptions are all in Welsh,' said Penny. 'What an alien language it looks – all ys and double ls. I can't make head or tail of it.'

'Well, half of them seem to be Jones,' Pippa said, pointing to a name in crumbling stone. 'And that's easy enough.'

'Or Evans,' added Penny. 'Though I can't see any Gwynfryn Evans. Perhaps she's a one-off!'

'Blast!' said Daniel, looking up in alarm as a heavy drop of rain stung against his forehead. 'The rain's begun already. Quick – back to the car!'

Although they ran full tilt, they were drenched by the time they scrambled back inside. The rain was sheeting down, lashing the roof of the car, beating against the windscreen, obscuring their surroundings. Dusk had fallen instantaneously; the glinting gold of evening swallowed up in storm clouds; summer doused in wintry cold.

'I think we'd better wait till it eases off. The windscreen wipers won't be able to cope with this lot.' Daniel tried to ignore his intense craving for a cigarette, and also his idiotic feeling that Wales was pouring down on him a storm of disapproval; positively wanted to be rid of him. After all, they hadn't forecast rain (as Penny had just pointed out), so this unexpected cloudburst did seem slightly ominous. Penny and Pippa's silence seemed an additional source of reproof, and he guessed they were both thinking of Mrs Gwynfryn Evans's haven, where they might now be lying in their warm and cosy beds if he hadn't dragged them heartlessly away. He was especially worried about Pippa, who had become tense and sullen again – little wonder in such weather: the rain hammering down relentlessly and the wind keening like a demented mother mourning her dead child. If only it wasn't so difficult to know what course to follow. It might be wiser to turn back, as Penny had suggested earlier on, but he had no idea which way was 'back', and any road he took might actually lead him further and further astray. Yet they could hardly pitch a tent in the middle of a downpour which looked as if it had set in for the night. Another option was to sleep in the car – cramped, cold and uncomfortable, and quite impossible for him. He could no more sleep in a car than run naked through a crowded store. No, the only sensible plan was to wait until the rain had eased and then press grimly on, in the hope of finding either the camp or somewhere else to stay.

At length the deluge did begin to slacken, so he nosed the car forward and ploughed through the huge puddles which already swamped the road. Leaving the derelict village, he came to another crossroads and took the right-hand fork. It gradually narrowed to a single track with passing places every hundred yards. Though there *were* no other cars to pass – the last one had been ten or fifteen miles back. The deserted roads were unsettling, as if he had left the normal world behind and was battling through a dream-landscape where the colours were all grey, the outlines blurred, surreal. He was forced to go at a snail's pace, not only because of the still pelting rain, but because of the high ridge in the middle of the narrowed pitted lane, which kept catching on the exhaust. Overhanging branches closed him in, engulfed him, the dark itself a blindfold. He could see nothing of his surroundings except fragmentary glimpses caught in the headlamps' glare, which served only to increase his claustrophobia: ivy smothering tree-trunks; densely tangled undergrowth strangulating hedgerows; the road itself shrouded in thick cloud. He was driving ever deeper into a confining labyrinth; the windscreen wipers rasping and complaining as he was swallowed up and lost. Penny and Pippa had both dropped off to sleep, intensifying his sense of isolation. It was as if they had disappeared completely; left him quite alone in a dark and choking maze.

On his first ever trip to Wales, he remembered feeling equally alone. He had been picked up from the airport by a tall and nameless shadow-man who drove him to Greystone Court. The long, despairing journey had been conducted in strained silence, and on arrival at the fortress-school, the stranger shook him by the hand, informed him that his father was a fine and worthy man and that he must never let him down; then vanished whence he had come. (It had been out of the question for either of his parents to accompany him themselves. He was one small boy, and their work involved a thousand boys, none of whom had his advantages, his chance of a superior education. He soon came to understand that education meant banishment, and privilege was another word for pain.)

He reached out for a cigarette, brought his hand back empty to the wheel. It was food he needed, not nicotine. He had eaten nothing since Mrs Gwynfryn Evans's meagre lunch – macaroni cheese without the cheese. Penny and Pippa must be starving too, but they had solved the problem by closing down in sleep. He checked on them again to make sure they were still there; that this journey wasn't a mirage, a nightmare of his own.

He returned his attention to the road, slowing to a crawl to coax the car through a stretch of swirling flood-water. He was beginning to worry about the electrics. If the engine failed, they would be stranded all night in a freezing car – maybe stranded all week in this barren wasteland, miles from anywhere.

He jolted up another hill, braking when he reached the top and staring in incredulity at what he saw below. Eerie lights were flickering in the darkness, and he could just make out the ghostly shapes of tents. No, he wasn't dreaming. As he drove on down the hill, he could hear the barking of a dog, echoed by a crying child. They had actually arrived! He glanced at the clock on the dashboard. Both hands pointed to twelve. It seemed extraordinary, almost magical, that not only had they found the camp precisely at the stroke of midnight, but also that the weather had changed.

He switched off the windscreen wipers, listened to the silence. Both dog and child had quietened, and the merciless rifle-fire of rain which had assaulted the car windows for the last two hours or more had unaccountably ceased. He cleared his throat, feeling strangely disconcerted. He could do with a stiff drink, a shot of instant courage.

'We're here!' he said, shaking Penny's arm.

She woke with her usual languor, too inert and sleep-dazed to take in what he was saying. Pippa didn't even stir, but remained huddled in the back.

'Look, I'm going to have a recce,' he said, having explained once more that they had reached their destination. 'See if I can find some way of driving up a bit closer. You stay here, okay? I won't be long.'

He grabbed his torch and anorak, and slipped between the trees which lined the lane. The heavy clouds suddenly gaped apart, to reveal a bold three-quarters moon, its light silvering the hills, spangling the wet undergrowth. He stood motionless and marvelling, savouring his reprieve. He had come through his ordeal and been rewarded.

'Claptrap!' he muttered, rubbing his cricked neck. For a man with years of study behind him and a reputation for rational thought, he was becoming alarmingly susceptible to woolly superstition, if not self-delusion. Still, deluded or no, he did find the whole thing singular – the abrupt lull in the downpour, that imposing midnight moon.

He stumbled on, concerned about the fact that he'd left Penny and Pippa alone, yet magnetized by the scene ahead – this unlikely fragile settlement in the middle of a wilderness. He could discern a few parked cars and vans, the embers of a dying fire, a washing-line strung between two trees. The camp was small – about six or seven tents in all and a couple of more striking tepees – though there was no sign of their occupants; no sound except the snarling of a dog. Praying it was tethered, he edged towards the tents; starting in alarm as a shadow fell across his path. Someone was coming towards him; a small man, slight in build, though his long, distorted shadow made him taller, even dangerous. It was too dark to see the detail of his face, but his hair fell past his shoulders and his eyes were piercing points of light.

The man stepped forward, blocking Daniel's path. He tensed, ready to defend himself, but the man's voice was low and gentle – a mother's reassuring tone.

'Welcome,' he said, stretching out his hand. 'I've been expecting you a long time.'

15

DANIEL LAY ON HIS BACK, staring at the darkness. The darkness was alive. It pressed down on his eyes and nose, tried to stop him breathing. It was also very cold, so he'd lost his toes and fingers. Maybe he was going to die. Dead people were cold. They must have sent him away to die.

At home he had a night-light – a nice, friendly lamp which shared the night with him – and his bedroom door was left ajar, so another piece of light came in and lay down on the floor beside his bed. And his tall safe parents slept next door, so he could call them if he had a frightening dream. There were eleven other beds in here, with eleven other boys, but no one he could call. The boys jeered at him because of the funny way he talked. But what was so funny? He had always talked like that.

It was too dark to see the boys, but he could hear their snuffly breathing. They all breathed different ways. Thompson made a whistly noise and McKenzie had a cold and sounded all bunged up. McKenzie's name was Michael, but you weren't allowed to call him that. They took your names away here, like they took away your sweets. 'Daniel' had been confiscated.

He'd learned that word on his first day, along with 'slave' and 'beato'. 'Beato' was a funny word which hurt. They beat you quite a lot. Last week, he'd run away – run back home to Africa. He didn't know the way, but he walked for ages and ages and cut his leg crawling through barbed wire. Mr Newman found him and drove him back in a big blue shiny car. Then they took his trousers down and hit him twelve times on his bottom. It left red marks, but you weren't allowed to cry.

The first night, he cried for hours. In the end, Matron came in and said he was disturbing the whole dormitory and had he got a pain? He was crying too much to answer, so she took him to the washroom and told him to wash his face. It was horrid in the washroom. There were white tiles on the floor and the windows had ghosts' faces in.

Matron was a woman, but she didn't look like one. She had a stiff white cap instead of hair, and she was flat in front where his black nanny had a big soft wobbly cushion. They didn't have real women in Wales, or girls, or dogs and cats, or any colours except grey. Everything was grey – the sky, the hills, the school, the food, and the uniform was scratchy grey. Tonight they'd had rhubarb and that was greyish pink. He had never heard of rhubarb. It was very sour and had lumps in like the stew.

McKenzie had poured water into his stew and made him eat it with his pudding-spoon. And after supper, he'd told him about the ghosts. Ghosts were white, not grey, and sometimes they'd had their heads chopped off, so they carried them under their arms. There were loads of ghosts in Wales, and two at Greystone Court. They came out at night and sort of floated along the corridors like smoke. He hadn't seen them yet, but they'd probably come tonight – creep into the dormitory and rise up over his bed.

He closed his eyes to keep them out, but the dark got even thicker then, heavy like his new school coat. He had never had a coat before, but the sun didn't reach as far as Wales, so you had to wear more clothes. He was freezing now, and the sheets were stiff like Matron, and his heart was ticking so loudly, he was frightened it would wake her and she'd come storming from her room. He tried to burrow further down the bed. Someone was sneaking in. Not Matron, but a ghost. He could hear its scary breathing. It hadn't got a head. He could smell it too – like frogspawn and wet socks.

'Help!' he screamed, struggling to sit up. Something was wrapped all round him, getting in the way. He lashed out with his feet and fists, yelling for his mother, begging her to come.

And suddenly she did come. A torch was bobbing across the landing, and he could see her long brown hair, wavy and unbraided, the way she wore it at night. He grabbed the hair, twisting his fingers through the strands, to keep her there for ever. His tears were making wet marks on her nightdress, but he clung on even tighter, sobbing 'Mummy, Mummy, Mummy,' over and over, because he knew her name would scare the ghost away.

He felt her arms close round him, cried louder in relief, shuddering and gasping, as if once they'd started, the tears refused to turn off. His chest hurt from the sobs, which were exploding through his body like bubbles in a can of Tizer, popping in his throat. A hand began to stroke his hair, rhythmically and slowly, feathering down from his forehead to the back of his neck. She had never stroked his hair before, never let him press so close. Usually she told him to be brave and dry his eyes; that big boys didn't cry and that he mustn't wake his father. Then she would tiptoe back to her own room and leave pieces of the nightmare still twitching in the folds of the sheets. She never stayed for long. Both his parents were Busy – always Busy, even in the middle of the night.

But tonight she didn't go. She hadn't even ticked him off, or used her dark blue voice, which meant that she was cross with him and would have to tell his father. Perhaps she'd let him stay with her, and he could persuade her not to pack that loathsome trunk; not to send him back to school at all. The trunk was locked and roped, and he often wished they'd rope his mouth as well. Then he wouldn't let them down by crying when it was time to say goodbye. 'Goodbye' was worse than 'beato', a word which throbbed and stung.

'No!' he panicked, hammering with his fists against her shoulder. 'I'm not going back. I hate it there. I tried to run away.'

'You can never run away, Daniel, not from your own pain.'

He jumped. The voice was wrong – a kindly and soft-timbred voice, but a man's voice, not a woman's. He hardly dared to open his eyes, and when he did he jerked away in horror. He had been clinging to another man: arms around his neck, head against his chest, fingers twisted through his long brown wavy hair. He was so mortified, so embarrassed by his outburst, he could only stare down at the ground, still confused as to where he was. The bare floorboards of the dormitory had changed into stones and rubble; a pile of bedding lay jumbled in the corner, his sleeping-bag still tangled round his ankles where he had tried to kick it off. His eyes moved slowly upwards, taking in the details of his prison. Not the bleak school billet with its metal beds, barred windows, but a ruin on the hillside, with crumbling rough-stone walls and a makeshift tarpaulin roof. The wavering pencil of torchlight seemed to emphasize the vastness of the night. Through the empty window-frame he could see only a small square of darkness, but he knew it stretched to infinity. He could hear its heavy breathing as it pressed down on the hills; could still taste its bitter blackness in his mouth.

He shivered. He was wearing two thick jerseys over his pyjamas, as well as woolly socks and a scarf, but there was no warmth in his body. He cast his eye over the other man's clothes – that ridiculously impractical robe which did look like a night-dress (and concealed God knew what beneath it); the long untidy hair – none too clean, and unnerving on a male.

'Look here,' he stormed, turning on him furiously as a way of defusing his embarrassment. 'It was an insane idea – making me sleep here.'

'Yes.' The voice was soft. 'Madness is sometimes very power-ful. It can show us things we'd be blind to otherwise.'

Daniel ignored the cant. 'Christ knows why I agreed,' he snapped. 'I must have been mad myself.' He was enraged at his spineless submission; hardly able to believe that he had let himself be talked into spending this night alone – maybe several nights alone – away from all the others, even segregated from Penny, who was sleeping in the tent. It was to be his 'initiation' period, but initiation into *what*, he wondered with a shudder of distaste?

'You *are* mad, Daniel. You're angry. Angry with me, and still more angry with your parents.'

'My parents? What the hell d'you mean? You've never met my parents. You know nothing whatsoever about me, and you're not likely to find out. We're leaving the moment it's light.'

'That's a pity, Daniel, when it cost you so much to get here – so much indecision, so many sleepless nights.'

Daniel slumped down on the ground, startled once again by the man's uncanny insights. *Now* he remembered why he had agreed to be imprisoned here: he'd had no defence against such power. He had also been beguiled by his first night's remarkable sleep – a longer, deeper sleep than he'd had literally in years; lying in a tepee with a smoky wood-fire belching in the centre, and sharing the cramped space not just with Penny and Pippa, but with several other campers – the old and sick and halt – who were too frail to withstand the rigours of an ordinary tent. It was a miracle he had slept at all, let alone so well, and it had seemed further proof of the healer's mysterious skills.

Now he wondered if it had been a fluke, simply exhaustion after the drive. No, there was more to it than that: an overwhelming sense of peace, which had touched them all, even Pippa; a sense of genuine welcome and unquestioning acceptance into the family.

He had met more of the so-called family next day, but recoiled in dismay from the prospect of community living. He had assumed all along that he and Penny could pitch their tent at a distance; avoid living cheek by jowl with a bunch of total strangers and being sucked into the maelstrom of the camp. Yet the healer was a magnet, drawing everyone towards him, issuing his orders, deciding who slept where and who did what – a tyrant who could mind-read. Wasn't it peculiar, to say the least, that he should have materialized at the very moment he was screaming for his mother? The fellow couldn't possibly have heard him – not from four hundred yards away. He slept in his own tepee at the bottom of the hill, alongside the other campers, whilst this ruined house was halfway up the slope. So what had brought him dead on cue?

There was a sudden shift and clink of stones outside as an intruder or an animal disturbed them. Daniel squinted through the blank hole of the window, but could see nothing except darkness. The place was beginning to get to him, and the man's continued presence made him more and more uneasy. He was still overcome with shame that he had blubbed in his arms like that; utterly aghast that he could have mistaken a living man for the long-dead mother of his childhood.

'Look, if it's all the same to you,' he said, wincing as he recalled his near-hysteria, 'I'd rather you pushed off, okay? I want to get back to sleep.'

'Yes,' said the healer, 'you need to sleep soundly like a child – that child you weren't allowed to be. Goodnight.'

Daniel watched him go, the puny torch-beam swallowed up in blackness; the soft footsteps fading into nothing. He felt irrationally annoyed that the fellow should keep making such percipient remarks, but at least he was wrong in one respect – no way would he sleep soundly, not after what he'd been through. Never, since the age of eighteen, had he come so close to

183

Greystone Court, not just geographically but in memory and emotion. And there were other, darker memories he dared not even confront, but which might erupt in his nightmares, waking him in panic again. Best not to sleep at all. He had no idea what time it was. One of the idiotic rules here was a ban on clocks and watches; a reliance on so-called 'natural time'. It made him feel totally disoriented, as if he had lost the basic structure of his life. And what use was 'natural time' when it was pitch dark outside and there was no way of telling if dawn was mercifully close or still endless hours away? He didn't even have a book to read. No wonder he had dreamed of school when his possessions were being confiscated with as much tyrannical relish as they had been thirty years ago – first his watch, then his books and radio. The healer called such things an obstacle; an escape from pain and therefore an impediment to healing; an interruption of 'interior silence', whatever that was supposed to be.

The exterior silence was spooky enough. When he lay awake in Wandsworth, there would always be a symphony of sounds – the drone of distant traffic, a plane rumbling overhead, the over-grown forsythia next door which rustled against the windowpane whenever it was windy; Mrs Mason's tomcat on its prowls. And although such noises often annoyed him, at least they proved the presence of humanity; reinforced the sense of a solid street around him, its tall brick walls enclosing him, keeping out the void. But here the night was gagged, and he felt alone with alien nature; the only sound the rushing of the stream. Its relentless babble seemed threatening and intrusive, as if he had become a helpless pebble tossed headlong in its current; swept inexorably along to some dark and dangerous sea.

Never, since he'd quit smoking, had he felt so intense a craving for a cigarette. Lighting up would provide a tiny ritual, a source of instant comfort. So many comforts had gone – light, heat, hot water, his wife's body next to his, his cigarettes, his music, his normal routines and boundaries. He searched his trouser pockets for a sweet; found only fluff and a few odd coins. Money had no value here. However much he had, it wouldn't buy the things he needed.

He stamped his feet and pummelled his hands in an effort to keep warm. The cold had seeped into his bones, made him stiff and sluggish. He was tempted to creep back down the hill and join Penny in the tent, but that would mean disturbing Pippa who was sleeping with her mother. There was nothing for it but to crawl into his sleeping-bag, pile the two spare rugs on top, and sit the rest of the night out. The minute it was light he would wake his wife and daughter and insist they left immediately. Maybe they could drive on to the sea, which couldn't be that far away, and find a guest-house with comfortable sprung mattresses, a plug-in fire, and proper windows with glass and even curtains. Meanwhile, he'd have to imagine such luxuries; convince himself he wasn't cold and that he couldn't feel the stones and shale digging into his back beneath the groundsheet. He wormed into his sleeping-bag, plumped the one thin pillow, then closed his eyes in order to withdraw from his surroundings.

Once he'd shut out the rough walls and the claustrophobic tarpaulin lowering over his head, his mother leapt into his mind again – the mother who had stroked his hair – now very clear and solid against the black velvet of his eyelids. She must have slipped back into his room and sat down on the bed. It was extraordinary, unheard of. She never spoiled him in that way; would have been tight-lipped and steel-voiced if he'd dared to disturb her twice in the same night. But she was smiling unconcernedly and her new un-Busy hands were stroking not just his hair but continuing right down his back; easing his stiff spine, soothing all the pain away. He could even feel her own hair tickling on his neck; smell her smell of flannelette and talcum powder. She was rubbing peace into his skin, and the peace was pink and silky like the calamine lotion she used when he had sunburn. But he wasn't burnt, nor freezing any more, just luxuriously warm; her indulgent hands radiating heat. He was becoming irresistibly drowsy; sinking down and down into some feather-bedded world where everything was hushed, and where his mother was a fire, a hearth, a roof. He was so relaxed and heavy-eyed, it was an effort to speak at all, but there was just one question he had to ask. He forced his lips to move. 'You won't go away and leave me on my own again?'

'Oh, no,' the deep, male, mother's voice assured him. 'I'll be here with you all night.'

16

DANIEL OPENED HIS EYES to the sun, which was flooding through the window-frame, gilding the bare walls. He sat up slowly, fumbling for his watch; remembered it wasn't there. He threw off the tangled covers, wriggled out of the sleeping-bag, then picked his way to the door across a carpeting of rubble. The hillside reared above him, dotted with white sheep; the sky was benignly blue, a light breeze ruffling his hair. Even without his watch, it was obvious he had overslept. The sun was well up in the sky and everything around him was wide awake and busy: birds swooping overhead, crows cawing at each other, two wild ponies cantering down an incline, the exuberant stream gushing over stones – no longer sounding menacing, merely energetic. He was amazed he hadn't woken before, but his cocoon of sleep had cut him off from the morning's lively stir.

Exhilarated, he ventured out himself, only pausing to find his shoes and discard his woolly scarf. He went striding along a sheep-track which zigzagged up the hill; bounding across the springy turf as if he were wearing seven-league boots. He knew he should be going in the other direction – downhill to the camp, where he would be expected to join in the morning chores or ceremonies, or perhaps some healing session. And he ought really to see Penny, to decide if they should leave or not. Yet his body seemed to want to climb, and his mind recoiled from arguments, decisions. His simple instinct was to enjoy the golden morning and his new sense of well-being, to pursue the sun to the crest of the hill and look down at the landscape spread below. So far, he'd hardly moved beyond the confines of the camp. He'd been too busy getting organized; trying to come to terms with the strangeness of the situation, to sort out names and faces. But now he was curious to explore, especially since he'd heard that this bleak and lonely moorland had once been the site of a lead and silver mine – a whole prosperous community battening on its riches. He found it hard to believe. True, the hill was strewn with the wrecks of miners' cottages, like the one he'd been sleeping in himself, but they had long since become part of the landscape, overgrown with grass and moss; less an eyesore than a type of outdoor sculpture, erected here by some eccentric minimalist artist, and gradually softened by the hands of time.

Little remained of the mine save the odd rusting pipe or rail and a couple of stone-arched tunnel openings, flooded inside with pools of stagnant water. Yet once there must have been huge water-wheels, lines of mule-drawn trucks clattering back and forth along the rails, sweaty workmen toiling in the heat and grime. Now a spindly rowan tree sprouted in the winch-house, and placid sheep munched rhythmically among the crumbling stones.

He stopped to get his breath, gazing up at the mountain peak which put the whole thing in perspective. These husks and dregs of man's past wealth were little more than scratches on the hillside; odd remnants which had been absorbed back into nature and hardly counted in the vast scale of things. And as he climbed still higher and left the site behind, he could see only folds and curves of hills, rising one beyond the other; their foreheads barred with shadows, their scalps wreathed in blue mist.

He peeled off his two sweaters and tied them round his waist. He was wearing far too many clothes for a strenuous summer walk, but he had set out on an impulse, without any thought for his normal morning ritual of razor, comb and soap. Actually, it had given him a sense of liberation to step straight from bed to hillside, like an impetuous child absolved from the constraints of boring things like washing or searching for clean socks. He finger-combed his hair, used his sleeve to mop the perspiration off his face, then continued across the brow of the hill. There was something wonderfully elating about looking down on everything, as if he had reached the lower rung of heaven and could pity the poor mortals still scurrying around on earth. He stretched his arms like wings, almost expecting to lift off, like the sparrow-hawk above him, soaring in the playground of the sky. He shouted, just to hear his voice; was answered by a plaintive 'ba-aaa' – a sheep watching him inquisitively as he clambered up on a boulder and surveyed the sweep of countryside below.

He was as high as he could go now, and the path plunged down again, following a dip between the hills. It was so steep in places he had to use his hands to steady himself; palms soon grazed and muddy, feet sliding on loose stones. All at once, he slithered to a halt, grabbing at a clump of rough-leaved ferns. Only now had he seen the lake below him – a stretch of silent water shimmering in the sun; the hills huddled closely round it, as if to protect it from intruders. He felt a trespasser himself in this remote and secret spot, yet he also had the eerie feeling that he was not in fact alone. His consciousness of some other presence was so palpable, convincing, that he actually glanced round to check on who was there. Nobody and nothing. Even the sheep were keeping their distance, and the darting swallows crisscrossing the sky had dwindled into tiny specks, leaving only the unruffled clouds.

Furtively, he stole down to the lake's edge, as if scared of being apprehended if he disturbed that awesome silence, which made even his own heartbeat seem insensitively loud. His feet scrunched from flinty stones to softer sand as he approached the rippling water; his shadow trembling in its polished blue–black mirror. It seemed devoid of any fish – indeed devoid of any life at all – a lake in some dark myth, mysterious and unfathomable. Again, he looked surreptitiously behind him, certain he was being watched, but again he could see nothing save sun and shadow, hill and sky. He searched for a flat pebble and sent it skimming across the surface; listened to its final plop, wondering how far it had to fall before it reached the bottom. The sides of the lake shelved steeply, suggesting it was very deep.

Impulsively, he tugged off all his clothes, left them in a jumbled heap, and waded into the water, catching his breath as its icy claws shocked his naked limbs. He struck out briskly, to defeat the numbing cold; threshing with great force, and revelling in the commotion he was making now that he'd dared to break the brooding spell of silence. This place was so unspoilt, he felt like the first living creature who had ever lighted on it, ever left his footprints here – no, more than that, he felt like the first man on earth: a just-created Adam, free to sample his new world; to try out water and declare that it was good. He splashed and ducked and circled, playing childish games with himself – he would reach that patch of shadow in under twenty seconds; he would curl up and turn a somersault, and then try swimming with his eyes shut, as if he'd yet to receive the gift of sight.

Next, he took a deep breath in and dived under the water, using really vigorous strokes to prevent his natural buoyancy from bobbing him back up again. There was no sign of the bottom, just the water growing darker and darker as he spiralled further down, struggling now to hold his breath. He was forced to surface, spluttering and coughing, ears aching from the pressure, heart hammering in complaint. He floated on his back to recover, the huge clouds staring down at him, the sun bedazzling his eyes; then dived again, determined to touch bottom. Fighting his own limitations – mortal lungs and finite breath – he swooped down and down and down; entering an alien world of cavernous black water. He tried to ignore the tightness in his chest, the increasing shock of cold as he ventured even deeper, still encountering no end to the abyss.

Lungs bursting from the strain, he catapulted up again, through water changing rapidly from black to slate to sapphire; then exploded into warmth and light as he broke the silver surface. Gasping in relief, he trod water for a while, too exhausted for more effort, screwing up his smarting eyes, shaking his wet hair.

At length, he swam slowly to the shore, let himself dry off in the velvet-fingered sun, then scrambled back into his clothes. He was still cold, despite the sweaters – cold and starving hungry, his stomach rumbling shamelessly. He careered back up the path and across the brow of the hill, startling the stolid sheep which went skittering away. His seven-league boots seemed still in perfect order as he raced along the track, relishing the glow of warmth returning to his body, the blood pounding in his veins. He was surprised how soon he reached his 'house', panting to a halt outside it, and only now seeing it as the sturdy serviceable shelter it was, rather than a prison. It was the only one of the cottages with all four walls relatively intact – the others were pathetic heaps of stones. He felt something close to pride in it as he knelt inside to fold the rugs and sleeping-bag, gazing through the window-frame at the stupendous view, which reduced his Wandsworth garden to a diminutive cabbage-patch. It suddenly occurred to him that he had indeed slept soundly like a child, despite all the discomforts and the intensity of his fear. And the sleep had done him a power of good, since he had actually spent the morning living in the present – not anxious, not self-judging, not brooding on his problems or those of the Third World, but enjoying simple pleasures, which for him was quite remarkable. In short, he'd been a child again.

'The child you weren't allowed to be.'

He stood up so sharply his head grazed the tarpaulin roof. That brief but disturbing phrase had brought his apprehension surging back. He would have to face a man who had seen him sob his eyes out, whom he had clung to in hysteria. And he would have to rejoin the others, overcome his shyness and unease. Automatically he looked at his watch, then cursed his naked wrist. He'd lost all track of time, had no idea how long he'd been out walking, but Penny must be wondering where he was. She and Pippa had probably come up here to look for him; returned mystified or worried.

He pulled off his two sweaters, then emerged into the sun again and trudged dutifully downhill towards the camp. His disquiet increased with the noise – screams and shouts from unruly children playing round the tents, and the yapping of some obstreperous dog shattering his new-found peace. He wrinkled his nose at the stench of the latrines, which were sited on this westward side of the camp – the most primitive of earth-closets and surely a health risk in themselves. He simply couldn't bring himself to use them. They turned his stomach, put him off his food.

The lack of privacy reminded him of school – having to share his most intimate smells and noises with less fastidious boys, perched side by side in a row of chilly cubicles, separated only by the thinnest of partitions. And there was the same distasteful sense of humanity *en masse*: being lumped together with people he hadn't chosen as his companions, and didn't necessarily like, but who had to be put up with since there was no chance of avoiding them.

His steps began to falter as he reached the outskirts of the camp. He dodged from tree to tree so that nobody would see him, then skulked behind the bushes until he had rustled up his courage. Now he could see faces, recognize the people he'd met yesterday – that pigtailed girl who believed in reincarnation and hoped to establish a permanent community on the lines of an Indian ashram; the middle-aged woman losing her sight (who would actually look more at home at a suburban coffee-morning); the two young gays, whom he suspected might have AIDS. How in God's name had he landed up in such eccentric company and living in such a tip? The once grassy field was a sea of viscous mud, churned up by a dozen cars and vans. And the tents themselves were mud-splashed, dotted untidily around the field, each surrounded by its flotsam: washing bowls and gumboots, pushchairs, broken toys. Washing-lines were strung between the trees, festooned with socks and pants (and a few weird and wonderful outer garments), while a row of polythene bags dangled from another string, for the different forms of rubbish – paper, glass, compost, metal, plastic. The whiff of rotting food was overlaid with less obnoxious smells: paraffin and woodsmoke, the aroma of a simmering onion stew. A meal was being prepared by half a dozen would-be chefs, squatting on their haunches around the communal fire, poking various messes in blackened pots and pans.

He edged a little closer, looking out for a blaze of carrot hair, but there was no sign of Penny or Pippa. Perhaps they had set out on a search-party and were halfway up the hill. He scanned the slope behind him, but could see only the inevitable sheep still mechanically cropping the grass. He turned back to the camp, suddenly glimpsed the familiar red hair, with a darker head behind it – Penny emerging from their tent, followed by the healer, who was stripped to the waist and displaying a luxurious pelt of body-hair.

Daniel clutched at the tree-trunk, nails digging into the bark. What the hell had they been doing? Did the man go on his nocturnal rounds from sleeping-bag to sleeping-bag, first soothing motherless schoolboys, then inveigling his way into the tents of husbandless wives? How long had they been together, and what were they up to now? They were still standing disturbingly close to each other, deep in conversation, the healer's fanatic gaze boring into his wife's blue eyes.

He couldn't shift his own eyes from the fellow's naked torso and those whorls of coarse dark hair. He himself could boast little more than half a dozen puny hairs sprouting round his nipples, and Penny had once upset him by her tasteless jibe that he buy a sack of lawn-seed and sow it on his chest. The healer wouldn't need such help – his chest was thatched already – and his skin was so tanned from his healthy outdoor lifestyle, he made most boring city-dwellers seem pallid and unwell. Even without the mane, he looked much more disturbingly masculine than he had done in the middle of the night, when his voluminous robe had disguised the curve of his rump, now brazenly defined by tight blue jeans. And his long effeminate hair was tied back in a ponytail, revealing a strong jaw. Yet he had no height to speak of, no broad and burly shoulders, and was certainly no muscle-man. So why did Penny seem so fascinated – practically flirting with him, for heaven's sake – her face glowing as she hung on his every word? And *he* returned the compliment; totally absorbed in what she was saying in reply, then suddenly placing both hands on her shoulders.

Daniel blundered towards them, tripping over a guy-rope in his fury. What right had this man to paw his wife, hypnotize her almost? His angry words aborted in his throat as the healer moved from Penny to embrace him in his turn. He stood rigid and embarrassed, recoiling from the smell of sweat, from the warm and hairy nakedness pressed against his chest. Too shaken to resist, he waited for the ordeal to end, then ran a nervous hand across his shirt, as if trying to remove the healer's traces. Penny smiled a greeting – so casual and perfunctory, they might have been parted a mere hour or two, instead of the whole night.

'I was beginning to think you'd run away,' she laughed.

'No, I . . . went for a long walk.'

The healer laid his hand on Daniel's arm, as if he found physical contact a necessity, and had no objection to starting on the husband once he had softened up the wife. 'I'm glad you slept so well, Daniel. It was already past eleven when you woke.'

'Eleven?' Daniel sounded incredulous as he shook off the hot hand. Never in his life had he slept so long – even half-past seven was late for him, and nine was truly decadent. But perhaps the man was bluffing. How could he be so precise about the time when all watches were forbidden, or see through stout stone walls from four hundred yards away? Unless he had some bugging device trained on the ruined shack. Whatever the truth, it made him feel uneasy. In some way, he was being watched; his very mind open to inspection. He immediately tried to quash his thoughts before they too were scrutinized; adopted a less hostile tone. 'Well, I only hope I haven't missed lunch. I'm absolutely ravenous.'

'No, we always have lunch late. Everything takes longer here – preparing food and cooking it, chopping wood for the fire. You'll have to do your bit, Daniel. We live as a community and aim to share everything – our experiences and states of mind as well as just the chores.'

Daniel said nothing, feeling both resentful and rebuked. It was also beginning to annoy him that the fellow should keep trotting out his name – Daniel this and Daniel the other – when he had no name of his own beyond 'the healer'. Yesterday, at lunch, another of the new arrivals had asked what they should call him, and he had answered 'Anything', then gone on to explain that he deliberately avoided one restricting name, because he aimed to be a different person for each of them; becoming male or female, child or sage, according to their individual needs. The girl in question had then insisted on addressing him as 'master', which must have been most gratifying when he was probably a Joe Bloggs. There was no trace of a Welsh lilt, and the voice, though soft and caressing (dangerously so, as he had found to his own cost), was basically South London – hardly a sign of exotic ancestry. The whole story of his descent from Merlin seemed more and more preposterous. More likely he was just a dropout, or perhaps someone who'd been made redundant and was now seeking a new role, a new source of self-esteem. It must give him quite a buzz becoming 'guru' or 'master', in place of a mere number on a social security form.

'Where's Pippa?' Daniel asked brusquely, turning back to his wife.

'In her element! Stephen put her in charge of a sick dog.'

'*Who?*' He didn't remember a Stephen. There had probably been an influx of new invalids or hangers-on – more smells to pollute the privies, more faces to get straight.

Penny indicated the healer, flashed him a coquettish smile. 'I've decided to call him Stephen.'

Daniel frowned his incomprehension, mouthed a silent 'Why?'

'My father's name, of course.'

Why 'of course', he wondered? The healer was nowhere near old enough to be a father figure – though when he came to think about it, he had no idea of his age. Last night he'd seemed ageless and eternal, as his mother had done herself during the first decade of his life. But today he had shed that gravity and appeared younger altogether – a lover, not a father. He supposed he should be grateful that Penny hadn't opted to call him Phil.

He asked again about Pippa, anxious at the thought of her running around with a pack of unknown dogs. The Alsatian, in particular, seemed alarmingly fierce, and even the spaniel had already nipped a younger child.

'She's quite all right. Don't worry. She's in Rainbow Lodge with Esther and Doris.'

He noticed how quickly she had picked up the terminology. Apparently tepees were called 'lodges', and Rainbow Lodge was the big communal tepee where he'd spent his first extraordinary night. Its name derived from the rainbow painted on the canvas, though the once-brilliant spectrum of colours had been so assailed by the elements, it was now little more than a smudged and faded motley.

'But what about the dog?' he pressed.

'Oh, he's in there as well – along with the other invalids. The poor thing's got a really nasty leg. He tore it on some barbed wire and although their vet in Yorkshire stitched it up and gave him penicillin and stuff, the owners say it just won't heal. It shows how your fame has spread,' she added, turning to the healer with another radiant smile, 'when people travel two hundred miles for the sake of the family pet!'

'Hey, Penny!' someone called – a low-pitched breathy voice.

Daniel saw the pigtailed girl approaching them. She was dressed in a bikini top and brief blue denim shorts – incongruous with her heavy rubber boots.

'Pen, we're going to build a labyrinth for the new-moon celebrations. I wondered if you'd help?'

'Yes, 'course I will, Corinna. What d'you want me to do?'

Daniel hardly registered the reply. That brief exchange was enough to disconcert him. He had been separated from his wife for just one night and a morning, and already she was 'Pen'; already on intimate terms with the healer, and throwing herself into the activities of the camp. How could he suggest they leave, when both she and Pippa had settled in so rapidly and were evidently enjoying their new roles? Yet the thought of having to participate in some whacky new-moon junket made him still more nervous.

He realized he was staring at Corinna's ample breasts, which threatened to overflow her skimpy top. Guiltily he looked away, only to encounter another girl in a low V-neck, worn without a bra, the clingy fabric outlining her nipples. Almost everyone he had seen so far seemed in a state of half-undress, and his own conventional shirt and trousers looked completely out of place amidst the shorts and caftans, the cropped jeans and the swimming trunks. Only Margot, the woman with the eye problems, still stuck to her neat uniform of navy pleated skirt and gingham blouse, though even she had resorted to wellington boots to cope with the thick mud. Daniel glanced down at his own spattered shoes and trousers. He would be better off in a diving-suit, he reflected with an ironic shrug. Not only would it spare his clothes, but he could remain thankfully anonymous behind the mask and goggles.

He started at the sepulchral sound of a conch-shell – the signal for their meals. It was being blown by a small mousy girl, who, he'd heard, had changed her name to Happy, after the healer had cured her of 'cancer of the mind'. She refused to use a surname, because she insisted she was neither her father's child nor her ex-husband's wife, and claimed that her efforts to fulfil both roles had caused her health to break down in the first place. She had returned to the camp as a sort of acolyte, assisting with the laying on of hands. Both she and Corinna had made the place their home, and it was obvious both were besotted with the healer. He had an arm round each of them as they sauntered towards the fire to join the other campers, who were perched on wooden crates or sprawled on groundsheets or black dustbin-bags. Daniel wished the healer would use his magical powers for something truly philanthropic, like conjuring up a proper table and chairs. He found it very awkward eating off his lap, while the damp seeped into his bottom and his back ached from the strain. Penny took his arm and steered him in the direction of the food, asking how he was feeling.

'Okay,' he answered guardedly. 'Hungry more than anything.'

'Well, I can guarantee you won't starve. I spent half the morning peeling enough potatoes for an army, and chopping a mountain of leeks and swedes.'

And the other half being mauled by the healer, Daniel thought tetchily, his spirits sinking lower at the mention of so many dreary vegetables. What he needed was a pound of best rump steak and a pint of beer to wash it down, but both meat and alcohol were forbidden at the camp. 'Isn't Pippa coming too?' he asked, recalling his daughter's revulsion at last night's lentil hotchpotch.

'No. She's eating in the lodge. Esther and Doris aren't well enough to sit outside, so they have all their meals in there, and Stephen thought it best for Pippa to join them, at least until Bernard's settled down.'

'Who's Bernard?' he enquired. Would he ever memorize these names? He certainly hadn't met a Bernard. Fellow males were thin on the ground, outnumbered by roughly three to one.

'He's the dog – the one with the bad leg. He's really gorgeous. A boxer.'

'But is he – you know – safe?'

'Oh, yes. All slobbery and soppy, with big brown pleading eyes.'

Daniel contented himself with a grunt. The description seemed more appropriate for the 'master' – or JB as he'd decided to call him: a respectful-sounding shortening of Joe Bloggs – but he and Penny were now in earshot of the others, so he was obliged to hold his peace. He lowered himself to the ground, trying vainly to get comfortable on the rough-textured wooden plank which had been laid across the mud, and watching with impatience as the contents of the cooking pots were slowly ladled out and handed round. Everyone was so laid-back and disorganized, the food was cold by the time he got his portion. On this occasion, he was eating out of what looked like a dog-bowl – Bernard's possibly – while Penny had been given a chipped enamel plate. He took a cautious mouthful, gagging on a slimy lump of something unidentifiable, then made a manful effort to force it down. Whatever it was, it must be intrinsically healthy, since JB insisted on 'natural food' in the same way as 'natural time'. Additives were anathema, refined food strictly shunned, sugar and white flour regarded as hardly less horrendous than nicotine and booze.

He tried to keep his mind off steak and kidney pie and treacle tart, swatting crossly at a wasp which had alighted on his doorstep of black bread. (The bread here was so coarse and heavy it might have served better as building bricks, for the construction of more solid quarters than flimsy canvas tents.) All meals were shared with God's creation – wasps and flies, bluebottles and midges. It was best not to ponder on hygiene, or to wonder if those cooking the food remembered to wash their hands between the privies and the saucepans. Actually, there was little chance for reflection of any sort in the ceaseless buzz of conversation, and he was finding it a strain to answer intimate personal questions at the same time as demolishing his stew.

'Are you in therapy, Daniel?' asked a girl whose name he'd forgotten, her long greasy hair dangling in her food.

'Er, no.'

'Pity! I went to a Jungian for years, and it really opened me up. I was a bit like you before – frightened of getting to know myself, and putting on a front to face the world.'

Daniel removed a potato-peeling from his mouth. How the hell could this infuriating woman know anything about him? He had only met her at the meal last night, barely exchanged two words with her.

'Therapy makes you far too self-absorbed,' Corinna interjected. 'We've got to look outwards to society and the community, instead of focusing all our energies on our individual psyches.'

'Anyway, Jung was a racist,' Happy said dismissively.

'*And* sexist,' Corinna added.

'Not as bad as Freud, though. All *he* did was patch people up to make them fit for the patriarchy. We need to be in touch with the feminine side of things, instead of everything in nature being labelled "phallic". I mean, what a bloody cheek! Why on earth should storms and sky and mountains all be seen as masculine?'

JB removed his arm from Happy's shoulders and gestured with his spoon. 'But you can go too far the other way,' he warned. 'After all, feminism stresses separation as much as patriarchy, and separation is isolating. We tend to split things into opposite poles – male and female, God and man, right and wrong, you and me – when we ought to seek harmony instead. We really need to understand that we're all men and all women, and both at the same time.'

Daniel glanced from Corinna's breasts, still straining against the confines of their top, to JB's hirsute chest. The proposition seemed unlikely, if not downright ludicrous, though he had no intention of arguing the point. He was intensely grateful that the spotlight had shifted away from him, and that the girl who'd originally challenged him was now busy feeding her toddler with a boulder of the bread, first softening it in a highly-coloured concoction of beet and carrot juice. He had declined the drink himself, preferring to stick to water (which had been served in a baby's plastic beaker, with a bear on the side and a dead insect floating on the surface).

The conversation had returned to feminism; Happy championing someone called 'the goddess', while Corinna berated the missionary position which she described as a variety of rape, since the woman was pinioned by the man and often found it impossible to reach a climax. Margot was plainly shocked, pursing her lips and complaining to her husband George that this was not a suitable subject for discussion during a meal, let alone in front of impressionable children.

The half-dozen children were not, in fact, listening, but providing their own counterblast; arguing and fighting, or complaining about the food; one boy even demanding a Big Mac. Daniel could sympathize on that point, though he found the noise demoralizing, and wondered why it was so difficult to like or even tolerate other people's offspring. If he shared JB's philanthropy, he would love the whole world for what it was, instead of pondering on the advantages of a different sort of set-up, where neither wasps nor dogs nor under-twelves existed, or where infants reached the age of reason while they were still safely in the womb.

This place was seeding in him a whole series of new guilts: guilt at craving steak, for instance, when Corinna had expounded to him how much cruelty meat-eating caused. And what about the missionary position? Of course it didn't turn him into a rapist, but just listening to the endless talk about women's rights and satisfactions made him depressingly aware (again) of how far he had failed Penny in the last few months.

He abandoned his spoon and fork. (Knives were in short

supply – or perhaps contrary to the principles of peace and non-aggression – but since the bulk of the food was mushy and there was no butter for the bread, they were not essential anyway.) He mopped his face, unfastened a couple of buttons on his shirt. Sweat was beading on his forehead, snailing down his back. It was far too hot for a fire, and although the flames were dying down, they were still roasting him on one side, while the sun grilled him on the other. He couldn't understand why they cooked on an open fire at all, when many of the campers had brought Calor gas or oil stoves, but presumably it was connected with pollution. That was another thing which niggled at his conscience – he knew he didn't share the others' overriding passion for the welfare of the planet. All in all, he was beginning to suspect that he was not a particularly creditable member of the human race; continually preoccupied with his own concerns rather than those of Mother Earth. To expiate his sense of shame, he had chipped in far more money than the surprisingly small sum which had been requested as his contribution. All the expenses were shared; each family or individual making a donation to cover basic necessities, with Corinna in charge of the kitty. (He would have contributed a great deal more if it would have guaranteed him proper meals, eaten in the normal fashion in privacy and comfort.)

He looked up from his plate, aware of a sudden lull. For the first time since they'd started lunch, absolutely no one was wrangling, preaching or holding forth, and even Margot and Corinna must have made their peace, since Margot seemed much more relaxed, and was reverting to her coffee-morning chitchat.

'Well, it's really lovely weather,' she enthused, squinting up at the sun with her all but sightless eyes. JB had assured her that she didn't need her thick remedial glasses, which made eating something of a problem for her. She had spilled a trail of stew from mouth to lap to groundsheet, and drunk in error from someone else's glass.

'Yes, I bet it's not much hotter on the Costa Brava,' Len observed in his no-nonsense Brummie accent, obviously relieved that he could now contribute to the conversation. He and his wife Jeanette had nothing in common with the new-age acolytes. Len was a builder and Jeanette worked as a hairdresser, and they had clearly never heard of Jung, nor of esoteric concepts such as auras and past lives. They were here for the sake of their daughter – a girl of eight or so, who had suffered since birth from eczema and asthma, and found no relief from drugs. Daniel noticed that they, too, were struggling with their food. Len had left the bulk of his stew, and Jeanette was crumbling her bread into morsels, to tackle it piecemeal. Both were distracted by the flies, Jeanette flapping her hand back and forth across her daughter's plate to try to shoo them off, and Len shaking his head irritably every time they hovered near his face.

'You've caught the sun already, Daniel,' Jeanette pointed out. 'Have you been working on your tan?'

'No,' said JB softly. 'He's been swimming in the lake.'

Daniel tried to hide his consternation. 'How did you know that?' he muttered.

JB smiled. 'I led you there myself. You needed to drown your fear, wash away your pain and grief from the past.'

Daniel felt himself blushing furiously as every eye was trained on him. Any moment now this tactless creep would be telling the whole company how the poor scared little schoolboy had mistaken him for his mother and lain sobbing in his arms.

'We're all men and all women, both at the same time.'

Daniel stared down at his hands. The words took on a deeper meaning as they re-echoed in his mind. The healer *had* been his mother, protecting him all night. Yet now he felt threatened by the fact. He had learned, at the tender age of seven, to do without a mother; to reject all weakness and dependency, all need for female cossetting. JB's mystic meddling could tear down the armour he'd spent so many years constructing, reveal the frailties beneath.

He was saved by the toddler tipping over his drink – purple slush seeping into his pale blue dungarees. Jeanette ran to fetch a cloth, but another child – the oldest there: a teenager called Rick – chucked a mud-ball at her retreating back and hit her between the shoulder blades. She wheeled round in astonishment, only to be thwacked a second time; her shirt and slacks besmirched with mud.

Len sprang up from the groundsheet, turning on the healer in a fury. 'What's the fucking use of talking peace and harmony, when these kids are allowed to behave like bloody savages?'

'I'm not standing for language like that,' Margot protested in a tight-lipped voice. 'I'm as disgusted by the children's behaviour as you are, but you can hardly complain if you set them such a bad example.'

'Hear, hear,' grunted her husband George, running a nervous finger round his perspiring red bull-neck.

'There's no such thing as "bad language",' Corinna remarked serenely. 'Words only have the power we choose to give them.'

'I'm sorry, young lady, but you don't know what you're talking about.' George had scrambled to his feet as well, and was standing over Corinna. 'There's some words I don't want to hear, not in any company, and especially not with ladies present.'

Then Happy started sounding off in support of Corinna's viewpoint, and a general argument broke out about whether any words should be taboo, and if so, which ones and why? The healer took no part in it, nor had he defended himself against Len's indignant outburst. Instead, he was talking softly to the culprit, trying to control a subdued and sullen Rick through a combination of humour and sweet reason.

Daniel sat in silence, welcoming the uproar. Probably no one would remember the reference to his own fear and grief, now that everybody else was so upset – Rick's embarrassed mother stammering her apologies, Jeanette in tears, and George and Len still sparring. He caught Penny's eye and exchanged a surreptitious smile with her – the first time she'd thought to acknowledge his existence since the beginning of the meal. She was sharing her upturned orange-crate with the younger of the gays, a lanky boy called Dylan, all bones and eyes and hair, and had been talking to him *sotto voce* throughout the rackety lunch. Their private conversation had made him feel excluded, especially as he'd been hoping to sit next to her himself so that he could hold her hand, metaphorically at least. But she was holding Dylan's hand, literally and blatantly. It appeared to be an unwritten rule to fondle anyone within reach, and at every opportunity. Well, he was damned if he'd hold Len's hand, or his other neighbour's on the plank – Dylan's partner Gerard (Gerald? Something like that anyway) – who had a crew-cut and a cold, and had hardly spoken yet beyond a few 'Excuse me's when he sneezed.

'I'll get the pudding,' Penny volunteered, shrewdly asking George for help, to put a stop to his shouting-match with Len. Her bid for peace was effective; the fractious voices petering out as she and George returned with two large bowls of something brown again. All the food seemed to be mud-coloured, whether bread, stew, soup, dessert or cake. Everybody wiped their plates with the square or two of kitchen towel doled out at each meal, which served as paper napkin, handkerchief, sweat-rag or whatever. Then Penny sloshed some soupy stuff on to the same (still greasy) plates. Dishes were in short supply, and using the same receptacle for both the first and second courses at least encouraged you to finish up your food. Otherwise a dollop of prune mousse or organic brown-rice pudding would land on top of a discarded swede or a half-chewed stringy parsnip.

He declined dessert altogether, since he had no idea of how to dispose of his uneaten stew (not to mention the plum-stone and the feather which he'd extracted from it earlier). He sat nibbling at his bread – which seemed the safest of the food, if not the most original – gazing up at the distant (silent) hills. Whatever the deficiencies of the cuisine, at least the view was some compensation; the sun so brilliant on the peaks he had to shade his eyes to look at them; the white clouds trailing wisps and shreds like Mrs Gwynfryn Evans's leaking duvet. His thoughts returned to the lake, his private sanctuary enfolded by the hills. He longed to plunge into its depths again, cool himself in every sense. Just recalling it had changed his mood. He could feel his former peace returning, a languor stealing over him, as if he were stretched out on its pillowed shore, drying in the sun.

He glanced furtively at the healer, though hardly knowing why. JB was sitting motionless, head erect, palms uppermost; the dark hypnotic eyes fixed unwaveringly on his own. Confused, he tried to look away, but he seemed somehow mesmerized – compelled to hold that gaze, even against his will. Yet all the while the sense of peace was growing stronger; the people around him dwindling, their chatter fading out, until he was alone again, and naked again – a newly-created Adam disporting in his paradise.

Somewhere in the distance he could hear the healer's voice, though it barely grazed the bewitching healing silence of the lake.

The enigmatic words were mere ripples on its surface, a flicker in his consciousness.

'*I led you there myself.*'

17

'HOW LONG HAVE YOU BEEN HERE?' asked Daniel, swishing another plate in the scummy near-cold water.

'Oh, it must be over a week now.' Claire flicked her tea-towel at a midge. She had already been bitten and kept rubbing at the red bumps on her arm.

Daniel scratched his own bite – a large one on his neck. Washing up outside meant not just the lack of running water or a proper sink and draining-board, but being subjected to the attentions of the insect population. On the other hand, the sun was wonderfully warm and he was enjoying the sensation of having the unbounded sky above him, rather than a confining Wandsworth ceiling. He had even gone so far as to remove his shirt, and could feel his grateful skin soaking up the heat. 'What's your impression of the place?' he pressed, hoping to glean some information from a friendly fellow inmate.

'Well, it's been quite a strain in some ways, but Rick's definitely getting better. His stomach pains aren't half as bad, and he's not so anti-social. Oh, I admit he can be bolshie, and I almost died when he threw that mud at Jeanette, but he actually apologized when Blue had a word with him. He wouldn't have done that in a million years if *I'd* suggested it.'

'Blue?'

She flushed. 'That's my name for the master. I know it must sound silly, but blue's always been my favourite colour – the colour of big peaceful things like sea and sky and . . .' She faltered, as if afraid he'd think her pretentious. 'What do *you* call him?' she asked.

Now it was Daniel's turn to hesitate. Studiously he attacked a blackened saucepan with his dishmop. 'I . . . I haven't quite decided,' he replied. 'I can't make him out at all. I mean, I really don't know the first thing about him. Does anyone? Do *you*?'

'Oh yes! That's the only reason I came. I live in Wales myself, you see – only thirty miles away – and someone in our village knows this man who had cirrhosis of the liver, but was cured by Blue within three days of arriving here.'

'Oh, really? And have you *met* the chap, questioned him yourself?'

'No, he lives in Shrewsbury. But apparently it was almost like a miracle, and even his doctor said he couldn't believe his eyes.'

'Mm, that's the trouble, though, isn't it? It's always "apparently" or "a friend of a friend", never anything more precise. I think we need to check up on him – ask to see his credentials, so to speak.'

Claire twisted the damp tea-towel in her hands. 'But that would look as if we didn't trust him. And it would be a bit ungrateful, when he does all this for free. Yes, I know a few people make donations, and we all share food and stuff, but basically he's giving and we're taking.'

'Maybe,' said Daniel tersely. 'But if it's our children's health at stake, then we shouldn't take any risks.'

'But what risks could there be? I mean, it's not as if he uses drugs or surgery. And Happy told me he learned his healing methods from really amazing people like Australian Aboriginals, and shamans in Peru, and Pueblo medicine-men. He's actually *lived* with them, Daniel, travelled all over the world, from one tribe to another.'

Daniel tossed aside the ineffectual dish-mop and seized a scouring pad, venting his frustration on the saucepan. Claire's disclosures had made him still more alarmed. Wasn't it the height of irresponsibility to allow his daughter to be used as a guinea-pig for the dubious (if not dangerous) remedies of some Pueblo medicine-man? He glanced around at the various bodies sprawled out on the grass – they might be sunbathing on holiday rather than here in search of cures. Did no one share his apprehension, or at least his belief in basic standards and precautions? Most of them looked half-asleep, lulled by the fine weather, or perhaps drowsy after the meal. And those still awake seemed absorbed in some weird rite or other. Happy and Corinna were performing an exotic dance underneath the trees, circling with slow rhythmic steps and semaphoring with their arms. Another girl sat cross-legged outside her tent, meditating presumably, with her hands resting palms up on her knees. She was humming on one note, the low drone occasionally punctuated by the laughter of a child. Outwardly, the scene was tranquil enough – the stream burbling over stones, white butterflies alighting on gold buttercups, the sheep still placidly grazing. Only he was out of tune with the general air of peace; his mind churning with unanswered questions; suspicion of the healer overlaid with a grudging respect and a streak of indefinable fear. He was also worried about Penny. She had disappeared straight after lunch – and so too had JB. He only hoped they weren't closeted together in the intimacy of the tent, he giving and she taking.

'Another thing,' said Claire, drying a clutch of forks and packing them in the cardboard box which served as a cutlery drawer. 'He's been ill himself – quite seriously ill – and I'm sure that makes a difference. If you've experienced suffering first-hand, you're far more likely to sympathize. He confided in me the first night I arrived, which I thought was really touching. I was pretty low at the time – in tears and everything – so I suppose he realized it would help to know *he'd* been through the mill as well, and yet survived and come out stronger for it.'

'The healer healed,' Daniel murmured.

The irony was lost on Claire. 'Yes, that's right,' she enthused. 'He says we're all wounded and all capable of being healers, but we deny our natural powers.'

Daniel scrubbed vigorously at the pan, cursing the ban on detergents. A slimy bar of household soap was no match for burned-on sludge. 'Has your son had any healing yet?' he asked. 'I mean, a proper kosher session with the laying on of hands, or whatever?'

'No, and even if it was offered, he'd resist it at this stage. He's very shy and suspicious, you see. But Blue always takes his time. He won't force himself on people, but waits until they're ready. And anyway, there are others here who need him more than Rick does. Take Doris, for example. She's got MS, but she hasn't had a session either. You just have to be patient. It's all part of accepting things, and acceptance is really crucial. He's taught me that already.'

Daniel resisted the temptation to argue the point that if

acceptance of one's ills was healing, then all and sundry could set themselves up as Magic Men. He had taken an instant liking to this woman, despite her simplistic views, and had no wish to upset her. In appearance she was plain and rather gawky – not the sort of female he would normally look at twice. She was an inch or two taller than he was, and although she stooped to disguise her height, her apologetic posture only emphasized it more. Her hips were narrow, boyish; her breasts indiscernible beneath the baggy shirt. She wore glasses which seemed frivolous and completely out of character – magenta-coloured frames with little specks of glitter on them – as if she had allowed herself just one stab at glamour, and then settled for drab clothes and lank straight hair. But the eyes behind the spectacles were sensitive and trusting, and her warm outgoing manner put him at his ease.

'Are you Welsh?' he asked, moving to a less contentious topic.

'No, but my husband is – or ex-husband, I should say. It's stupid, I suppose, but I can't bring myself to use the word.' She swallowed, made a pretence of re-arranging the forks. 'He walked out three months ago.'

'I'm sorry.'

'It's okay. And oddly enough, I really mean that now. Blue's helped me to see that it *is* okay to be depressed. He says depression's simply part of life – the shadow side or dark side. We shouldn't call it an illness, or suppress it with electric shocks or pills, but actually try to welcome it instead, because it teaches us compassion and develops what he calls our soul. Not soul in the religious sense, but . . .'

'Mum!'

'What?' Claire turned to see her son approaching, cradling something in his hands.

'Look! I've found a sheep's skull. Isn't it fantastic? It's still got all the teeth in.'

'So it has.' She took it from him, stroked a careful finger around the hollow of the eye-socket. 'It must be pretty old. It's completely smooth and clean.'

Picked clean by the crows, thought Daniel. He could picture the cruel birds circling; the foxes tearing flesh from bone. It disturbed him somehow – this reminder of clean death. 'Where did you find it?' he asked.

'Just in the next field. I'm going back there now to take another look. There might be other bones and things, to add to my collection.'

'Quite the little ghoul, isn't he?' Claire grabbed Rick's sleeve before he could dash off again. 'You're not going anywhere, my lad, until you've had your medicine.'

'Oh, not again!' Rick groaned. 'It's absolutely foul.'

'That's as may be, but Blue says it's doing you good, and he wants you to take it every two hours.'

Daniel returned to his improvised sink: a battered plastic bowl perched precariously on two upturned crates. 'I thought you said Blue didn't believe in drugs?'

'He doesn't. This is based on plants. In fact, I collect them myself each morning, now he's shown me which ones to use – comfrey, and burdock, and red valerian, when I can find it.'

'And deadly nightshade,' Rick muttered, 'and great big flabby toadstools.'

Daniel laughed. He felt a certain sympathy with Rick. The boy was tall and gangling, as *he'd* been in his teens, and seemed constitutionally unable to keep still; continually shuffling his feet, flicking back his hair or gnawing at his thumbnail. He remembered his own restlessness at school; being forced to sit quietly at his desk while inwardly he was exploding through the roof, streaking to the nearest airport and hurtling back to Zambia. The change from prep-school to senior school hadn't ended his unhappiness. It was still the dreaded Greystone Court – just a transfer to another building (bigger, colder, greyer than the Junior House). As if prompted by the move, he had grown six inches in as many months, shooting up from dwarf to beanpole; wrists protruding from his blazer sleeves; trouser-legs embarrassingly short. He recalled the hated nicknames: 'Stick Insect' and 'Broomstick', even 'Twiggy', worst of all. If Rick was suffering similar taunts, then it was quite possible his pains were psychosomatic. Being so much taller than your classmates could prove a heavy cross to bear, especially if you were the shy type and longed to be invisible – not exactly easy when there was so much of you to hide.

'It's amazing,' Claire was saying as she poured some murky greenish liquid from a Thermos flask into a glass, 'how Blue's changed my attitude to things. Even gathering these plants is a sort of sacred task. You have to speak to them first, not just grab the leaves or flowers as if they're your natural God-given right. He says we need to respect them, ask their permission before we help ourselves.'

'Well, I wish they'd said no,' groaned Rick, as she pushed the glass into his hand.

'Go on – be brave!' she urged. 'Remember what Blue said: "Close your eyes and down it in one go!"'

'You must be joking.' He took a tiny sip and gave an extravagant grimace, clutching at his throat and pretending to gag. 'I refuse to drink another drop of this vile stuff unless I can have a sweet or something, to take the taste away.'

'Blue doesn't approve of sweets, Rick. You know that perfectly well.'

Rick aimed a kick at the cutlery box. 'He doesn't approve of anything, if you ask me. No crisps or Coke or telly – not even a flipping biscuit. This place is worse than a prison camp.'

'Well, you could have a piece of carrot cake. Or there may be a bran muffin left. I'll go and check the tin.'

'I don't want that muck, Mum! I want some proper sweets.'

'I've got some toffees in the car,' Daniel admitted, giving the word 'toffees' a whispered emphasis, to stress their status as contraband. 'Almost a full packet. You're welcome to them, Rick, so long as your mother doesn't object.'

'Well, I do,' retorted Claire. 'They'll undo all the good Blue's done, *and* it's going behind his back. I just don't think that's fair.'

'You're such a fuss-arse, Mum! One little sweet can't hurt. And anyway I reckon I deserve one. I'm stuck here with nothing to do, the food's disgusting and you keep shoving that shitty medicine down my throat. No one in their right mind would come here in a thousand years. Can you imagine what my friends would say? They're all away on proper holidays stuffing themselves with burgers and chips, and probably beer and fags as well.'

Much the same as *my* friends, Daniel thought wryly. Except with them it would be entrecôte and *pommes dauphinoises*, washed down with a good claret and perhaps followed by a cigar. He could already smell the whiff of the cigar, taste it in his mouth.

The mention of 'fags' had roused in him a sudden intense desire to smoke.

'Don't be silly, Rick,' said Claire. 'I'm sure your friends don't drink. Their parents wouldn't allow it.'

'Get a grip, Mum! You really are pathetic! Pete and Darren have been swilling lager since they were ten, and Barry often helps himself to his dad's whisky.'

The argument continued, until Claire reluctantly gave in, though probably more to spare Daniel the embarrassment of a protracted family tussle than from any real conviction that a bag of Creamline toffees was any less heinous than cigarettes and Scotch.

'Okay,' said Rick to Daniel. 'Let's go.'

Claire took over with the scouring pad, tackling the last cooking-pot – a heavy iron contraption even more charred than the previous ones – while Rick and Daniel strode off to find the car. All the vehicles had been moved to higher ground to prevent any further mishaps. George and Margot had told him that when they first arrived, their spanking new Cortina had stuck chassis-deep in the mud, and could only be hauled out with a tow-rope. He was surprised that they had actually stayed the course, rather than turning tail for home, or swapping the healer's ministrations for those of Thomas Cook. He was sure they would be far happier in a nice hotel in the Algarve, with all mod cons and a courier on hand.

His thoughts returned to Rick. He wondered if his truculence was a reaction to his father walking out. Away from his mother, he seemed far less outspoken, retreating behind a façade of glum reserve. Was it worse to lose your father in your teens, or when you were only four, as Pippa had been?

'How old are you, Rick?' he asked, instantly regretting the question. He had hated it when grown-ups asked his age. Whatever answer you gave, it was invariably the wrong one, and you'd be judged too big, too small, too old, too young, too something.

Rick evidently felt the same. 'Nearly fourteen,' he mumbled, picking up a stick from the ditch and slashing at the grass with it.

Daniel refrained from comment. He'd have guessed fifteen at least, but he suppressed his exclamation of surprise. So the boy was little older than Pippa. Perhaps the two could be friends – both silent types and both deprived of their fathers. He hadn't seen Pippa since last night, and was struck with new guilt about how little he'd actually thought of her. They were only here for her sake, yet he had no idea how she was. Had she opened up and blossomed now that she had new responsibilities, or was she feeling still more miserable? She had said very little yesterday, but that was hardly surprising in such unconventional surroundings. He really ought to find her; reassure himself that she was not at any risk from either the healer or the injured dog.

'Hey, look!' said Rick, nudging him as they crossed the muddy ditch.

Daniel glanced in the direction Rick was pointing. A girl appeared to be making love to a tree – the girl who'd talked to him at lunch about her therapy. Well, it had certainly succeeded in removing her inhibitions, since her arms were flung tightly round the tree-trunk, her face pressed against its bark, eyes closed in ecstasy. She was crooning to the tree – a stunted blackthorn with several dead or broken branches and a scattering of sickly leaves.

'I offer you my love,' they heard her whisper. 'And I ask for yours in return.'

Rick caught Daniel's eye and tapped his forehead with his finger. 'Another nutter,' he mouthed.

Daniel nodded in complicity. If *he* found this place hard to take, especially its lunatic fringe, then it must be even worse for an adolescent boy deprived of *Neighbours*, Nintendo, and his normal high-tech life. The two of them were standing only a few feet from the girl, yet she was oblivious of anything beyond her wounded lover.

'May you and I be at one in the sacred circle of life,' she confided to the tree. 'I feel your sap rising in me. I feel my roots growing as deep and strong as yours.'

Daniel gave her a wide berth, shepherding Rick past. It was easy to scoff, dismiss the woman as mad, but her utter concentration, the solemnity in her voice, was somehow most unnerving. And anyway suppose such things were catching? Would he be able to return to the real world, to do his job administering scarce resources for deprived and suffering Africa, without being affected in some fundamental way?

He quickened his pace, half-running to the car, fighting a sudden urge to get in and slam the door, drive away from the whole crazy bunch – tree-amorists, and healers, and gullible depressives developing their souls. Instead he hunted for the toffees, eventually locating them underneath the front passenger seat. He helped himself before passing them to Rick, deciding to join him in the crime, if only to douse his craving for a smoke.

'I've got a crate of apples here as well,' he said, remembering Claire's reference to the campers pooling food. He was probably breaking another rule by hoarding all this fruit, when the principle was share and share alike. 'If I dig you out a carrier, perhaps you'd like to take some?'

'Thanks,' said Rick, tearing the wrappers off two toffees and cramming both sweets in his mouth at once.

Daniel unwrapped his own more slowly. 'They look a bit squashed,' he observed.

'I'm not complaining!' Rick handed back the bag. 'Here, have another. They're nicer two at a time.'

Daniel complied. At least it solved the problem of any further conversation. He locked the car and they set off again, cheeks bulging, chomping in a companionable sort of harmony. It did feel truly wicked to be guzzling sweets like this, imbibing banned white sugar. He had rarely broken the rules at school – he'd been too frightened of letting his parents down, when they continually impressed on him how fortunate he was compared with the poor African children. He had never really understood that 'fortunate'. The 'poor African children' weren't parted from their families for three-quarters of the year, nor did they get chilblains or detentions, and certainly nobody dinned into them what fearfully bad form it was to cry, or whinge, or admit you missed your mother.

They skirted the blackthorn votary, who was now lying at the base of the tree, fondling its sinuous roots. There was something overtly sexual about the way she touched those roots; her bare arms stretched along them, her lips murmuring endearments. Daniel felt strangely threatened. Supposing Penny left him for a tree? Oh, he knew the thought was ludicrous, but his confidence had hit rock bottom after his recent potency problems, and there was no way he could compete with the phallic might and majesty of some vigorous young oak.

He picked his way despondently between ruts and bramble-bushes, Rick following at his heels. As they approached the huddle of tents, the boy stuffed the bag of toffees right down inside the carrier, covering it with apples. 'Gotta be careful the Mega-Wanker doesn't see!'

'The Mega-Wanker?'

'Well, Blue, if you prefer. If Mum *has* to call him a colour, I think slime-green suits him better. He's such a creepy toad.'

Daniel dislodged a lump of toffee from his teeth. Yes, Mega-Wanker was bloody good! He amplified JB to JBMW, deriving a definite satisfaction from putting the healer down. He needed to get his own back for the way the fellow had undermined his defences, infiltrated his mind.

He sidestepped a coil of dog-shit, stopping abruptly as his wife's flamboyant hair flashed into view. She and Corinna were about fifty yards ahead, both crouching on the ground, examining a plant. Perhaps Penny had been instructed to gather herbs, like Claire, to make some vile concoction for poor Pippa. He was about to call out to her and ask what she was doing, when suddenly he froze. Corinna had put an arm around her and was giving her a kiss – not a sisterly or friendly kiss, but a fervently erotic one, full on the lips. And Penny appeared to be responding, kissing Corinna back no less eagerly. He stared in disbelief. He had considered semi-seriously the risk of losing his wife's affections to a tree, but this was even worse – more immediate and more real. Corinna must be lesbian. No, that was hardly likely when he'd seen her in a clinch with JB, and when Claire had told him (not without a hint of jealousy) that Corinna had a crush on Blue and wore a snippet of his hair in a locket round her neck. But perhaps *Penny* had made the overtures; encouraged Corinna somehow. Now he came to think of it, everyone she met, regardless of their gender or sexual proclivities, appeared compelled to grope her: first the healer, then Dylan, and now this wretched woman. Only *he* was excluded – the legal wedded husband ousted from her tent.

He felt the more humiliated because Rick was watching avidly, and would be adding Penny to his list of nutters and/or nymphos. He expelled his breath in relief as the two women disengaged; Penny blithely unaware not only of his presence but of the turmoil she had wreaked in him. She and Corinna ambled off together, arms entwined, like lovers. He followed at a distance, still shaken and suspicious, watching as they stopped to talk to various of the campers – laughing, joking, exchanging hugs – utterly relaxed and so . . . so *physical*. It was years since he'd seen his wife like this: radiant and carefree, as if released from her normal worries and concerns. He realized with a surge of guilt that here in the camp she had regained the things she'd lost when she had married him and left the Streatham madhouse – the company, community, the dogs and kids and mucking in, the chatter and the sharing. Without intending to, he had imposed restrictions on her life, and now she was retaliating – ignoring him, in short; far more interested in a female she had known a mere two days. And she was probably neglecting Pippa too – so blissfully absorbed in seducing her new playmate that she had neither time nor energy to bother with her daughter.

Well, if that was the case, he'd better go and sort Pippa out himself. He'd take Rick with him (once he'd had his medicine), so he could introduce the pair, and perhaps Claire would come as well, to provide some moral support. Pippa had gone to the Healing Dome to find some ointment for the dog – or so he'd been told by Len – and the Healing Dome always made him nervous. The few times he'd ventured in there, he'd been frightfully embarrassed – unfamiliar faces smiling at him as he entered the green gloom; unfamiliar bodies in various stages of undress; worthy people offering him weird things he didn't want: nettle tea or carrot juice, or lumps of different coloured crystals which apparently could affect your state of mind. He had forgotten now which one promised peace – amethyst, was it, or rose quartz, perhaps? – but anyway, whatever, he shouldn't have been so quick to refuse. He could do with some inner serenity to cope with this new shock.

Rick had run on ahead to rejoin his mother, and was craftily brandishing an apple, whilst concealing the criminal sweets. She had finished the washing up and everything was shipshape, Daniel noted approvingly – plates stacked in one box, beakers in another, the dirty water emptied, mops and cloths wrung out. A woman after his own heart, at least as far as domestic order was concerned.

'Great news!' she smiled, standing over her son with the medicine-glass in one hand and the Thermos in the other.

'Oh, really?' Daniel was unconvinced. His own definition of 'great news' would be Penny agreeing to leave this place and spend a month in Rome instead, with no hangers-on, no threesomes; or a scientific breakthrough proving nicotine to be highly beneficial; or a guarantee from the Great Roué in the Sky that he would never lose his erection in his life again.

'We're going to have a healing session,' Claire announced triumphantly. 'This evening, after supper. And guess who Blue wants there?'

'You and Rick?'

'Yes! Who else?'

'Er, let's see – how about Margot and George?'

'Gosh, you're clever, Daniel! That's absolutely right. Who else though?'

'I've no idea. I assumed everyone could wander along if they chose.'

'Oh, no! Blue can't concentrate with so many different energies – some of them might oppose his. Healing works at a very subtle level, you see, so he has to be careful that his channels don't get blocked. One last guess – go on!'

'Um . . .' Daniel frowned, trying to recall the circle of faces at lunch. 'I know! Jeanette and Len's daughter. What's her name? Sharon?'

Claire shook her head, beaming in delight. 'No, *your* daughter, Daniel – and you!'

18

DANIEL REMOVED HIS MUDDY SHOES and placed them with the other footwear which had been left outside the tepee. Then he ducked in through the entrance, glancing over his shoulder to make sure that Pippa was still behind him and hadn't taken to her heels and fled. The instant he stepped in he was lassoed by a circle of faces, assailed by murmured greetings. Why so many people here, when Claire had mentioned only six? She gave a cheery wave and he stumbled gratefully towards her; sat down on the dirty folded duffel coat she had saved as a cushion for him. He shuffled up to make room for Pippa; introduced her to those who hadn't met her yet, praying he'd remember their names. Her shyness only increased his own. Her face was scarlet beneath the freckles as she mumbled her 'hellos'.

'And this is Rick,' he concluded. The boy was sprawled beside his mother, picking little bits of fuzz from his sweater and rolling them in balls between his fingers. 'Or do you prefer Richard?'

'Don't mind,' Rick shrugged, scrambling up to a sitting position and darting a sidelong glance at Pippa. 'Dad calls me Richard when he's mad with me.'

They all laughed except Pippa, who had shrunk even further into herself, and had actually cut Rick dead by deliberately turning her back on him. Couldn't she make an effort, Daniel fumed? Claire had been so friendly towards him, this was no way to repay her. Rick slumped down on his rug again, chewing at his thumb.

'Rick's thirteen, like you, Pippa,' Daniel continued doggedly. 'And he lives in Wales, not far from here.'

Still she didn't respond. She had drawn up her legs, clasped her hands around them, and put her head down on her knees; her body language signalling complete shut-off and withdrawal. Daniel's self-control was stretched to breaking point. This was downright rudeness, not just shyness. 'Pippa, I'm *speaking* to you,' he rapped.

There was no reaction whatever, but he sensed her silent rejoinder: Shut up and go away!

'She's got her mother's lovely hair, I see,' Doris put in tactfully. She was sitting next to Pippa, her wasted frame supported by nothing more than a single flimsy cushion. On her other side was Gerard, still wretched with his cold, then George and Margot, looking peeved, Dylan, with wet hair, and a woman he'd never seen before, wearing a pink home-knitted cardigan over what looked like a nightdress.

'I thought you said there were only going to be six of us?' he whispered to Claire, deciding to ignore Pippa for the present.

'There were,' Claire whispered back. 'I can't understand why Blue's called in these others, or where on earth he's disappeared to.' She removed her glasses and rubbed her eyes – undoubtedly her most attractive feature, being luminous and large, though they were screwed up at the moment in dismay. 'And we should be in the Healing Dome, not here. It's got much better vibes.'

This was the nearest she had come to criticizing the master, though he didn't share her objections. As far as he was concerned, the more people there, the less conspicuous he and Pippa would be, which was definitely an advantage. As for the healer's late arrival, well, the later the better – just so long as he wasn't dallying with Penny. (It was difficult to know which was the more galling: the thought of Penny snuggling up to Corinna, or lying in the Wanker's hirsute arms.) The change of venue from Healing Dome to Rainbow Lodge was also to his liking, since he found the former claustrophobic and loathed the reek of incense. He was happier here in the tepee, with its memory of that first night's blissful sleep, which still seemed quite extraordinary.

On that occasion, he'd hardly noticed his surroundings – simply sunk into the black balm of unconsciousness – but now he had a chance to look around. The central fire had been banked down and was only gently smouldering, but there was a stack of fresh-cut logs beside it, and an ancient kettle steaming on a trivet. The canvas, dirty-grey inside, was hung with shawls and rugs, which gave colour and a sense of warmth; one especially striking batik depicted a vibrant purple sun above a golden mountain peak. To the right of the entrance, a tray of chipped mugs sat balanced on a crate, with various jars labelled Barley Cup, or Fig and Millet 'Coffee', plus a few large battered cake-tins, which (he remembered with distaste) were used to store Happy's specialities – damp and sugarless flapjacks, dry and fatless cakes. Opposite stood a sort of makeshift altar, which seemed more a shrine to Nature than to any God he recognized, being heaped with flowers and fruits – mostly wilting buttercups and knobbly mottled apples, but also a bunch of whiskered grasses and some overripe red plums. Stones and pebbles had been arranged around the edges of the altar, and three gleaming magpie feathers were stuck in an empty jam jar. Another, smaller, jar held a single plain white candle, which, though unlit at present, had drooled writhing coils of wax down its sides. The whole thing looked amateurish, yet was also quaintly touching, as if constructed by an eager child as an offering to its teacher.

'And how's the poor dog getting on?' Doris asked Pippa brightly, trying to break through her reserve.

Pippa, hunched up blind and deaf, gave no sign that she had heard, so Daniel answered for her, mumbling some inanity. No one else was talking much, and the atmosphere seemed strained – hushed like church, but with a growing air of restlessness as still the healer didn't come. Daniel wondered how long the others had been waiting. He had turned up late himself because it had taken time and tact to prise Pippa from her precious dog. Bernard had rolled in some cow-dung and Pippa had volunteered to clean him up, then been highly indignant at having to leave the job unfinished. He wished to God they'd start the proceedings, for her sake as much as his. He could imagine what she was thinking: 'I could have cleaned up half a dozen dogs by now. We're just stuck here doing nothing.'

He looked down at his watch, only to realize for the umpteenth time that it wasn't on his wrist. Now he understood why no clocks and watches were allowed – it forestalled all protest about exactly how much time was wasted, since people could only guess the length of the delays. In the sequestered gloom of the tepee there was no means of telling if the sun was going down or not. They were cut off from time and weather, and even the noises of the camp were muted by the thick canvas.

By way of diversion, he scanned his companions' feet, which, in their shoeless state, provided an intriguing guide to each person's state of mind. George's – large and clad in navy woollen socks – were drumming angrily, while Dylan's, bare and slender, betrayed his nervousness, clinging to each other for mutual comfort and support. Gerard, sporting short white socks, kept clenching up his toes, as if his partner's apprehension had afflicted him as well. Doris had misshapen feet, but they rested serenely side by side, whereas Rick's dirty grass-stained pair twitched and jiggled constantly – in sharp contrast to Pippa, whose whole body remained ominously still. His daughter appeared to have closed down altogether, which provoked in him a feeling of mingled resentment and despair. He reached out to touch her arm, made a jokey remark about earning Brownie points with his long stint of washing-up, but she only flinched and moved huffily away.

He turned to Claire in desperation, but she too seemed on edge. 'You know, I'm getting really worried about Blue,' she said. 'Suppose something awful's happened – an accident, or . . . I mean, why should he summon us all for a session, then not turn up himself?'

'He's here!' cried Gerard, and everyone fell silent, listening to the footsteps just outside, then a scuffle of shoes being taken off and dropped. A frisson of expectancy rippled round the tent, and all except Pippa sat up straighter. Even Daniel caught the general mood; felt Claire's relief in particular wash over him like a wave.

'Hi, everyone!' a breezy voice announced, and a bearded face thrust itself through the flaps – grey hair thick and curly, complexion ruddy with a drinker's broken veins. Tony from Leeds, the owner of the injured dog, which limped in after him. His wife Judith brought up the rear – a plump and kindly woman with salt-and-pepper hair escaping from its bun, and eyes so intensely blue they looked younger than the rest of her.

Their friendly smiles were not universally returned. Claire, for one, made no pretence at hiding her disappointment, while George, muttering to himself about the squash, grudgingly made room for Tony's fifteen stone. But the effect on Pippa was startling. Instantly, she uncurled and came to life, jumping up to embrace the dog, as if they had been parted half a lifetime instead of half an hour. She left her place next to Daniel to sit between Judith and Tony, speaking to them in a perfectly normal fashion, and even managing a smile. The boxer settled at her feet, his coat still damp; the dressing on his wounded leg covered with a sock. Daniel recognized the sock as one of Pippa's – her favourite pair, in fact, which he had bought for her himself: black and yellow stripes with bumble-bees round the top. Bernard was chewing at it impatiently, but Pippa gently restrained him, petting him and stroking him and whispering blandishments in his ear.

Daniel could hardly bear to watch. He had spent most of the afternoon brooding on his wife's defection, and now he had the same unpleasant feeling of being excluded and rejected, but this time by his daughter. He wasn't so much jealous of the dog (though its impressive male equipment was conspicuously on show), but of the way that Pippa had bonded with its owners, as if *they* were her rightful parents. He had felt it straight away, the first time he'd seen them together – the way she seemed to trust them, relaxing in their company as she never did with him these days. Okay, Judith was the sort of woman nobody could fail to like, easy-going, affectionate and motherly, but what on earth did Pippa see in Tony – a bearded slob with a jolly (jarring) laugh and a maddening habit of cracking his fingers and addressing everyone as 'love'? Yet there was Pippa, literally rubbing shoulders with him, while studiously ignoring the man who'd been her father for the last seven years, in every sense except the biological.

Claire seemed as dispirited as he was, though for rather different reasons. 'I don't understand,' she whispered, 'why Blue had to ask that pair. I mean, how can a dog have the same importance as a person with MS, or someone who's going blind? I can't think what he's up to, or why he isn't here.'

Daniel found himself in a role reversal, offering sympathy to the woman who had previously listened to *his* troubles. Rick was no help at all, now openly rebellious and threatening to walk out if they didn't get a move on. Then suddenly the woman in the nightdress began a loud and rambling conversation with an invisible companion. Every eye swivelled round to look at her, but she continued unconcerned, nodding and smiling to herself as the stream of aimless prattle burbled on. The two gays were looking horribly embarrassed, while George and Margot exchanged glances of distaste, and Rick was unable to suppress his giggles as he watched in fascination. Daniel cleared his throat, fighting a wild urge to escape. Here was madness, real and unadulterated, and again he was too close to it, frightened it might taint him. He liked well-defined boundaries between things – sanity and madness on each side of a deep divide – but since he'd set foot in this outlandish place, the divisions in his own mind were becoming perilously confused. He blessed the resourceful Doris, who saved the situation by suggesting that the woman might like a breath of air, and leading her out of the lodge. She went willingly but volubly, leaving a silence pregnant with unspoken questions – who *was* she, and should she be here at all when the healer already had his hands full with more conventional cases?

It was George who finally broke the silence, remarking to Margot in what he intended as a whisper, but which was clearly audible, 'Phew! That dog does smell.'

'He *doesn't*!' Pippa retorted. 'He's just a bit damp, that's all.'

'Wet dogs always pong a bit,' Tony put in jovially. 'You should have smelt him earlier on, George! He'd rolled in something unspeakable – hadn't you, Bernard old chap?'

The dog pricked up his ears at the sound of his name, and Pippa laid her cheek against his flank, kissing him and telling him what a lovely darling boy he was.

Daniel pummelled his fist in his palm. Pippa had actually overcome her reticence, speaking out undaunted in front of the whole assembled company, to defend that wretched animal. Yet she had refused to talk to *him*, even one to one. He looked to Claire for some support, but she was still preoccupied with Blue.

'Perhaps he's ill again,' she fretted. 'I mean, he gets so little rest looking after everyone else, I often wonder how he manages to keep going.'

As if in answer to her speculations, there was a flurry outside the tepee and Happy pushed her way in, resplendent in an ankle-length filmy skirt and an ornate brocaded waistcoat, her mousy hair concealed by a tie-dyed scarf. 'Mitra's so sorry to have kept you, but . . .'

'*Who?*' Daniel whispered to Claire.

'That's Happy's name for the master. Mitra – the Hindu god of harmony and light. Beautiful, isn't it?'

Daniel made no comment. Happy was recounting what had befallen her God of Light: there had been a minor crisis involving some new arrivals, who turned out to be trouble-makers rather than people seeking help. And although Mitra had succeeded in ejecting them, he now needed a brief respite to rid himself of the negative energies and cleanse his healing channels. 'So he's asked me to stand in for him,' she said, her elation at the privilege glowing in her face. 'Or at least take over till he gets here. And the first thing he always does is to ask us all to send out light and love to the universe. So as a symbol of that light and love, I'm going to light the candle on the altar.'

She prostrated herself a moment in front of the pebbles and the plums, then bobbed back up again, producing a box of matches from the voluminous folds of her skirt, and lighting the blackened wick with a ceremonious flourish. The candle took a while to light, but it caught at last, throwing eerie flickering shadows around the tepee, which only increased the general apprehension. Even Bernard was whining and gnawing at his wound again.

Bloody hocus-pocus, Daniel thought. What had incense or candles to do with healing – or with conventional religion, come to that? It was all done for effect, to disarm the rational mind. Well, *his* mind wouldn't be disarmed, whatever Happy's ploys. He would simply observe the proceedings like some visiting anthropologist studying the rituals of a newly-discovered tribe.

'Ready everyone?' Happy had adopted a low and stagy voice, which only made her sound pretentious. 'First we'll try to centre ourselves and focus our attention. And I'd like you to hold hands. That helps to channel the energy in the circle.'

At first only Dylan and Gerard complied, touchingly relieved to be allowed to hold hands in public without attracting comment. Then Judith and Tony each offered a hand to Pippa, who insisted on holding Bernard's paw as well. The rest were more inhibited, especially Rick and George, and Daniel himself felt utterly ridiculous as Claire slipped her sweaty palm in his, and Gerard on his other side gripped his fingers shyly. Never in his life had he held hands with another man, but it was impossible to refuse without appearing churlish, or, worse still, homophobic.

'Close your eyes and breathe in very deeply,' Happy ordered from her position near the altar, where she was squatting on her haunches, unaware that one end of her flowing scarf was trapped beneath her thigh. 'And I want you to imagine that the boundaries and divisions between man and man, and man and beast, and man and his surroundings, have dissolved and disappeared. We're all one, all at peace.'

Daniel, eyes still open, glanced around the circle. Peace and love seemed thin on the ground. Claire's jealousy of Happy was all too obvious on her face; Margot's expression combined bewilderment and pain; while George's hostile frown cut deep between his brows.

'Now, as you exhale, slowly and deliberately, send out your light and love – first to the earth and all who live on it.' Happy let out her own breath with a dramatic hissing sound.

Judging by the tense silence, everyone else seemed to be holding their breath rather than expelling it, but Happy continued unperturbed. 'Breathe in once again, and as you exhale this time, send out your light and love to all the seas and rivers and lakes and ponds, and all the creatures that live in water. I want to hear that breath – let it out with a great big sigh.'

Again she demonstrated, apparently quite unabashed by the exaggerated sound she made (which set Rick off in giggles again). Tony did his best to copy her, using all the power of his burly chest, then Gerard gave a faint apologetic gasp, and Dylan followed suit, looking painfully self-conscious as his breath came out in a strangulated whinny.

'And now another deep breath in, and let out your light and love to the sky, and all the birds and angels in it, and also send your love to outer space and to the beings who may live there, and to any other forms of consciousness we don't yet comprehend. Come on, everyone – the biggest sigh of all.'

They all obeyed this time, except a defiant Rick, munching his last toffee, and Pippa, fussing over the dog. George's sigh, however, was undisguised exasperation, and Claire's sprang from dejection rather than light or love.

'Fantastic!' Happy said. 'Now, open your eyes, but stay sitting where you are, because I've brought my feeling-stone and I want to pass it round the circle.' She reached out behind her and picked up something from the ground, cupped it in her hands. 'Stones have tremendous energies, so if we hold one in our hands like this, we can connect with all that energy. I found this particular stone on a lonely beach in Ithaca, and, as you'll see, it's breast-shaped – the symbol of nurturing and healing. Just think – it may be millions of years old! And we can absorb that ancient wisdom simply by touching it; tuning in to it through our nerve-endings. I'd like each of you in turn to hold it for a minute or two, and then share with the rest of us what it makes you feel. I'll start, shall I, to give you the idea.'

She got up from her knees and went to sit cross-legged between Judith and Gerard. Daniel peered at the stone, which did look unnervingly like a breast – one of Corinna's voluptuous pair, with a prominent brown nipple at the top. Happy sat with her eyes closed, tuning in to the stone; a blissful expression on her face as she rubbed her palm slowly back and forth across the nipple.

After a while, she opened her eyes, blinking several times, as if surfacing from some far domain where darkness was the norm. Then she said solemnly, 'This stone reminds me of all the help and comfort I've been honoured to receive from Mitra – especially the great gift of healing. Yet I also feel privileged to have undergone the suffering which brought me to him here, because he's made me see that those of us who suffer pain actually help to redeem the world.'

'Crikey!' Tony said.

Happy merely smiled at him, then passed the stone to Gerard. 'We go round in the direction of the sun,' she explained. 'That also helps the energies. And as you pass the stone on, I want you to engage in eye-contact with the person who takes it from you – just hold their gaze a moment and look deep into their soul.' To illustrate, she fixed her eyes on Gerard, who flushed and began to fidget, clutching the stone awkwardly, as if ashamed to be seen with it. Several minutes passed. The others were looking at him expectantly, but he didn't say a word.

'Try to tell us what you're feeling,' Happy prompted.

'Er . . . I've got a bit of a headache.'

'D'you get a lot of headaches?' she enquired.

'Yes, he does,' said Dylan. 'Really bad ones sometimes.'

'They may be connected with one of your past lives. Mitra had a patient who suffered from constant pains in his neck, and it turned out that he'd been guillotined in the French Revolution. In fact, Mitra said he actually chose that form of death, as atonement for an even earlier life, where *he'd* been an executioner. It's the Law of Karma, you see, and once you understand that law, you'll find it . . .'

George could contain himself no longer. 'Look here,' he interrupted, brandishing his fist. 'My wife and I were invited to a healing session, and it's pretty damned clear to me that there's not going to be much healing when the healer isn't here. Is he on his way, or isn't he? I'm not hanging around much longer, I assure you. Margot's in a lot of pain and she can't cope with all this claptrap.'

'Forgive me, George,' said Happy in a calm sweet-natured tone, 'but I wonder if it's *you* who can't cope?'

'There's nothing wrong with me, young lady.'

'And perhaps there's nothing wrong with Margot,' Happy countered. 'After all, many of us are blind in the sense that we have no inner vision, no spiritual far-sightedness. We see truth only partially, so that everything is blurred and . . .'

'I've never heard such poppycock! I'll have you know my wife's been seen by three top Harley Street specialists and had every test in the book. She may lose her sight completely in a matter of a year or two, and even now it's got so bad, she's seriously disabled. Wait! I'll show you. See that sign over there?'

They looked where he was pointing. 'EARTH FIRST!' urged the placard, in big black capitals. George lumbered to his feet and snatched it up.

'Six months ago, my wife could read quite normally – books, papers, magazines – even really small print. Reading was her favourite hobby. She'd get through half a dozen novels in a week. But now her sight's deteriorated so much, I'll bet she can't even make out those huge letters.' He stuck the sign under Margot's nose, stabbing his broad finger at the E. 'Can you see that, dear, or not?'

She shook her head wordlessly, upset and disconcerted at being made the centre of attention.

'It's getting rather cold,' said Judith diplomatically. 'Why don't I put some logs on the fire?'

'Good thinking!' Tony beamed. 'I'll do it, love, don't worry. And while I'm up, how about a nice hot cup of tea? I see we've got a kettle here and enough mugs for us all.'

'I'm afraid tea's not allowed,' Happy reproved him gently. 'And anyway we never eat or drink in the middle of a healing session. If our bodies are busy digesting, we resist the higher energies.'

'Rubbish!' George exploded. 'Nothing's going on here except an ego-trip for you, my girl. And a complete waste of time for the rest of us. Well, enough's enough, as far as I'm concerned. Margot and I are leaving. And I don't just mean this so-called healing session, I mean leaving for home – right now.'

Rick's hunched form snapped upright. He tugged at Claire's sleeve, hissing urgently, 'Mum, can *we* go home as well?'

Happy remained unruffled, brushing George's outburst aside like a speck of dust on her skirt, and addressing the boy instead. 'Home is where you feel safe, Rick. So long as you're at peace with yourself, you can make anywhere your home, even a foreign country, or a prison cell.'

But not Greystone Court, Daniel thought bitterly, reflecting once again that he had lost his sense of home when he was only half Rick's age. He had spent the Christmas and Easter holidays with unknown English relatives, only returning to Lusaka for the longer summer vacations, and by then he was a stranger – the boy who'd gone away and come back as someone else. But perhaps it was his own fault. He hadn't been 'at peace with himself' as Happy put it so glibly; hadn't felt 'safe' – still didn't, come to that.

'And remember, Rick,' Happy was saying, still eponymously benign, 'the whole world's your home, in one sense. You see, you're part of the great universal . . .' She broke off in mid-sentence and scrambled to her feet, her floaty scarf billowing out behind her. 'Mitra!' she exclaimed.

At once Claire jumped up as well and rushed over to embrace the healer, who was suddenly standing at the entrance to the lodge. Daniel simply stared. How had he materialized like that, unheard and unannounced, and why did he look so different? True, he had changed his clothes, but it wasn't a matter of mere dress – rather something much more subtle and disorienting. Each time he appeared, his bearing and expression seemed to have altered in some inexplicable way, as if he had become another person. On this occasion, he was wearing a white shirt – less a man's shirt than a woman's blouse, loose in style with soft, full sleeves gathered at the wrist. More notable than its style was its dazzling whiteness, which almost hurt the eyes. How could he keep it so pristine white, when clothes were only washed in the stream, without bleaches or detergents? His eyes, in contrast, looked even darker than usual, glinting like jet in the candlelight as he turned from Claire and Happy to greet the others.

Daniel continued scrutinizing this man of many faces. His hair was plaited, Red Indian style, in a single pigtail hanging down his back. The effect might well have been comic, but on the contrary, it gave him a new dignity; emphasizing his high cheekbones, his sensuous full lips. And although he'd barely spoken, the whole atmosphere had changed. Everyone seemed calmer, even George and Rick; the former settling back beside his wife, the latter gazing at the new arrival with something close to interest.

JB joined the circle, easing himself between George and Tony, as if sensing instinctively that the two were better parted. Happy slipped in, too, tucking her long skirt over her bare feet and fixing her hazel eyes on Mitra's darker ones. Daniel expected him to apologize, or explain his long delay, but the man sat utterly silent, communicating only with his eyes, which moved slowly round the circle, studying each face in turn.

When he spoke at last, Daniel was startled by the sound of his voice, which, like his appearance, had undergone a subtle change: it was now slightly deeper, as if he had become more man, less mother.

'Before we start,' he said, 'I'd like you to invite anyone important to you to be here with us in spirit. Anyone you feel you've lost through death, divorce, or distance, can be summoned here to join our circle – perhaps parents who've passed on, or people we once loved . . .'

Daniel thought of his own parents, especially his mother, whose presence he had felt so strongly last night. But the memory had receded now, and anyway he was sure that neither one of them would have time or patience to be sitting in this circle. They would undoubtedly be too busy, toiling in the realm of the dead as assiduously as in life.

Perhaps he should invite Penny's father, who had died when she was only ten. She never talked about him, but it must surely be significant that she had chosen his name for the healer. Stephen – the name so long unspoken had taken him by surprise. He had always prided himself on being sensitive and perceptive, yet he'd

227

obviously failed to understand how much that loss had meant to her. Perhaps he'd missed other things as well – in Pippa's life as much as Penny's – the caring husband and father blind to their true feelings.

He felt JB's eyes flick over his face, bringing him back to the present, commanding his attention.

'We also call on our spirit-guides, and on the unseen powers and presences, the deities and angels which influence our lives.'

Daniel shifted uneasily. A reference to the dead was one thing, but this was getting ridiculous. George grunted in impatience, and even Tony seemed bemused. A bluff Yorkshireman like him might be at home with dogs – the boxer here and three labradors in Leeds, so Pippa had informed him – but he was probably not over-familiar with spirit-guides or angels.

There was silence again. JB appeared to be praying, an expression of the utmost concentration on his face; his body so still it might have been cast in bronze. Then he fixed his eyes on Margot, touched her gently on the shoulder. 'Margot, I'd like you to lie down here in the centre of the circle.'

Happy spread a rug on the ground, and helped Margot to stretch out on it, making sure that she was comfortable. The others watched, absorbed, while JB positioned himself at her head, sitting back on his heels with his palms upturned and his back effortlessly straight.

'I need your help,' he told them, 'the help and support of every person present. You're not here just as passive spectators, sitting on the sidelines. Your own faith and mind-power are an important aspect of the healing, and you, too, have a role to play.'

Daniel was instantly on his guard. No doubt this was another ruse to subdue their rational minds, so they'd all manage to convince themselves they had witnessed some amazing feat and give JB the credit for it. Nowadays, it seemed, people were so hungry for miracles and saviours, they were only too ready to turn off their critical faculties and turn on their credulity. Well, he for one refused to be taken in. His whole way of life was founded on reason and logic, and he didn't intend to abandon them for superstitious wish-fulfilment.

JB placed his hands on Margot's forehead, gently stroking her eyes shut with his thumbs. 'Let's all focus our minds on

Margot – really concentrate, so that our combined energies are directed to her eyes. And I want you all to believe that she can see – see without strain, see without her glasses, see as easily and clearly as she did a year ago.'

His voice was becoming incantatory. All part of the spell, thought Daniel – a voice to lull and mesmerize, so that these credulous 'participants' could invent their comforting fantasies, untroubled by the need for dispassionate thought.

JB had moved his hands to Margot's eyes, covering them with his palms. His body remained completely still, but he took several deep and sighing breaths, as if daunted by the task before him – or was he simply making a show of summoning up his powers? No one said a word. He had won their full attention; even Rick and Pippa looking impressed and overawed. Daniel was tempted to remove his daughter; insist she left this masquerade. He shouldn't just sit here and let her be bamboozled when she was too young to know trickery from truth.

JB was making gentle rhythmic motions with his hands, moving them from Margot's eyes, slowly down across her face, down lower to her neck, then resting them on her chest. Daniel stifled a protest. What the hell was the fellow up to? Margot might be fifty-something, but her breasts were still attractive: firm and nicely rounded. He was astonished she hadn't objected, especially as the trespassing hands began to exert more pressure on her chest. Certainly, her husband was frowning in alarm, but even he refrained from comment – so desperate for a cure, perhaps, that he was willing to condone this breach of propriety. Daniel glanced at the others, wondering if they too were shocked. Apparently not. They'd been so well and truly duped by all the mumbo-jumbo, they couldn't see how preposterous it was for the laying on of hands to be applied to Margot's youthful breasts rather than her failing eyes. Well, one thing was for sure: no way would he let his daughter be subjected to the Wanker's ministrations. He could just imagine the cheap thrills such a charlatan would get from 'healing' a pubescent girl; pawing at her budding virgin breasts.

At that moment, JB looked up, his eyes troubled, almost stern. 'One of you is resisting,' he admonished. 'The negative energies are exceptionally strong.'

Heads turned furtively, each wondering who was guilty. Daniel felt condemned already for failing to meet anybody's eye, yet he would judge himself every bit as severely if he believed for the sake of believing, merely to conform.

'All I ask,' said JB, 'is that the person should *wish* to believe. There's no need for actual faith, just an open mind and a willingness to participate. He needs to get out of his mind and into his heart; not to make harsh judgements, or separate himself from the healing power. He *is* that power – we all are.'

Another trick, thought Daniel, nails digging into his palms – making you feel so guilty and uncomfortable that you had no choice but to submit. Happy was sitting beside him and he was aware of her eyes fixed on him with a spaniel-like concern. She leaned across and whispered, 'Relax, Daniel. Let go. Just open your heart and surrender to Mitra.'

'Look, I'm quite okay,' he mumbled, recoiling in horror as she suddenly placed her hands on his head in full view of the others. He wished the earth would swallow him up. How the hell could he relax when every eye had turned to him, including his daughter's? An adolescent blush suffused his face and chest, as if he were fourteen rather than forty. Pippa was the one normally given to blushing, yet at present she seemed maddeningly composed, leaning against Judith's shoulder, with her arm around the dog.

'No, Daniel,' Happy persisted, 'you're *not* relaxed at all. You're extraordinarily tense. Just lie back and let me massage your neck and spine.'

'*No!*' he growled through clenched teeth. This was worse and worse. Unintentionally, he'd become the focal point, stolen Margot's thunder. George looked ready to lynch him for obstructing his wife's healing, and even Claire was regarding him with irritated pity.

Defeated and demoralized, he let Happy push him gently back until he was lying on the ground. Anything was better than having all the rest of them turn on him in fury or contempt. Wretchedly he peered up at the tepee-poles which converged at the topmost point of the tent. If only he were a bird, he could fly up there and squeeze out through the gap.

'Close your eyes,' Happy murmured.

'But what about Margot?' he protested. 'Surely *she's* the . . . ?'

230

'Leave her to Mitra,' Happy urged. 'He can work far more effectively if you're relaxed and don't resist him. And it's best not to speak. Silence is more powerful.'

That at least was a relief: the quieter he kept, the more likely it was that the others would forget him and concentrate on Margot. He lay as if dead, eyes closed, body inert, trying to convince himself that Happy wasn't there – not exactly easy when her hands were lapping down his body. Was this another try-on? Happy using him for a spot of titillation, as the Wanker was using Margot? Well, she had him in her power: there was no way he could object without (God forbid) making a further exhibition of himself.

Actually, he had to admit her hands felt wonderfully soothing – small and deft and cool; homing in with undoubted skill on all his tension-spots. It was the girl herself who irked him: her idiotic posturing, her incongruous form of dress. Still, if he kept his eyes obediently shut, he needn't look at her, and could pretend her hands belonged to someone else – Penny, or his mother, perhaps.

Yes, that was better, definitely. His annoyance and resentment were beginning to subside as he submitted to their touch. He hadn't realized how tired he was, nor how much energy he'd wasted screwing himself up into a huge knot of resistance. Even now, his hands were clenched, but those other calming hands were persuading his stiff fingers to uncurl, smoothing out each one in turn, softening their coiled steel. He had never had his hands stroked, and the sensation was quite magical – a light pressure feathering down the palms, then lingering on the fingertips – astonishingly intimate. His eyelids were becoming heavy. It was a luxury to keep them shut, no longer just a duty, and he was aware that he was sinking down, blind to his surroundings, letting go, surrendering. He could smell a musky perfume which seemed to be lulling him to sleep. His mother must have rubbed scent on her hands, wafting him in a fragrant cloud of frangipani, orange blossom, bauhinia, acacia – all the exotic African flowers he'd known as a young boy. Time was drifting back to childhood, and beyond. Or maybe there wasn't any time. Yes, that was it – he remembered now. Time had been extinguished, and he no longer had to worry about being late, or rushed, or holding up the others. There was only now, and now, and now – soft hands on his naked flesh; female hands giving him the things he craved: care, concern, the intense, exquisite luxury of love.

The hands were rubbing oil into his brow, then a gentle finger eased his lips apart and placed a droplet of the same oil on his tongue. His taste-buds flinched in shock as the drop exploded in his mouth into a tingling shower of forbidden childhood sweets – marzipan and sherbet, sugared almonds, candyfloss. Nothing was forbidden to him now, not even the most sensuous touch. The hands continued their caress, stroking oil along his eyelids, then down behind his ears. He must genuinely have died, and this was the anointing. Strange how sweet death was – peaceful and sweet-scented.

He lay delighting in it – the pampering, the safety, the miraculous fact that his mother had time for him in a world where time had vanished. Whole decades sauntered by and he watched them pass in luxurious sloth, reaching out for the odd shining day as he might net a butterfly. Then, through the perfumed haze, he heard a familiar voice echoing from somewhere far away – a whole continent away – summoning him back.

Unseen hands helped him up, and he saw a blur of faces, a haze of flickering lights; the shadows in the background mingling with the phantoms from his past. He gazed up at the shrouding walls, trying to remember where he was. Only slowly did he realize that he was sitting in the circle; Margot stretched out on the ground still, with JB kneeling at her head, exactly as before. He rubbed his eyes, confused. Perhaps no time had passed at all, and he had merely dreamed his mother's hands. Certainly, the atmosphere was dream-like. Although more candles had been lit and the fire was banked up with logs, the tepee was much darker; a stark contrast between the eager tongues of flame and the areas of murky gloom beyond. Smoke was swirling round the lodge, adding to the air of unreality, though no one appeared to notice. They were too engrossed in Margot, who suddenly began shivering and trembling, as if gripped by a high fever, or threatened by an attacker. Yet the healer himself sat motionless, his hands resting on her eyes again, and his face expressing such a ferocity of concentration that words like 'con' or 'trickster' seemed invidious. Daniel realized with a flash of insight that this was genuine *work* – and work which demanded total dedication. No charlatan would look like that: so ardent and committed, so utterly caught up in the intensity of his task. And all the rest were affected by his fervour; their faces rapt as they willed him to succeed.

JB began to speak, more slowly now, as if each word were being painfully chipped out like silver from a mine. 'Margot – open your eyes. I can feel the power of sight returning, being channelled through my hands. It only needs you to accept it. Do you wish to see as you once did?'

Margot nodded, too overwrought to speak.

The healer lifted up his hands, addressing the whole gathering. 'Do you all wish Margot to see?'

The response was so impassioned, Daniel had no choice but to add his own wary mutter of assent. He watched with growing consternation as Happy and the healer helped Margot to sit up. Far from opening her eyes, she was actually covering them with her hands, as if the risk of failure were too terrible to contemplate. George, however, crawled over to her side and prised her hands away, demanding in a hectoring tone, 'Well, *can* you see? For God's sake, Margot, put us out of our misery and tell us.'

Reluctantly she raised her head and looked falteringly around, blinking in the firelight. The next moment she burst out crying, hiding her face in her hands again. There was a shocked silence from the others; no noise except her muffled sobs – enough in themselves to damn this whole charade. Then a murmur of dismay began to buzz around the tepee; some scrambling to their feet to comfort Margot, one or two sitting rooted to the spot, too upset even to express their disappointment. George was clearly devastated, so that it took him a few minutes to realize that the source of all the uproar had conveniently fled.

'Good God!' he yelled in fury, lunging towards the entrance of the tent. 'The blighter's done a bunk. Well, he won't get away from *me* so easily. Just you wait, you fraud!'

'George, no! Please stop!' called Margot, darting after her husband and pulling him back by the sleeve. 'Don't you understand, I'm crying for *joy*! I can see, I can see! It's true – my sight's returned.'

Claire too burst into tears of joy; Tony crushed Judith and Pippa in a wild exuberant bear-hug; Dylan and Gerard embraced each other, and Happy poured out praise and thanks in an ecstatic monologue. Only George stood rigid, staring at his wife with a mixture of wonder and disbelief. Suddenly, he fumbled in his blazer pocket and brought out a small diary, which he thrust in front of her.

'Read that!' he ordered, turning to the opening pages with their lists of public holidays and tables of weights and measures, all in tiny print.

Margot dabbed her eyes, half-laughing and half-crying as she took the diary from him and recited like an obedient child: 'Good Friday, April the ninth; Easter Monday, April the twelfth; May Day Holiday, May the third; Spring Bank Holiday, May the thirty-first; Late Summer Holiday, August the thirtieth . . .' She paused after each date to smile rapturously at her audience, and they smiled back, equally elated.

Daniel felt no elation, only a sense of shock and continuing suspicion. This could all be just a trick. Margot might know those holidays by heart, or simply have a good memory for dates. And surely JB had damned himself by sneaking out like that, unwilling to face the storm of disapproval? Rick appeared to share his misgivings. He was pulling a comic from the pocket of his jeans – a forbidden *Beano* he had saved from confiscation by folding it to passport size. He smoothed it out and handed it to Margot.

'Here, have a go at Dennis the Menace,' he urged.

First she had to dry her eyes again. She was still caught between laughing and crying; her face radiant beneath the tears. She scanned the tattered page, Rick hovering just behind her, jabbing an impatient finger at the text.

'"Snarl, snarl!"' she began, giving a sudden delighted chortle as she continued in her incongruously ladylike voice: '"Let's go and get those softies, Gnasher! Okay, chaps, let 'em have it! Take that! Take that! Yeuch! Blat! Splatter! Gneuch!"'

'Yeah, dead right!' crowed Rick, his usual shyness overcome in the excitement of the moment.

'Bravo!' shouted Tony, and there was a spontaneous burst of applause; Margot submerged in a tide of hugs and congratulations. Even Pippa was doing a sort of triumphal jig with Judith, while the dog joined in with a fanfare of wild barks.

Daniel glanced at George. The man stood openly weeping, all his bluster and bombast ebbing away like sawdust from a stuffed

234

lion. Everyone seemed to be crying, or hysterical in some way – Daniel alone as cold as ice.

Claire gripped his hand, her eyes suffused with tears behind her glasses. 'Oh, Daniel, I'm so thrilled! Isn't it absolutely amazing?'

'No,' he said, so softly only the shadows heard. 'It's absolutely terrifying,' and he turned on his heel and bolted from the lodge.

19

DANIEL HURLED ANOTHER STONE into the water, welcoming the disturbance it made – the satisfying splash, the ring of ripples drifting away in slow motion. He needed to break the silence, which afforded no distraction from his thoughts. He must have been sitting here an hour or more, alone beneath the stars, looking out at the dark surface of the lake and trying to make sense of what he'd witnessed. 'Miracle' was so glib a word, yet he couldn't deny that *something* had taken place – and something pretty shattering. But he had to be on his guard. Because he was living in a sort of tribe, close to nature, removed from all the usual rational restraints, it was all too easy to become prey to superstition. Even being in a country like Wales tended to influence one's outlook, make one more susceptible to mystic (woolly) thinking. It was such a remote and enigmatic place, which had always believed in wizards, saints and seers, and famed since pagan times for its megaliths, its magic, its so-called supernatural powers. If JB did possess such powers, then might they not be a force for harm as well as simply for good, and should he allow Pippa to be mixed up with such things anyway?

He longed to discuss it all with Penny, but she had made it depressingly clear that she didn't want him with her in the tent tonight. The entire camp was buzzing with the news of Margot's cure, and his wife had chosen to celebrate it with Happy and Corinna, rather than with him. Oh, she'd put it very tactfully: how he and she needed 'space to grow' – which made it sound as if they were runner beans, for God's sake, instead of man and wife. The jargon was JB's, of course, but he could guess the real reason for her rejection. If a husband couldn't satisfy his wife, then it was only natural for her to seek companionship elsewhere.

He gazed up at the sky: the moon near-full and silvering the lake; the stars brilliant but inscrutable. That breathtaking expanse above made him a nonentity; impotent in a different sense. Already, he'd felt dwarfed by the surrounding blue-black hills as he climbed into their silence; his scrabbling footsteps as puny as a rabbit's. There had been no sign of any rabbits, nor of any other life: no light-footed fox or lumbering sheep; no hooting, flapping night-birds. Yet the stillness was deceptive. The sky itself was a seething soup of electrons, quarks, neutrinos, and one of those apparently tranquil stars might be exploding as he watched it. He had been reading about star-deaths only a week or two ago – the reeling sense of shock when man first discovered that what had always been regarded as eternal and immutable could expire in such a catastrophic fashion. And now his own eternal verities seemed to be going the same way; debris from the collapse of reason choking his dazed mind.

He perched on a craggy boulder close to the lake's edge. The moon was ogling the water; the flirtatious, shimmering water trembling in response. The stone felt cold beneath him, in contrast to the black velvet air, still warm from the day's unbroken sun, as if the night were a vast storage-heater warding off the usual midnight chill. He was reluctant to return to his ruin of a bedroom, which he knew would seem oppressive in his present state of confusion. And anyway his legs ached from the climb – much more taxing at night, despite the generous moonlight and the ally of his torch. Yet he'd felt drawn towards this place, already regarding it as his own private lake – a sanctuary where he could escape the noise and shock-waves of the camp.

He craned his neck again, trying to picture the stars as he knew they were in reality: gigantic lumps of whirling white-hot matter or huge swathes of swirling gases, not the tiny pinpoints of light twinkling there above him. The last time he'd sat and star-gazed had been with Juliet some months ago. Returning from a dinner out, they'd stopped by the river near Putney Bridge, intent on finding Venus, then spent half an hour picking out the various constellations. He grinned to himself as he pictured her here in the camp: her immaculate high heels would sink into the mud, and she'd be lost without her hair-dryer, aghast at the thought of washing in a stream. He closed his eyes, felt her long and glossy hair brushing his bare body as she changed position in bed. It had excited him, her hair – its straight cascading smoothness after Penny's wiry crop; the teasing way she had once shaken it across his thighs, enclosing his enraptured prick in a canopy of chestnut-brown.

He thrust his hands through his own hair as he recalled her angry letters – letters sent care of his office in response to his curt note, and bristling with hurt pride disguised as sarcasm. If things had turned out differently, they might be in Rome together now; that luxuriant hair enveloping him again as they savoured the pleasures of a double bed; the chimes from some church clock tolling a slow and sensuous midnight.

'Daniel,' breathed a voice behind him.

Startled, he wheeled round, half-expecting Juliet to have materialized in the flesh. But of course he should have known: there was only one person who crept up on him unawares like that, and who always knew his whereabouts, even when he was seeking to escape. And of course the man looked different again – in place of the dazzling white blouson an old and shapeless sweater; his hair tucked down inside the polo-neck, so that in the murky light it appeared conventionally short. Now he was just anyone – Joe Bloggs in reality – a bloke in muddy boots and Oxfam jeans. Except he'd just worked an almost-miracle, which put him on a par with Christ: Jesus Bloggs, in short. And already that mesmeric voice had sparked off the usual reaction of resentment, awe and fear, made stronger by the healing session.

'I thought you might still be awake.'

Daniel shrugged, adopting a deliberately flippant tone to conceal his agitation. 'Well, I suppose it's not that easy to drop off to sleep after witnessing a miracle.'

JB squatted on the sand beside him, leaning against the rock. 'I don't think I'd call it a miracle.'

'Oh, I see. So it was all an illusion, was it, or some sort of confidence trick? Well, congratulations. You almost had me fooled.'

JB said nothing, just shifted slightly on the sand. Daniel forced a laugh to show he was only joking. The silence was uncomfortable. Why did JB keep pursuing him, for heaven's sake? Did he never sleep? And if he was suffering from insomnia, couldn't he use his time productively by working a few more miracles – or whatever it was he called them? Take that poor soul with MS, for instance, or the logorrhoeic madwoman. Both were in dire need of help, whereas all *he* wanted was to be left in peace.

Perhaps Penny had sent him up here. She could have told 'Stephen' about his failings in the marital bed and begged him to effect a cure. Also, if she hoped to further her relationship with Corinna, it might suit her very well to have him out of the way. He lobbed another stone into the water, determined to wrest his mind away from sex of any sort. 'Do you happen to know how deep it is, this lake?'

'Unfathomable, apparently. They say there's a whole drowned city at the bottom.'

'And I'm expected to believe that, am I, on top of everything else?'

'You're not expected to believe anything.'

The quiet reply only accentuated his own unfriendly tone. Why the devil was he being so defensive? The man had done him no harm and had just transported George and Margot into a state of genuine bliss. Even if Margot's sight deteriorated as soon as she got home, at least she had enjoyed one night of triumph.

'Look,' he said less brusquely. 'D'you think there's any chance of helping Pippa? I mean, in her case it's not a simple illness or . . .'

'Illness is rarely simple.'

'No, I suppose it isn't. What I meant was . . .' What the hell *did* he mean? He had just resolved not to get his daughter mixed up in things he couldn't understand. Yet his recent thoughts of Juliet had brought other painful memories surging back – Pippa sitting listlessly at the breakfast table, staring at her uneaten toast as if she could see horror-pictures in it; or behaving like a deaf-mute in the sports shop where they'd taken her to buy new trainers, showing not a spark of interest in any of the shoes. Yet she had lost her own expensive Reeboks which she had bought six months earlier – and bought with great excitement. *That* shopping expedition had been happy for them all: Pippa darting around the shop, pouncing with delight on neon-coloured leggings and garish satin cycling-shorts; trying on baseball caps and ski-goggles. So what had brought about the change in her, and why did she keep losing things? Could there be a link with the loss of her real father – the deprivation she'd suffered at the age of four causing symptoms only now? Or was it even possible that Phil had got in touch with her, written to her secretly from Bahrain and put her in some terrible dilemma – maybe suggested that she join him and Khadisha?

Appalled by the idea, Daniel glanced at JB's face, now turned towards him with palpable concern. There was no trace of malice in it – that he had to admit – and if this extraordinary man could actually restore sight, then why not speech as well?

'I've thought a lot about your daughter,' he was saying, 'and I have this feeling that the problem's coming from outside. It's as if another person is threatening her whole security and happiness – someone with his own problems, who is suffering in his turn.'

Daniel grazed his hand along the jagged surface of the rock. The pain was nothing compared with the sharp jolt in his mind. The 'someone' must be him. He had always feared he was to blame – that his own affair and betrayal had affected Pippa somehow – and now JB was confirming it. It was also increasingly obvious that Penny had been blabbing, using 'Stephen' as her confidant. She was probably more upset than he'd ever let himself admit. Or had she some suspicion about Juliet? What if she'd discovered an incriminating letter, or a restaurant bill he couldn't explain away?

He jerked up from the rock and began pacing to and fro. He had come to Wales not just for Pippa's sake, but in search of that idyllic peace his mother-in-law had lauded, to lure him from unhealthy, noisy Rome. Yet here he was in a state of utter turmoil, no nearer solving anything, either in his own life or in Pippa's. If she needed a new father (a proper one this time, to replace the previous two incompetents) well, perhaps she'd better return to Leeds with Tony – a kind and jolly Dad who wouldn't 'threaten her whole security and happiness'. It was evident that he had failed his wife and daughter, and taking Juliet into account as well, had cast a blight on three separate lives.

He stopped his pacing to slump down on the rock again. There was no point in asking help for Pippa. If she could find her tongue for a different set of parents – dance a jig with Judith, let Tony hold her hand – then it wasn't healing she needed, but the love and understanding he had withheld from her himself. His only course of action was to tell JB he'd changed his mind, phrasing it in some tactful way which wouldn't sound ungrateful. 'Actually, we . . . er . . . can't stay long in any case. I'm already rather worried about problems in the office. So it's probably best if I get back and . . .'

'Still running away?'

'I'm not running anywhere, dammit! I'm a busy man, with certain responsibilities I can't just leave behind.'

'But that's the problem, Daniel, isn't it? You can't leave anything behind – not the past, not your pain and suffering as a child. I've been trying to understand why you're so desperate to escape, and it came to me this evening that you associate this part of Wales with death. It's not completely clear to me as yet, but I had this image of a child of seven or eight or so, who died not far from here – a child with your own name.'

Daniel simply stared, too shaken to respond. It *had* been a sort of death – the death of childhood, death of hope; the darkness and incarceration. But how on earth could JB have known? No amount of heart-to-heart with Penny could explain his insights this time, because Penny didn't know herself. He had told her very little; despised those men who kept banging on about the horrors of their schooldays, in search of easy pity. Such memories should be buried, or discarded with the uniform, the rugby kit, the tin trunk. There was something mawkishly self-indulgent about displaying childhood wounds and expecting people to rally round with the emotional equivalent of cold compresses and Band-Aid.

He stole another glance at JB, whose face expressed the same fierce and almost frightening concentration as when he'd been healing Margot. The word 'work' came to mind again, although muddied with less flattering words – fanatic, preachifier.

'You see, if it *was* a death, you've probably never mourned it, Daniel, never even faced up to it before. We all prefer to run away from death, but life is actually a whole series of deaths. Though it's also a series of births. You can be reborn into the present, which is a sort of resurrection. Living in the present moment is the only form of deathlessness worth having.'

'Look, I'm sorry, but I don't know what you're talking about.'

'Yes, you do. You understand extremely well – far better than I'd hoped.'

'What d'you mean, better than you'd hoped? You keep making out that you know me, when we're complete and utter strangers.'

JB laughed. 'Human beings are never that.'

Oh no? thought Daniel bitterly, remembering Greystone Court again. The only reason he'd been sent to that particular school rather than one less isolated was that his father knew the chaplain there, and perhaps assumed that he'd befriend his son, or even be something of a substitute father. But the Reverend Mr Hanbury-Webber had proved as icily remote as the school itself; a punctiliously strict man who was determined not to expose himself to accusations of favouritism. 'Complete and utter strangers' seemed precisely the right phrase to describe both him and most of the staff – tyrants ten foot tall who inhabited a different world and flew into terrifying rages over nothing.

But he didn't want to dwell on all these memories, nor on pain or death or childhood, or any of the other things he had managed so successfully to confine in locked compartments, but which this dangerous man was now dragging out for inspection. He grabbed a fistful of sand, let it trickle slowly through his fingers, then rooted for a pebble, sat tapping it against the rock. He was unable to stop fidgeting, whereas JB preserved a total stillness, as if hewn from rock himself.

The muffled chink of the pebble seemed magnified in the silence of the night. Daniel strained his ears, listening for some other noise – a restive sheep or rustling bird, the faintest plop or stirring from the lake. But there was nothing save his own stealthy tap-tap-tap, which only emphasized the fact that he hadn't really responded to JB's last remarks. He cleared his throat, trying out various openings in his mind, but dismissed them all as threatening – too likely to lead on to further inquisition. All subjects seemed taboo, in fact. If he returned to Pippa there would only be more blame, and if he started probing Margot's cure he would be trapped in awkward questions about acceptance and belief.

It was a relief when JB spoke himself, even accompanying his words with a slight gesticulation, as if to prove that he was flesh, not stone.

'You see, I too was living in the past, and actually became quite ill because I couldn't seem to let go of it. I was very closed like you, Daniel, and it took something really violent to shake me out of my misery – a shock to the whole system.'

'What *was* the shock?' asked Daniel, jibbing at the label 'very closed'.

'My life changed – totally.'

'But what happened?' Daniel persisted, considerably relieved that the focus appeared to have shifted from *his* problems to the healer's.

'It's difficult to find the words.' JB leaned forward and brushed his hand across the sand, as if smoothing out some obstacle in his mind. 'And anyway most words are misleading when it comes to spiritual change. I suppose you might say it was a question of grace breaking and entering my soul.'

Daniel only grunted. Religious terminology always made him defensive. He'd had enough of it at school – the Reverend Hanbury-Webber expatiating on the soul when he clearly lacked a heart. And as for grace, he had never really grasped it as a concept: not surprising, perhaps, when his initial introduction to it was as 'the grace of God which passeth all understanding'. He was aware of JB's eyes on him – that penetrating gaze again, which seemed to bore through to his marrow, or to the soul he wasn't sure he had.

'I have an intuition that the same will happen for you, Daniel. That may be why you're here. Often, there's a higher consciousness which plans things out for us, so perhaps you needed to come to Wales to confront that early death. In fact, it would probably be enormously helpful if you returned to the place where it happened . . .'

Daniel sprang up to his feet. *No!* he shouted silently. Never in a million years. Keep your crack-brained notions to yourself.

He realized he was shivering. It must have turned cold suddenly; the night storage-heater running out of power. 'I . . . I'd better get to bed,' he said aloud, already striding from the shore towards the path. 'It's bloody chilly up here in the wilds.'

'It's actually quite warm,' the impassive voice corrected. 'Surprisingly muggy, considering it's the middle of the night.'

'Okay, it's warm,' Daniel muttered, anger surging up in him, exploding through his body, as if he were breaking out in shingles or a rash. 'Have it your own way! Black's white, isn't it, and blind people can see.'

'Yes,' JB said softly. 'Just occasionally they can.'

20

DANIEL PUT HIS FOOT DOWN, watching the speedometer climb to seventy-five, then eighty. It was exhilarating to roar along a decent stretch of road, after his tortoise-like manoeuvrings on the narrow country lanes. He was out for the whole day, footloose and fancy-free. The radio was playing a jaunty piece for strings by a seventeenth-century French composer whose name he hadn't caught – perfect for the occasion since it matched his sense of spree. He'd been released from boarding-school and allowed to visit the real world again – a peculiar and wicked world, containing all the things discouraged by JB, and where people wore conventional clothes, instead of bikinis teamed with wellingtons or (in Happy's case this morning) a caftan and a coolie hat.

He could hardly believe how strange things looked around him. Passing through a town, he had gazed afresh at supermarkets, petrol stations, video arcades, marvelling at their novelty like an alien from another planet. He had been out of circulation only for a week, but the daily round of life in the camp had become almost second nature, so that it was so-called ordinary life which now seemed unfamiliar. He'd been tempted to sneak out before, but there was always some compulsory meal, or vital communal meeting to attend, and he'd found himself increasingly caught up in interests and activities which his more inhibited London self would never so much as contemplate. One attraction was the company of Claire. Penny and Pippa might have written him off, but she and Rick thought otherwise, and seemed actively to seek him out. He'd spent a good deal of his time with them, discussing life or God or Greenpeace with the mother, or damming streams and watching birds with the son. He had to admit he'd actually quite enjoyed it, and the weather was so blazing hot, there was every incentive to stay put and laze around.

It was JB who'd suggested that he break free of routine, take himself off for a drive or an excursion – all day if he liked. He'd been suspicious of the suggestion at first. Did the healer want him out of the way, so that he could deepen his relationship with Penny? No. Penny simply wouldn't have the time: too busy with Corinna, or learning overtone chanting and the theory of the chakras. After his initial hesitation, he had agreed with growing enthusiasm, and had set out after breakfast (heavy gritty muesli, washed down with fennel tea). Now it was nearly twelve and he was watching out for a decent pub, where he could stop and have a drink – not some fig and rhubarb brew, murky and lukewarm, or colon-cleansing liquorice-root, but a pint of ice-cold lager.

He retuned the radio to catch the midday news. He had heard it twice already, at ten and then eleven, hungry for information after seven newless days. But it was only a repetition of the previous two bulletins – mostly bombings, muggings, shootings, strikes and wars. Perhaps there was something to be said for banning newspapers and radios: without them you could almost believe in universal brotherhood and peace. And he no longer even missed his watch, but was beginning to appreciate the freedom from all time-pressures; the sense of days being baggy, shapeless, voluminous things, like comfortable old clothes, instead of rigidly restricting corsets stretched to breaking point.

He coasted down a hill, slowing to a stop as he saw a pub sign on the left – the Plough and Harrow, a pleasant grey-stone building softened by a flowering creeper, with more flowers on the curtains and a board outside announcing 'home-cooked meals'. As he walked into the bar, he could smell the rich aroma of roast beef, and realized how he'd been missing good red meat. The pub was almost empty, and much more peaceful than the camp – no children, dogs or chanting – yet he felt a frisson of unease at being there at all. Things he would never normally notice sprang out at him as crimes: sandwiches made with sliced white bread, oozing mayonnaise; sugar-loaded chutney, bars of chocolate, crisps. A man was sitting at the bar, peeling the cellophane off a glistening Walls pork pie. He looked remarkably complacent, considering the offences he was committing: cruelty to pigs, adulterating his body with preservatives and additives, consuming saturated fat, and despoiling the environment with non-biodegradable packaging.

Daniel watched him bite into the crust, the smell of greasy pastry tantalizing his nostrils, so that it was all he could do not to reach across and take a bite himself. Instead, he ordered his lager and scanned the menu chalked up on the blackboard. Damn the guilt – he'd enjoy himself for once: tuck in to steak and chips, or roast beef and spotted dick. Penny was learning not just healing methods, but a new philosophy (taught by gurus Happy and Corinna) for developing her 'real' self, as against the self which served man or child or state. He found it extremely threatening, but today, he decided, he would follow her example and develop his *own* 'real' self; indulge his gluttony to the full.

He took his beer to a table in the window and rummaged for his handkerchief – already unpleasantly damp. He'd gone down with Gerard's cold. In fact, half the camp had caught it, which seemed a shade ironical when not only was the weather so benign, but they were all expending so much energy on living a healthy life. It also gave Penny another reason to banish him and his germs from the tent. He was still sleeping in his lonely shack – sometimes even contemplated asking Claire to share it.

He booted Penny from his mind again, and turned his attention to the middle-aged brunette who had come to take his order. Her top half and her lower half didn't seem to match – the neat white blouse and stylish chignon spoilt by veiny legs and down-at-heel scuffed shoes. He spent some minutes with her discussing the relative merits of the chicken, beef and steak, partly for the pleasure of listening to her musical Welsh lilt, and partly because he was determined to spin out the rare treat of a normal meat-based meal. He was already savouring his beer, revelling in the taste of each slow mouthful, its tangy coolness soothing his dry throat.

He glanced across at the bar once more. The man had finished his pork pie and was now lighting a cigarette. He felt no envy this time, but a smug glow of satisfaction. In the last few days, his once desperate urge to smoke had dwindled into nothing more than an occasional wistful pang. Claire had been a great source of encouragement, telling him about an article she'd read which said it was more difficult to stop smoking than to come off heroin, and that a smoker on twenty a day raised his hand to his mouth seventy-three thousand times a year, which – according to her calculations – meant that he was seventy-three thousand times healthier than he had been a year ago.

Instinctively, he raised his hand to his mouth, though only to take another swig of beer. He wasn't totally convinced by her claim, nor by the accuracy of her maths. Still, she'd meant it well, and had even mixed him up a herbal potion which she assured him would alleviate any last faint cravings. Who knows? – it might actually have worked. Certainly he had no inclination now to go rushing up to the bar to buy a stash of Camels.

He lounged back in his chair, admiring the simple room. No video games or jukeboxes, but an interesting collection of old farm implements hanging on the walls: a primitive-looking hay-rake, an elaborate leather horse-collar and some ancient scythes and gin-traps. A couple of equally ancient codgers had just come shuffling in – regulars, by the looks of them – dressed in heavy tweed jackets despite the heat. They ordered pints of scrumpy and stood leaning against the bar, conversing loudly in Welsh. Daniel cocked an ear. What an extraordinary language it was – so utterly foreign-sounding, so unlike any other tongue he knew – a private language, spoken by a mere half a million people, compared with the hundreds of millions of English-speakers across the globe. He itched to learn it, to penetrate its secret structure, understand its sagas and its songs. One of the men was speaking with great emphasis, his face solemn and intense. Was he expounding the meaning of life – or merely complaining about his prostate?

Daniel blew his nose again, concealing the grubby handkerchief as he saw the waitress heading for his table with a tray. There was almost too much luxury to take in all at once: a proper china plate on a proper wooden table, instead of a chipped enamel dog-bowl on a groundsheet or a cardboard box; a sizzling slab of meat which didn't taste of wood-smoke; a bread roll so light and soft he half-expected it to float up to the ceiling; real forbidden butter, and a pile of chips so large it reminded him of the firewood he was constantly chopping at the camp, although on this occasion his hands weren't red and aching from the axe. And – bliss! – no vegetables at all, save for a minuscule parsley sprig and half a sliced tomato. He'd had enough of vegetables – soggy marrow, worthy swedes, so-called 'edible' fungi, flatulence-inducing beans – all cooked without salt or fat.

He showered salt on his steak and bit into it with relish, imagining Rick beside him, shovelling in a cheeseburger and chips. It was strange, the bond between them – a surprise to him as much as to Claire – the rebellious teenage boy and the middle-aged recluse. Except he was no longer a recluse, but had been out and about with Rick, helping him hunt bones, or explore foxes' holes and rabbit warrens. Rick was a true country boy and his interest in the natural world had brought back happy memories of his own time in the bush. He'd forgotten the simple pleasures of messing about in streams, identifying footprints in the mud – stoat and weasel, vole and heron – even climbing trees, which he hadn't done since the age of nine or ten. His only regret was that Pippa refused to join them, despite his continual efforts to include her on the expeditions, his attempts to arouse her interest by showing her rare bird feathers or treasures from the abandoned mine. She hadn't simply declined: she'd been uncharacteristically rude, shunning Rick completely as if he had some infectious disease, and resisting any overtures even from good-natured Claire. He'd suspected she was jealous, and had contrived to talk to her on his own, but had only been resisted in his turn. Finally he had complained to Penny, who had merely shrugged and said if the child was happy with her dog (and the two were indeed inseparable), then why not leave her be?

It was stupid to harbour a grudge against an injured slobbery boxer, but it did hurt to see her conferring with the dog's confounded owners, discussing canine matters with placid Judith and ever-cheery Tony while she cold-shouldered her own father. He had also seen her talking to JB, and immediately feared that the healer might be influencing her against him – that baneful 'someone' who threatened her well-being.

Well, he mustn't let her spoil his steak, nor his cup of strong black coffee which had never seen an acorn or a dandelion, and which he sweetened with two spoonfuls of wonderfully poisonous white sugar. By the time he'd drunk a second cup, he was in urgent need of a pee, so he slipped out to the gents, nodding to the two old men en route. He shut himself in a cubicle just for the joy of having peace and privacy; peeing in a proper porcelain toilet-bowl behind a locked and solid door, rather than a fly-infested hole-in-the-ground with dogs sniffing and kids sniggering if he took his trousers down. He flushed the cistern gratefully: so much more hygienic than covering up one's droppings with a handful of damp sawdust or a few tastefully arranged leaves. And what luxury to have a proper basin, with unlimited hot water gushing out at the flick of a tap, when he was used to boiling it in a slow and stubborn billy-can over a temperamental fire.

He glanced at the mirror over the basin, recoiling in shock at the unkempt character staring back at him. He had given up shaving after two laborious attempts, and followed Tony's jokey exhortations to 'grow a beard like mine, mate'. The stubble had been itchy and uncomfortable, but only now did he realize what an utter tramp he looked. A Hollywood suntan gave a chap distinction, but his own burnt-almond skin smacked more of the swarthy gypsy than the film star. There were scratches on his face where he had battled through the undergrowth with Rick, insect-bites pockmarked his neck, and his hair hung limp and greasy. It was a wonder they had agreed to serve him at all, rather than ejecting him from the pub on sight. He slunk back to the bar and bumped slap into the waitress, hurriedly stammering an apology, less for the collision than for his general slatternly state.

'I've been camping in the wilds, you see, and I simply didn't realize what a mess I looked. I'm afraid I need a shower and shave before I'm fit to be seen in public.'

'Well, you can always have one here. We've got two nice rooms upstairs, both with their own bathrooms, and both empty at the moment. It's normally twenty pounds a night, but I'll charge you just half-price if you only need the room for a couple of hours.'

She was clearly touting for business, though a tenner seemed inordinately steep for a simple wash and brush-up. On the other hand, the thought of lying in a bath, soaking away his stiffness, scouring off the dirt, was definitely appealing. And anyway could he really face the rest of the world for the remainder of the afternoon looking the way he did? He probably smelt foul, too – a pungent cocktail of sweat and dog and wood-smoke.

She finally settled for seven-fifty, and threw in a disposable razor – a pink plastic one which he suspected she had used already for shaving her stout legs. He was too contented to object, however, pottering round the bedroom trying out delights such as electric light, electric kettle, and comfortable sprung mattress, then wallowing up to his chest in a capacious modern bath.

Shaving was more of a problem, the insubstantial blade resisting his tough beard, but eventually he cleared the stubble – and then the clogged and scummy basin. He drifted back to the bedroom and stretched out naked on the bed. He'd half-drawn the curtains to keep the room cool, and the muted light and his torpor from the bath combined to make him drowsy. He closed his eyes, recalling his last bath, the one he'd shared with Penny, attempting to make love to her in a boudoir of pink foam. He stiffened at the memory, trailed his hand down to his prick, imagining not just Penny, but Happy and Corinna too, all lazing in the bubbles. Corinna's buxom breasts were flushed from the heat and steam; Happy's legs were open and he could glimpse her moistening lips just showing beneath her thatch. She and Penny were comparing pubic hair – Penny's thick and flaming; Happy's soft and fair.

He cupped his balls in his other hand – they felt heavy, over-full – continued stroking his stiff prick. The women were all watching him, becoming more and more excited, all wanting him, on heat for him. He stretched luxuriously, ran his tongue slowly round his teeth, still tasting beer and steak. He'd take his time, spin out this last pleasure like the rest; wait till he was so worked up that he could have all three women at once.

He let his fingers tease down between his thighs, then deep between his buttocks; slicked them up again, grazing with his nails from root to tip. He glanced back at the bath. Penny wasn't looking at him, but had turned towards Corinna and was tonguing her taut nipples. Happy, for her part, was fondling Penny's breasts, rubbing her warm body not against the husband but the wife. He felt himself go limp; grabbed another woman in his mind – naked panting Claire. No. She, too, was resisting, and, however hard he tried, he couldn't get excited by her gawky boyish figure. He attempted to change her shape, add voluptuous breasts, but above them were her glittery glasses, which refused to go away; her lank and dirty hair.

He shifted on the bed, still only semi-erect, but restive after eight days without sex. Noises were drifting up from the bar below, cars passing on the road outside, but all the sounds seemed muffled, as if he were sealed in a cocoon of indolent heat. Another car purred past. He turned it into Juliet's car – a sporty little Alfa in gleaming silver-grey. He could see her at the wheel, clothed only in her hair, which was streaming out in the wind. He leapt on board, ran his fingers through it, let them feather down her body to her thighs. The car began to buck and veer as he kissed her while she drove, kissed between her legs. They were heading for a peach orchard in southern Italy, and suddenly they'd arrived and were lying on soft grass. She was feeding him with peaches, pressing their soft fuzz against his naked skin; juice trickling down his belly, dribbling from his mouth. Juliet was Eve – Eve to his Adam, who'd been disporting in that lake. They'd been created for each other, created to do nothing else but swim in cool green grass, suck peach-juice from the other's mouth, entwine their languorous limbs.

He was so stiff it was hurting; his breathing heavy, feverish. A lorry rumbled past, followed by another, and the roaring from the road outside seemed to reverberate with the rhythm in his head. Now he was in Rome – the holy, dangerous city – Rome pulsing and vibrating under Juliet's white thighs; Rome fermenting in its seethe of summer heat. His hand pistoned up and down – whole body braced, eyes shut – and he was shout-ing to her, 'Come, yes *come*!'; incapable of holding back even a second longer. He was bursting like an overripe peach, juice spurting on to his chest, oozing slowly down his stomach. The rhythm was resolved now, and the whole of Rome lay hushed; the traffic at a standstill, listening as he panted out, 'I love you, Juliet.'

He flung the map on the passenger seat. He was bloody lost again. The ruined Cistercian abbey he was looking for must have crumbled into dust. The guide-book had marked it 'worth a detour', but hardly worth a fruitless thirty miles. He had passed a host of other ruins – castles, quarries, mines, and especially ruined holy places. Wales seemed strewn with the hulks of its discredited beliefs: once-sacred wells now fetid, or used as rubbish-bins; moss-grown stumps of Celtic shrines; roofless abbeys; dilapidated monasteries; Nonconformist chapels open to the sky. Did he really need to see another heap of holy stones in this suffocating heat?

He used his sodden handkerchief to wipe the sweat off his face. He had better stop in the next town and buy a giant-sized box of Kleenex. His cold was worse – like his mood. All his earlier elation was punctured like a pricked balloon, despite his lavish meal and luxurious bath. He should never have had that bath, then he wouldn't have been tempted to lie on the bed and make love to Juliet. He was furious that she'd returned, after his heroic efforts to leave her in the past, and a ton-load of new guilt (especially for the 'I love you') hung round his neck like an albatross. He also felt a vague sense of betrayal towards his fellow campers, however crazy that might sound. He had broken the rules, which somehow wasn't fair; could imagine Claire's reproachful expression if he admitted what he'd eaten and drunk. And he was bound to get ribbed by Tony when he appeared at the next meal clean-shaven and spruced-up, in contrast to the others' general scruffiness.

The road led past a cemetery – ruined bodies, this time – and he realized he was approaching a town, as scrubby trees and scrappy fields gave way to rows of houses. It was still oppressively hot, although the sun had disappeared. Everything was grey now, and there was a brooding stillness in the air, as if the sky were holding its breath; the town beneath it paralysed. It was only four o'clock, yet all the shops looked shut; no one in the streets save a perspiring woman pushing an old crock in a wheelchair, and a long-haired hobo hunched up on the pavement.

He parked in the main street, scanning the immediate shop-fronts: a deserted flyblown café, an Oxfam shop with limp dresses from another era hanging in the window, and an alarming-looking establishment selling trusses, medical corsets and orthopaedic footwear. He trudged past knee-supports and bunion-bracers, and on to a stretch of narrow terraced houses, wedged between more shops. He increased his pace deliberately, hoping he might boost his spirits by putting a spring in his step. There was no reason for his gloom, for heaven's sake, beyond his usual niggling guilts. He was still out on his spree, with several hours in front of him, and now that he was here, he might as well explore this town, which must surely have a few redeeming features. Perhaps there was an interesting old church, or a local museum or building of some note, and he could always stop for tea and Welsh-cakes.

He continued up the street, crossing the road when he saw a general stores – a tiny dingy-looking place which just might just run to paper hankies. He entered to a fusty smell of aniseed balls and carbolic soap. The shop was dark inside, and a few loaves of none-too-fresh bread sat like unclaimed luggage beside a tray of wilting vegetables. The woman behind the counter was talking to two customers in Welsh, but she broke off as he approached, and all three women turned to stare accusingly, as if he had gatecrashed a private gathering. He stuttered out his request, embarrassed to be addressing them in English. The shopkeeper merely pointed to a shelf, and her two compatriots eyed him in beady silence as he grabbed the first box he could see and searched through his pockets for some money.

'Thanks,' he said, scooping up his change. 'Good afternoon.'

His words went unacknowledged, but the minute he'd slipped out, the women resumed their talk, as if the power had been switched back on – doubtless now condemning his intrusion.

He quickly crossed the road again, to escape their recriminations, yet aware that he was becoming really paranoid, over-reacting to everything. They had probably meant no harm, but were just sparing him the discomfiture of having to listen to a language he couldn't understand. He opened the box of tissues, only to discover that they were flimsy squares of pastel-pink, when he wanted man-size white. He plucked out half a dozen and had a really good blow, then walked briskly up the hill, keeping a constant look-out for anything of interest. But once he reached the top, he was faced with virtual wasteland; the road trailing away past vacant lots and ancient tattered hoardings. So – that was the town! He had more or less explored it, without stumbling across a single building of any grace or merit. There wasn't even a tea-place, let alone a book-shop or an art gallery.

He felt a sudden pang for London, where he'd have the choice of going to a cinema or theatre, sitting in an air-conditioned wine-bar, visiting any number of churches and museums, or sampling every cultural delight from medieval music to modern ballet to exhibitions of rare manuscripts or prints. Yet wasn't it perverse to be hankering for a city of seven million strangers when he'd so recently discovered the simple pleasures of living in a community in the wilds? JB would say that his apparent thirst for culture was really an attempt to deny his inner emptiness. By overloading his life, first with work, then with so-called leisure interests, he was seizing on anything he could to fill the void. Without such pursuits, time stretched ahead empty and unending, as it had at Greystone Court. The problem was, he felt torn between two worlds; actually missing the camp, strange as that might seem, while tempted to return to his usual round of safe distractions.

JB was certainly right in claiming that he couldn't enjoy the 'now', the precious present moment – at least, not for very long. He had managed it this morning, but already he was back to dejection and regret. He was like an adolescent, continually changing moods, and unsure of his identity. But then Wales was much the same: scowling and sullen one week, with grumblings of thunder and heavy lashing rain, then smiling and coquettish the next, with disarming sunshine and blue skies.

He mooched back to the car, passing a gaggle of teenage girls emerging from a sweetshop, armed with dripping ice-lollies of a violently orange hue. They were talking in Welsh – of course – and once again he felt totally excluded. The language no longer sounded intriguing, only impenetrably foreign.

He fumbled for his car-keys and drove off from the town, not bothering to consult his map. He was heading south, and that was good enough: he should eventually find the camp, allowing for various wrong turnings and meanderings off-course. The houses thinned out rapidly, and he found himself in a parched and barren landscape; its shallow soil too poor to conceal the rock beneath, which was thrusting through relentlessly. This was a hard country – hard in every sense – once a battle-land, steeped in the blood of maurauding English and fiercely defending Welsh.

He passed an abandoned copper mine – a scrawny desolation which had poisoned all the vegetation; scaly orange deposits blistering the ground like puckered scabs on old wounds. Everything looked sterile, as if man had extracted not just wealth and ore, but every spark of life and scrap of green.

It was a relief to leave it behind and follow the course of the river, whose glints and dappled shadows restored his faith in nature. He even caught a fleeting glimpse of a heron – a patient feathered fisherman, motionless at the water's edge, waiting for the split second to pounce down and seize its prey. Then the road curved up again, veering away from the river and proceeding through a woodland copse until it reached a deserted crossroads. He slowed to peer at the signpost. 'Llancaern Castle, seven miles'. He slammed on the brake, the car shuddering to a halt. Llancaern Castle had overlooked his school, its forbidding tower dominating the countryside around. His hands tightened on the steering-wheel as he stared at the sign in shock and disbelief. How could he be this close to Greystone Court? The healer's insinuating voice echoed in his head: '*It would probably be enormously helpful if you returned to visit . . .*'

'*No!*' he protested, as vehemently as he had before. And he was even shivering the same way, too – an unnerving sensation in such sweltering heat. Yet his mind was working at fever pitch, trying to make sense of what had happened. His day's excursion had taken on a completely different complexion: no longer a simple escapade in which he was free to go where he chose, as whim dictated, but the healer's way of ensuring that his words were not ignored. Somehow, JB had directed him here; was controlling his every move, even from a distance.

Ridiculous! It was pure coincidence. Central Wales wasn't that extensive, so motoring anywhere around here was bound to bring him close to the school. What seemed more extraordinary was that the possibility had never even occurred to him; that with all his fear and dread of the place, he hadn't made a deliberate effort to avoid the whole area and head resolutely for the mountains or the sea. Well, he could always do that now. A sea-breeze would be glorious on such a stifling day.

He wrenched the car into reverse, turning it round so violently that it scraped against the hedge, and hurtled off in the opposite direction from the dreaded Llancaern Castle. The coast couldn't be that far. He'd start again, set off on a second jaunt – sunbathe on the beach, remove his sweaty shoes and socks and cool his feet in the shallows, buy an ice-cream cornet and saunter along the promenade – above all enjoy the 'now'.

He realized he was driving dangerously fast. If another car came round the corner, there could well be a collision. He forced himself to slow, suddenly noticing that the scenery looked familiar – ominously so. He knew this road, didn't he? – that jagged spur of hill with a single skinny poplar on the skyline, this series of gentle bends winding its way through a tunnel of trees, whose enclosing shade stippled the car with flickering light and dark. How could things still be the same after twenty, thirty years – his feelings still be the same: hopelessness and terror? Yet, this time, he didn't stop, didn't run away, didn't even ask himself how he could possibly be approaching the castle again, when he had taken the other road. Of course, it was perfectly feasible that the locals had turned the signpost round, as they often did in this part of the world, to spite the hated English. But it was just as likely that, with JB in control of things, *all* roads led to Greystone Court.

He drove on in subservience, losing half a dozen years with every mile he covered, until he was back in short trousers; his scratchy socks too tight around his knees, his feet locked in heavy clomping shoes, when he was used to barefoot Africa. There were snakes in the pit of his stomach, a writhing tangle of slithery yellow vipers, poised to strike as soon as he reached the school drive. That drive was as tortuous as they were, serpenting its way between sombre speckled laurels and darkly poisonous yews, and so close now he could feel himself being drawn into its coils. The castle was just looming into sight, glaring from its promontory – a nightmare castle, forlorn yet menacing; the ramparts crumbling and weed-infested, the tower impregnable. It had always seemed like a second prison, but despite its massy walls and real-life dungeons, it had never induced the same blind fear as Greystone Court itself.

And yes, here was the drive; its entrance half-concealed by shrouding trees; the wooden plaque announcing the school name masked by tendrilling brambles. He looked away. He had no need to spell it out – the name was tattooed deep into his flesh. He signalled right and turned in; wheels scrunching and protesting on the gravel, as if the very car was expressing its revulsion. He remembered how deceitful the approach was; tempting him into believing that there was nothing sinister at the end of all those bends. They simply meandered lazily towards some nature park or pleasure garden, or even a palace from a story-book. But then suddenly, horrifically, the grim grey buildings reared up in reality, dwarfing the scared seven-year-old and demanding his submission.

He switched off the engine and silence swooped down over him, as if he'd been caught in a black net; all his futile flutterings and strugglings restrained by its fine mesh. But, however faint his voice, he knew JB would hear him.

'Okay,' he murmured, glancing over his shoulder, surprised he wasn't hovering there behind him, wielding that cruel net. 'You win. You always do.'

21

DANIEL WAS SHAKING as he got out of the car. He stumbled towards the main building with its lowering granite walls, its grey slate roof, its huge squat chimneys, hungry to incinerate small boys. It was strange to see the school in such hot weather, when he remembered it as always being cold. He supposed there must have been summers, but his memories were of shivering on the games pitch, scratching frost off windows with a flinching fingernail, crawling out of çhilly sheets on a raw November morning to face the shock of a cold shower. His first term had been especially bitter, and he was astonished how each day got slowly darker as the term snailed its way to Christmas, until dusk was falling at half past three, when it would still be dazzling hot in Lusaka.

He looked up at the drainpipes, in sore need of a coat of paint; the upstairs windows with their peeling, scabrous frames. The place had always been shabby – ancient buildings in a state of genteel disrepair – yet when he'd first arrived here, thirty-odd years ago, everything had struck him as bafflingly new: new clothes, new food, new words, new games, new tribe. He himself was a 'new bug', and new bugs must be broken in by various well-established methods. Live worms were dropped down their necks, and older boys would whip them round the shower-room, bashing them on the head with wet knotted towels (which might conceal an enamel mug or a cricket ball). And then there was his initiation, when he was led blindfolded and gagged through a large expanse of stinging nettles – still in his short trousers, of course. Afterwards, his so-called friends had taunted him unmercifully because he had never heard of stinging nettles, let alone set eyes on any.

Were the nettles still there, he wondered, stealing round the side of the building to see if he could find the site of that and other tortures. Probably everything would have changed after so many years. In fact, maybe the place was no longer a school at all, but had been turned into a hotel or conference centre, or sold to some developer who was about to pull it down. It certainly looked deserted, though of course it was the holidays, so the boys would have gone home. He had hated that word 'home', which his classmates used so glibly. *They* went home not only for the holidays, but each half-term as well, whereas home for him was restricted to the summer break, and so different from the others' homes that it attracted yet more ridicule. So many aspects of his life were a source of deepest shame: he'd brought the wrong sort of tuck box, wore the wrong pyjamas, spoke the wrong sort of English, asked the wrong questions, and had the wrong sort of parents (who let him down still further by never actually visiting, giving rise to the suspicion that they were dead or even in gaol). Interesting, he reflected wryly, as he ambled down an overgrown path, that to be sent away to boarding school was regarded as a privilege, but to be taken into care was seen as a disaster. Yet both involved the same loss of normal family life, the same upheaval and emotional abandonment.

'Excuse me!' someone called – a well-modulated female voice behind him.

He swung round to see a middle-aged woman dressed in a business-like blue linen suit, her greying hair cropped severely short.

'May I help you, sir?' she asked, bearing down on him with a not entirely convincing smile, the 'sir' tinged with a slight irony. He noticed that the blusher on her face, which gave her cheeks a youthful bloom, was undermined by the age-lines round her eyes.

'I'm s . . . so sorry,' he began, his boyhood stutter instantly returning as he realized he was trespassing and might be ordered to report to the Headmaster for a 'beato'. He blurted out a few names and dates to justify his unauthorized arrival: he had been at the school from 1960 to 1971, when Dr Robert Hamilton was Head, and had started off in Raleigh House, the preparatory department, under the ex-professional cricketer, Mr Baines.

'I . . . I do apologize for just breezing in like this, but I happened to be in the area and thought it would be rather fun to pop in and see the place again.'

Fun? His enthusiastic chirpy tone seemed to emanate from someone else – some clown in a sitcom for whom school life was all midnight feasts and jolly-hockey-sticks. But it had evidently paid off: the woman was visibly thawing as she saw that he was a bona fide old boy, rather than an intruder.

'I wondered if it would be possible to have a quick look round – see my old dormitory in R . . . R . . Raleigh House.' God! That infernal stutter wouldn't help his cause. The woman's expression had become dubious again, as if she might be content to let him wander round the grounds, but was reluctant to admit him to the inner sanctuary.

'Well, I'll have to ask Major Potts. He's the assistant bursar. We're the only two here at present, and I'm afraid we're very busy.'

He apologized again, feeling afresh that sense of being perpetually in the wrong, which he was sure the school would have managed to instil in Albert Schweitzer himself. He followed the woman back along the path, stopping abruptly as she stepped through a small side door and motioned him to follow. She could have no idea how intimidating it was for him to step over the threshold. He was the rabbit approaching the trap, the bird fluttering into the snare.

'Do come in. The office isn't far, and it's much cooler inside than out.'

He returned her still half-hearted smile, steeling himself to walk inside. In a flash the season changed. It was winter again and everything was cold – cold stone walls, cold floorboards underfoot, cold north light filtering through cold uncurtained windows. He was assailed by familiar smells of chalk, boiled cabbage, wintergreen, and it was some moments before it dawned on him that he was actually smelling nothing more than a faint whiff of sweetish face-powder. The woman had come back for him, frowning impatiently as he stood frozen in the doorway. How could he explain to her that he was petrified by those long-dead headmasters, sneering from their elaborate gilded frames? He had forgotten how they patrolled this stretch of corridor; their gimlet eyes swivelling round to follow any unfortunate wretch who dared to have his tie askew or his socks around his ankles. He kept expecting to see the boys – not one, but tramping hordes – to experience that panic at being herded along in a scrum of jostling strangers, all bigger, brasher, louder than himself. But the place was utterly deserted, only the woman's brisk tap-tapping footsteps disturbing the grey silence.

She seemed to be pulling him in her wake, compelling him to march along at her own no-nonsense pace, when he needed time to let his fears disperse. And so many half-forgotten things were diverting his attention – these ornate wooden scrolls listing all the school prefects since 1886; those chilling rolls of honour inscribed with the names of old boys killed in both world wars. He remembered other names: of torturers, of cronies, of sadistic masters now rotting in their graves. And he was still smelling smells not there – sweaty plimsolls, tepid watery cocoa, spilt ink, wet beds; the smell of cold and fear.

He made himself walk faster. The woman was waiting for him to catch up, and had stopped at a wood-panelled door further along the corridor.

'This is Major Potts' office. Would you wait outside a moment please, while I go and have a word with him.'

He nodded deferentially, feeling the self-same surge of guilt which used to churn his stomach as he stood outside the Head-master's study waiting for a caning. He paced up and down, up and down, trying to distract himself by studying the school photo-graphs arranged in serried rows on the wall, and dating from the 1920s. The boys themselves were also arranged in rows, and all reduced to conformity by identical grey blazers, uncompromising haircuts and expressions of dazed solemnity. In the more recent years, black and white gave way to colour, but there were still no individuals – no spiky-haired punks or oddballs – and not much colour anyway beyond that sea of grey, grey, grey. He returned to the older photos and found himself aged twelve, look-ing ridiculously young: skinny legs, childish rounded face, dark unhappy eyes.

He drifted to the window and glanced at his reflection in the pane, noting the changes wrought by almost thirty years. The eyes were still unhappy, but the face – thank God – had lost its vulnerability, its unhealthy, haunted air. Indeed, he was relieved to see he looked reasonably presentable, and not the tramp of several hours ago. If he had turned up here unshaven and unwashed, he would have been turfed off the premises without any more ado. Perhaps JB had stage-managed that as well. After all, it did seem rather odd that a waitress in a pub should offer him the use of a room with so little prompting. He had accepted it at the time as an opportunist bid for custom, but now he was less sure. If the healer had the gift of restoring sight, then luring him to Greystone Court in a salubrious and well-groomed state would scarcely tax his powers.

'Mr Hughson?' a voice boomed from the door. Daniel straightened up instinctively when confronted with the imperious figure stepping out to meet him. The Major's cursory handshake was no more than a formality. In the fleeting moment of contact with the cool, dry, bony hand, Daniel registered how hot he was himself – his palm unpleasantly clammy, his shirt sticking to his back.

'The name's Potts – assistant bursar. Come in a moment, will you?'

Daniel entered the spacious office with a growing apprehension. Had they been checking on his records, unearthed some heinous crime? In fact, he'd won a scholarship to Cambridge – and scores of other prizes before that – but academic prowess was of minimal importance here. There might be other records: of his secret rebellious thoughts, his plans to burn the school down, shoot the physics master. And what about the notorious Black Book, which, rumour had it, listed all the pupils' sexual peccadilloes? No one had actually seen it, but it had always loomed in his imagination – every page covered with a scrawling mass of horrendous accusations.

'Take a seat, Mr Hughson.' The Major nodded to a chair. Daniel sat obediently, looking down at his shoes, which were dusty from his long day out. An ex-military man would expect highly polished shoes; hair cropped to a well-disciplined length, like those shorn boys in the photographs. He would also highly disapprove of runny noses, and Daniel realized to his horror that he had left his paper hankies in the car. He sniffed surreptitiously, praying that the Major would turn his back or walk over to the window, which would give him a chance to wipe his nose on his sleeve.

'I believe your father was a friend of the Reverend William

Hanbury-Webber. I never knew him when he was chaplain here – before my time, I'm afraid – but I understand he was quite a saintly man.'

Daniel nodded, composing his face into what he hoped was an expression of respectful gravitas. So they *had* been checking up on him. The Major asked him next about his time in Raleigh House (where the brutal Mr Baines had wielded the cane with as much zeal and professionalism as he'd once shown with a cricket bat). Daniel uttered some inanity about his early love of sport and how Mr Baines had encouraged it. He could see clearly now that this was indeed a vetting process, so it was in his own best interests to answer the questions as politely as he could. He also made a conscious effort not to slouch or cross his legs, and to keep his voice considerably low, to avoid disturbing the woman who'd brought him here. (She must be the bursar's secretary, since she was working at an adjoining desk – a much smaller and less imposing affair than the Major's mountain of mahogany.)

'Anyway,' the Major concluded, rising from his chair and thus presumably satisfied with the results of his inquisition, 'I understand you're keen to see your old dormitory in Raleigh House. Of course, you'll find a lot of changes, but I trust you'll find they're changes for the better.'

Daniel sprang to his feet on cue, again making the right gratified response. He offered the woman a silent smile of thanks as Major Potts ushered him through the door, but the smile went unacknowledged.

'I'll escort you to Raleigh, Mr Hughson, then I'm afraid I'll have to leave you to your own devices. Unfortunately I'm extremely busy, and I've already kept Mrs Austin late. She only comes in part-time in the holidays, and I don't like to take advantage of her.'

Another reprimand, thought Daniel, as he strode along the corridor, trying to keep up. It was *he*, not the Major, who had kept Mrs Austin late, 'taken advantage' of them both. Yet uppermost in his mind was the terrifying sense of being led deeper and deeper into a dark confining labyrinth, with no means of escape. He became aware that the Major was talking to him, and tried to pay attention; express his admiration for the just-completed art block he was being proudly shown. There *had* been changes, yes, but they were strictly superficial. A coat of paint here, a new facility there, dwindled into insignificance when compared with what was still the same – the hostile echoing corridors, the lack of any softening touch such as pictures, curtains, easy chairs; the bleak grey quad (with not a tree in sight) which led across to Raleigh.

The Major was frowning at the door, his fingers flicking expertly through the heavy bunch of keys. 'I shall have to get our caretaker to take a look at this lock. I remember it sticking the last time I tried it. It probably only needs a drop of oil.'

The door creaked as he pushed it open. Daniel, too, gave an inward groan as he stepped into his past once more, hardly daring to look up.

'You'll find most of the other doors inside are open. We don't tend to lock the dormitories or classrooms, because, frankly, there's nothing in them to steal. We remove any valuable equipment and store it during the holidays in our strongroom.'

Was that a warning, Daniel wondered, in case he himself might be planning petty larceny? He remembered school assemblies when the Head would make an accusation: 'somebody (and that boy knows who he is)' was guilty of 'removing' a brand new leather sports bag from the junior locker-room. Invariably he would blush to his ears, feeling the finger of suspicion pointing to his own squirming form. He had never actually stolen so much as a toffee or a ruler, but the more scarlet and contorted his face, the more conclusive was his guilt.

Even now, he knew he was flushed, though as much from heat and fear as guilt. Major Potts, in contrast, appeared enviably cool. Despite the sultry weather, he was wearing a three-piece suit with a stiff white shirt and formal tie. Yet he betrayed no hint of discomfort; his clothes immaculate, his face imperturbably pale.

'I'll leave these keys with you, Mr Hughson. Can you please be sure to lock the door behind you, then drop them back to my office? And I'd appreciate it if you could return by half past five. I have to get off prompt today.'

'Y . . . yes, of course,' Daniel stuttered, adding a belated 'Sir', and realizing to his discomfiture that he should have called him 'Sir' throughout the interview. More black marks – this time for disrespect. Yet, as he watched the lordly figure stride back across the quad, he was almost sorry to see him disappear. Now he was on his own, with no distraction from his fear. Yet how shameful to be frightened of walking into a perfectly ordinary building, which didn't even look as big as he remembered it, and by no means as oppressive. Raleigh House had been built on a less daunting scale than the main school buildings and the seven Senior Houses, and was definitely less bleak inside. Yes, here was the small entrance-hall, with the staircase leading off it, and the Day Room and the classrooms at the back. He paused to get his bearings, noting the new lino and the almost-cheerful orange walls. The huge noticeboard which covered one side-wall displayed nothing more alarming than games fixtures and duty-rosters, lists of dormitory monitors and details of various school activities and clubs. A portrait of Sir Walter Raleigh, with high-domed forehead and pointed beard, hung on the opposite wall. That was a new acquisition, as was the table-tennis table in the large though shabby Day Room, the television set, and the squashy vinyl chairs in a shade of ardent marigold, which seemed blasphemous in their hedonistic brilliance. Changes for the better, as Major Potts had said.

Further such changes awaited him upstairs: duvets on the beds instead of scrawny blankets; even a cuddly toy, for heaven's sake – a goggle-eyed giraffe which must have been left behind by its owner. He remembered some godforsaken new bug turning up, aged seven, with his teddy bear. The bear had lasted half an hour before being ceremoniously dismembered and drowned in the school pond. When the bereaved child howled his protest, he was threatened with a similar fate. But perhaps nowadays it was no longer *de rigueur* for the under-nines to put away all childish things.

Blast! His nose was running again. He dived into the washroom to fetch a length of toilet paper. The place had been modernized almost beyond recognition – no longer the cesspit he remembered, with its growling water-pipes and total lack of privacy, but a pleasant blue-tiled shower-room which would do justice to a leisure centre.

He walked on to the end of the passage to search out his own dormitory – the one he'd been allocated at the start of his first term, when he, too, was only seven. He stood in the doorway, hardly seeing the brightly patterned duvet-covers, or the prints of ships around the walls. This room could never be brightened, never modernized. The pain and grief it contained would seep through any whitewash like fungus on damp stone. He had realized on his first night here that his life was over. Officially, he had eleven more years – an eternity of wretchedness which would be impossible to endure. He had lain awake, considering how to end it all: he could starve himself to death, or take some sort of poison, or jump from a top-floor window. But all such things were against the rules. You had to eat up every scrap of every meal; all medicines, let alone poisons, were kept strictly under lock and key, and all top windows barred. But although he himself had lived, hope had died within him, and from that day on he had walked around weighed down by its corpse.

God – what pretentious rubbish! He turned on his heel and marched back down the stairs. Children as young as seven didn't harbour thoughts of suicide. He was merely indulging in self-pity again. Perhaps that was the reason JB had brought him here – to make him see that he'd got the whole thing out of proportion, blown up a few privations into a reign of unadulterated terror.

He seated himself in the Day Room on one of the orange vinyl chairs and looked out at the lawn, parched and brown in patches, but as meticulously clipped as the Major's iron-grey hair. Beyond it stretched the games fields – rugger and cricket pitches, tennis courts, athletics track. Despite his effusions to the Major, he had never excelled at any sport, except long-distance running, which had given him a welcome chance of being on his own. He gazed beyond the grounds to the surrounding countryside, trying to remember exactly where he had run, but recalling only the tight bursting feeling in his chest as he pounded up a hill or through a wood. The horizon was a blur of bluish-grey; clouds beginning to build; the week of sultry weather threatening to explode in rain. He closed his eyes, feeling utterly wrung out. The strain of being here at all had left him like a rag doll, spineless–limp.

He slumped back in his chair, half-drifting into sleep; memories and images floating through his mind, forming and reforming like the fractured shifting colours in a kaleidoscope. Except the colours were all grey – the grey of ash, of rain. He could hear rain drumming softly in his head, then – suddenly – a different sound: muffled shouts outside the window from the rugger match in progress. He fumbled in his pocket for another square of toilet-paper, mopped his sore red nose. He had been let off games this afternoon on account of his bad cold, and was making the most of being on his own, allowed to sit and read without the usual tormentors snatching his book and calling him 'Snot-nose'. It was far too wet for games – a drizzly February day with a cutting wind and a dank greyness in the air, making him feel that the English sun (which had scarcely put in an appearance all the term) had now gone for good and been buried in its grave.

He rubbed the misted pane and peered up at the clouds – big bulging mounds of them, like the mounds of stodgy dumplings which sat heavy on the stew each Tuesday, and were covered with a greasy scum. Despite the winter, he wasn't cold at all today, but boiling trembly hot, as if he'd been simmering in the stew himself, trapped beneath the dumplings. His clammy hands were sticking to the book and little prickles of sweat were making his nylon shirt feel horribly slimy. Perhaps he had a temperature, or maybe the radiators were turned too high (although usually they were only lukewarm). Anyway, the room was stifling – but you weren't allowed to open windows, not without permission.

He moved closer to the window, laid his forehead against the cooling glass. He was surprised at the power of the rain – not so much today, when it was only really spitting, but other days when it wham-slammed down, flooding drains, overflowing gutters, transforming dull slate roofs to glistening black. He liked to watch the puddles in the quad: fresh rain lashing into them in frenzied hissing circles; puddle merging with puddle like amoeba under the microscope, until tarmac changed to lake. And of course *every-one* was off games then, a whole herd of them imprisoned, becoming ratty and impatient as rain steamed all the windows, built up a cocooning fug.

He turned another page of his book, a really super story about two boys called Tim and Kipper who lived in the wilds and dressed in animal skins. He glanced down at his own grey-clad legs. Thank goodness he had gone into long trousers. That had happened last September, when he was eleven and three-quarters. Shorts were fine in Zambia, but not here in Wales, where winter ran its icy hands up and down your bare legs.

He skipped a boring passage of description, to get to the exciting bit where Kipper had to fight a wolf single-handed. He continued reading, pausing now and then to blow his nose, but only looking up when an extra loud cheer erupted from the rugger game outside. Then, suddenly, behind him, he heard the door-knob turning and footsteps coming in – the sort of slow and scary footsteps only grown-ups had. A low voice spoke his name.

He sprang to his feet, wondering what new crime he had committed. Perhaps he shouldn't be reading, or shouldn't be alone, but Mr Baines had said particularly that he was *allowed* to read in here, and that he needn't go to the Sick Room unless Matron decided otherwise. So why had Mr Sayers come to find him? He didn't like the new chaplain, though he wasn't half as strict as Hammy-Webb (who had left last year to be a missionary in Borneo). In fact, Sayers tried to be matey and made God sound like a nice kind Uncle who was always shelling out pocket money and ordering ice-creams all round. But since you never saw the ices or the cash, it was all a bit of a chizz, and he almost preferred Hammy's tight-fisted God. Where Hammy-Webb was beaky-thin, Sayers was flabby-fat, with a loose and jowly neck, and a paunch pushing out the waistcoat of his baggy old tweed suit (which was a nasty dirty-green colour like the mould you got on bread). His voice was flabby, too – a mixture of slugs and hymns – and the hair around his bald patch was straggly-grey and stained yellow at the ends.

'Ah, Hughson, there you are! You're off games, today, I gather. I thought we could take the opportunity to go through your Divinity prep. You did jolly well, by the way, but there are just one or two points I'd like to go over in more detail.'

Daniel shut his book. Shouldn't he have known that being allowed to read in peace was too good to be true? The last thing he wanted was to talk about Saint Paul and his crummy Missionary Journeys, which he'd heard more than enough of in class. Saint Paul had been born round about AD 5, which was such yonks and yonks ago, it was hard to get worked up about him. And, anyway, he seemed rather a crotchety person (like most of the masters here), who would insist on going to places which were impossible to spell – Laodicea, Bithynia, Beroea – where all the e's and a's and o's got muddled up.

'Fetch your coat, Hughson, and we'll go up to my study. How are you feeling, by the way?'

269

'Fine, sir.'

'Well, you look rather flushed to me. Has Matron taken your temperature?'

'Yes, sir. And she's going to take it again this evening, sir.'

'Good, good. *She'll* sort you out. Now, do up your coat – we don't want you getting wet. I think we'd better make a run for it.'

He dashed across the quad, the chaplain lumbering beside him, out of breath and wheezing. Daniel shook the rain off his hair as they entered the main building, noting how the chaplain's suit was flecked with little damp spots. His clothes all looked grubby anyway, as if he dribbled down his front. His spittle was probably yellow from his pipe. He had fourteen pipes in all. He'd told Blake Major so, in confirmation class. Daniel wasn't sure what confirmation had to do with pipes, but he had decided he'd never smoke himself, because it turned your fingers yellow, and your hair and eyes and spit, and probably your insides as well.

Blake called Sayers 'St Bruno', after his tobacco, which came in small cream tins that were awfully hard to open. Yet shreds of the tobacco seemed to be constantly escaping, and would scatter on his books and clothes, or get caught in his moustache. The moustache was two-tone grey and yellow, like his hair, with the same sad straggly ends.

'Buck up, Hughson! You're walking in a dream, boy.'

'Sorry, sir.' Daniel trotted to catch up, following the chaplain up the staircase. It was deserted at this time of day – everyone was either out on the games field, or still in class, waiting for the bell.

'Right, shut the door and I'll fetch your book. I was very pleased with your piece, Hughson. You're showing great promise in Divinity, you know.'

Daniel squirmed with embarrassment. He wasn't used to praise. He was also having trouble with the door – or rather doors. The chaplain's study had an outer and an inner door, both difficult to close. On Mr Sayers's first day at the school, a boy called Mycroft, a famous practical joker, had placed a long-dead bird in the gap between the two. The chaplain had tripped over its rotting smelly carcass and banged his head badly on the door-frame. (Mycroft was expelled.)

'Is that door playing up again? It never seems to shut properly. Hold on, I'll turn the key. We don't want you sitting in a draught, with that bad cold of yours. Right – take a pew by the fire, and let's have a look at what you've written.' The chaplain eased his bulk into a shabby leather armchair, drew it up beside Daniel's chair, opened the small blue exercise book and gestured with his pipe to the page.

'This Second Missionary Journey needs a bit more detail. You wrote quite a lot on the first and third, but tended to skimp on the second. That's the one where Saint Paul had an important dream, remember, instructing him to cross to Macedonia?'

Daniel nodded. He never had dreams like that himself, where God told him what to do or where to go. He only wished He would – instruct him to leave for Zambia right now; not even pause to pack his trunk or return his library books. It would be warm and bright in Lusaka and he wouldn't have a cold, and perhaps he'd go for a swim in the dam with the geese and cranes and heron, and float on his back and look up at the huge shining space above him – sky and sky and sky.

'Hughson, are you listening?'

'Yes, sir.'

'Well, what did I just say?'

'The dream, sir. I think you said in class last week that Saint Paul called it a vision.'

'Very good! He did. Mind you, I must admit you don't look at all well today, so perhaps I'm being unfair.' He smoothed back Daniel's hair and placed a hand on his forehead. 'Yes, you do seem rather feverish. We'd better put the work away. I'm sure we'll find some time tomorrow to go over it again.'

'Thank you, sir. Can I go back to Raleigh now?' Daniel didn't like the feel of the pudgy hand clamped against his brow, or the smell of the gas fire (which made a little snarly noise, as if annoyed that he was there), or the dingy room, stuffed with hulking furniture, or the books in the bookcase, which all looked old and boring – the sort with no pictures in, about people who were dead.

'Not so fast, Hughson! I've been wanting to have a chat with you, to find out how things are. It's part of my job here to make sure each boy is happy, and that there aren't any little problems which might need sorting out. Mr Baines says you're doing very well, but I realize it must be difficult with both your parents abroad. I've lived in Lusaka myself, you know. I was there just after the war, though I expect it's changed completely since the forties.'

Daniel didn't answer. The forties seemed as long ago as Saint Paul and AD 5. The chaplain had removed his hand, which now rested on the chair-arm. It was very large and fleshy, with long sandy hairs tangled on the back of it. Perhaps his head-hair had been sandy once, back in the age of dinosaurs, or whenever he'd been young. Daniel wriggled in his seat, thinking enviously of Tim and Kipper, who never sat in chairs, but swung from trees like Tarzan, or crawled through the undergrowth in pursuit of man-eating lions.

'You're fidgeting a lot, Hughson. Are you uncomfortable in that chair? It *is* rather lumpy, isn't it? Why not sit on the sofa? Come along, we've got to spoil you a bit this afternoon!'

The chaplain heaved himself to his feet, offered a hand to Daniel and led him to a huge broad-shouldered sofa, which was also shabby leather, but a different colour from the chairs. Having ensconced him at one end, he shambled to the bureau, opened the bottom drawer and extracted something from it. He returned to Daniel with a large box of Black Magic, its lid embellished with a scarlet satin bow.

'I expect you're fond of chocolates, aren't you?'

Daniel nodded, though his experience of them was limited. Sweets were restricted to Saturdays and Sundays, and then it was mostly acid drops or humbugs, never swanky boxes. Even now, he felt he shouldn't take one. The rules were etched so deeply into his brain, he feared instant retribution if he reached out for a strawberry cream. Actually none of the creams were there. The whole top layer had gone, and all the nicest centres on the second layer. He took the smallest chocolate left – a long thin one with a squiggle on the top, which looked almost like a D.

'Go on – tuck in! Have two or three, if you want.'

Daniel took a nougat and a caramel, wondering if there was some mistake. No one urged you to tuck in at Greystone Court. Anyway, it was difficult to eat them because the chaplain kept on asking questions and expecting instant answers. He had lowered himself to the sofa and was sitting so close that one fat thigh was nudging against his own captive grey-serge leg.

'Now tell me, Daniel, are you having any problems with the older boys at all?'

'No, sir,' Daniel mumbled through his mouthful of sticky nougat. He was confused by the reappearance of his Christian name, which had been kept strictly under lock and key since he'd arrived at Greystone Court.

'I know when *I* was at school, there were certain boys who used to get up to all sorts of things – especially in the dormitories at night. I expect that happens here, does it?'

'Er, no, sir.' Daniel blushed as scarlet as the ribbon on the chocolate box. He stared down at the carpet, which was faded-brown and stained.

'You don't have to call me "sir", Daniel. This is just an informal little chat between the two of us. And there's no need to be shy. You can tell me anything you like.'

Daniel sat in rigid silence. The nougat was lodged like an obstruction in his mouth, refusing to be swallowed.

'I mean, if another boy has approached you, or done anything you found a bit confusing, perhaps you'd like to talk to me about it. It's always better to share such worries with someone more experienced, who knows about these matters.' He leaned down with a encouraging smile, his face looming into Daniel's. Daniel could smell his breath, see the tiny dirty craters in his skin, the black hairs in his nostrils.

'Look, you mustn't be ashamed, my boy. These things are only natural. In *my* day we were taught that everything was wrong, and that God would come down on us like a ton of bricks if we ever touched ourselves. But God's not like that, Daniel. He understands. He had a body just like ours, so He knows exactly how we're made and what our needs are.'

Daniel found it hard to listen. He was transfixed by the plump hand, now advancing in his direction. He felt it latch on to his own hand and remain glued there, hot and heavy. He prayed the chaplain would light his pipe again, then he'd need both hands, and would be so busy puffing and sucking he wouldn't be able to carry on with this creepy conversation. But the pipe sat in the ashtray, cold and dead.

'And you mustn't worry about size. That'll come – just give it time. You probably think you're small for your age, but boys come in a whole variety of shapes and sizes, and there's nothing wrong with any of them.' He squeezed Daniel's hand confidingly, gave a throaty little laugh. 'I expect you'll find this hard to believe, but when *I* was twelve, I was quite a little tiddler. I used to think I'd never grow. But I *did* grow, Daniel, and you will, too, believe me.'

Daniel felt his hand (which was still clamped inside the chaplain's) being manoeuvred slowly down between the private folds of the baggy mould-green trousers. The tweed was thick and prickly, and the shiny little fly-buttons were pressing right into his fingers. Sayers's voice had changed – no longer the voice he used in chapel, but a soft and sort of fluttery voice, like moths' wings. Daniel hated moths, but his hand was trapped, the whole of him was trapped – walls and bulky furniture closing in on him.

'There! Would you like to be as big as that?'

Daniel couldn't speak. The bulge felt hard and solid, unimaginably huge. And he knew he shouldn't be touching it at all. God's cold blue eye was peering through the ceiling – Hammy's God, not Sayers's – a furious God who would send him straight to Hell.

'All I'm trying to do, Daniel, is to show you that any fears you may have are totally unfounded. It's just a question of confidence, you see, of believing that a young boy like you can grow into a big man like me. Let's take a little look, shall we, and then you'll see exactly what I mean.'

He fumbled with his fly-buttons, then slipped Daniel's hand down inside his underpants, guided the boy's fingers up and out again, still clasped around the bulge, which was now on public view.

Daniel stared in horror. It seemed not just huge, but ill: hideously swollen, with its blue veins standing out, and inflamed and awfully flushed around the tip. It was rooted in a nest of coarse brown hairs; straggly hairs sprouting through the limp white underpants. It looked all the more alarming because nothing else in the cluttered room was naked or exposed. The windows were concealed behind dark and heavy curtains; the desk was covered with a cloth, and the people in the pictures on the walls were wearing layers and layers and layers of clothes – crinolines and wraps and shawls; waistcoats and long overcoats; boots and hats and gloves.

'There, that's more comfortable, isn't it, and it's important we're both comfortable. Come on, my lad, relax. You need to loosen up a bit, that's all. I promise I shan't hurt you. All I want you to do is rub your fingers up and down like this.'

Daniel wished his hand would shrivel up and die – anything to prevent him having to touch that ghastly thing. God was in the room with them now. He'd just glimpsed His picture on the wall – eyes so sad he could hardly bear to look at them; crown of thorns skewered into His bleeding head. Hammy-Webb had said that every time you committed a sin, especially those called 'sins of the flesh' (which were never fully explained), you put Christ on the cross again, hammered in the nails yourself.

'Come along, Daniel, you can do better than that, I'm sure. Keep your hand much firmer, and go right down to the bottom, and then slowly up again. That's it! You're learning fast. Now put your other hand just there. No – further round, like that. And move in a bit closer. I promise I won't bite!' He gave a jovial smile, and Daniel noticed tiny gobbets of moisture on his lips, as if the inside of his mouth was sweating. 'Clever boy! You're doing jolly well, really beginning to get the hang of it.'

A fat finger tweaked the back of Daniel's neck, while warm tobacco breath whiffled in his face. 'And now, my lad, I think you deserve a little reward. Let's do the same for *you*, shall we, and see how big we can make you. I expect you're getting nice and big already. As big as me, do you think?'

Daniel looked around in desperation, seeking some escape. But the door was locked and the chaplain had the key. If only the people in the pictures could help – that woman in the crinoline, with her kind, sweet, smiling face. But she'd be appalled at what he was doing; wouldn't want him anywhere near her.

'Keep stroking, boy. You're slacking!'

Daniel sucked a final smear of nougat from his tooth, tasting castor oil, not chocolate. He could hardly get his hand round the thing, which seemed about to burst in red-hot fury. The chaplain held his other hand cupped beneath two lumpy puckered swellings, also covered with coarse hairs, which felt itchy and repulsive.

He looked away, disgusted; suddenly remembering Tim and Kipper. If only they could rescue him – come swinging past the window in a spaceship or a helicopter and whisk him safely aboard. Travelling at the speed of light, they could leave Wales behind in seconds, reach Zambia in a trice. Yes, there they were already, zooming over Mazabuka, about to touch down in Nsefu Park. He was vaguely aware of fumblings round his trouser-top, gropings at his zip, but he fixed his total concentration on clambering out of the spaceship into the waiting jeep.

He let the fingers carry on their business down below, while he stayed higher up, safe inside his head. There were lots of things to see in the park – elephants and rhinos, snapping lurking crocodiles, a flock of ha-de-dahs screeching to a halt on the lake. He wished they'd make less noise. He was getting rather confused, couldn't keep his attention where he wanted. It kept straying back to what was happening further down. He didn't like it happening, and the sad God in the picture was watching with His mournful eyes. But the other feelings were stronger – wicked shameful feelings, which were terribly exciting. He *was* getting bigger, bigger than he'd ever been. And suddenly the chaplain sort of slid down from the sofa – still holding him, still fondling him – and knelt on the carpet right between his legs. He must be going to pray, to his own kind God, who understood, who let you do these things. But he didn't pray – he couldn't – he didn't have a mouth any more, not a chaplain's mouth full of sermons and Saint Paul. He didn't even have a face. That, too, had disappeared, pushed deep into his own grey flannel thighs. All that remained was his shiny scaly bald patch, and the fastening on his dog-collar, digging into his red and bulgy neck.

Daniel closed his eyes, determined to shut out everything but the feelings in his thing – soft and hard, warm and cool, slippery and tight – all at once, all mixed up together. Digby-Jones had told him that some men put their willies in other people's mouths, and he'd simply refused to believe it. It was too horrible to think about. But it wasn't horrible at all. It was the best feeling of his life. The mouth was sliding up and down, and felt very firm and tight, and the fingers on his balls stroked slowly back and forwards, softly round and round. And he was soaring up in that spaceship, higher, faster, weightless, until he knew the ship would burst, blasting off in a fabulous explosion and shooting him into outer space – no, further still – to Heaven itself.

'You enjoyed that, Daniel, didn't you?'

He crashlanded back to earth, slowly opened his eyes. Kneeling at his feet was a sweaty man with a damp squashed-looking face, which he was wiping with a grubby handkerchief. The man leaned forward and wiped him too, dabbing between his legs. Daniel tried to pull away, but his thing was wet and sticky, did need cleaning up. Whatever had been going on? He dared not think about it, or imagine what Hammy-Webb would say, or Mr Baines, or – worst of all – his parents. Just thinking of his parents made him burn with shame. They'd be so shocked and sickened, they'd never allow him to come home again.

'There's no need to look so worried, Daniel. You've done nothing wrong at all. It's just a natural way of getting relief, and we all need relief from time to time. God made us that way, didn't He, so it's perfectly all right.' He stowed the hankie in his pocket and coaxed Daniel to his feet. 'Now I'd like you to help me to get my own relief. That's only fair, isn't it? Your turn first, then mine. You'll need to take your trousers down and lean over this sofa-arm.'

Daniel stood paralysed, listening to the instructions. Impossible instructions – but equally impossible to refuse. The chaplain was fussing with a cushion, slipping it under his head, to make him comfortable, as he put it. Comfortable! He felt utterly humiliated, bent almost double, with his sore and bunged-up nose jammed against a musty cushion, and his trousers round his ankles. He hated having his trousers down; he looked stupid in his socks and shoes with his legs so thin and white. It was probably all a trick and the chaplain was only pretending to be nice, and was actually going to beat him on his behind, as a punishment for what he'd done.

He shut his eyes, waiting for the thwack. His nose was making the cushion all soggy, and the stale smell of the leather reminded him of the dead and rotting bird. The chaplain must have gone to fetch the cane. He could hear a few soft scuffling noises, then footsteps stealing back. He tensed, but all that touched him was a gently fluttering hand, stroking along the crease in his behind.

'Relax,' the voice kept saying, the excited twittery moth-wing voice, which seemed to match the tickly hand. The fingers had moved lower and were creeping down the back of his left thigh. 'Relax, my boy, relax.'

How could he relax, when something was pushing at his bottom-hole? He didn't know what it was, but it felt small and sort of snakey, and was making him all wet. Then rough hairs prickled on his skin, and he realized with disgust that it was the chaplain's bristly moustache. So the other thing must be his tongue. The very thought of it made him feel sick, and he was scared he might actually throw up. He tried to wriggle away from the tongue, but it refused to stop – only poked in further.

'You're frightfully tense, my boy. Can't you try to let go? I'll tell you what'll help – pretend you're going to the toilet, having a lovely little crap and emptying everything out.'

Daniel tensed even more. You couldn't go to the toilet in the middle of a master's study. It would make an awful mess. He was terribly afraid now. The chaplain's voice had changed again, become louder and more impatient. 'Relax, relax!' he snapped.

There was nothing for it but to do as he was told and pretend he was on the lavatory. He bore down as hard as he could, and at once felt something being eased into his bottom-hole – not the tongue, but something much much bigger. It was only pushing slowly, but it was still hurting him and stretching him, and he was terrified he'd cry. It must be another sort of punishment – far worse than a beating because it made him so ashamed. Tears welled into his eyes, but he bit his lip, bit his knuckles, did everything he could to stop them spilling over. You weren't allowed to cry. That was the worst humiliation of all, and you were called blubber-guts or spastic. (Even Digby-Jones hadn't cried last week, when he'd got half a dozen strokes for cheating in a maths test.) If only he could move. His back was aching terribly and he couldn't breathe or speak. The cushion was half-choking him, and the sofa underneath was so hard it hurt his forehead. He dared not even think of God – not now – he'd go to Hell, without a doubt, the very instant he died.

He imagined he was dead already and let himself go limp like the dead bird. Immediately there was a stabbing pain, and the flood of tears he'd been holding back overflowed in great shuddering hurting sobs. The thing pulled out abruptly, and he felt a spurt of hot wet sticky stuff ooze slowly down his behind. He didn't move a muscle, but remained cowering over the sofa-arm, his nose-snot and his tears all revoltingly mixed up.

'Quick, boy! Dress yourself.'

The chaplain chivvied him upright and mopped him with the handkerchief again, then wiped himself and fastened his flies, hands clumsy on the buttons.

'Come on, don't just stand there! It's getting late.'

He pulled Daniel's trousers up for him, helped him tuck in his shirt. He was doing everything in a rush, and looked cross and also nervous, continually glancing over his shoulder, as if Hammy's God might burst in at any second. Daniel was still feeling sick and couldn't make his limbs work. The chaplain was treating him like a first-year: smoothing his hair, dabbing at his tear-streaked face, even doing up his belt. Then he sat him on an upright chair, and stood directly behind it, with one arm on the chair-back, as if to stop him escaping.

'Now listen, Hughson' – his voice was low, but dreadfully stern – 'what we've done just now is our little secret, only between us and God. There's nothing wrong about it, so you don't have to feel guilty, but it's very important all the same that you never mention it to anyone. Am I making myself clear, Hughson?'

Daniel nodded. It was hard to speak. The tears had started up again and were sliding slowly down his face into his mouth. He had lost his Christian name once more; felt that he'd lost everything.

'There's no need to cry, Hughson. If I hurt you, then I'm sorry, but it's all over now, and it's far better for both of us that we simply remove it from our minds. You see, if anyone should hear about it, they might not understand, and it could get us into trouble – extremely serious trouble. You don't want that, do you, Hughson?'

'N . . . no, sir.' He knew he must say 'sir' again, now that he was Hughson four times over.

The chaplain suddenly veered away from the chair and blundered to the mantelpiece to fetch a second pipe. Daniel noticed that his hands were trembling as he struck four matches in a row, but still failed to get it to light. He strode back to the desk, seized the other pipe and started poking it with a matchstick, scraping out black gungy stuff. 'I . . . I understand from my predecessor that your parents are obliged to make considerable financial sacrifices to send you here, Hughson.'

Daniel mouthed a silent yes. The mere mention of his parents had deprived him of all speech.

'Well, imagine how they'd feel if the Headmaster had to inform them . . .' The matchstick snapped between his fingers. He flung it in the bin, swearing under his breath; began to fill the pipe, pressing down the tobacco with a grimy shaking thumb.

Daniel felt shaky himself. That terrifying sentence was still hanging in the air. If the Headmaster wrote to your parents, it meant you were really for it. He tried to swallow, but there was a huge lump lodged in his throat – a block of rough grey stone which wouldn't budge.

The chaplain had finally succeeded in lighting his pipe and was sucking it and puffing; all but burning his thumb as he continued to push down the tobacco. He gave a spluttering cough, blew out smoke and words. 'You see, the Headmaster might well feel, Hughson, that it would be better for all concerned if your parents were to remove you from the school.'

Daniel broke into violent sobs, hunching over his lap to hide his face, his terror.

'It's all right, my boy.' The chaplain leaned towards him, dried his tears on the damp and smelly handkerchief. 'I can make sure that doesn't happen, and that your parents aren't involved in any way at all. But I shall need your solemn word that you'll never speak of it yourself. Now can I trust you, Hughson?'

Daniel responded with a vehement nod, which sent a pain shooting through his head. His ears hurt, too, and there was a dull ache in his behind.

'Right, I want you to kneel down on the floor here, and make a vow in the sight of God that no mention of this afternoon will ever pass your lips, so long as you shall live.'

Daniel fell on to his knees in a frenzy of remorse. He would do anything, anything, to prevent his parents finding out. If he was expelled from school, all the sacrifices they'd made to give him special privileges would have been a total waste. He might not *want* the privileges, but they expected him to want them, and he knew they would never forgive him if he threw them all away.

The chaplain was kneeling beside him, speaking in his chapel-voice. Daniel joined his hands and shut his eyes.

'Now, repeat these words after me: "I promise in the presence of Almighty God . . ."'

Daniel swallowed, making a supreme effort to hold his tears back. 'I . . . I promise in the presence of Almighty God . . .'

'"That I, Daniel Hughson . . ."'

'That I, Daniel Hughson . . .'

'"Will never . . ."'

There was a brisk tap at the door. The chaplain sprang to his feet, straightening his already straight dog-collar and thrusting the chocolates back into the drawer. 'Stay where you are!' he ordered Daniel, as he crossed the room and unlocked the inner door.

Daniel shut his eyes again, at the sound of urgent footsteps striding in. Perhaps it was his parents, already summoned to the school to take him home in disgrace . . .

He recognized the Headmaster's steely voice; squinted between his eyelids to make sure. He glimpsed the flowing black gown, the thin lips and silver hair. Instinctively, he made to stand up. You were supposed to snap to attention the instant any master entered the room (especially the Headmaster), but perhaps it was different when you were in the middle of a solemn vow. He subsided to his knees again, hands clasped tightly together, listening to the chaplain, who was still talking in his chapel-voice.

'Yes, of course, Headmaster. I'll come immediately. No, it's no trouble whatsoever. Hughson and I were just finishing anyway. Hughson, on your feet, boy! The Headmaster is here.'

Daniel struggled up and gave a timid bow in the direction of the Head, though keeping his eyes fixed firmly on the carpet. You didn't ever look at Dr Hamilton. He could strike you dead if you met his gorgon's eye.

The chaplain placed a paternal hand on his shoulder – for the briefest of brief moments – then turned to Dr Hamilton.

'Hughson is off games, Headmaster, so I was taking the opportunity of giving him some spiritual direction. He's having a few problems with prayer – the usual sort of thing: difficulty in concentration, the odd doubt about his faith . . .'

Dr Hamilton glanced at Daniel as if not quite sure who he was. 'Good,' he murmured vaguely. 'I hope you're grateful, Hughson.

The chaplain's a busy man, so you're lucky to get some individual attention. Now, run along, boy, will you. The chaplain and I have some important work to attend to.'

22

DANIEL OPENED HIS EYES. He had lost all track of time. The heavy wooden panelling and sombre stained-glass windows gave the chapel an air of permanent gloom, so whatever the weather or the time of day, here inside it was always a wet Sunday, always winter dusk. He was surrounded by grim-faced saints watching from each window: Saint Paul, Saint Peter, Saint John the Baptist, and a score of other martyrs or apostles, holding palms or swords or staves, and, beneath them, painted on the glass, the names of various school benefactors in spiky italic script. The Reverend Mr Walter Sayers stood praying at the altar, resplendent in white vestments; his brocaded chasuble glistening with silken lilies – symbols of innocence, of purity.

'I am the resurrection and the life,' his solemn voice intoned.

'You fraud!' yelled Daniel, springing to his feet. 'You filthy hypocrite! All you brought was death.'

He leapt up the steps to the altar, fist clenched, arm raised in violence. His blow struck empty air. He was alone in the chapel, Mr Sayers gone – now food for the worms, or ashes in an urn.

He stood leaning on the altar-table, stripped bare of its lace cloth, its heavy silver candlesticks, its vases of stiff flowers. Winter changed to summer, his prickly grey school uniform to Marks & Spencer trousers and open-necked check shirt. He was no longer twelve, but forty, yet the memory of that February afternoon was so precise, so vivid in its detail, he could scarcely believe that he had somehow managed to suppress it for almost three decades.

He grasped the edge of the altar, feeling the need to anchor himself to something sharp and solid. He had been sitting in the Day Room in a state of total shock, then – without quite knowing how – had found himself stumbling towards the chapel, as if lured back into the chaplain's domain, still mesmerized, still terrorized, still with that dull pain in his behind. Was he man, or child? He stared at his large, adult hand – capable, broad-palmed; then, slowly and deliberately, he compelled his powerful grown-up legs to walk down the altar steps again and take him to the door. Before he reached it, he hesitated, then, on impulse, he slipped into the third pew from the back – the exact spot where he had knelt that first Sunday in the chapel after his 'session' with the chaplain. It was Founder's Day and there had been a special service, the organ booming out its jubilation, the choir embroidering the hymn with hosannas, alleluias. He could hear the sound again, whooping to the rafters; felt a sly nudge in the ribs as Collins, kneeling next to him, hissed, 'Shut up, Snot-face! Your sniffling makes me sick.'

He too felt sick, sick with terror. He couldn't pray – God wasn't there – no longer simply deaf or stern, but vanished altogether. He felt completely lost without a God, especially here in chapel, where everyone was praising Him, including Mr Sayers. The chaplain had turned to face the congregation, a silver cross gleaming round his neck, a second cross embossed into the fabric of his chasuble; his voice shiningly devout.

'May Almighty God, our heavenly Father, have mercy upon you, pardon and deliver you from all your sins, and bring you to everlasting life, through Jesus Christ, our Lord.'

Murmurs of 'Amen' rose from the surrounding pews, but Daniel remained in silence, cowering beneath the black cloud of his thoughts. If the chaplain had the power to deliver people from their sins and promise them eternal life, then he *must* be holy, mustn't he? He couldn't be a bad man. Anyway, a bad man wouldn't wear those swanky robes, or stand there so importantly and preach about God's Word. So *he*, Hughson, must be bad – wicked through and through – the whole thing his own fault.

He stood up automatically as the rows of boys shuffled to their feet. Another prayer or hymn, though he hardly heard the words. He was thinking of Divinity tomorrow – the first lesson since his private 'tutoring', which had moved so hideously and swiftly from Saint Paul. How could he meet Sayers face to face, in public, in the classroom, to answer questions about missionary journeys, or – worse – about sin and Hell? In the last three days, his stutter had become so bad, he could manage little more than nods or mumbles. Every time he saw the chaplain, he began to shake with nerves, fearing another invitation to 'go over his work'. And the briefest glimpse of the Headmaster made him go hot and cold, imagining the summons to his study, to be told he'd been expelled. He couldn't eat at all. The food just stuck in his throat, and there was no room in his stomach for anything but fear.

'O come, let us sing unto the Lord; let us heartily rejoice in the strength of our salvation . . .'

He glanced up at the choir. His friend Forbes was singing solo, except he wasn't his friend any more – he hadn't any friends. He dared not talk to anyone in case he broke his vow of silence and blurted out something he'd regret. He was utterly alone – alone with a dark secret which was poisoning his mind like a deadly black mamba. He longed to share his secret, confide in someone brave and wise who could suck out the poison for him, but there was no one brave and wise at Greystone Court. Anyway, if he broke his vow, the God who wasn't there might strike him dead. And even if he did tell, no one would believe him. It was his word against the chaplain's, and the chaplain was a master, a grown-up and a clergyman – overwhelming odds. The other masters would beat him black and blue for even suggesting such a thing; the boys would only jeer, and probably accuse him of being a poofter.

'Prat!' Collins taunted, as Daniel dropped his hymnbook and scrabbled on his knees to pick it up. He would be called much more spiteful names than that if Collins and his cronies ever found out what had happened – nancy, fairy, faggot, pansy. And maybe they were right. If the chaplain had picked on him rather than one of the others, it *must* be because he was queer. God hated queers. He sent them all to Hell.

He looked furtively at Collins's book to see what hymn they were singing – number 184: 'Dear Lord and Father of mankind'. He kept thinking of his own father, wondering with sick dread if his parents had been told about his crime. But even if they hadn't, he knew that from now on they'd be forced to live in separate worlds – they in their high shining world with principles, ideals; he stuck on his foul rubbish-heap. But however far removed they might be in conduct and in actual miles, never before had they seemed to loom so close; continually watching him, accusing him, even in his dreams. They had slipped into the chapel, replaced the stern saints in the windows; his father's face glowering at him from beneath each stained-glass halo; his mother's staff raised threateningly, to strike her wicked son. Terrified, he switched his gaze to the smiling wooden cherubim carved beneath the frieze, but they were smiling with the chaplain's smile, and their tobacco-breath was hot and vile. Wherever he looked, the chaplain's face leered back at him. The plaster saints were slobbering with his yellow dribble; the tapestry of Christ the King had the same long straggly moustache, with little flecks of food caught in it. And the hymns and prayers kept repeating 'Father, Father' – Almighty Father, Merciful Father – shocked, disgusted father, white with rage in Lusaka.

He plunged to the door; stood breathless, his heart pounding, looking back at the silent empty chapel. '*Damn* you!' he whispered to the chaplain's mocking ghost. 'You wrecked my life here totally.' He'd been a harmless, self-effacing boy, whose most heinous crime was losing his Latin primer, or being late in returning a library book. Yet he had been made to believe that he was rotten to the core, and that however hard he worked at school, however many prizes he won, he had neither hope nor future. All those years of guilt and shame, when he'd done nothing more reprehensible than miss a Tuesday rugger game on account of a bad cold.

His nose was running now. He wiped it on the back of his hand; rested his throbbing head against a brass plaque beside the door. There were plaques all round the walls, commemorating past headmasters and chaplains, though none for Mr Sayers. He had left in 1967, not as Hammy-Webb had left, with a special service of farewell – fulsome tribute for years of sterling service – but suddenly, inexplicably, and almost overnight. Probably another buggery, Daniel realized bitterly, as he paced up and down the aisle. At the time, his first euphoric relief had turned swiftly to new terror. He had recalled the chaplain's words: 'If anyone should hear of this, it could get us into trouble, Hughson – very serious trouble.' Sayers had said 'us', not 'you', including himself in the reprisals. So perhaps that trouble had come at last; someone had found them out. And if the chaplain had been dismissed, then his own expulsion was bound to follow. Much as he longed to leave the school, escape its grim barbarities, he couldn't bear the disgrace of being expelled, or the thought of facing his parents' outrage. So, once again, he began living through a nightmare, instantly interpreting any sharp word from a master as the first step in his damnation.

By that time, he had transferred to the senior school and achieved his extraordinary growth-spurt. Looking back, it no longer seemed extraordinary, but simply a natural reaction to his rape: changing from little boy to brawny adult would protect him from further advances. But he hadn't liked the person he'd become. The small sweet child was gone, replaced by a gangling not-quite-man – isolated, wary, not daring to trust anyone, and certainly not God. In fact, he had never prayed again, except outwardly, officially, at services or school assemblies, merely to conform. He had lost his God along with his virginity – at least any loving, merciful God. He was left with Judge and Scourge.

His restless pacing had brought him back to the door. He yanked at the handle and slammed out of the gloom into the sunlight, striding across the quad to Raleigh House. He had left the place unlocked, the bunch of keys inside. He hoped there'd bloody well been a burglary – though Major Potts had told him there was nothing much to steal. Is that what Sayers had felt himself: that 'nothing much' had happened to the timid, snuffling twelve-year-old; that nothing had been stolen from him – only a mere matter of his virginity, his innocence, his happiness, his childhood? And not simply his childhood – it had affected his adult life as well. Even in his twenties, the fears had continued, wrecking both his sex-life and his confidence. That boyhood initiation had been so utterly repellent, he had mistrusted sex thereafter, always secretly fearing he was abnormal in some way.

He returned to the Day Room, unable to keep still, weaving in and out of the garish orange chairs as he prowled from door to window. He found the bunch of keys where he had left them on the table; swept them to the floor. Let the vandals ransack the joint. For all he cared, they could burn the bloody place down. There was bound to be a gang of local thugs, opposed to the snobbery of private schools, who'd get a kick out of breaking and entering . . .

He sank down in a chair. That last phrase seemed familiar. He could hear the healer's hypnotic voice sounding in his head again:

'You could say it was a question of grace breaking and entering my soul.'

He punched his fist into the chair-arm. What a wonderfully apt expression – if you changed grace and soul to cock and arse. It *had* been a breaking and entering, a forcible intrusion into his child's body. And JB had had the gall to use high-flown terms like 'spiritual change' and 'higher consciousness', then sent him here to re-live the sordid reality. If this was higher consciousness, he'd prefer to remain in Lethean amnesia. What point was there in recalling such cruel memories, which he had blocked off so successfully once the chaplain had departed – convincing himself that the incident had never happened; that no Mr Sayers had been at the school at all; had never even existed? Why change the scenario now, when there was no way to right the wrong? Sayers was dead, Hamilton was dead, and if he had any sense, he'd kill the memories themselves stone dead, before they drove him mad. JB was a powerful man, but power like that was dangerous, in the same way that a nuclear reactor could be programmed for great good, yet was also capable of wreaking vast destruction. He had resolved a dozen times already to take Penny and Pippa away from the camp, before they too were harmed, but on this occasion he'd act on it, drive back now – this instant – and insist they all went home.

He ploughed back to the window, a new worry seizing hold of him: did he confide in Penny about the rape, or would that only cause more problems? The word 'rape' itself set off a sort of panic. He certainly hadn't known it at age twelve, and even now, it made him shudder. It seemed too histrionic, a word best left unspoken. But Penny wouldn't share his scruples, would pounce on the term with burning indignation; jump in with both feet and want to take it up with the school; fight his cause, fight injustice generally. He recalled a recent programme he had watched on child abuse, the embittered victims (or survivors, as they were called these days) weeping on TV, openly arraigning fathers, uncles, teachers, to the prurient excitement of the public. He could just imagine some self-important therapist or media personality trying to winkle out all the juicy details in his own case, so that an audience of fifteen million-odd could sit slavering over Sayers's wicked ways. That would be another sort of nightmare. And even if he swore Penny to secrecy, she was bound to keep bringing it up in private, offering 'therapy' of her own.

No. He'd bury it again for another thirty years, by which time he'd be so ancient, it wouldn't matter any more. And he'd also bury the memory of his visit here, change the itinerary in his mind – not Greystone Court, but the ruined Cistercian abbey he'd intended to visit all along. He knew enough about ruined Cistercian abbeys to be able to supply a few plausible details if Penny asked about his day.

He strode into the hallway, paused a moment by the noticeboard. The present chaplain – a Mr Alan Rutherford – had written out a list of times for choir-practice and signed it in a neat italic hand. Daniel rummaged through his pockets, found an old pencil-stub, worn to almost nothing. He licked the point to make it write, then scrawled across the chaplain's notice in large untidy letters: 'FUCK YOU, SAYERS, YOU BASTARD!'

He tossed the pencil-stub away and blundered to the door, the twelve-year-old's hot stinging tears coursing down his cheeks again as it slammed accusingly behind him.

23

DANIEL PULLED OFF THE ROAD. He was only a mile or two from the camp now, but he'd been distracted by the violent scene in the field beyond the fence. Two rams were engaged in battle, their clashing horns disturbing the sultry silence of the country-side. He sat and watched the fight, alarmed by the ferocity of the implacable male rivals as they charged again, again; using the full force of their bodies to thwack against each other. There was a momentary lull as they braced themselves for another furious onslaught; heads lowered, muscles taut. He, too, sat rigid, hands gripping the steering-wheel, as he waited for them to return to the attack. He winced as it occurred; the savage crack of horn on horn sending shock-waves through his own body.

He turned away, imagining JB and himself locked in a similar contest; the former fighting to the death to stop him leaving the camp; he determined to do so. Driving back from Greystone Court, he'd become more and more angry with the healer, blam-ing him for all this new upheaval. Despite his resolve to suppress the hateful memories, they wouldn't *stay* suppressed. In fact, further sordid details kept bursting back into his consciousness, like a flood of dirty water breaking through a dam. He had come to Wales for a rest, and instead JB had plunged him into turmoil.

The rams had changed position, one pushing the other against the fence, but both still slogging it out with unabated aggression. Daniel almost envied them. How much simpler to fight physically like that – pawing the ground, butting with head and horns – than to fight silently and impotently inside. He jumped out of the car, slamming the door so hard he startled the two rams; all his rage with Sayers and the healer suddenly redirected at his parents. How could they have chosen such a benighted school in the first place, or left him there so long when it was obvious that he loathed it, and that his unhappiness was screaming out for anyone with an ounce of sensitivity to see? Were they cruel, or simply blind? Of course, it would suit them very well to have their time-consuming offspring five thousand miles away – out of sight and out of mind – leaving them free to live their unselfish conscientious lives.

He strode towards the fence. Unselfish? They had *never* been unselfish. The whole thing was a sham. They were too busy for a child, too engrossed in their careers, their desire for status and esteem. They loved children in the abstract – the unwashed millions, the disadvantaged blacks – but not their only son.

He leaned against the sturdy wooden fence, in need of its support. He felt as if he'd experienced a death. He had just lost both his parents – those altruistic parents he had revered throughout his life – and this new demise had shaken him as severely as their physical deaths. Only now had he realized, and with a painful sense of dislocation, how their high-minded philanthropy had led to his neglect. Service to black Africa was their all-important ideal, and since one insignificant white child had no such pressing claims, he'd been forced to remain more or less invisible. They'd hardly even *known* him, for God's sake; simply delegated his care to a succession of black nannies, or to remote and faceless relatives in England.

He paced back to the car, walking like a robot, blind to everything around him. He switched on the ignition and sat hunched over the steering-wheel, despising his self-pity. Countless children suffered *real* neglect – poverty and hunger, the lack of any home at all – so what right had he to complain? He longed to confide in Penny, if only to offload his own confusion. Perhaps he'd been mistaken in deciding to conceal the whole affair. Whatever his fears about her reaction, it seemed a heavier burden to keep it to himself, continually reliving the grim past while outwardly pretending that everything was fine. He could always give her a carefully edited version: spare her the grosser details, but explain how shocked he felt and how he had to leave this part of Wales at once.

Wearily, he drove off down the road, praying she'd be alone. No, that was hardly likely, when she'd become more and more involved in camp activities, but with any luck he could prise her away from some relatively low-key task, like carrot-chopping, or lentil-soaking, or building that infernal labyrinth. He needed time on his own with her, not just to relay the horrors of this afternoon, but to discuss the whole issue of why she was avoiding him, living her own free-wheeling life here, as if she were unmarried, uncommitted.

As he turned the final corner and descended the steep hill, he was astonished to hear the sound of drumming – a steady throbbing beat which instantly transported him to Africa: watching the .Kuomboka ceremony in western Zambia, or listening to a mother-drum echoing from the compound on a sultry summer evening. He glanced at the surrounding hills, the gnarled and twisted thorn trees, the stolid blackface sheep – hardly the setting for an exotic tribal rite. So what the hell was going on?

He parked the car in the tree-fringed lane and walked warily towards the tents. The campsite was deserted – unusual in itself. There was nearly always someone around, especially in this weather – some languid child or invalid sprawled out on a rug; some acolyte communing with the sky – but he couldn't see a living soul, except one somnolent dog. What struck him was the brightness of the colours: a pair of shiny scarlet wellingtons on the deep green of a groundsheet; an orange tent with a clutch of yellow mugs outside; a turquoise blouse on the washing-line. For the last two hours he'd been inhabiting his dead grey past, but these vivid colours seemed to jolt him back to life.

The noise of the drumming was coming from an adjoining field, one they sometimes used for healing sessions. (JB claimed it was on the junction of two ley lines, whose power would help the healing process.) But healing sessions were conducted in solemn silence, not accompanied by a drum. Daniel followed the insistent beat; glimpsed a crowd of people standing in a circle on the grass. Almost everyone was there – not just the zealots like Happy, Claire, Corinna (and a fervent-looking Penny), but even shy Dylan, sickly Doris and conventional Len and Jeanette.

He edged a little nearer, keeping well behind the clump of thorny bushes, which provided an effective screen. Though actually nobody had eyes for him – they were too intent on the ceremony. It was being conducted by a youngish man he had never seen before, dressed in what looked like an animal skin and holding a large cowrie shell. A ripple of smoke coiled up from this shell

292

and a sweetish aromatic smell seeped into the air: not incense, something herbal, though Daniel couldn't identify it at all. He peered more closely at the man, who was wearing frayed blue jeans, and above them, yes, a wolfskin – as disturbingly wild and primitive as the electrifying drumbeat. The drum itself, painted with a bear's head, was wielded by a second unknown man. He was taller than the first and wore nothing above the waist but an ornate silver pendant and a scruff of gingery chest-hair. As Daniel watched, the drumming gradually softened, subsiding to a gentle stroking movement, almost a caress. Was this the famous New Moon party he had heard discussed so often? No: that was over a week away, and surely even JB, with all his uncanny powers, couldn't tamper with the phases of the moon? He looked up at the sky, as if to check that hadn't happened, but it was too early for a moon of any sort. The last clock he'd seen (on the tower at Greystone Court) had said twenty-five past five, so it must be evening now. But the light was still undimmed; the weather suspended in a brooding tense humidity, which lay heavy on the hills and fields.

JB himself was nowhere to be seen, nor was there any sign of Pippa. Daniel was grateful for both mercies: he didn't want his daughter involved in way-out rites, and if he laid eyes on the healer, he was afraid he might lose his cool and actually attack him.

He emerged from the cover of the bushes and ventured into the field, fascinated and baffled at once. Two concentric circles had been marked out with stones on the grass, the campers forming a third circle around them. He was now in full view, but he realized no one was likely to spot him when they were so caught up in the ritual, every face rapt in concentration. All at once, he saw Penny step into the centre of the inner circle, to join the wolf-clad stranger. What on earth was the fellow doing? He had stooped towards her left foot and seemed to be wafting the smoke from his shell with a sort of feather-fan thing; his rough pelt almost touching her pale body. He continued to fan the fumes in a slow theatrical manner, proceeding up the left leg and the left side of her body, then around the top of her head, and back along the spine, and finally down the right leg to the right foot.

Daniel watched with increasing irritation as the entire process was repeated; the unsavoury-looking man squatting down once more to Penny's feet; his long hair brushing her bare leg. The drumbeats grew more intense, thrumming and vibrating in excitement, while all eyes were fixed on Penny. Suddenly, the wolf-man began to flap his feather-fan around her head, moving it faster and faster like a frenzied circling bird. The drumbeats matched its rhythm, finally pounding to a tumultuous climax.

Daniel turned on his heel and slunk back the way he'd come. He couldn't bear that noise a moment longer – it was too unsettling, even threatening. He also felt completely at a loss. He had returned after just one day's absence to find these two outlandish strangers conducting a ceremony more bizarre than any he'd yet witnessed. They made him feel like an interloper from a more conventional tribe, whose staid and sober members would never dream of prancing around with smoke and drum and feathers, but would remain tamely indoors with their improving books, their rational and demonstrable ideas.

He crossed to the next field, then picked his way through the camp to find his own tent – or rather Penny and Pippa's tent. He had scarcely set foot in it as yet. Inside, it was a tip: piles of dirty clothes left just anyhow; the bedding jumbled, streaked with mud; and a few discarded apple cores giving off a ripe and fusty smell. Penny's sundress lay crumpled in one corner. He picked it up and held it pressed against him for a moment; resolving there and then to sleep in the tent tonight, to get close to her again – close in every sense. Once he had her in his arms, it would be much easier to talk.

Elated by the thought, he set about tidying up; the simple routine task restoring some semblance of order to his life. He folded all the clothes, transferred the rubbish into one large plastic bag, then gave the double sleeping-bag a really vigorous shake. Several things fell out: a sock, another apple core, and an elaborate tortoiseshell hair-comb with a ruched velvet frill attached, which he remembered seeing Corinna wearing. So what was it doing in Penny's sleeping-bag? She couldn't have borrowed it from Corinna – it was useless for short springy hair. That left only one conclusion: they must have been sharing a bed. He slumped down on the groundsheet, staring miserably at the comb. The last thing he needed was any further complications – his mind was confused enough already. And he was worried about Pippa. Had *she* been there, watching her mother canoodling with another woman? And where was she now, for heaven's sake? Penny was obviously too absorbed in wolf-men on the one hand and female liaisons on the other to have time left for her daughter.

He rolled over on his stomach and buried his face in the pile of folded clothes, wishing he could cancel the whole day – the dalliance with Juliet, the horror of the Sayers thing, the disillusion with his parents, and now this new affront. He felt an overwhelming need to sleep; to sink down into a different world where partners were faithful to each other, chaplains were good holy men, parents loved you and protected you, and holidays meant pleasure.

'Gosh, darling, you gave me quite a shock!'

Daniel opened his eyes, found himself staring into Penny's freckled cleavage, exposed by the deep V of her tee-shirt. At first he couldn't remember where he was and took some time to surface; eventually struggling to sit up and rubbing his cramped limbs.

'I'm so glad you're back! I was getting really worried.' She didn't sound worried in the slightest, but bubbly and euphoric, as if she'd had one glass too many. 'I was afraid you'd miss the party.'

'What party?'

'You're not ill, are you?' she asked, ignoring his own question and squatting down beside him.

'No. Just knackered!'

'Well, tonight will perk you up. It's a sort of Native American pow-wow with drumming and dancing and all sorts of chants and songs and things, and it's going on till dawn, and then we greet the rising sun and . . .'

'You can count me out,' he grunted, flopping back on the bedding.

'Oh, don't be a spoilsport! Everybody's coming.'

'Well, *I'm* not.'

'What's the matter, darling?' She reached out and squeezed his hand. 'Has your cold got worse?'

'No,' he lied. 'It's better.'

'Well, didn't you enjoy your day?'

'Oh, yes. It was fantastic!'

'So what did you do? Tell me all about it.'

'I visited this ruined Cistercian abbey . . .' He watched her excitement fade to bored politeness. He couldn't tell her anything – not now. He kicked Sayers and the Cistercians to the cellar of his mind; tried to take an interest in her own day. 'But what about you? What's all this Native American stuff?'

'Oh, it really is amazing!' The exhilaration surged back into her voice. 'I hardly know where to start. We've learned such masses today, my head's in a total spin. You see, these two Robins showed up and . . .'

'Robins? You mean birds?'

She laughed. 'No, silly – *people*! Two marvellous men who both happen to be called Robin. They met in Dakota where they were working with healers from the Plains Tribes. We call one Robin and the other Rob, so they don't both answer at once! But they've got these medicine names as well – names the natives gave them, which they use in the formal ceremonies. Rob is Dancing Antelope and Robin's Wolf Warrior.'

Daniel bit back a retort. Perhaps he, too, should invest in a new name – Wounded Hart or Moping Ruminant. He did feel utterly deflated. How could he spend the night with Penny if she planned to sing and dance from dusk to dawn, and had two new rival healers to bewitch her? 'But where's what's-his-name?' he asked. 'Stephen, as you call him. Has he left, or something?'

'Of course not! Rob and Robin only came here because they're friends of his. Apparently, they all spent some time together in Peru. They were studying there with another shaman several years ago.' She unbuckled her sandals, wiggled her grubby toes. 'No, Stephen's gone on a mission of mercy. A local farmer called here, to beg help for his wife. I'm not sure what was wrong with her, but Stephen went rattling off in the farmer's ancient Land-Rover and told the Robins to hold the fort till he got back. Oh, Daniel!' She knelt up, took his hand again, her face radiant, alert. 'The native traditions are absolutely magical! We've just had this fabulous pipe ceremony . . .'

'Yes, I saw you.'

'You *saw* us? When?'

'Before I crashed out here. Heaven knows what time it was. I heard the noise and watched you for a while. Your Wolf Warrior chappie seemed to be blowing smoke on your legs. Funny sort of ceremony!'

'Oh, that wasn't the ceremony. That was smudging.'

'What?'

'Smudging. It's what you do first, to purify everything – the pipe, and all the people taking part, and the sacred space itself. It's like a sort of smoke-bath. You burn these special herbs, you see. Robin brought them with him. Desert sage – that gets rid of all the negative energies. And lavender, for forgiveness, and something called sweetgrass, which Robin says brings beauty into your life.'

Exactly what I need, thought Daniel: one waft from Robin's magic fan and I'll be able to forgive the beauteous Sayers, and everything will be sweetness and light.

Penny was still talking, leaning forward and gesturing exuberantly. 'You burn them in a shell because that's the water element. The herbs themselves are the earth element, and the smoke's the air, so you end up with all four elements – fire, air, earth and water. They're really keen on symbols. Rob explained it all. The bowl of the pipe represents everything that's female in the universe, and the stem is everything male. So when you join them in the Pipe Ceremony, that's a symbol of making love.'

'Penny . . .' He longed to stop her at that point; turn symbol into fact. But she hardly seemed to notice he had spoken.

'It's also a symbol of the whole of creation. In fact, what I really like about their ideas is the way they see everything as one, with no great gulf between animals and men, or even animate and inanimate. I mean, when Robin had finished the ceremony, and we'd each gone into the circle and offered prayers and things, he asked Great Spirit to hear our prayers and then he said, "for all our relations". At first I thought he was referring to his family, but Rob explained that the phrase means all of creation – what he calls cloud-people, and stone-people, and standing-people (they're trees), and winged people, and four-legged people and two-legged people. Don't you think that's beautiful – that clouds and stones and trees and birds and animals are all part of us and joined to us?'

'Yes, I suppose it is,' said Daniel bleakly.

'Actually, I kept thinking of you, darling, because there was so much stress on tobacco. It seemed funny really – there you are, trying to give it up as an anti-social vice, while for them it's the central part of a ceremony! Apparently, spirits love tobacco. So when you build the Medicine Wheel, you sprinkle some between the stones, to attract them. Then you fill the pipe with seven separate pinches of tobacco and offer the first pinch to Great Spirit and the rest to the six Directions – that's Grandfather Sky, Grandmother Earth, and each of the four winds.'

Daniel could suddenly see Sayers's pipe, sitting dead and cold in the ashtray; smell that tobacco-breath again. Would the vile smell ever leave him? He grabbed Penny's arm, tempted to blurt out the whole story.

She misinterpreted the gesture as interest in what she was saying, and continued with even more enthusiasm. 'I mean, what on earth would you have done, darling, if you'd been there when we smoked the pipe? We all had a little puff, you see, and I wondered if you'd find it just too tantalizing, and all your resolutions would go phut. Corinna and I were laughing about it afterwards.'

Daniel froze. 'Listen,' he said, distracted now from Sayers. 'You and Corinna . . .' What could he say without sounding jealous or offensive, or even slightly paranoid? He said nothing, in the event, since Penny had jumped in again.

'Oh, Corinna adored the whole thing! In fact, she and I did a lot of the initial work building the Medicine Wheel. You have to find these special stones to mark out the circles on the grass, so you go on what's called a power-walk and ask Great Spirit for help. Circles are terribly important, Robin says.'

Yes, he thought, and so is our relationship: it's falling apart, and you seem blithely unaware.

'We'll be doing circle dances tonight. You must come, Daniel, and meet the Robins for yourself. And there's another super couple who arrived today. You'll really like them – I know you will. She's an aromatherapist and he's . . .'

'Look, I'm sorry, Penny, but I don't feel up to a party.'

'But we've just had a whip-round to pay for all the food and stuff, and I chipped in a fair bit – enough for the three of us. In any case, it'll make you feel much better, darling. Drumming changes the energies. Robin says it's been scientifically proved. It actually influences the biochemistry of the brain, so if you're feeling down, it can alter your whole mood.'

Daniel blew his nose with unnecessary force. Already he disliked the Robins for no other reason than their hold over his credulous wife, who was parroting their every word. 'Where's Pippa?' he asked abruptly. It seemed unlikely in the extreme that his unsociable daughter would want to attend some raucous party, notwithstanding Penny's contribution towards her share of food and drink.

'She's gone to the coast with Judith and Tony. The dog's much better, apparently, so they're having a little jaunt, to celebrate.'

So everyone was celebrating on what for him had become Black Tuesday. His bitter thoughts of Sayers had seeded a new worry over Pippa. 'Do you think she's . . . you know . . . safe with them?' he asked.

'What d'you mean?'

'Well, we don't really know them from Adam.'

'*I* do! I've spent ages talking to them. They're absolute darlings, and solid as a rock. In fact, we're jolly lucky they're here. They've done more for Pippa than I thought anybody could. I must admit I'm a little disappointed that Stephen hasn't done his stuff and given her a private session. But then I suppose he's frightfully busy – not just with the people here, but being called out to all and sundry in the area. And anyway perhaps he's wise enough to know that Pippa can be helped best through the dog. I mean, we've seen it for ourselves, darling. It's really taken her out of herself and given her more confidence. Tony even suggested that she's got such a way with animals she should train to be a vet.'

Daniel made no comment. Secretly he had often hoped that Pippa would follow in his footsteps by going up to Cambridge, but he had never expressed the idea in so many words, being always very careful to leave her options open. Tony, clearly, had no such scruples, and had now added career-adviser to his role of substitute father. He fidgeted on the groundsheet. The tent was claustrophobic, and seemed to be sweating as they were themselves; the air inside stale and over-breathed. Noises drifted through the flaps – voices, laughter, the yelping of some other dog – but he felt cut off from that outside world; cut off even from Penny. She was sitting so close he could smell her flowery talc and the wood-smoke in her hair; could see the outline of her nipples pushing against her tee-shirt, yet it was impossible to touch her, to lean down and kiss the cleft between her breasts. He was so preoccupied with her body – the bare expanse of thigh where her full skirt had rucked up – that he was startled when she spoke again, returning his attention to Pippa and the problems.

'Actually, they should be back quite soon. They've only gone to Aberystwyth. Pippa liked the name! And tomorrow they're taking her to see a Roman gold mine. It's much better for her to be out and about. When she's here all day, she gets very edgy, especially with Rick.'

'There's nothing wrong with Rick.'

'Maybe not, but Pippa seems . . . well, frightened of him.'

'That's stupid. He's just a harmless boy. And anyway he's desperately shy – I bet he's more frightened of *her*.' He heard the tetchiness in his voice, decided not to pursue the matter. He was sick and tired of arguments, and was also beginning to realize that he'd never be able to leave the camp before the end of August – an eternity away. It would be cruel to sever Penny from her Robins, or to deprive Pippa of her pleasure-trips and her bond with Judith and Tony. So once again he was trapped.

'Look' – he tried again – 'why don't *we* go out, the three of us – say the day after tomorrow? I've hardly seen anything of you or Pippa, and this is meant to be our holiday. I wouldn't mind a trip to the coast myself. Or we could drive north to the mountains.'

'Listen, Daniel, darling,' Penny put her arm round him. 'It's good for us to have a break from each other – and that goes for Pippa too. We hardly ever do, you know, and the nuclear family can be awfully sort of stifling.'

So Corinna says, he muttered under his breath. Or maybe Rob or Robin. 'Nuclear family' wasn't an expression Penny used.

'What did you say?'

'Nothing.' He didn't trust himself to speak again. He had given up his own holiday plans and come to Wales for his daughter's sake, and now both Penny and Pippa were going their separate

300

ways. Yet he was uncomfortably aware that it was partly his own fault. From their first or second day here, he had noticed Penny slipping back into that gregarious and carefree lifestyle she had enjoyed before their marriage and which *he* had selfishly stopped. She was obviously so gratified to have her happy anarchy restored, he could understand her desire to escape the restrictions of a much narrower family life. He shook off her encircling arm, interpreting her embrace as a mere clumsy attempt to mitigate the harshness of her words.

'I don't know what's got into you, Daniel. You really seem down in the dumps. Which is all the more reason for you to come tonight. Drums are fantastically powerful. Rob says they're alive – living creatures like ourselves. They can heal us and transform us, connect us with the rhythm of the earth. And he's brought this marvellous rattle – a genuine native one, with bird feathers on top. You see, the sound of the rattle wards off evil spirits, so . . .'

'Oh, Penny, for God's sake! You can't expect me to swallow that.'

'Hold on a minute. You don't even understand. Rob says evil spirits can mean simply hatred or depression. You don't have to take it literally.'

'Rob says a lot of things.'

'Yes, he does. And some of them are brilliant. He really makes you think. If only you'd open your mind for once, instead of being so suspicious . . .'

He snatched up the tortoiseshell hair-comb, clenched it in his hand. He hated being labelled suspicious – Penny and Corinna condemning his closed mind (as JB had done already), then taking advantage of his absence.

'You can even play the drum yourself, if you like. Rob let me have a go. He told me in private that the rhythm works like an orgasm – a huge release of pent-up energy, then peace and relaxation.'

'Right,' he said through gritted teeth, 'I *will* come.' He gripped the comb so fiercely its teeth dug into his palm. If his only prospect of an orgasm was to be via Rob's libidinous drumming, well, he'd better seize his chance.

*　　*　　*

301

> '*Hey-ya Hey-ya We-ya, Hey-ya Hey-ya We-ya,*
> *Hey-ya-ya Hey-ye-ya, Hey-ya-ya Hey-ye-ya,*
> *Hey-ya Hey-ya We-ya, Hey-ya Hey-ya We-ya,*
> *Hey-ya-ya Hey-ye-ya, Hey-ya-ya Hey-ye-ya.*'

'Now howl like wolves,' Rob instructed.

Daniel's howl was the loudest and the longest, braying from his throat and ripping through the darkness. He was enjoying this, most definitely. He'd been several different animals in turn – a buffalo, a leopard, a bull, and now a wolf. Rob had taught them the Wolf Chant and was providing an accompaniment with native drum and rattle. Penny was quite right – the sound was immensely powerful and *did* change the energies. He hadn't understood her jargon at the time, but now he felt the change at some deep instinctive level. All the heavy head–stuff (as Rob called it) had disappeared entirely, and he had discovered a new self – supercharged, dynamic, and located in his body, not his inhibited mind. Of course, it could be connected with the contents of his glass. He had no idea what was in it (except it was something extremely potent), nor why indeed they were allowed alcohol at all. JB was still absent, so perhaps what the eye didn't see . . . Or maybe the Robins had different rules, or there were special dispensations for parties. He took another generous swig. Anyway, who cared about the reasons? The brew was tangy and full–bodied – exactly what he needed to get out of his head. Even his cold had improved dramatically. He was no longer so bunged up and had hardly needed to blow his nose in the last couple of hours.

> '*Hey-ya, Hey-ya, We-ya, Hey-ya, Hey-ya!*'

He gave every 'ya' a yodelling trill, drumming on his knees in time with Rob. He envied Robin his wolf-skin, though Penny had told him he looked pretty good himself. He had kestrel feathers in his hair, and Claire had painted his face for him, really taken trouble with it. Some of his fellow revellers were in full-scale fancy dress, improvised from rugs or bath-towels, or had borrowed each other's clothes – Tony in Jeanette's nightgown, Dylan in Happy's sari, and Happy herself looking quite spectacular in another animal-skin (presumably loaned by the Robins, who had also brought body-paint and feathers, various exotic headdresses and a second drum, wielded by a triumphant Rick).

Impulsively, Daniel pulled Happy to her feet, whirling her into a Dionysian dance, inspired by the rhythm of the rattle and the drum. Claire and Penny immediately joined in, then Corinna, Gerard, Dylan, Len – all cavorting round the fire and still whooping out their wolf-cries. Daniel watched their silhouettes crossing and re-crossing, converging in a flickering haze. He seemed to be fusing with the other dancing bodies, losing his own boundaries, merging with the night itself. The whole atmosphere was magical – the moon silvering the field, the flames casting leaping shadows, the smell of burning sage – and yes, the sense of being one with the spirit of the earth, as Penny had explained. Daniel had never felt so close before to the sky, the clouds, the stars; could touch them if he leapt a fraction higher; just as he could feel each blade of grass beneath his jouncing feet.

'We've lost touch with our roots,' Claire had told him while she was painting his face, 'which means we're cut off from the ground of our being, the dark eternal earth.' He had dismissed her words, like Penny's, as just more mumbo-jumbo, but again he'd been mistaken. He was aware now of those roots, anchoring him, supporting him; was experiencing that healing bond with the whole enchanted universe. He longed to do more than dance; to leave the confines of the circle and break free into the countryside. Robin had helped each of them to find their totem animals, and his was the Plains Buffalo, imposing and immense. He could see it pawing the ground, flicking its tail, snorting out great bison-breaths, in response to the wild drumming.

Suddenly, he *was* the beast – hooves pounding, nostrils flaring – charging across the field. And the field itself was changing – no longer bounded by a fence, no longer in mid-Wales, but expanding into the vast untrammelled prairies of primitive America, when buffalo were safe still from the white man's deadly rifles and roamed the plains in thousands. He was part of a vast herd, those majestic thousand thousands stampeding along behind him, throwing up the dust. The wild rhythm of their thundering hooves was combining with the frenzy of the drumbeat to pound away the horrors of his day. The harsh crack of the rattle was rooting out evil spirits, who were then demolished by those mighty crushing hooves – Sayers trampled into nothing, gored by ruthless horns. He could feel his own horns, curving from his massive head; the long shaggy hair heavy on his neck; the sheer power of his huge flanks. He bellowed in excitement as he plunged faster, faster, faster; swept along from Missouri to Dakota, from exhaustion to elation, until he was exploding in a tumult of sound and speed – release.

He stumbled to a halt, flung himself panting on the grass; gazed up at the stars. He was buffalo and white man; Indian and eagle; star and stone and tree. Grandfather Sky watched over him; Grandmother Earth enfolded him, and his racing heart was beating to her rhythm. He was united with the cloud-people, the winged people, the stone-people, and somewhere in the distance his own two-legged people were singing a new chant; their voices like a summons and a spell.

He walked slowly back to join them, still marvelling at his new-discovered world; the tender grass beneath his feet, the mysterious clouds above, the blaze of lamps and torches mastering the darkness. He slipped into the circle, Penny one side, Claire the other, Rob right opposite; the words of the chant now rising all around him:

> *'Air moves us*
> *Fire transforms us*
> *Water shapes us*
> *Earth heals us.'*

He was intensely aware of each element as they created it in song – the night air on his face, the convulsive crackling flames, the rippling water in the stream, the strong heartbeat of the earth.

> *'And the circle of the wheel*
> *Goes round and round*
> *Goes round and round.*
> *The circle of the wheel goes round.'*

He gazed round their own circle, feeling a deep bond with every person there; even with Corinna, who no longer seemed a threat;

even with the new arrivals, Andrew and Anita, who had struck him on first meeting as weird in the extreme. They had spent the earlier part of the evening semi-naked, engaged in their own mini-orgy underneath the trees. Now they had returned, however, Andrew hand in hand with Gerard, Anita next to Doris. Pippa had also kept her distance from the mêlée, and been sitting with Judith in another part of the field, but they too had joined the circle. Pippa seemed miraculously normal, actually singing with real verve, and exchanging smiles with Tony. Even Rick was transformed; no longer sullen or rebellious, but an enthusiastic shaman pounding his incantatory drum.

'Earth heals us,' Daniel sang, suddenly knowing it was true. Everyone was healed – pale decrepit Doris glowing in the firelight; Len's normally suspicious eyes shining with new fervour; Claire a soaring eagle in her dramatic feathered headdress. He relished the strong contrasts between light and dark, heat and cold: the black night closing in beyond the bright grin of the fire; the ground cool and damp beneath him, while his face was scorching hot; the moon gliding in and out of the clouds – now brilliant, now obscured.

> '*Round and round*
> *Round and round*
> *The circle of the wheel goes round.*'

As the last chorus died away and the drumming slowly subsided, Robin rose to his feet, resplendent in his wolf-skin.

'Great Spirit,' he prayed, extending his arms to the sky. 'We are one with you, one with the moon and stars and with all celestial beings. We are the old people; we are the new people; we are the sacred people, who come to you in wisdom and . . .'

His words were interrupted by a sudden squall of rain, falling with such force and fury it seemed as if Great Spirit was not benevolent at all, but was answering Robin's prayer with a torrent of abuse. There was a wild flurry of activity as everybody dashed for shelter; clothes and feathers sodden; flames hissing out their protest as the fire was doused in seconds. Tony hoisted Doris into his arms and ran with her towards the tents, while Rob tried in vain to protect his precious drum. Rick was hunched over his own drum, loping awkwardly along; his hair in rats' tails, his shirt clinging to his back. Happy shouted in alarm as the glass cracked on her gas-lamp. Dylan rushed to help, but tripped on his sari and fell headlong on the grass. Gerard doubled back to rescue him, dodging the gyrations of Andrew and Anita, who were performing an ecstatic rain-dance, water streaming down their still half-naked bodies. Daniel left them to it, more concerned for Penny. He took her arm and steered her across the field, which was already liquefying into mud. Pippa had gone on ahead with Judith, and he could just make out the pair of them lurching over the tussocky grass, trying to see their way.

He pulled Penny to a stop, kissed her there and then in the middle of the field, the rain slamming down on their heads. She didn't pull away, although they were in full view of Corinna, but responded to him ardently. He could feel her warm wet body pressed close against his own as she returned his kiss, prolonged it. They were both absolutely drenched, but he didn't give a damn. He was in tune with all creation, so if Sister Rain chose to drum down on the tent all night as he drummed into Penny, well, the best of luck to all of them. He, the Great Plains Buffalo, was about to claim his mate again, with the blessing of Great Spirit.

24

DANIEL JERKED AWAKE. Rain was lashing against the canvas, the tent straining at its guy-ropes like a panicked bucking horse. He disentangled his limbs from Penny's and fumbled for the torch. She didn't stir, only mumbled in her sleep. He was amazed that *he* had managed to sleep in what sounded like a force ten gale. But then he'd been awake the last three nights in equally wild weather, and was so exhausted yesterday evening he must have just crashed out. But now the alarm clock of the wind prevented any chance of further sleep.

He wormed out of the sleeping-bag and struggled into his waterproofs, cursing the constricted space. Before venturing outside, he went to check on Pippa in the other half of the tent – a separate sleeping compartment, slightly smaller than their own. She was wide awake, sitting up with her arms hugged round her chest, looking desolate and scared.

'All right, darling?' he whispered.

She nodded, shivering.

'I'm just going to tighten the guy-ropes.'

'Want me to help?'

'No, you sit tight. It's absolutely bucketing down.'

'I know! I've been listening to it for ages.'

'Why didn't you come and get us?'

She didn't answer. Daniel squatted awkwardly beside her, noting that her eyes were red and puffy. Judith and Tony had left two days ago, and she was so upset at their departure, she had been crying off and on since then, sobbing herself to sleep at night. He longed to comfort her, but there was little he could say to make up for the loss of that adoring faithful dog. And whatever words he chose, he knew they wouldn't get through to her. She was shut off once again in her own isolated world; her wretchedness

307

a barrier between them. He glanced at her peaky face. If he was tired, then she must be dead beat. The uneasy silence in the tent made the wind sound even louder. It was like another person who had joined them for the night – a demented lunatic who kept stirring everything up, becoming more and more hysterical.

'Well, I'd better brave the elements!' he said at last, with an unconvincing laugh. He touched her shoulder nervously, relieved she didn't flinch away from what he'd intended as a gesture of affection. Did he dare go further and give her a real hug? No. He still felt somehow dangerous – that baleful person who threatened her whole sanity and happiness, according to JB.

He crept back to the entrance of the tent, peering down at Penny's sleeping form. She was still dead to the world, despite the shuddering of the tent-poles, the frenzied canvas flapping back and forth. He pulled on his gum-boots, ducked out through the flaps. The wind hurled itself against him as if involved in some personal vendetta. He could barely withstand its savagery as it clawed his waterproofs, trying to tear them from his back; whipped his hair wildly around his face. The tent itself seemed about to blow away; one tent-peg out already, its guy-rope whirling helplessly, the others stretched to breaking point. He fought his way to each one in turn, the rain stinging on his face as he hammered in the pegs. The sky was remorselessly dark, but he could just make out two huddled figures engaged in a similar battle. He lurched across to see if he could help; found Gerard and Dylan, clad in dripping plastic macs, anchoring their tent against the gale.

'Need a hand?' he called, voice shredded into tatters.

'No, I think we're winning, thanks!' Gerard shouted back.

Over the last few days, a spirit of camaraderie had been building among the campers – the brave few who remained. The appalling weather had driven many of their band away, those too frail or too impatient to contend with continuous heavy rain. Doris and Esther had gone, as well as Len, Jeanette and their (uncured) daughter Sharon. The two Robins had also left, to run a Healing Circle in Glastonbury – out of doors again. How could anyone be healed, thought Daniel, living in such unspeakable conditions? His own cold had got worse, or perhaps he'd caught a second one from Andrew, whose semi-naked cavortings the evening of the pow-wow had brought retribution in the form of a sore throat. His nose was running now, though that seemed only natural, with everything around him streaming and dripping.

He struggled back towards his tent, his clumsy boots squelching in the morass of sticky mud. Every camper's clothes were spattered with that mud; every pair of wellingtons heavy with its coating; even the bedding caked with it, and every car brown-streaked. He kept his head bent low as he tried to stand his ground against the wind; stopping in his tracks as he heard a muffled shout from Claire's tent. The whole thing had collapsed and was reduced to a heap of tangled canvas; she and Rick were trapped beneath the wreckage.

He staggered over to rescue them, almost colliding with Anita, who had just emerged and was looking round in consternation; a garish yellow cycling cape bellying out above her pink pyjamas. She and Daniel scrabbled to find the opening of the grounded tent, and yanked it apart while Claire and Rick crawled out. Claire was whimpering with pain. She had been hit on the head by a tent-pole, and a second bruise was swelling on her knee. Rick meanwhile was complaining about the huge black slugs he had inadvertently put his hand on as he wriggled free of the canvas.

'Come and join us in our tent,' Anita offered, her drenched pyjama bottoms clinging to her skinny legs; her hair plastered to her head. 'Everything's wet through inside, but at least the thing's still standing!' She took Claire's arm, while Daniel clumped along behind with a still protesting (and bare-footed) Rick.

'I've just trodden on another frigging slug! They're ankle-deep in this lousy field. If this is Mum's idea of a holiday, she must be even madder than I thought.'

'Perhaps she's into Outward Bound,' Daniel suggested with a grin. He and Rick had developed a style of jokey solidarity, though it was difficult to sustain in this all-consuming fight against the elements.

He heard another shout behind him, turned to see Corinna and JB, armed with a powerful flashlight which cut a welcome swathe across the darkness.

'Quick!' Corinna called. 'Everyone into Rainbow Lodge! Forget the tents – they're useless in this weather.'

Claire doubled back to clutch Daniel's arm, all but sobbing with relief. 'Just the thought of a fire!' she exclaimed. 'And a cup of hot sweet tea. And something dry to sit on.'

'And more slugs, no doubt,' Rick put in, *sotto voce*, accepting the waterproof jacket which JB was holding out to him before the angry wind could snatch it up instead.

'I'd better get Andrew,' Anita said. 'He's feeling so lousy with his throat, even this gale wouldn't budge him from the tent, but a hot drink might change his mind.'

She veered away, soon obscured by the sheeting rain, while JB rescued Gerard, who was floundering in the mud. Dylan followed disconsolately, his frail form almost lost in his all-enveloping mac, his fading torch-beam bobbing about like a tiny helpless boat adrift on a black sea.

'I'll join you in a moment,' Daniel shouted, picking his way back to his own tent; each step slow and clumsy as the wind tried its vicious best to batter him off-course. Pippa was watching for him anxiously; Penny still miraculously asleep. He secured the guy-ropes once again, then went to wake her up; tell her they were transferring to the tepee. It was some time before she realized what was happening, although the tent was blowing almost inside out; the canvas heaving all around her and bulging down so low it almost touched her face. He passed her her mud-encrusted boots, helped Pippa into her anorak. Rain was spitting in at them from the entrance of the tent, and a black dustbin-bag suddenly whirled in from outside, spinning like a dervish.

'Can't we stay here?' Pippa begged, dodging out of its way.

'No, darling, I'm afraid we can't. This gale is really nasty and everything's getting soaked. It'll be much drier in the tepee – not to mention safer – and the fire will warm you up.'

'I'm not cold,' she said through chattering teeth.

'Come on – up and out!'

He marshalled them in front of him, shining the torch to light their path, though the lowering darkness seemed to swallow up the puny beam. The wind was like machine-gun fire, exploding in their ears, and the conditions did indeed remind him of a war: the same sense of fear and chaos in the blackout; the same disorientation as all normal landmarks vanished and they were assailed by hostile forces entirely beyond their control. The short distance to the tepee had become a daunting route march. They were blitzed by wind and rain, slowed by viscous mud, unsure what might hail down on them from the enemy in the sky.

They removed their boots outside the lodge; Pippa shrinking back as she heard the sound of singing. He, too, felt nervous at the thought of all that matey bonhomie, though Penny was already bounding in. He followed more reluctantly with Pippa; found the war spirit once again in evidence: tea being brewed; wet clothes drying by the fire; the troops belting out a rousing tune to keep up their morale. He hovered by the wood pile, self-conscious with so many eyes turned in his direction, but attracted by the cosy fug, the smell of fragrant wood-smoke and hot toast. This large and sturdy tepee provided a genuine shelter from the storm, and although the poles were creaking and the canvas straining like a ship under sail, it was a doughty ship which wouldn't sink or founder.

He knew he must join the circle, not stay skulking at the back. He'd been told often enough by Penny and Corinna that circles were not only companionable, but sacred – a universal symbol of wholeness and perfection, infinity, eternity (and also represented feminine power: unbounded, oceanic, and opposed to 'straight' masculine power, whatever that might be). Even living in a tepee was apparently healing in itself, not only through the potency of its circular shape, but because it allowed direct contact with restorative Mother Earth. He shuffled forward, Pippa trying to hide behind his back. Claire smiled at him encouragingly, beckoning him over with her eyes. He hesitated. Pippa would object to being dragged so close to Rick. She was still extraordinarily hostile to the boy, and though he was baffled by her attitude, this was hardly the time to challenge it. It was enough that they got through the night without any further crises.

He steered her firmly by the elbow, and squeezed between Dylan and Anita, judging them relatively innocuous, and certainly preferable to Megan and her vile son Tim, who had arrived the day after the pow-wow in a clapped-out Daimler hearse. Megan had brought her elder sister Pat, who was said to be suffering from a malignant tumour on her thigh, though her strapping build and ruddy cheeks made her look anything but ill. Tim was there on sufferance, since there was no one to look after him at home – a fractious, unattractive child, who, although he was almost four (and thus not far off school-age), was still being breast-fed by his doting New Age mother. Even now, he was pushing up her jumper to grab a floppy breast, cramming it into his mouth and sucking with a violent greed. Daniel switched his gaze to the fire. He knew that women such as Megan considered breast-feeding a natural healthy function which could be performed just as well in public as in private. But personally he found it an embarrassment. It also presented him with a dilemma: if he viewed the proceedings with no hint of reserve, he would feel like a voyeur; if, on the other hand, he averted his eyes, he would doubt-less be thought squeamish or reactionary.

He was relieved when Corinna passed him tea and toast: now he could concentrate on his own ingestion, rather than on Tim's. The toast was charred to a crisp and tooth-breakingly hard. But then cooking on the tepee fire was a hit and miss affair. Only yesterday Happy had ruined a bean and barley stew, which finally emerged as a manure-coloured sludge stiffening on their plates. Still, it would be churlish to complain when he had been rescued from the deluge, warmed from within by scalding nettle tea, sus-tained by dry black toast.

The wind's insistent howling sounded much more muted now, and apart from the odd drip or plop, the rainstorm kept at bay. It was also a relief to be sitting in the light, rather than lying in the endless dark, as he had done the last three nights. A pair of stalwart hurricane lamps cast a soft glow through the lodge, and the fire itself helped dissipate the black void of the night. Even the singing had mercifully petered out, while Happy and Corinna distributed not just sustenance, but relatively dry clothes for those like Rick and Anita who were soaked to the skin, or Andrew, who looked feverish and could speak only in a scratchy grunt. Daniel's eyes kept returning to JB, who was sitting opposite the door, with a rapturous Claire one side of him and a sleepy Pat the other. Wasn't it time he worked a few more miracles – cured Andrew's sore throat, for a start, or better still, followed Christ's example and calmed the raging storm? But his eyes were closed, his expression quite inscrutable, as if he had removed himself in all but bodily presence from the crush of damp humanity around him.

'Okay?' Daniel whispered to Pippa who had abandoned her own slice of toast; taken only a half-hearted sip of tea.

Her nod was equally half-hearted. But then he could hardly expect her to be bouncing with enthusiasm about this eccentric get-together in the middle of the night, cooped up with a bunch of offbeat people she would never have chosen as companions in a thousand years. He felt much the same himself about the company, but made an effort to be sociable, more for Penny's sake than anything. He turned to Anita with some comment on the storm; froze in horror as he saw the glass of golden liquor in her hand. He knew he should be used to it by now, but it never failed to revolt him – the fact that she and Andrew drank their own pee. She endorsed the practice with the name of urinotherapy, claiming that lamas and yogis had been doing it for centuries, which explained their radiant health. He watched her take a generous swig and swallow it with relish; quickly looked away, only to catch sight of Penny feeding Corinna with a flapjack, breaking it into morsels and popping each into her mouth with lingering sensuality. He snapped his own burnt toast between his fingers, crumbled it to dust.

Anita put her glass down, smiled at him encouragingly. 'I hear you're seriously considering living this way permanently?'

'*What?*' he said, aghast.

'Penny was talking to me about it just last night. You see, I used to live in a tepee village – a small one down in Devon. In fact, that's where I met Andrew. It was a wonderful experience! We were absolutely committed to the ideal of community, so we shared everything we had – food, clothes, vehicles – the lot. And there was no division of labour. We took turns at all the chores, whether it was changing dirty nappies, or digging the latrines, or carving tepee poles, or making bread and yoghurt. That broke down the usual barriers between men and women, and parents and non-parents, and drew us all much closer. I mean, Andrew knew nothing about kids. He was an only child, and didn't even have friends with children, so it was enormously enriching for him to share in the child-care and feed other people's babies.'

Daniel looked nervously at Tim again. 'Enormously enriching' was not the phrase he'd use for sharing in this particular child's care. Tim was swilling like a pig at trough; his mouth clamped to Megan's right nipple, while his fist was latched to her left breast, as if he were staking his claim to a second course.

'And we shared our feelings, too,' said Anita, tugging down her borrowed scarlet sweater, which was too short in the body and revealed a gap of naked flesh. 'We had meetings twice a day, when we all opened up and thrashed out any problems, whether it was jealousy, or anger, or maybe someone fancying someone else, or resenting them, or . . .'

'Oh yes,' croaked Andrew, leaning over to join in the conversation. 'I got to understand women terrifically well. I mean, once you've discussed PMT or painful periods, you've got a pretty good idea of what it's like to have a female body.'

'And another thing,' Anita pointed out, 'is that you relearn all the skills you've lost. When people lived more naturally and simply, every member of society could build a shelter, or weave a blanket, or make music, or heal the sick. But we've now handed over those roles to so-called "experts", and impoverished ourselves in the process. But in a commune, you can reclaim your skills, especially if you're living outside, in tune with nature.'

Daniel sipped his tea. He had no wish to weave a blanket, build a shelter, or learn to play a drum, and he felt totally incapable of healing anyone, but he feared Penny might be all too keen on reclaiming her lost skills. And in theory he could sympathize. The notion was actually quite a sound one, and he had to admit to a sneaking admiration for Anita and Andrew's ideals – urinology apart. He had heard them talking two days ago about co-operatives and permaculture, and had felt selfish in comparison: a small-minded materialist, more concerned with feathering his own nest. And although he shied away from the idea of sharing feelings and/or child-care, it couldn't be denied that he might be far less daunted by raw emotion and helpless screaming infants if he'd had more practice in handling both. Yet he doubted if he could change now – he was probably too set in his ways. What he feared was Penny changing – as she'd done already, alarmingly. They seemed set on a collision course: she embracing the community ideal, while he longed to have her to himself in the sort of bourgeois marriage abhorred by New Age thinkers.

'Listen, everybody,' Claire pronounced, breaking into his thoughts and interrupting the general aimless chatter. 'I think we ought to sing one of Robin's chants. They're just the thing for a time like this, because they'll help us to relax. Remember what he said about getting rid of tension by opening up the voice?'

Rick made a face, but the others agreed with alacrity, except for Pippa and JB (still locked away in their mute and private worlds) and Pat, who seemed to be in pain. Daniel had noticed her grimace as she accidentally touched her thigh, then bite her lip, as if trying to restrain her tears. If she did genuinely have cancer, this primitive lifestyle could be really dangerous. Surely she would be better off in hospital than lying sleepless in a tepee with a storm rampaging outside, and forced to endure a raucous singsong on top of everything else.

'Let's have "We Are The Power",' suggested Happy, who was wearing a long nightshirt beneath a shaggy afghan coat (both garments mud-adorned). 'To empower us through the night.'

'Great! I'll be the drum,' joked Anita, seizing two spoons and banging with them rhythmically on Daniel's enamel mug.

He winced. The night of the pow-wow, he'd been able to let go – had loosened up to an incredible extent, in fact – but he attributed that to alcohol. He could hardly get high on nettle tea (or pee). But he was aware of Penny smiling at him eagerly from the other side of the circle, urging him to join in. He mouthed the words at first, feeling inhibited and foolish in the face of Pippa's silent disapproval.

> 'We are the power in everyone
> We are the dance of the moon and the sun
> We are the hope that will never hide
> We are the turning of the tide.'

Tim stopped his suckling, as if affronted by the noise, and gave one last vicious pull before abandoning his mother's sagging breast. Then, continuing his baby act, he crawled into the centre of the circle and began rolling on the ground, milk drooling from his mouth. As he cast around for plaudits from his audience, he fastened on Daniel as his next source of diversion, and, without any warning, hurtled across and threw himself into his lap. Daniel went rigid with embarrassment. Megan was looking at him fondly, evidently expecting him to play father to her adorable little son. The shared child-care had been unexpectedly foisted on him. He tried to make his arms more welcoming, without betraying the distaste he felt. Tim was butting him with his bullet-head, dribbling into his groin, and he was so unnerved by his new role that he went wrong in the singing; his baritone booming up the scale while everyone else went down.

'*We are the hope that will never hide . . .*'

He longed to hide himself – better still to vanish altogether. He envied JB's knack of shutting himself off, as if the drumming rain, the rousing chant and Anita's jangling spoons were all happening on another distant plane. Tim began to scream, not in pain or misery, but emitting howls of sheer animal vitality, as if invigorated by the breast-milk. Daniel stole a glance at Megan (who was wiping her nipple with what looked like a paint-rag); imagined himself for one brief but startling moment suckling from that breast, instead of Tim. In his state of bleak exhaustion, he was attracted to the idea of plugging into an instant supply of nourishment and solace. And how fantastic to be able to sleep somewhere quiet and comfortable: even here in the lodge would do, if only the noise would stop. He wished he dared suggest that they all stretch out and shut up. There was room enough for everyone to lie down, a fire to keep them warm, plenty of rugs and pillows, and nothing to get up for in the morning save more rain, more wind, more mud.

The last words of the chant had died away, but the silence was short-lived.

'Now let's sing "Hepa Hey Ne Ne",' Penny enthused, cuddling even closer to Corinna. 'I really love that one.'

Well, I don't, Daniel thought, as the unearthly sounds soared up to the tepee-poles, merging with the descant of the rain. 'Hepa Hey Ne Ne' meant 'bless the earth', or so he had learned from Rob. At this particular moment, he felt more like cursing it: its damp hardness under his bottom; its refusal to relent and lay on a proper summer. Far from living close to nature, as Anita recommended, he was harbouring heretical thoughts of his house in urban Wandsworth – windproof, dry and probably environmentally unsound.

> '*Hepa hey ne ne, hepa hey ne ne*
> *Hepa hey yana, hey ne yo wey.*'

Anita was going wild with her spoons, Claire beating an accompaniment on her mug and then her knee. Rick added to the din by blowing a tin whistle he had scrounged from Rob before he left, while Penny and Corinna were singing in close harmony and rocking backwards and forwards together, as if they had fused into one body and one voice. Tim's screams had reached a crescendo – he was wolf, hyena, jackal, all in one; a wild uncontrollable animal still butting with its head.

'Stop it!' Daniel snapped. 'We can't hear ourselves sing.'

Tim's only rejoinder was another savage butt. Daniel stumbled to his feet, clutching his bruised chest. He couldn't stand this child a moment longer, nor the general pandemonium. And it was beyond his comprehension how anyone with cancer, who was obviously in pain, could tolerate it either. The decent thing to do would be to invite Pat to sneak out with him, but that was hardly feasible. Instead he whispered to Pippa that he was going to check the car and would she like an excuse to leave? He was stunned when she shook her head. She must fear him more than Rick, if she preferred to stay in this uncongenial company rather than take her chance to escape. JB was truly psychic to have picked up the antipathy between them, when he was only vaguely aware of it himself.

He started edging to the doorway, suddenly realizing that the chant had ended and everyone was looking at him. Even the healer had ceased his self-communing and was gazing at him fixedly. (He had already worked his magic on Tim – the child had quietened instantly and returned tamely to his mother.)

Daniel lowered his own eyes, stood dithering at the entrance. 'I'm . . . er . . . just going to see if the car's all right,' he stammered. 'I'm afraid it may be bogged down in the mud.'

Unlikely, when only yesterday they had moved all the cars to higher ground. Claire and Happy shouted after him, urging him to stay put – the weather was atrocious still and he already had a cold. Even Andrew grunted a hoarse warning, but Daniel ignored them all, went blundering out into the night, the relentless rain drowning every protest.

He rummaged in the back of the car to find another sweater. It was freezing cold without the heater, but he dared not switch it on when he was so worryingly low on petrol. The nearest service station was a good ten miles away, and the narrow lanes had become even more treacherous after four days of non-stop rain. He switched on the radio instead, tuning and retuning in search of the World Service, but all he could get was a crackly Welsh-language broadcast, which sounded as foreign as the 'Hepa hey ne ne', and definitely less benign: some angry man pontificating, by the sound of it. For all he knew, it could be a call to arms; the entire English nation threatened with extinction. He turned it off and listened to the rain, feeling a sense of total impotence that he had no off-switch for the weather; couldn't tune from foul to fair. Irrationally and absurdly, he blamed JB for the storm – it was all part of some malignant plan to test his endurance to the limit, then finally break his spirit. Since arriving at the camp, he seemed to have been living on a roller-coaster – up with Margot's 'miracle'; plunged down at Greystone Court; up again for the pow-wow, but staying down since then. Was there about to be another high?

He peered out at the night: the wind still blustering and whining; no break in the dense clouds; no glimmer yet of daylight. Any improvement seemed unlikely unless JB used his powers; hung a blazing sun in a blue and cloudless sky and ordered the bad weather to stay away for a week or more, until everything was dry. Camping was impossible in these conditions, when they were confined to claustrophobic tents, with damp matches, sodden clothes, a plague of slugs which crawled into the bedding, and a spiteful wind which blew everything away. Washing, dressing, cooking, had all become ordeals, and his thoughts had long since shifted from Third World deprivations to his own longing for the luxury of an electric kettle or tumble-dryer. In the middle of last night, he had drunk a mouthful of fruit juice from the carton and choked on a dead wasp. Then he'd struggled out of the sleeping-bag for a pee, stood behind the tent, with the rain lashing at him – *laughing* at him – while he tried to unzip his flies. (He slept in jeans and sweater – it was too cold for pyjamas.)

And yet, according to Anita, Penny wished to adopt this way of life for good – maybe not living in a tent, but at least in some community. He knew that both Happy and Corinna were keen to start one up, so doubtless Penny had been willingly co-opted as another founder-member. He couldn't quite work out how he fitted into the picture. Would he be expected to give up his job (and Pippa quit her schooling, to learn yoghurt-making or shamanic rites, in place of maths or history), or would a husband and a daughter be regarded as an irrelevance – like sex? He still hadn't managed to make love to Penny, no longer even wanted to. It was too cold and too uncomfortable, and there was rarely any privacy – always some emergency or interruption, as had happened the night of the pow-wow. Just as he'd stripped Penny of her rain-drenched clothes and was about to remove his own, he had heard an anxious Claire shouting from outside: her tent was leaking and could he help her patch the hole? In a matter of seconds, the lusty Great Plains Buffalo had changed to paltry handyman.

Despite the problems, Claire seemed remarkably cheerful. She insisted Rick was cured, although Rick had told him privately that he only pretended his stomach-pains were better, to be excused the odious potions. She had nothing to go home for, except the dole and an empty house, and, like Penny herself, enjoyed the company, the communal meals, and the sense of being part of a fraternity (or sorority he should say, since females still out-numbered males). The more he reflected on it, the more he realized he was out of tune with the others, woefully lacking in community spirit. In theory, he might endorse their principles. Indeed, the whole concept of collectivism and co-operatives struck a chord with his own socialist ideals. But it was much easier to approve such things on paper, or to support them in, say, Israel, or in a safely generalized Third World context, than to rethink one's personal life and maybe lose one's home and whole security.

He fidgeted on the seat, stamping his numb feet to restore the feeling to them. He had no idea what time it was – except it had been night for far too long. He fought a sudden panic. Suppose dawn never came, but darkness followed darkness for the entire rest of his life? He had felt the self-same terror his first night at Greystone Court, lying in his dormitory watching the black fanlight stay black, black, black, black, black. No, he mustn't think of school. It would lead on to thoughts of Sayers, another source of darkness which he was determined to suppress.

He jumped out of the car, slammed the door behind him and dived into the back, shutting out the wind and rain which had seized their fleeting chance to beleaguer him again. He shook the wet off his hair, tried to get more comfortable spread across the seat, first removing all the clutter – the mouldy apples, rotting food, abandoned summer clothes and untouched books. He would relax here for a while, enjoy a brief respite before returning to the fray. He hardly dared imagine what might be happening in the lodge now: rebirthing sessions (Anita's speciality), or shiatsu massage (Andrew's), or working out their astrological compatibilities? Claire had asked him only yesterday if he was Scorpio or Pisces, and when he'd told her neither, she'd seemed genuinely disappointed that his earth sign and her water sign were not altogether harmonious. He tried to keep his mind on fire signs, to provide a spark of inner heat to thaw his frozen limbs. He could scarcely believe it was August, rather than mid-February. He shivered at the allusion. February was Sayers again. Would he ever quash the memories, ever recover from this horrendous trip? Everything was dark – inside, outside, past and future.

He shut his eyes, hid his face in the musty-smelling seat. 'Help me,' he begged silently, wondering who the hell he was addressing – Great Spirit (who had departed with the Robins), his dead and buried childhood God, or that infuriating healer he seemed unable to escape.

25

DANIEL RUBBED THE STEAMED-UP WINDOW and stared out in astonishment at full impressive daylight, shreds of blue in the sky, even glints of sunshine. Once again he had slept – overslept, in fact – in impossible conditions, even in his boots! He had cramp in his left foot, his back was stiff, and his forehead ridged and furrowed from the imprint of the seat. Yet he hadn't woken once – hadn't so much as stirred – despite his uncomfortable position, his restricting waterproofs, and the fact that never in his life before had he managed to drop off in a car.

He refused to give the credit to the healer. It was a fluke, that's all, a proof of how exhausted he was. He opened the door, stepped out and stretched himself, gulping down great draughts of clean fresh air. He was starving hungry, but had probably missed breakfast, if not lunch as well. His thoughts shouldn't be on food, though, but on Penny and Pippa, whom he had abandoned in the middle of the night. Were they anxious, or annoyed with him for managing to sleep, while they'd been forced to stay awake till dawn?

He set off to find out, apprehension weighing on his mind in the same way as the mud dragged at his boots. The weather was much warmer, though; an airless, humid sort of day, which made him sweaty in his layers of windproof clothes. The camp-site looked a wilderness: Claire's tent still horizontal, and several others sagging; plastic bags and empty tins scattered by the wind; branches broken off the trees, and a flotsam of small twigs and leaves clogging every surface. He was surprised that no one was around, clearing up the mess, but the place seemed totally deserted.

He crawled into his own tent, found Pippa curled up in a ball, lying on her sleeping-bag. She sat up as he entered, looking anxious and forlorn.

'What's wrong, darling?'

'N . . . nothing.' Her voice faltered on the brink of tears.

'You're not ill, are you?'

'No.'

'Where's Mum?'

'In the Healing Dome. Everybody's there.'

'Everyone except you and me,' he smiled, trying to create a link between them, however tenuous. 'I'm sorry I disappeared. Believe it or not, I fell asleep in the car, and I've only just come to. Did Mum wonder where I'd got to?'

She shook her head, pulled down her crumpled skirt. He struggled out of his waterproofs, then sat awkwardly beside her on the sleeping-bag, shocked at how damp it was. He heard her take a deep breath in, as if preparing for some physical feat.

'Once the rain had stopped,' she said, her voice so soft he had to strain to hear it, 'Mum and Corinna went to find you in the car and saw you were fast asleep. She said you looked so peaceful, she didn't want to wake you.'

Again, he felt a twinge of disbelief. Could he really have continued sleeping with people peering in at him, or looked peaceful in that cold cramped car? But more important was the fact that Pippa had responded to him; actually uttered two long sentences – well, long compared with her usual terse replies. If only they could continue talking, he might find out what was wrong with her, get close to her once more. She was clearly tired and miserable, cowering here alone, with not so much as a book to distract her, and lying on wet bedding amidst a tide of dirty clothes. He was beginning to feel resentful that JB had done nothing for her. His cures might be spectacular, but they were few and far between. Penny had tried to convince him that their daughter would find healing through her bond with Bernard the dog, but now that bond was severed, any hope of a recovery appeared to have vanished with the dog itself.

'Would you like to go home?' he blurted out impetuously, feeling an instant sense of disloyalty to Penny. 'I mean, all of us? Today?'

He was startled by her response: the way she gripped his arm and whispered '*Can* we?' with such urgency, such a note of desperate longing, his guilt immediately redoubled, and he stammered out a promise to arrange it. He had obviously underestimated how much she loathed this offbeat way of living, without her beloved Bernard to compensate. He was determined now to leave, whatever Penny said. It was unfair to keep the child here when she was so utterly dejected and had no one her own age but Rick.

'Look,' he said, shifting in the restricted space and rubbing his stiff back, 'this thing with you and Rick – he hasn't hurt you, has he, or . . . ?' The memories of Sayers had made him inordinately suspicious, though it seemed unlikely that a shy lad such as Rick, who was usually tongue-tied in her company, would have abused her in any way. Yet he noticed her expression change, the look of fear, distaste. He had been miserable at her age, locked in his own nightmare world, but his parents hadn't known about it. He still felt angry with those parents (or strangers, as they seemed now), who'd been so laudably overburdened with the sufferings of the entire Third World, his own woes had failed to register at all. He couldn't bear to think that he was equally insensitive to what was going on in Pippa's life; ignoring a weight of private pain. Somehow, he had to get through to her. She hadn't answered his question, so he repeated it, rephrased it.

Any reply she might have made was drowned by shouts from outside – eager footsteps, shrill elated voices.

'What on earth's going on?' he frowned.

Pippa shrugged, flinching back from the disturbance into a corner of the tent.

'It sounds like another pow-wow, God forbid!' He ducked out through the entrance, saw all the others streaming from the Healing Dome, babbling with excitement. Andrew and Gerard had lifted Pat shoulder-high and were carrying her in procession. Megan followed with Tim in her arms; she crying, he laughing; both sounding near-hysterical. Claire and Happy were clinging to JB, Claire kissing his neck, twining her fingers through his long loose wavy hair. Penny and Corinna were almost dancing along, exchanging jubilant glances, while Dylan and Anita brought up the rear, leaning on each other, as if too dazed to walk without support. All the faces wore a look of triumph, like victors in a war, or devotees who had attained a state of nirvana.

He felt totally excluded – the loser, the non-combatant, the uninitiate.

'What's happened?' he asked Penny, sidling up behind her; his curiosity overcoming his embarrassment at being the only one in ignorance.

'Pat's been healed! Completely. Her tumour's disappeared.'

'Another miracle!' Claire exulted, stroking the healer's arm, to absorb his magical energies.

'I prefer not to use that word,' JB reproved her gently.

'Why not, when it's the right one? Pat's doctor said her cancer was incurable.'

JB stopped, as if to give his words more weight, addressing not just Claire, but all of them. '"Incurable" only means that medicine can do no more. It takes no account of higher forces. There are no limitations to healing, other than those we set ourselves. If we truly believe we can recover, then we will.'

'That's bloody nonsense!' Daniel exploded, thinking of his father, who'd had almost superhuman confidence in his ability to survive a stroke and then a heart attack, but had died still fighting death. He backed away in confusion when he saw the hostile glances aimed in his direction. He had discredited their miracle; the once euphoric revellers now patently resentful, and Megan complaining fiercely about his rudeness to the healer.

He hardly knew whether to apologize or to return to the attack. These people had become his friends, or at least his comrades in adversity. The hazards of the last few days had created a sympathy between them. Yet now he was the killjoy who had stopped the joyous cavalcade; thrown cold water on their flames of triumph. Gerard and Andrew set Pat down on her feet, while Claire gazed at him reproachfully, as if he were Judas to the healer's Christ. He was closer to Claire than anyone, yet when he watched her fawning on JB, smothering his neck with kisses, it aroused an incoherent rage in him. He was overreacting again, of course, but the horror of the Greystone Court affair had stirred up an inner ferment he found it impossible to control.

Penny reached out and squeezed his hand in an attempt to calm him down, include him in the group. He drew her back the other way, safely out of earshot. 'I need to talk to you,' he whispered, cursing the fact that it was virtually impossible ever to get her on her own.

'Can't it wait?' hissed Penny. 'We're on our way to Pat's tent, to celebrate her cure.'

'No, it can't,' he griped, suddenly enraged at her obtuseness. If she was close to him at all, she should *know* he was upset; use her intuition to detect his inmost feelings. Couldn't she see that something had happened to him, and what a bad state he was in? And what about her daughter? It didn't appear to bother her in the slightest that two out of the three of them were loathing every minute of this so-called holiday.

Lowering his voice still further, he turned his back on the group, deliberately avoiding Corinna's cold blue stare. 'I've just promised Pippa that we're going home today.'

'*What?*'

'Well, she really does seem miserable. And I honestly don't think it's fair to inflict another fortnight on her.'

'Look, we can't talk here,' said Penny, frowning at Rick, who had pushed his way towards them and was trying to catch Daniel's eye.

'No,' said Daniel, 'you're right.' He took her arm and marched her away, she protesting at his vehemence.

'Not so fast! I'll break my ankle if you drag me along like that. Where are we going, anyway?'

'Just somewhere we can sit in peace and talk without an audience.'

'Well, I can't be long. I want to get back to Pat.'

'For Christ's sake, Penny! We've hardly had a moment to ourselves since we arrived here.' He strode on up the hill, making for a stump of wall – wreckage from the lead mine. He brushed the debris from it and sat down.

Penny panted after him, tripping on a half-hidden ledge of stone. 'Listen, Daniel, will you? I've just witnessed something absolutely riveting; something which has changed my life – and might change yours as well, if you weren't so self-obsessed – and you have to go and ruin it.'

'That's not fair,' he countered, wounded by the 'self-obsessed'.

'Yes, it is. You've upset all the others by your attitude, and you're so concerned with going home to your petty little comforts, you don't seem to understand that we're living in the company of an amazing man who can actually work miracles.'

He sprang up to his feet again, his anger surging back. 'You've no proof it was a miracle. How the hell do you know the tumour's gone? Did you rush Pat to the hospital for x-rays?'

'There's no need to be sarcastic. And anyway I *have* got proof. I felt the lump myself, last night. It was really quite grotesque – very big and hard, rather like a cricket ball. And now it's vanished – just like that.'

He began pacing to and fro, hands thrust in his pockets, brow creased in a frown. Penny might be scatty, but she had never been given to delusions. And what about the earlier healing he had witnessed for himself – Margot's sight restored?

'Look, I'm sorry,' he said gruffly. 'I just find all this miracle stuff pretty hard to take.'

'Well, so do I, if you really want to know.' She slumped down on a pile of shale, grimacing at the sharpness of the stones. 'I was a bit suspicious when Pat said she had cancer in the first place. I mean, she looks so hale and hearty. But Megan told me that's deceptive and she's lost all her usual energy and had to give up her job. And she's also in a lot of pain, but because she's a real fighter, she tends to play it down, so that people think it's nothing. Well, I misjudged her myself, didn't I, and even Corinna had her doubts. I think that's why Megan suggested we should all *feel* the lump for ourselves – to prove her sister wasn't a fraud.' Penny picked up a large stone, as if to demonstrate, running her hands across it. 'Then, later on, Pat told me the whole story. Apparently the lump was only small when she first noticed it, and she thought she must have banged her leg or something. But it gradually got bigger and bigger, so after about six months she went to see her GP. He arranged a biopsy, and they told her at the hospital that it was what they call a sarcoma – a malignant tumour of the bone – and there was no hope of a cure. In fact, they even hinted that it could be fatal within a matter of months.'

Daniel wrenched out a fistful of grass and started shredding it between his fingers. 'But how could anything as serious as that just . . . just melt into thin air?'

'Search me! The whole experience was absolutely shattering.' She drew him down towards her, placed her warm hand on his arm. 'Oh, Daniel, let's not quarrel. This is such a special day, it seems criminal to spoil it. I only wish you'd been there.'

'So do I!' How could he make a judgement, either favourable or hostile, if he hadn't witnessed the proceedings for himself? It seemed ironic that he should have slept through Penny's 'shattering experience', when his usual problem was insomnia.

Penny slipped an arm around his waist, gazing into the distance with a look of baffled wonder. 'It wasn't just the miracle, it was the extraordinary way it happened. You see, Stephen seemed to be struggling at first, as if the healing wasn't easy for him, or he was being tested to the limit. In fact, it all got rather heavy, and we were sitting there screwed up and tense, and hardly daring to breathe. And then gradually he changed before our eyes.'

'Changed? What d'you mean?'

'Became a different person.' She noted his incredulous look, pounded her fist on her lap. 'Oh, it's so frustrating, darling! I knew when I told you, you'd say it was preposterous, and I honestly don't blame you. If I hadn't seen it with my own eyes, I wouldn't have believed it either. Look, let me try to explain.' She chewed her thumb a moment, straining to find words. 'First of all, his voice changed. It went really deep and rumbling, which was uncanny in itself. I mean, he's never spoken like that before. And it didn't fit his age or build or anything, but seemed to be coming from someone else. And then his face and body changed. He became older, bit by bit, and his skin got dark and swarthy, like an Indian's, and he even had a beard.'

'Oh, Penny, that's crazy! You sound as if you're off your rocker.'

'I know I do. But everybody saw it – not just me.'

'Well, you must have been hallucinating – the whole damned lot of you. A case of mass hysteria, I reckon.'

'That's hardly likely, is it, first thing in the morning in the cold clear light of day?'

'But you were awake the whole of last night, weren't you? So it could have been caused purely by lack of sleep.'

'No, it couldn't. We all kipped down soon after you'd gone. The rain stopped very suddenly, and once I'd been to check you were okay, I came back to the tepee and went out like a light.'

Daniel didn't answer. It seemed his wife had been bewitched, though he suspected it had less to do with the supernatural than with the compelling force of Eros. She was clearly infatuated with 'Stephen' – her father-figure/lover. And Claire, Corinna and Happy were all equally adoring, and could easily have convinced themselves that their hero had uncanny powers. As for Andrew and Anita, they were so way out themselves (believing in Tarot cards and angels, and refusing to wear shoes, for fear of harming the ground), that their testimony would hardly count in any case. But what about Dylan and Gerard? He had got to know them better in the last few days, and though they were both highly strung and shy, they were undeniably intelligent; not the types to swallow signs and wonders without demanding evidence. And Pat herself seemed very down to earth; a no-nonsense sort of woman, who, he'd heard from Megan, had a degree in biochemistry. A scientific training would surely make her wary of using words like miracle too glibly.

He was aware that Penny was watching him, looked up to meet her eyes.

'You don't believe me, do you, Daniel? It's written all over your face.'

He plucked another handful of grass; contradictory arguments swarming in his mind. 'I just don't know what to think.'

'Look, I felt that lump with my own hands. I can describe it to you in detail if you want. It was so horrible, I'd hardly have imagined it. And anyway, you're forgetting Pat herself. She felt something really violent actually happening in her body – like an electric shock, she said, shooting through her leg. And before that, she was conscious of waves of . . . sort of energy, streaming from Stephen's hands. And a sensation of quite stupendous love.'

'*Love?*' he echoed mockingly.

'Yes. Andrew questioned that as well, and she said she knew it sounded vague and rather soppy, but it was the only word which seemed appropriate. In fact, she got a bit embarrassed when we asked her about it. She doesn't strike me as a hype-merchant, or someone who embroiders the truth, but she said she felt as if the most powerful source of love she could imagine in a million years was shining like a beam of light directly into her cells. She tried to make a joke about it – said it was like a chicken being microwaved. But we could all see she was shaken to the core.'

Daniel snapped the head off a plantain. The cynical retort he was on the point of making was silenced as he recalled his own sensations when Happy had laid hands on him, just prior to Margot's healing. He, too, had experienced love – a mother's love, so extraordinarily intense it had overwhelmed him completely. Yet he hadn't mentioned it to anyone, and had even blocked it from his memory till now. Was that because it didn't fit his scheme of things – what Penny would condemn as his narrow blinkered outlook? He caught her eye and immediately she challenged him again, her voice more determined than ever.

'Okay, Daniel, forget all the stuff about love. I know that's not your thing, but just answer me one question. A big hard solid lump which twelve people examined – thirteen, if you count Tim – has vanished without trace. So what's *your* explanation?'

He crushed the plantain stalk to pulp, wiped his green-stained hand on his jeans. 'I'm sorry, I don't know. It could be spontaneous remission, I suppose.'

'But that's a sort of miracle in itself. And it's still connected with Stephen, because it happened while he was healing her, and – wow! – did he work hard! You should have seen his face!'

'I wish to God I had.' He was feeling increasingly frustrated at having missed this phenomenal session, and was even conscious of a certain irrational jealousy that it was Pat who had been singled out for healing, when she had only just arrived. Why not poor Dylan, who had stood the course for almost a whole month, and was HIV-positive (so Gerard had confided when they'd been chopping wood together). Or why not Pippa, come to that? His daughter might not have a terminal illness, but she was still in need of help. His earlier annoyance with the healer intensified as he recalled her despairing face: its air of desolation; the dark-circled eyes, which seemed to be looking always inward.

He eased himself up from his stony seat, reluctant, as ever, to dwell too long on miracles. Like the stones, they were uncomfortable. 'Listen, Penny, wonder-cures apart, we've got to do something about Pippa.'

'We *are* doing something. Just being here is good for her. She's learning a whole new set of values.'

'I don't think she's learning anything – except how wet Welsh rain is.'

Penny grinned and stood up too; gazing round admiringly at the range of purple-browed hills. 'Give her time. She's already shared in a few rituals, and they're important in themselves. They break down the division between mind and body, and between different parts of our self, and they help to . . .'

'For God's sake, Penny, all that malarkey may be food and drink to you, but it's hardly of any interest to an isolated thirteen-year-old who's pining for her dog.'

'But she'd *not* isolated here, Daniel. That's the whole point of community living. We're part of something bigger than our-selves.'

'That's all very well in theory, but in actual fact she's sitting on her own in a dank and airless tent, staring into space and looking the picture of misery.'

'That's her choice, though, isn't it? She could have come to the healing if she wanted.'

'I don't call that a choice! Other girls her age are busy playing tennis, or going to the cinema, or being taken to the zoo by doting aunts or grandmas.'

'She can do all that the rest of the year. She'll never learn spir-itual values stuck in Wandsworth.'

'What's wrong with Wandsworth? You've never complained about it before.'

She stretched out her arms to the sky in what he felt was an absurdly theatrical gesture, a parody of Happy. 'It's too far from our roots,' she said, face upturned to the sun, expression madden-ingly smug. 'People need a sacred space where they're more in touch with nature, and with the whole world of myth, which links them to the past. There's no sense of continuity in cities. Everything's too new and artificial.'

He wheeled away in irritation. She had been brainwashed by Corinna, or JB, and was spouting their pet theories secondhand. He stumbled along the path, suddenly noticing a clump of flowers – tiny bell-shaped trumpets with striking glossy leaves; two pea-cock butterflies hovering above them. Higher up, a buzzard circled slowly in the sky, its movements as unhurried as the lazy clouds themselves – pearly wisps merging into blue. The countryside *was* beautiful – there was no denying that – and he would never get this sense of space in Wandsworth, this view across lush fields and dramatic dappled hills. As usual, he was torn: one part of him pining for London and the comforts of his home; another part exulting in the grandeur of the landscape. But it wasn't simply a matter of fine views and pretty flowers – his daughter's health and happiness were at stake. Should he keep her here in the hope that she'd be cured, or return her to the safety of Elveley Road?

He drifted back to Penny, who was absorbed in watching the buzzard; the majestic bird soaring almost out of sight towards gold-tinged swathes of cloud. It seemed unkind to drag her back to petty arguments, or to break the all-embracing silence, which was now so profound he felt it should be put in a glass case and labelled 'utter peace'. But this was their only chance of talking. 'Look,' he said, taking both her hands in his as a gesture of appeasement, 'apart from anything else, I'm worried about Rick. Pippa seems to absolutely loathe him.'

Penny slipped her hands free, as if unwilling to be fettered. 'Maybe she does, but he's the means to her healing. Stephen told me yesterday.'

'Oh, that's idiotic, Penny! How on earth can she be healed by a whippersnapper schoolboy?'

'You've changed your tune, I must say! Rick was supposed to be so wonderful, I thought.'

'Not wonderful, just ordinary. And hardly likely to be working miracles in conjunction with your Stephen.'

'He's not "mine".'

'Oh, really? You could have fooled me. Anyway, this is beginning to sound more and more ridiculous. First she's meant to find salvation through some wounded dribbly dog, and now through a boy she shuns like the plague and who has problems enough himself.'

'Daniel, what's got into you? There's no need to be so scathing.'

'What's got into *you*? You're not thinking about how Pippa feels at all. Why the hell should you foist her on someone she obviously detests?'

'I'm not foisting her on anyone. I'm just giving her the chance to see things from a different point of view. Anyway, if she does go home, what then? D'you think she'll magically recover there?'

'At least she'll have more to do.'

'She's got masses to do here. And it's good for her to be with other people.'

'But she's not with other people, is she? What you really mean is it's good for *you*.' He broke off in annoyance. Half a dozen sheep were edging curiously towards them, as if attracted by this marital altercation. He shooed them away, resumed his argument. 'Just because you're the centre of attention, with Stephen and Corinna fighting for your favours, you assume that Pippa and I should be equally keen on living like a band of gypsies.'

'Don't be stupid, Daniel. You sound inanely jealous. And anyway, you were enjoying it yourself last week. What's happened to make you so stroppy all of a sudden? Okay, I know the weather changed and we had a few bad days, but the rain's blown over now, and with any luck it'll stay that way.'

He stumbled towards her, embraced her almost violently, burying his face in the soft bolster of her breasts. 'It isn't just the weather,' he admitted, smelling the chaplain's evil pipe again, feeling that obscene moustache prickling on his bottom.

'Well, what then?'

He muttered something inaudible, wounded by her rebuff. Her tone had been impatient, and she had all but pushed him off. He had evidently made a *faux pas*. Only Corinna was allowed unrestricted access to her body.

He pulled away and started striding up the hill; the chaplain in pursuit. He was unable to rid himself of Sayers, especially now he had come so close to mentioning his name, blurting out the whole grotesque experience.

'Daniel, for heaven's sake, where are you off to now? I thought we were trying to talk about Pippa.'

'Oh, don't worry about Pippa,' he retorted, shouting over his shoulder as he continued his furious climb. 'You get back to your darling Corinna. Perhaps you'll have another miracle – she'll turn into a man, so you can get married and live happily every after.'

26

DANIEL BUTTONED HIS SHIRT with cold and clumsy hands. He was still shivering from his swim, but relaxed at last, at peace. Every time he came here he experienced the same calming effect, as if the lake were a source of healing in itself. Its very seclusion acted as a palliative, and its water appeared to have the power to wash away not just sweat and grime, but anger, fear, regret. The rocks beside the shore were some of the oldest in the world, and the thought of such a time-scale put things in proportion. Or maybe it was the almost religious process of immersion. He grinned to himself. Some of Penny's hokum must be getting to him, despite his strong resistance. As for Pat's 'miracle', he had decided to reserve judgement. Not having witnessed it in person, he didn't feel he was qualified to make an objective comment. And anyway, it was much too soon to declare her permanently cured. She would need to return to the hospital, have her case reviewed. But he wasn't going to let it upset his peace of mind, as Margot's cure had done. For three or four nights after that, images of blindness had crept into his dreams, so that *he* was the one who couldn't see; groping through the interminable dark until, suddenly and shatteringly, the full light of dawn restored his eyesight, as JB rose resplendent in the sky.

He shook his head to dispel the dazzling image; concentrated instead on the mundane task of putting on his socks and shoes. His fingers were still numb, bluish round the nails. It was probably idiotic to swim in sub-zero temperatures when he already had a cold, but he felt far better for it. Certainly when diving deep, deep down, he had experienced a sense of total release, and had successfully drowned Sayers, whose body had sunk lumpenly to the bottom.

He smoothed his dripping hair, broke into a run. The best way to warm up was to jog around the shore, get his circulation going. The air itself was warm; the day still close and humid. It was only that unfathomable black water which never seemed to lose its jolting chill. He pounded across the sand, glancing up at the encircling hills, barred with sun and shadow; a lone sheep standing on a spur of rock, looking like a large white stone itself.

His mind was surprisingly clear and, even as he ran, he was working out a solution to the problem of the holiday, or what remained of it. He could hardly understand his earlier indecision. It all seemed perfectly simple now that he had rid himself of resentment and self-pity. He would keep his promise to Pippa and take her home for a week or two, thus giving Penny the freedom she craved, and removing the pressure from all three of them. It would also allow him to check on things in the office, and deal with any urgent post or phone-calls. And when he and Pippa returned here for a final week with Penny, he could bring a good stock of warm dry clothes and, he hoped, more tolerance. He had heard from Megan that while they'd been battling with rain and storms in Wales these last few days, London had been basking in a sunny spell. So, with any luck, he and Pippa would enjoy a fortnight's calm – in every sense. He would take her out, let her choose the excursions for a change, do his best to heal the breach between them.

He veered towards the water's edge, slowing his pace to a walk. He wanted one last look at the lake before he left for London, so that he could take something of it with him – its tranquillity and composure. He had never seen the slightest sign of life in the water, yet it seemed to *give* him life, like some baptismal rite. He remembered what Penny had said about people needing a sacred space where they could be more in touch with nature. It had annoyed him at the time, but this particular spot did indeed feel sacred; stirred in him some deep response to what he could only call the numinous. He watched his reflection trembling on the surface of the water, bent towards it like a modern-day Narcissus, finally thrusting his fingers through the shadow of his face and dispersing himself into fragments.

Reluctantly, he turned away, walked across the sand towards the path, and began the long trek back. It must be early afternoon by now, and he had eaten nothing since last night except a few ripe blackberries he'd gathered on the way. He must grab some leftovers from lunch, then have a word with Penny; try to make her see that, despite her earlier arguments, it was not in Pippa's interests to stay here any longer. Actually, he didn't anticipate any major opposition on her part. It was pretty clear to him that she was so caught up in this tribal way of life, she was merely using Pippa as a convenient excuse. She might well be secretly relieved to have her daughter off her hands, but probably couldn't bring herself to admit it, especially as the whole purpose of their coming here had been to help Pippa over her problems.

He strode on down the path, making a mental list of what he had to do: pack his things, check the car, make sure the tent was sound, ask Gerard to give Penny a hand if anything went wrong, and explain to Claire and Rick why he was leaving. He hoped to be on the road within an hour, though he had no real idea of the time. He stopped a moment to cram in a few more blackberries – small mean things with no taste to them and pips which stuck in his teeth. He also picked a flower or two for Pippa, and kept a look-out for bones to add to Rick's collection. Flowers were rare up here, so he pounced on any tiny bloom as a treasure, especially pleased to find a spire of toadflax: each pouting pair of yellow lips complete with protruding orange tongue. As he stooped to pluck it, he was suddenly aware that this stretch of lonely moorland would probably have looked the same five thousand years ago. The remains of the lead mine were a long way further down, and all he could see around him was hill blurring into sky, green merging with grey-blue, chameleon clouds forming and re-forming, and shadows like mauve bruises on the crags.

He lengthened his stride, actually relishing the prospect of tepid chick-pea fritters or congealing fungi fricassee, or whatever they had left him. He was too hungry to be fussy, and anyway, he could compensate tonight with steak and strawberries in the French bistro round the corner. He'd treat Pippa to a slap-up meal, with not a slug or wasp in sight.

At last he reached the final lap, the steep and muddy sheep-track which led down to the camp. Far below, he could see three figures crouching on the ground, unrecognizable at this distance. The details gradually sharpened as he approached, until he could make out Penny's beacon-head – the only splash of colour in the

335

surrounding hazy-green. Corinna was on one side of her (of course), Claire the other, and all three women appeared totally absorbed. He shouted to them, and waved, but they didn't seem to hear. Well, however engrossed they were, he would have to beg a minute of Penny's precious time, to tell her he was leaving. He jogged over to the group, lurching abruptly to a panicked halt. It looked as if they were peeing, all three of them, together. But surely community living didn't go as far as that, and why should they choose so exposed a spot, instead of seeking cover? Unless it was connected with Anita's urinotherapy. She must have talked them into it, and this was some communal collection rite. He was about to take to his heels and run, when Penny called him over.

'It's . . . okay,' he mumbled. 'I can see you're busy.'

'No, don't go away. It's lucky you're here. Come and join us, will you?'

He edged towards them warily, his face flaming with embarrassment as he saw that they were naked from the waist down, and although not apparently urinating, seemed on the point of doing so. He averted his eyes and stared fixedly at his feet, studiously counting the eyelet holes in his shoes.

'We were just saying that we ought to have a man present,' Corinna informed him in an accusing tone of voice. 'After all, it's men who are to blame for making a natural function a taboo.'

'I . . . I'm sorry, but I don't quite . . .'

'Oh, men always deny it. But it was a brilliant manoeuvre on their part – the perfect way of undermining women's power and confidence. Every month our already shaky self-esteem receives another kick in the teeth.'

'Look, wait a second,' Penny interrupted. 'What's the point of attacking Daniel – or any man, come to that? We've got to make them understand, Corinna.'

She beckoned him closer, rewarded him with a smile – a patronizing, parental sort of smile, he felt, as he squirmed beneath their scrutiny. It struck him that he must indeed look childish, if not downright absurd, clutching a droopy bunch of flowers and with a rabbit's skull bulging from his pocket.

'Now listen, darling,' she continued, 'let me try to explain. All three of us started our periods today, and that's quite important in itself. Women in primitive tribes used to menstruate together, at every new or full moon. Their periods were synchronized, you see, and the same thing's happening with us. Apparently it *does* happen when women live in communities.'

'Look, Penny, I . . . I'm . . .' He was lost for words in such intimidating circumstances. He had already caught disturbing glimpses of pubic hair, bare and fleshy thighs, and felt like some shameful pervert gawping at forbidden sights.

'Hold on!' said Penny, sensing his desire to escape. 'I haven't even told you what we're doing yet. This is a very ancient rite, a shamanic rite, in fact. Robin was explaining to us that the first shamans were women. The original form of the word actually means a female rather than a male. And he said they used their menstrual blood in ceremonies and rituals – let it flow on to the ground as an offering to the earth. And apparently some tribes still do it today. Well, we're doing it ourselves, to regain our sense of power, and to re-connect with all those ancient women who were revered as priestesses or healers, rather than made to feel inferior.'

'It's a sacrifice which takes no life,' Claire said solemnly, sitting back on her heels. 'And,' she added, 'a natural fertilizer. You can put it on your house-plants.'

'Don't be silly, Claire,' Corinna frowned. 'That may be true, but it sounds plain daft. This is a really serious issue. The last thing we want is to trivialize it and make men still more hostile.'

'I . . . I'm *not* hostile,' Daniel stammered, lowering his eyes again. The sight of his mud-caked shoes seemed infinitely safer than the terrifying prospect of three converging streams of menstrual blood.

'The whole of society is hostile,' Claire pronounced. 'You only have to look at the word "curse". I mean, I've always used it myself, but it's completely negative. And when you think that we grow up in an environment which actually hates and fears women's core biological function, is it any wonder that so many of us feel bad about ourselves?'

'That's because it's a patriarchal society,' Corinna said with a dismissive shrug. 'In other, wiser societies menstrual blood was seen as sacred, the most potent healing medicine there was, and of value to the entire community. And when a woman had her period, she was specially honoured and respected. They believed

337

that she had psychic powers and was more intuitive at that time – in touch with the cycle of the moon, and the ebb and flow of the tides.'

Daniel shifted uneasily. He could see they had a point, one he might find fascinating if he was ensconced safely in a library, reading it in an academic journal. It was quite another matter actually to be confronted with three half-naked women, squatting right in front of him, letting their blood flow on to the ground. He had no idea what was expected of him, nor what part mere men were supposed to play in such shamanic rites. Did they touch the blood, or taste it, or smear it on their faces, God forbid? He forced himself to look at it, as the first stage in his initiation. It had soaked into the grass, making a deep scarlet stain, with one or two blackish clots still glistening on the surface. He quickly looked away. Rick's murky green concoctions seemed innocuous in comparison. In his fantasy at the Plough and Harrow, he had imagined these same women naked in the bath, but that had been soft-focus, an erotic panorama he could switch off if he chose. The reality was different: mortifying, inescapable, and repellent in its detail.

Claire was speaking again – something about the spiritual significance of woman's menstrual cycle. He couldn't really take it in; was wrestling with a sense of isolation. He had regarded Claire as his special friend and ally, yet now she seemed a stranger who had gone over to the enemy. Except even words like 'enemy' only went to show how basically aggressive he must be; his whole view of men and women conceived in antagonistic terms. He felt thoroughly demoralized, not to mention trapped. He couldn't simply walk away after such impassioned homilies, unless he took his courage in both hands and confessed to all three women that he was driving back to London and had to leave forthwith. He could always stress it was for Pippa's sake, and indeed he did feel more determined now to remove her from this company, before she, too, was pressured to take part in these distasteful primitive ceremonies. She was so excruciatingly shy about her periods, the very notion would appal her.

'Listen,' he blurted out. 'I . . . I've decided to go home – now, I mean – this afternoon. My cold's so bad, it'll never clear up here. And Pippa's not well either. I think she's sickening for flu or something, so I felt it might be wiser for me to take her back for a week or two, then return here when we're better.'

He was blushing again in confusion. He had seized on the first lame excuse which popped into his head, but only now did he realize how illogical it sounded. If he and Pippa were sick, then all the more reason for them to stay at what was after all a healing camp, not flee their chance of cure. And, still more reprehensible, he had failed to comment on their rituals, but simply interrupted them, behaving like those boorish males Corinna so abhorred.

'Look, don't think I'm not interested,' he added desperately, racking his brains for something meaningful to say on the subject of lunar cycles or menstrual taboos. His mind remained a blank, so he muttered some excuse about having to get off before the traffic started building up; trying to imply that he would willingly hear more, if only he had the time.

'Have you told Pippa yet?' asked Penny. 'I mean, does she *know* she's leaving?'

'Well, no, I suppose she doesn't. Though I did sort of promise earlier on. I'll go and tell her now.' He was already backing away, terrified she might detain him, or that Corinna might begin some new tirade.

'I'll come and wave you off,' called Penny, settling back on the ground. 'Oh, and I'd better help you sort out Pippa's stuff. Give me five more minutes, okay?'

'Fine!' he shouted, slithering gratefully down to the bottom of the slope. She hadn't tried to stop him, hadn't raised the slightest objection. He was free to leave, almost had her blessing – certainly the promise of a fond farewell. Extraordinary how light he felt. It must be that magical lake again, drowning not just *his* resentment but Penny's ill will, too. My own minor miracle, he thought, as he ran towards the tent. Not quite in the same league as a tumour being spirited away, but a most welcome little favour from JB.

He traipsed back up the hill. Penny hadn't budged; was still sitting between Claire and Corinna, fertilizing the ground. These shamanic rites were certainly long-drawn-out; the earth greedy for its full libation of blood. 'Give me five more minutes,' she'd said,

339

and at least twenty must have passed – frustrating, fruitless minutes. Pippa had categorically refused to leave unless Penny came as well. He was not only disappointed, but severely shaken. Wasn't this the final proof that *he* was that guilty 'someone' cited by JB? Pippa had been desperate to leave when he'd suggested that all three of them should go, but had done an instant U-turn once she'd discovered that her mother wasn't coming, as if terrified of being left alone with him. He felt like some abuser, a dangerous, unpredictable brute, yet he didn't actually understand in what way he was harming her. The business with Juliet was over, but perhaps she didn't know that. If she had stumbled on some proof of his affair (and though utterly unlikely, the chance of it kept haunting him), she might well assume that he was still betraying Penny. Or maybe it was something less specific. She found him crass, as Corinna did, or just too self-absorbed, or . . .

He tripped on a deep rut and swore under his breath. Pippa had put him in a dilemma. How could he push off now for a week or two, as planned, and leave her to her own devices, especially when Penny seemed so supremely unconcerned? However much his daughter might resent him, he couldn't simply wash his hands of her; make his own escape, while she sat moping in a tent, more or less abandoned by both parents. Yet it would be humiliating in the extreme to tell Penny and her fellow shamans that he had changed his mind, after making such an issue about leaving. He was only fifty yards from them, but still hadn't worked out what to say. He edged a little closer, cleared his throat to catch his wife's attention, then beckoned her towards him. He was enormously relieved when she got up – even put her pants back on and walked in his direction. He led her away from the others, shamefacedly admitted that Pippa wasn't wildly keen to leave with him.

'But I think I'll still go home myself – just for a couple of days. It'll give me a chance to check on the house, tidy up the garden, all that sort of stuff.'

'Good idea!' she said. 'But why only a couple of days? Wouldn't it be better to spend a bit longer at home – I mean, do some things you enjoy, for once, not just dreary old chores. The Proms are in full swing now, and there's that weird Polish play at the National. And didn't you want to see the new film about Van Gogh?'

He nodded miserably. She couldn't wait to get rid of him; was offering him a whole menu of diversions to keep him away as long as possible. He glanced over her shoulder at the two still squatting women. How could he compete? *They* had periods – the most potent of all medicines – and they were psychic and intuitive, in tune with moon and tides. They were also bonded by this intimate rite itself, and by centuries of male oppression; by the fact that they had breasts and wombs, and were the very source of life. He saw that he might lose Penny, as he seemed already to have lost Pippa. There was no way he could counter these heady ideas of feminism, freedom, the sense of continuity with powerful ancient priestesses.

He took a hesitant step towards Claire and Corinna. He was still nervous of approaching them, yet felt it would be unforgivably rude to walk off without a word, when they'd been sharing a life for the last two weeks. He was just stammering his farewells when his eye fell on the flowers he'd picked for Pippa, lying wilting on the ground. He didn't even remember putting them down. Although it was just as well he had – she wouldn't want presents from a father she despised. It also appeared that Penny's offer to wave goodbye applied only to him and Pippa as a pair, not to him on his own. She hugged him briefly and wished him a good time, but then went straight back to her companions, rather than accompanying him to the car. And when he turned to look at her from the bottom of the slope, she had shrunk again to a blur; even her distinctive hair drained of all its fire.

27

DANIEL EMPTIED THE GRASS-CUTTINGS and stared approvingly at the closely-shaved lawn. It hadn't really needed mowing again, after only three or four days, but he had been looking for a job: something physical and practical, to stop him pacing aimlessly around. He wiped his sweaty forehead and decided to go inside for a drink. It had been uncomfortably hot all week, and today was particularly close, so that he'd felt sticky from the moment he got up.

He poured himself an ice-cold beer and took it into the sitting-room with *The Times*. Lounging in his favourite chair, he riffled through the Saturday supplement, looking for the film reviews. At least he could read in peace today, without that horrendous noise outside the window. They were digging up the street to lay a cable, and every time he settled down with a book or piece of work, his ears would be assaulted by the whine of electric drills, or by the pounding vibrations of earth-movers, snorting like great angry bulls.

But this afternoon, perversely, it was almost too deathly quiet. August was a vacuous month: most people were away, including the neighbours on both sides. He turned the page to the travel section, realizing he hadn't taken in a word about the films. What was wrong with him, for heaven's sake? In Wales he'd been frustrated because books were strictly forbidden, and in any case there was little time for oneself. Yet now that he had both time and reading matter, he couldn't seem to concentrate.

He laid the paper down, drifted to the mantelpiece and re-read the postcards from his friends enjoying hedonistic holidays on sun-drenched beaches or palm-fringed tropical islands. All the locales seemed unimaginably distant – as did Wales itself now. He glanced out at the deserted street, wondering if he was the only person left in London. Every other living soul appeared to have fled across an ocean, or immured themselves behind a mountain range or coral reef, or some emotional Iron Curtain. Even his colleagues at the office had been rather unforthcoming when he had called in during the week, as if they suspected him of snooping, or of trying to reassure himself that they weren't slacking in his absence. Although he had disarmed them over a coffee, he'd decided not to go back again before the official end of his holiday – still a fortnight away. It was something of an irony that this was his longest summer break for several years, yet secretly he was longing to curtail it. Last August, there had been complications (a colleague sick, another on compassionate leave) and he'd managed only a week away from his desk. This year, they'd made it up to him, yet he was chafing at the bit and would gladly forgo this enforced period of leisure to resume the challenges of work.

He replaced the postcards carefully on each side of the clock, surprised to see it was only five to two. Time was really dragging, and he resented the number of clocks in the house, all reminding him that an hour took twice as long here as it seemed to do in Wales. The first few days hadn't been too bad, since there was plenty to keep him busy: sorting out the dirty clothes he had brought back from the camp, generally tidying up the place and dealing with his mail, then turning his attention to the garden. But now everything was shipshape (unnaturally so, Penny would complain); every letter answered, every message on the answerphone returned. Actually, he wished the phone would ring more, break the sluggish silence.

He mooched back to the paper, leafing through the pages until he found a piece which caught his eye, entitled 'MORE SEX, PLEASE – WE'RE SPARROWS!' Apparently sparrows were irredeemably promiscuous; in fact, according to the article, some thirty per cent of *all* birds were cheerfully sleeping around, and even so-called faithful swans frequently cheated on their mates. The piece went on to claim that there was hardly a single species of mammal, rodent, fish or insect which wasn't adulterous, polygamous, or worse. He thought of Penny, his own once-faithful mate, now entwined with Corinna in the double sleeping-bag, or tiptoeing to JB's tent to find comfort in the middle of the

343

night. And what about poor Pippa? Would she be cowering in the tent alone, crying over the dog; or forced to participate in some outrageous communal rite which involved removing half her clothes? He really ought to get back to the camp, if only for her sake, but how could he inflict himself on his wife and daughter when both of them had made it clear that he simply wasn't wanted?

He flung the paper on the table and went to find his keys. A bracing walk on the common would take him out of himself, put a stop to this fatuous self-pity. It was really quite pathetic to keep dwelling on his solitary state, when he'd deliberately chosen to be on his own. But now that he'd changed his mind – well, the common would be crowded on a Saturday afternoon, which would help to make him feel that he was still a paid-up member of the human race.

He picked his laborious way between the obstructions on the pavement. The workmen had left piles of earth and rubble, mounds of damply orange sand. Every few yards were deep and dangerous holes, each one marked by warning signs and a small battalion of red and white striped cones. Short lengths of plastic piping lay abandoned in the gutter, with a scattering of fag-ends and the odd Kentucky Chicken carton. The surface was so pitted and uneven, he was relieved to reach the common, yet even there he couldn't keep his thoughts away from Wales. In fact, he was forced to admit that Penny had been right about the majesty of the Powys landscape, in contrast to this urban recreation ground. He'd always regarded it as an oasis – one they were lucky to have, so close to central London – always admired the oak and chestnut trees, the attractive pond with its flock of Canada geese. But today he was more aware of the noise and general scruffiness. A railway line ran right across the middle, with trains continually shuddering by, and planes droned overhead, effectively drowning any bird-song. The grass looked parched and brown, and several of the trees had been defaced by crude graffiti carved into the bark. And in whichever direction he walked, the greenery soon petered out and gave way to congested roads.

Doing his best to ignore the traffic noise, he struck out across the grass, smiling at an elderly woman walking her chihuahua. His smile was not returned. She stared coldly past him, probably assuming he was a potential rapist, or at least an unsavoury character. He strolled on past a clump of trees, noticing how many people were on their own: young girls plugged into Walkmans; lone foreign-looking students lying on the grass, engrossed in books or papers; an old man limping along on two sticks, and a few joggers panting by. Everyone seemed isolated in their own sequestered world, the faces shuttered or suspicious; reluctant to make contact or even exchange a few innocuous words – all strangers here in London.

He stopped to watch a tramp rooting through a litter-bin and extracting half a dirty sandwich; was tempted to invite him home for tea. Perhaps there was something to be said for living in a community, sharing food and conversation. Yet he realized how contrary he was being: he, the arch-critic of communal life, now felt nostalgic for it.

He sat down on a bench and surveyed the scene around him. A family group were picnicking under a tree; the children feeding the pigeons, trying to coax the shy birds nearer with scraps of chocolate cake. The elder girl reminded him of Pippa – long coltish legs, curly hair and freckles – but there was one overwhelming difference: this child was happy. He watched her animated face as she giggled with her sister, then rushed back to her parents to wheedle a further supply of cake. Her father cut her off a slice and she hugged him as a reward – only a fleeting hug, but evidence of their mutual trust, her spontaneous affection.

He shut his eyes, turned his world to black. Was Pippa glad he'd left, relaxed and even chatty now that he was no longer any threat to her?

He dragged himself up to his feet again. No wonder he felt morose when he'd done nothing more constructive all week than restore the house and garden to rights, then moon around feeling sorry for himself. He hadn't been to a single play or concert, nor out for a single meal. Why spend another evening cloistered at home on his own, his restless mind racing back to Wales again while his body slumped inertly on the sofa? He could go up to the West End now, drive to Leicester Square and see the new Van Gogh film, as Penny had suggested; maybe pop into the National Portrait Gallery, if there was time before it began, then treat himself to Peking duck at Young Chen's.

He already felt more cheerful with a definite plan of action and his Saturday night no longer just an empty stretch of time. He was whistling as he reached the house, and ran straight upstairs to change; relishing the luxuries of an electric razor, a full-length mirror, and clothes which were neither wet nor creased nor stained. The car, too, was transformed – its mud-coating hosed away, its smeary windows polished, and the inside so immaculate Penny might well ask him if he had ambitions in the chauffeuring line.

He drove to an accompaniment of Mahler's *Song of the Earth* – somewhat ironic in the circumstances, but exhilarating none the less. The journey was painless altogether; no hold-ups or diversions, and the traffic relatively light. He even found a parking space a stone's throw from the cinema. The next programme didn't start till six, so he had almost an hour to kill. Perhaps he'd have a stroll, instead of going to the gallery; look at living faces rather than the dead and painted kind.

He set off down the street, although it was difficult to make much progress with crowds of tourists sauntering along, continually stopping to take photographs and generally obstructing the pavement. How could he have been so naïve as to imagine he was the only person left in London? While his friends had departed for foreign shores, the rest of the world converged on Merry England, or so it seemed from the babel of disparate languages and the different shades of skin. Of course he was used to cosmopolitan London and its flock of summer migrants, but they struck him much more forcibly today. His spell in Wales had made him see everything anew, and he still felt slightly alien, even in the city he knew best. It was almost as if he'd gone abroad himself; arrived from the wilds of the country in some huge metropolis, where everyone was on holiday and dressed to fit the part. He kept passing people in Bermuda shorts or garish patterned shirts and a whole variety of headgear, from plastic pork-pie hats printed with Union Jacks to romantic boaters wreathed with flowers and ribbons. There was even a girl in a bikini top, displaying her deep tan (and deeper cleavage) and dripping ice-cream down her front from a fast-melting Mr Whippy.

Practically everyone was eating: licking ice-lollies or choc-bars, or pouring toffee-coated popcorn down their throats from huge

346

waxed cartons embellished with pink dinosaurs, or biting into slices of hot pizza – strands of melted cheese crisscrossing their chins. At each street-corner, rival take-away stalls were all doing a brisk trade: squirting mustard on frankfurters, or syrup on waffles; handing out burgers and kebabs. The reek of grease and onions collided with the sickly-sweet smell of candyfloss, and as he passed a tandoori restaurant, a belch of curry blasted through the open door right into his face.

He wondered what the healer would say to all this contraband; could almost see him rushing into the square, clad in his long robe, overthrowing kiosks like Jesus in the Temple and driving out the vendors. And he'd doubtless also disapprove of the raucous music pumping from a record store, amplified to deafening volume, and outshrilled only by a car alarm (whose persistent yowling was generally ignored, even by the pigeons). Daniel was more aware than he'd ever been of the contrast between this rackety West End and the staid grey weekday ambience of the Albert Embankment (where he worked in an drab office-block five hundred yards from Vauxhall), which boasted neither buskers nor video arcades, attracted no tourists, and had only a handful of restaurants where people ate decorously indoors.

He turned into a side street and elbowed his way to the crossroads at the end. Waiting for the lights to change, he winced again at the din, not just from the motorbikes roaring past at full throttle, but from a half-demolished building being attacked by two machines. They were biting into the masonry like greedy yellow monsters; gobbling bricks and mortar, crunching metal struts, then vomiting out great clouds of snot and dust. Their lethal claws tore voraciously at the structure; smashed through gaping windows and unresisting doors, leaving a trail of devastation. As he stood and watched, a familiar phrase flashed into his mind: 'breaking and entering'. And with the words came Sayers – the Sayers he'd thought drowned – leering at him once again, pursuing him even here.

He blundered across the road against the lights, dodging the stream of cars and plunging blindly ahead. A dozen Japanese youths were clustered around a camera shop, forcing him to slow down. He cursed them under his breath, then pounded on again, oblivious to his surroundings; seeing only Sayers's fleshy face, his grossly swollen penis.

He dived across another road, then stopped dead in his tracks. Somebody was speaking to him, a soft but compelling voice: '*You can never run away, Daniel – not from your own pain.*'

He swung round towards the voice. No one was there save a rather frowsty woman totally absorbed in reading the menu tacked up outside a café. Yet the words had been spoken aloud and enunciated clearly – soft, maybe, but absolutely distinct. He pinched himself to make sure he wasn't dreaming; registered the twinge, as tangible, unmistakable, as the words themselves had been. Yet JB was in Wales, so how could he have heard his voice? And it *was* his voice, beyond any shadow of doubt: the same timbre and inflexion; the exact same phrase as had been addressed to him when he'd woken in terror, clinging to his 'mother' that first night on the dark and lonely hillside.

He stared at his reflection in a window – yes, he still looked perfectly normal. Then he did some mental arithmetic, working out a few square roots and reciting Pythagoras's theorem. Yes, his brain appeared to be functioning with no obvious loss of power. How then could he account for so unnerving an experience?

He walked back the way he'd come, considerably shaken, but determined to regain his self-control. He must keep to his plan for the evening, not give way to panic. He could still go to the cinema, but choose a different film. Van Gogh's vision of the world would be too disturbing for his present state. He was beginning to feel menaced by his surroundings: the buildings slightly distorted, as if they were closing in on him; the cars tiny metal boxes hurtling to destruction. And there were far too many people – scores of faces looming up, then vanishing into the crowd again; hostile eyes, chewing mouths, flashes of white teeth, snatches of conversation which sounded foreign even in English, surreal non-sequiturs.

He found himself back in Leicester Square, surrounded by giant film posters for horror movies and spine-chillers. He couldn't escape the images: dismembered corpses, smoking guns, teeth sunk into virgin necks, robots on the rampage. He shuddered at the thought of two hours of blood-soaked violence, but the sex-films looked no better: a woman's spiked stiletto heel being rammed into her lover's face; a man threatening a half-naked girl with his gleaming phallic pistol. Surely there must be something less horrific. He liked the idea of an erotic film, but a gentle and alluring one without the blood and gore. It would be far easier to immerse himself in some saga of seduction than to watch a crazed artist hack off his own ear.

He leaned against a shop-front, wiped his face on his sleeve. The stifling heat seemed to have sapped his powers of decision. Sweaty bodies were milling all around him; countless restaurant kitchens pouring out their steamy breath; exhaust fumes polluting the air, and the sun beating down relentlessly. If the cinema wasn't air-conditioned, he might well expire from heat-stroke.

He still couldn't make up his mind; stood envying his fellow humans who appeared to have an aim in life, even if it was nothing more momentous than window-shopping, or camera-clicking, or sitting at a pavement café with an espresso or a beer. Should he go and have a drink himself, or take the tube to St James's Park and walk among the trees, or head straight home and slam the door? No, he needed a diversion; something to quash the healer's voice, help him forget he had ever heard it.

He traipsed back to the Odeon, which had half a dozen screens in all – one showing a French movie with *amour* in the title, and a less salacious poster than the rest. Now that his thoughts had strayed to sex, he couldn't get the subject out of his mind. The celluloid variety would be better than nothing and at least he could cool off. There was a large notice propped outside the door, saying, 'THIS CINEMA IS AIR-CONDITIONED – COME IN AND ESCAPE THE HEAT!'

He followed their suggestion, queuing at the kiosk for a ticket. He was directed to Screen 3, and stepped into the dark; the cold air like a jolt against his skin. Blinded for a moment, he paused to get his bearings in the aisle. A young voluptuous Thai girl was ogling at him from the screen, her sultry scarlet lips parted in a smile, her eyes passionate, provocative, promising untold delights. He returned her gaze, but saw a different face – a woman with less blatant eyes, cooler lips, pale English skin.

Impulsively, he ran back the way he'd come, down the flight of stairs into the foyer. He emerged into the heat once more, striding across the square towards the car. It was suddenly so clear. He'd been starved of sex these last three weeks and needed a real woman – a flesh and blood woman, who also had a mind and heart – and he knew where he could find her; knew at last where he was going.

28

DANIEL STOOD OUTSIDE the French-blue door. A tasteful colour
– naturally – to match the tasteful window-boxes, planted with
variegated evergreens and edged with trailing ivies. No strident
reds or yellows here, no litter on the path, no screaming children
or scruffy dogs to detract from the atmosphere of elegant restraint.
He gazed along the tree-lined road which led to Hampstead Heath,
and was only a few streets away from the so-called village, with
its pretentious restaurants and designer boutiques. He always felt a
stranger in north London, especially in this exclusive little enclave,
where there were no corner shops, no hoardings, no sign of
common humanity – nothing to lower the tone. Though he was
doing that himself, of course: a dishevelled individual in his shirtsleeves, who had been loitering on the doorstep for the last ten
or fifteen minutes, trying to summon up the courage to ring the
bell.

He smoothed his hair, wiped his clammy palms on his trousers,
then pressed a timid finger to the buzzer. At first he thought she
wasn't in, and felt a rush of disappointment and relief (in more
or less equal proportions), but suddenly the familiar voice crackled
down the entry-phone.

'Yes, who is it?'

'Daniel,' he said softly.

The silence seemed to scream.

'Daniel,' he repeated, but he was speaking to empty air. The
intercom had been shut off; the door slammed in his face, at least
metaphorically.

He pressed the buzzer again; this time keeping his finger on it,
amazed at his own audacity. But he refused now to be thwarted,
when coming here had cost him so much anguish – fear and guilt
and scruples on the way. (Several times he had actually stopped

the car, on the point of turning back.) She would soon tire of that tenacious bell reverberating through her flat.

'Daniel, will you kindly go away and leave me alone.'

Her tone was sharp, almost out of control. He made his own voice milk and honey. 'I need to see you, Juliet. Only for five minutes. I won't stay any longer, not if you don't want me to.'

'I'm sorry, but I've nothing to say.'

'Yes, but *I* have.'

A blue-rinsed matron was peering at him crossly from the open window of the spacious ground-floor flat. He was disturbing the peace, the general air of decorum and tranquillity expected of Woodleigh Chase. (Specious name, he'd always thought, for an apartment block in London.)

He gave another determined jab at the buzzer. 'Look, I think you'd be wise to let me in, if only as the lesser of two evils. We appear to be upsetting all your neighbours. I've gathered quite a little audience down here.'

Another lie, but he knew it would gain him admittance. Juliet loathed 'scenes', or breaking the proprieties. The door shuddered in submission as she snorted an abrupt 'Come in.'

He walked slowly up the stairs, his steps faltering as he reached the second landing. He wished she had come to meet him, instead of forcing him to ring a second bell. Though she answered this one promptly, wresting open the door and flinging him a look of such resentment, he felt himself shrinking beneath her scrutiny.

'You . . . you've cut your hair,' he stammered, appalled to see the long, swinging glossy curtain replaced by a short bob.

'Hm – a pity about *yours*.' The cold grey eyes appraised him. 'What on earth have you done to yourself?'

'What d'you mean?'

'Well, you're much thinner to start with. And you've got dark rings under your eyes. And just look at all those scratches on your hands!'

He glanced down at his hands, surprised to see the network of red lines, sealed with tiny blackish scabs. 'Oh, those are just from brambles, and from collecting wood and chopping it. Most of the trees were thorny ones, so it was easy to get scratched. And I'm sure I can't have lost weight. I've been eating like a horse, and stodgy food for the most part.'

He was still standing outside the door. It struck him as bizarre that they should be discussing the paltry details of his camping trip before she had invited him over the threshold or asked him why he had come.

He took a step towards her. She immediately shrank back as if he were infectious, but he continued through the doorway; half-triumphant and half-panicky that he was actually inside. As he pushed the door shut, a new rush of apprehension flooded over him. This flat was full of memories – full of *him*, for heaven's sake. He had sat so many times on that elegant chaise-longue, or eaten at that bijou table, which always seemed too cramped. He had made coffee in her kitchen; showered in her dauntingly feminine bathroom (everything shell-pink, even her toothbrush and the weighing-scales); rumpled her neat bed. Yet all she could do now was turn on him with venom.

'You've got a bloody cheek, you know, showing up like this when you told me loud and clear that things were over between us – finished, dead, kaput.' She gave each word a clipped sarcastic emphasis. 'And you might at least have phoned first. I could have had a visitor.'

Another lover, you mean, he thought. The notion made him irrationally jealous. Was *that* why she was wearing a new scent? It was so heady and oppressive, he could almost taste it on his lips; its musky fragrance provoking the whole flat. He couldn't take his eyes off her; completely unprepared for the maelstrom of emotions the mere sight of her aroused: guilt, fury, lust, desire. He glanced at her breasts, their curve only just discernible beneath the ivory silk blouse; then down at her long legs, made longer still by flimsy gold-strapped sandals with impossibly high heels. He felt attracted and repelled at once, seeing her not only through his own lascivious eyes, but also as Claire would view her: affected, superficial, and absurdly overdressed. The immaculate red talons (and matching scarlet toenails), the elaborate make-up, even the perfection of the flat itself, all riled him in a way he could barely understand. How dare she criticize his own unkempt appearance when she would never have lasted five minutes at the camp?

'I thought you had something important to say? I'm still wait-ing, Daniel.' She subsided into a chair, giving the impression that she was infinitely wearied, and crossing one leg over the other with an alluring flash of black-stockinged thigh.

He cursed himself for looking, started pacing restlessly around. All the speeches he'd prepared seemed utterly inadequate. Yet he was uneasy at the silence, the sense of things unspoken on both sides. He stopped in front of the sideboard, suddenly catching sight of himself in the gold-framed antique mirror on the wall. Yes, she was right, he *did* look a mess: gaunt and almost haggard, with purplish circles under his eyes and a deep scratch on his chin which hadn't healed. He could imagine what she was thinking: he had spent three weeks with a healer and returned sickly and exhausted.

'Look,' he said, at last, 'I . . . I owe you an apology. I came to say I'm sorry.' That wasn't true at all. He had come because he craved her naked body; longed to feel her magnificent hair swathing his stiff cock. But she had cut her hair, castrated him. He could hardly bear to look at it; felt it was a desecration, almost an act of spite. It changed her face, emphasizing her cheek-bones and making her look older, yet also somehow vulnerable; her neck too pale and slender, an exposed and fragile stalk.

'Sit down,' she urged, less harshly, gesturing to the chaise-longue.

He perched on its velvet edge, feeling, however inanely, that he was defiling it in some way. His swarthy skin with its bumps and bites and bruises (all a further legacy from Wales) seemed as inappropriate here as Juliet's own stylishness would have been in Rainbow Lodge. He cleared his throat, tried to hide his navvy's hands. 'I should have said sorry before.'

'Yes, you should.' She tossed her head disdainfully, the tiny pearl-drops in her ears twitching in reproach. He remembered her birthday earrings (pearls as well, ironically) which now sat, unworn, in Penny's drawer – another source of reproach.

'Things were difficult – at home, I mean.'

'So I gathered.'

'And it was hard to write that letter.'

'It wasn't particularly easy to read it.'

He registered the hurt in her voice; lapsed again into silence. It did now seem reprehensible to have ended things between them so abruptly. He had written a second time, in fact, to tell her he was going to Wales, but had kept it short and curt; whereas *her* second letter had covered three whole sides. Its accusing phrases were flooding back, fuelling his embarrassment and guilt. It surprised her, she had written, in a caustic but still measured tone, that his family meant so much to him – that was certainly not the impression she'd received. Indeed, had he forgotten how he'd begged her to make more time for him, to keep every weekend free, not to book a summer holiday because the two of them must go away together, spend more time together overall? He blushed as he remembered those wild impassioned pleas (usually whispered desperately when he was forced to leave her bed and return guilty but well-gratified to an unsuspecting Penny).

He stared down at the carpet: a thick plush pile in an impractical shade of cream. He had treated them both badly, his mistress and his wife, yet neither had sought vengeance. Penny was still in ignorance, of course, but Juliet could have made trouble for him; even phoned his home and created a furore by revealing the affair. He felt an overwhelming urge to apologize again, to make it genuine this time – ungrudging and unambivalent. Did he dare to take her hand, even prise her from her chair and persuade her to sit beside him? Such gestures had been so easy before, but were now impossible or dangerous.

She appeared to read his mind, forestalled his overture by reaching out her own hand and offering him a cigarette.

'So you still smoke Camels?' he observed.

She had changed to his brand a few weeks after meeting him, complaining at first that they were far too strong, and only smoking them on sufferance because she had run out of her Silk Cut. But she had soon become accustomed to that strength and started buying them herself. In fact, it had created a further bond between them, along with their mutual taste in books and wine and music.

She was still holding out the packet, her hand all but touching his knee. He was sorely tempted to take one. A refusal would seem churlish, as if he were rejecting any peace-offering, not just the cigarette. Yet it would be crazy to give in after a full nine weeks of abstinence, not to mention Claire's encouragement. Claire had helped him more than anyone, praising his strong will and constantly reminding him how much good he was doing himself. He could imagine her disappointment if she were ever to find out;

her sense of almost betrayal. But why in God's name had his thoughts returned to Claire? Her presence in Juliet's flat only added to his confusion, especially when he realized that he was still seeing his past mistress through her eyes; his excitement undercut by disapproval.

'Daniel! D'you want a cigarette or not?'

'N . . . no, thanks, I've given up.'

'What, again?' She raised a quizzical eyebrow.

'Yes. And I'm serious this time.'

'Congratulations! Will it worry you if *I* smoke?'

'No,' he lied, slumping back on the uncomfortable chaise-longue. It was an ordeal to watch her light up. The smell was tantalizing enough, but, worse, it evoked those ritual-times they'd smoked together – after meals, and especially after sex – lying naked on the duvet, still flushed, elated, damp; his heart thumping out its gratitude and guilt. She exhaled a wisp of smoke, which drifted slowly past him, dispersed to airy nothing. Had their whole affair been as tenuous as that, as fleeting and insubstantial?

'You won't say no to a drink, I hope?'

'No,' he smiled; quite ludicrously relieved that she no longer sounded cross, and was even treating him like a normal guest.

'No drink, or no "no"?'

'No "no",' he replied. 'I'd love a drink.'

'Your usual?'

'Please.' The phrase jolted him as the Camels had done. 'Your usual' implied that nothing had changed; that those cold, accusing letters had never actually been written; that he was here to take her out to dinner as a prelude to making love. Perhaps she was secretly glad to see him, pleased that he'd come back. Her initial anger had subsided remarkably quickly, considering his audacity in turning up on her doorstep. (He was astonished now that he had ever found the courage.)

Warily he followed her to the sideboard, where she was pouring his Martini; put his hand on her arm; the silky coolness of her blouse enticing him with memories of her coolly naked body. 'Juliet . . .'

He stalled. He seemed to have lost the knack of talking to her; could hardly believe they'd once spent hours discussing Africa, or music, or even footling things like the respective merits of Swiss and Belgian chocolate. Yet she hadn't shrugged his hand off, was standing so disarmingly close, he could see the faint gold down on her cheek, smell her smoky breath.

'Let's have dinner,' he blurted out. 'I'll take you to Chez Antoine's.' The best restaurant in Hampstead, with prices which would bankrupt him – but what the hell? Somehow he had to bribe her, keep her with him longer.

'I'm already going out to dinner. In fact, I mustn't be too long.' She pushed up her cuff to consult her small gold watch, removing his hand in the process. 'I'm being collected at eight-fifteen.'

He recoiled as if she had slapped him in the face. So there *was* another man: a man who liked short hair and had persuaded her to cut it; a man who had no commitments, no wayward wives or moody, silent daughters; a man who bought her earrings and was able to present them to her, instead of using them as a sop to ingratiate himself with his wife.

'Look, you can't!' he almost shouted. 'We've got to talk.'

'What d'you mean, I "can't"? You really have got a nerve, Daniel! You finish things between us in the most high-handed way imaginable, then start behaving as if you own me.'

'I'm sorry, I was wrong – I mean wrong about finishing things.'

She gave a bitter laugh. 'So I'm expected to follow your every whim, and chop and change along with you? Can't you see how unreasonable you're being?'

'Yes,' he said. 'I can. But . . .'

'But what?'

'I don't know.' He sank back on the chaise-longue, aware that he was saying things he had never planned to say and probably didn't mean. He, too, glanced at his watch – a quarter to eight. How on earth could it be so late? He had thirty minutes left with her – less if she got rid of him well before her visitor arrived. As far as he was concerned, his rival was already there, haunting him, disturbing him, overlaying his own traces in the flat – worst of all, displacing him in her bed. No doubt the wretched man could stay the night, make love to her next morning, instead of being forced to leave at some schoolboy hour and sneak ignominiously home.

She was advancing from the sideboard with his drink, leaning forward to give it to him; another waft of her seductive perfume

357

sapping his good sense. He took the glass, then grabbed her wrist, his fingers snapping round it like a padlock. 'I've just got to see you, Juliet.'

'You *are* seeing me. You're here. But there's no need to hold me captive.' She shook her hand free, grimacing at the faint red weal he'd left. 'I'm already hanging on your every word without your having to resort to violence. I just wish you'd get on with it.'

'It's not that easy,' he countered. 'We can't pick up where we left off, as if nothing's happened in the interim.'

'Well, that's your problem, isn't it? No one asked you to come back.'

It would be impossible to talk at all if she took that hostile tone. 'Look, all I'm saying, Juliet, is that I need to see you for longer than five minutes.'

Studiously, she checked her watch. 'We have twenty-seven and a half, which seems extremely generous for someone who told me a couple of months ago that he had nothing more to say.'

He ignored this second taunt, swallowing his pride to plead, 'Is there any chance you . . . you could cancel your dinner?'

Her angry exclamation was deserved. He knew the suggestion was preposterous, and only sparked by jealousy. If he wasn't careful, she'd throw him out. He had better keep away from the minefield of the past and embark on humdrum conversation – find out how she'd been, ask her how her job was. He watched as she returned to her chair, noting with annoyance how she edged it away from his own.

'So how have things been going?' he asked.

'Fine,' she said, noncommittally, taking a long luxurious drag on her cigarette, as if it were considerably more satisfying than anything he could say.

His next words fared no better, drowned this time by the shrilling of the phone.

'Excuse me, will you, Daniel? I'll take that in the other room.'

Decisively, she closed the bedroom door. He suspected it was another man, since she was so keen he shouldn't hear. Or perhaps it was the suitor expected at eight-fifteen, phoning to say he'd be late – or early – and should he bring red roses (or a priceless antique pendant to match the new pearl earrings), and could he move in permanently?

Look, stop this nonsense, he told himself, appalled at the way he was overreacting. He'd assumed he'd cut all emotional ties, so the intensity of his present feelings had left him severely shaken. He strode to the open window and took a breath of calming air. There was no proof whatsoever that the caller was a man. It could just as easily be Juliet's aged mother, or a colleague from work, or a casual friend ringing for a chat. He picked up a small bronze on the windowsill – a young child's head, sculpted with great energy and vigour. That was new, as well. Another gift, perhaps? There was no sign of his own presents, which he had chosen with such loving care. Had she consigned them to the dustbin?

He prowled up and down, the bronze still in his hand, looking out for 'evidence' – some clue as to her lover's taste; some proof the man had stayed there. He slunk into the kitchen, feeling like a trespasser, gave a swift glance round. Everything seemed much the same: no new foods or acquisitions which might point to a frequent visitor who expected more for breakfast than Juliet's stern morning fare of black coffee and a slice of diet bread. He peered into the fridge: no sausages, no fattening foods, no celebratory champagne. He longed to inspect the bedroom, too, but the door remained firmly shut. He could hear her voice – animated, exuberant, a completely different tone from the one she had used to him just now. She wouldn't talk to her mother like that, and if it was just a casual friend, why couldn't she ring them back, explain she had a visitor?

He snatched up *The Times*, took it with him to his chair and started flicking distractedly through the pages, as he had already done this morning.

'MORE SEX PLEASE – WE'RE SPARROWS!'

Oh God! Not that again. Every species unfaithful, including cast-off mistresses. He ditched the paper and resorted to his drink, lacing it with self-recrimination. Not only was he overreacting, he was being totally inconsistent and unfair. If you gave up a woman for well-considered reasons, convinced yourself, and her, that there was no future in the relationship, then you could hardly object if she found solace elsewhere.

359

Except he *did* object – vehemently – and also felt resentful of the fact that she should be prattling on so avidly, as if she had forgotten his existence. He checked his watch again: two minutes to eight. Her escort would be here in fifteen minutes, unless that was him on the phone. Either way, his own presence in the flat could only be a nuisance and embarrassment. Juliet must wish him at the bottom of the ocean, and he felt much the same about her new companion. He was bound to be young and attractive, with no hint of receding hair – some yuppie in the City who bought his suits in Jermyn Street and owned a private plane, or a dashing trendy heart surgeon with a box at the Royal Opera House.

It would be better if they didn't meet, to prevent awkwardness on both sides. Yet he couldn't simply creep away without saying goodbye to Juliet. He paced back to the bedroom door and stood listening just outside, but could hear no sound at all. Was the other person speaking now, or had Juliet rung off at last?

He banged his glass down and began tramping back and forth with deliberately heavy steps, but the noise he made produced no response. Perhaps the call was over and she was lurking in the bedroom to avoid him. Dare he look in, or knock? He remained hovering outside, despising his own vacillation; finally gave a faint tap-tap and opened the door a crack. She lay diagonally across the bed, cradling the receiver; her tight skirt riding up, displaying long black silky legs; her head thrown languorously back, as if she wasn't simply talking on the phone, but making love to it. She hadn't heard his knock, so he pushed the door a little further open. She turned towards him, her radiant flirtatiousness capsizing in an instant, replaced by an indignant frown. She held up her hand like a barrier and shook her head in annoyance; both gestures signalling 'Keep out!'

He backed away, anger taking over from discomposure as he returned to the lounge and drained his glass in one long resentful gulp. He'd been crazy to come here in the first place. Juliet was bad for him; made him act like a jealous adolescent. He would never set foot in her flat again, but would erect a high brick wall around the whole of Woodleigh Chase.

He seized a pen and paper from the bureau, and, still standing up, started scribbling her a note. 'I'm off,' he wrote, 'since you haven't time to talk. And anyway, I hate to interrupt your busy life.'

He underlined the 'hate' three times, feeling that emotion flaring in his chest: hate for his rival, hate for his ex-mistress, hate for his own crass and puerile self.

29

DANIEL FIRED MALTESERS into his mouth like a succession of small brown bullets, then crunched them to a satisfying pulp. He was starving hungry, yet he didn't dare go near a Hampstead restaurant for fear of meeting Juliet and the man he'd already murdered in his mind. He tried to keep his attention on the screen, though the film had started long before he'd wandered in, so he couldn't make much sense of it. It was trendily obscure – shot in black and white, and sub-titled – and apparently set in pre-war Lithuania. The dialogue was scant and interspersed with moody shots of desolate streets, or sudden startling close-ups of old men's faces, pocked with grief and stubble. Long periods of silence alternated with wailing bursts from the depressing and atonal score. Even in normal circumstances, he would have found the thing hard going, but in his present state it was more or less impossible. The meagre plot was inextricably confused with the more dramatic sub-plot of Juliet and her co-star. His mind kept jumping from Lithuania to Chez Antoine, wondering if they were eating there, or already writhing between the sheets.

His eyes strayed back for the umpteenth time to the illuminated clock, though its hands moved just as sluggishly as all his clocks at home. No, wherever they had gone to eat, they couldn't have finished dinner yet; would still be drinking to each other; feet touching under the table, fingers intertwined.

He shook the last Maltesers into his hand, feeling it was insensitive to munch them while the white-haired crone on screen wept for her dead son. (At least he *assumed* the boy was dead. She appeared to have three near-identical sons – dark, gaunt and tragic-looking – so it was all too easy to confuse them.) It would be even more insensitive to nip out to the foyer and buy an ice or a hot dog, yet he found himself on his feet, blundering down the aisle. There wasn't much risk of disturbing his fellow cineastes: he was almost alone in the place, apart from one canoodling couple at the back, and a solitary Indian boy.

Blinking in the bright lights of the foyer, he ordered his hot dog, which was handed to him in a skimpy paper napkin marked 'Keeping You Satisfied'. The tautly glistening sausage, lying pink and naked in its soft white yielding bed, left him so unnerved that he was unable to bite into it. He returned to his seat in the dark; the warm damp package heavy in his hand. He, too, felt damp in the sweltering heat of the cinema, as if he were sitting in a tropical swamp. No wonder so few people had turned up for the film. There were better things to do on an evening in high summer, and if he had any sense himself he'd be relaxing at home on the patio with an iced drink in his hand and the cool night air restoring him to sanity. He had intended to go home, in fact, even driven as far as the end of the Finchley Road. But then he'd driven back again, unable to drag himself away from Juliet country; his dread of laying eyes on his successor mixed with an overwhelming urge to see the competition. After driving round in circles, cursing Hampstead's twee congested village, he had finally found a parking-space and stalked into a cinema, reverting to his original plan. And he'd been here for the last half-hour – half-century.

He made a renewed effort to follow what was happening on the screen, though the images seemed tediously repetitive – further combinations of weeping, angst and stubble, accompanied by the keening of a cello. He shut his eyes to watch the second film: Juliet disrobing in the bedroom, her wild dark bush surprising him, as it never failed to do. It was so different from her head-hair: not a glossy well-tamed chestnut, but much darker and unruly, with defiant whorls escaping from her ultra-brief silk pants.

Still clutching his hot dog, he crept towards the exit again; managed to get as far as the street this time. When he and Juliet went out to dinner, they had always made a point of returning early; skipping coffee and liqueurs for more intimate delights at home. Juliet and partner might be doing the same this evening. All he really wanted was a brief glimpse of the fellow, then he'd go home satisfied – or at least with his curiosity assuaged.

He drove to Juliet's street once more, parking in a shadowy

spot a safe distance from the flat. Woodleigh Chase was mercifully well-lit, Victorian-style lamps throwing obliging swathes of light across every door and pathway. No one seemed to be about, but he settled himself in the driving-seat, with the uncomfortable sensation that he was behaving like a teenager, spying on a couple like this – and fruitlessly, he was beginning to suspect. They might have gone to *his* place, which could be the other side of London – gone anywhere, for God's sake: Surrey, Scotland, Wales.

Wales! He'd actually forgotten its existence; nor had he spared a thought for Penny since that fleeting memory of her earrings in the drawer. Yet it was for *her* sake that he'd finished things with Juliet, so how could he be so devious as to sneak back to his mistress's lair?

Exasperated, he switched on the ignition and was about to pull away when he saw two figures turning the corner and strolling along the pavement towards the elaborate wrought-iron gates of Woodleigh Chase. One of them was instantly familiar, but she was accompanied by another woman – a younger, plumper girl with fairish hair. He stared in disbelief. What a complete and utter fool he was! All that jealous anguish and she'd merely been out with a girlfriend. Well, thank God they hadn't spotted him. The sensible thing now would be to drive straight home, as he had originally intended, and leave Juliet alone.

Except she wasn't alone – not yet, anyhow. He craned his neck to watch, saw both women slip through the front entrance. For one ridiculous moment he wondered if they were going upstairs not for coffee or a nightcap, but for kisses and caresses like Penny and Corinna.

He thumped his fist on his knee. He was getting worse and worse, becoming almost paranoid. Did he intend to stay here all night, checking every creak and whimper of that inscrutable blue door? Admittedly the alternative was little more appealing: to return to an empty house (and bed), and then wake to the prospect of an empty, endless Sunday.

He switched on the radio and caught the last few minutes of a quiz show: how many square yards in an acre; why was Aethelred the Unready so called? He got both answers wrong: he was out by eight hundred as regarded the square yards, and thought Unready meant 'indecisive', instead of 'lacking counsel'. Daniel the

Indecisive – well, that was right, at any rate. He dithered for a further fifteen minutes, flicking along the wavelength from one station to another, without finding any programme to rival his compulsive interest in Juliet's front door.

Halfway through the Jasper Jones Request Show (which in normal circumstances he would have avoided like the plague) the young plumpish female re-emerged, this time on her own. She slammed the door behind her and stood buttoning up her jacket, then strode purposefully away, down the path and along the shadowy street. Was it just his imagination, or did she look a shade dishevelled, her hair more tousled than it had been earlier?

He snapped off the radio and jumped out of the car, darting through the gates of Woodleigh Chase. If he rang Juliet's bell now, she would assume it was her girlfriend, doubling back to fetch something she'd forgotten. He wouldn't even have to give his name, just sidle in as she released the door.

'*If* you're lucky,' he told himself, pressing the buzzer with a nervous but determined finger, and praying to the gods he didn't believe in.

One of them must exist. The door opened with no question and no fuss, and he sprinted gratefully upstairs; his panicked heartbeat resounding through the stairwell.

He stubbed his cigarette out in the ashtray, staring at it with fury and disgust. The crumpled fag-end seemed to be snuggling up to Juliet's red-stained one – the only kind of closeness they had achieved. He'd been so disconcerted to find her already undressed (and absolutely beside herself with fury – accusing him of spying on her, behaving like a lunatic), that he had snatched a cigarette almost in self-defence. He could hardly deny the charges when he'd condemned himself in almost identical terms. None the less, he'd shouted back, and things had spiralled out of control into a vitriolic row, which had left them both shaking – and both smoking.

He closed his eyes for a moment. The strained, resentful silence was almost more disturbing than the slanging match. He felt so ashamed, so tired, he hid his head in his hands, as if to creep into oblivion. He could smell nicotine on his fingers, taste it in his mouth – a harsh repellent taste, which didn't stop him craving a second cigarette. He reached for the packet, but all at once a different smell engulfed him: the reek of Sayers's pipe, as the chaplain's foul and pungent breath whiffled in his face. The effect was instantaneous: tears pricked at his eyelids, started sliding down his cheeks – the traumatic tears of a twelve-year-old. Horrified, he tried to blink them away, but they continued unabated, in full view of Juliet. She had never seen him cry – the very thought was mortifying. She would despise him even more now.

He turned his back on her, but he couldn't stop his shoulders shaking, nor control his violent sobs. He was cracking up, revealing himself as a spineless sissy to a woman he respected. He was aware of her arm creeping round his shoulders, her perfume in his nostrils, displacing the tobacco. She had come to sit beside him, and instead of angry words she was whispering soothing phrases, like a mother calming her hysterical child. He tried to speak and couldn't. It was so extraordinary, so startling, to be close to her again, to feel her arms encircling him. She was wearing nothing but a housecoat, tied loosely at the waist, and her bare feet looked strangely vulnerable without their usual stylish footwear. It was as if by taking off her high-heeled shoes and formal navy skirt she had also removed a barrier between them. Admittedly, she'd been incensed when he'd first caught her dishabille, but she was now speaking to him more tenderly than he had ever imagined possible.

'Daniel, darling, please don't cry. Don't you realize, you've just made everything all right? I mean, that was the whole problem – I thought I meant nothing to you. But now . . .' She broke off, as if embarrassed herself; the pale satin of her housecoat spotted with his tears.

He pummelled his eyes with his fists. God! She assumed he was crying over *her*; had even called him darling. Whatever could he say? It would be impossible to tell her about Sayers, and if he alluded vaguely to some recent shock he'd had, she'd only insist on knowing all the details. 'Look, Juliet, I . . .'

'It's all right – you don't have to explain. I was horrid – I admit it. I said some really vicious things. But you must understand, it upset me too, your appearing like a bolt from the blue, when I assumed I'd never see you again.' She retied her sash, smoothed its tasselled ends, then took his hand in hers. 'Forgive me, darling, for putting it so bluntly, but it's the best thing which could have happened – your breaking down like this, I mean. I can see now that you value the relationship, and that our time apart has been a frightful strain for you. In fact, I noticed when you first came in how ill and tired you looked, but I put it down to that damn-fool camp.' She forced a smile, squeezed his hand affectionately. 'If you really want to know, you couldn't have said sorry in a more effective way. When you apologized before, it sounded sort of brusque and insincere, and I suspected you'd come round here just to . . .'

'Juliet, it's *not* that.' He couldn't get the words out. Even now, the tears refused to stop. He felt utterly humiliated, totally confused; no longer even knew why he was crying.

'I'd better get you a hankie.' Juliet stood up, ran barefoot to the bedroom.

He blundered after her, grabbed the proffered box of paper tissues and tossed it on the dressing-table without bothering to take one. He pressed himself against her, burying his wet face in her shoulder. He felt her tense and feared she'd pull away. Desperately, he clung to her, holding her so tightly he could feel every curve and contour of her body. He had never had an erection while he was crying – hadn't even realized it was possible. But then never before had he experienced such a turmoil of emotions: explosive reckless anger, bewildered rutting shame. Nor had he ever kissed her quite so fiercely; biting her lips, searching out her tongue with his, as if determined to devour her. He clawed her sash undone and wrested off the housecoat, drawing in his breath as his eyes moved from her breasts to the dark blur of her thatch. Then, somehow, he was on his knees, kissing the coarse hair, mumbling his lips against it, flicking his tongue between her legs. He realized she was still tense – dry and unresponsive. Had his crying turned her off? Was she feeling only pity for him, and no desire at all? He tugged at his belt and clumsily unzipped his jeans while continuing to tongue her. He dared not break the contact, or try to undress fully, fearing he'd lose the urgency of the moment and his passionate resolve. Nothing mattered any longer except manoeuvring her to the bed.

He all but dragged her, arranging her body as he wanted: on

her knees, face down – then pinioning her beneath him and entering her more roughly than he'd meant. She was still dry and still reluctant, but he had to have her; had to thrust away this terrifying anger. He was building up a rhythm, heaving himself against the crouched and passive form, lunging wildly back and forth; the defenceless bed shuddering on its springs. She was trying to speak – protest perhaps, or stop him – but he put his hand across her mouth. He mustn't hear her voice or see her face; must block out his surroundings: the pretty-pretty bedroom with its flower-sprigged walls and virginal white coverlet. He was somewhere else entirely – in a dingy study with a stained and faded carpet, heavy velour curtains shrouding all the windows; a deep male voice crooning in his ear.

'*You mustn't be ashamed, my boy. These things are only natural.*'

He *was* ashamed – horrified by his own brute violence – but he suppressed his feelings by thrusting harder still, in time to Sayers's bland disarming words. '*These things are only natural.*' The phrase throbbed through his head, drowning any scruples, inciting him to even greater ferocity. It was only natural to avenge himself, to prove he wasn't a poofter, or some cowering brat to be used as a receptacle, then tossed back in the shit. His hands were gripping the pale flesh; his rucked-up clothes uncomfortable; the soft purr of the gas fire goading and enraging him.

'*You've done nothing wrong at all, Daniel. We all need relief from time to time. God made us that way, didn't He, so it's perfectly all right.*'

Of course it was all right, and of course he needed relief – relief from days and days of fury and frustration; long nights deprived of sleep, or entangled in dark nightmare. The rage surged up inside him – exhilarating, horrible – until he was on the point of coming. He shut his eyes to concentrate; his breath hurting in his chest. The darkness turned to red beneath his eyelids: the red of Sayers's blood. He wasn't simply buggering him – he was murdering the bastard, and his crimson blood was flowing over the cold black leather sofa, seeping into the shabby balding carpet, oozing under the still-locked double doors, until the whole of Greystone Court had seen it, and he'd been expelled as a criminal.

Yes, he thought, as he slumped appalled across the unresisting body. They're right this time. No punishment could be severe enough for a rapist and a murderer.

30

DANIEL WAS IN DANGER of rolling off the bed. He edged in a few inches, afraid of waking Juliet, who had only just subsided into sleep. He couldn't endure another session of soul-searching. The last hour had been gruelling enough – her tears and his apologies, the storm of lies he'd been forced to produce to excuse his unspeakable behaviour, when there *was* no conceivable excuse. Yet Juliet had arrived at the conclusion that his violence was a sort of ardour, and though at first repelled by it, she was also somehow impressed; seeing him as a wild Byronic figure driven to excesses by the sheer strength of his passion for her.

He stared into the darkness; the only glimmer of light stealing through a crack in the curtains from one of the mock-Victorian lamps outside. While she lauded him as Byron, he'd been damning himself as a bully and a thug – in fact, little better than Sayers. He had kept offering to go home (longing to escape, if only to sort out the confusion raging in his head), but she had insisted that he stay, claiming he was still too upset to be on his own, let alone to drive. Despite his wretched state, he hadn't missed the irony of the situation: throughout their affair he would have given anything to stay the night with her, but now, when it was possible, he felt only dread and despair. The problem was that their whole relationship had become mired in misunderstanding, and although lying physically close, their bodies all but touching, he had never felt more distanced from her emotionally.

It was also oppressively hot. He was wearing nothing but his skin, but that skin was damp and sweaty, and he couldn't seem to get comfortable in the narrow too-soft bed. He tried to lie as still as possible, but Juliet herself was a surprisingly restless sleeper, turning over in her sleep and giving sudden violent shudders, which made him jump as well. He felt an overwhelming urge to have Penny there instead, but thoughts of Penny induced even fiercer guilt. Not only had he betrayed her yet again, he had proved himself a monster in the process. In fact, in whichever direction his mind strayed, some prosecutor would loom before him with accusations of baseness and neglect.

His stomach rumbled vulgarly, reminding him that all he had eaten since yesterday's breakfast was a packet of Maltesers and one bite of a hot dog. He tried ignoring his hunger, which seemed another dangerous appetite, best left unappeased. But a second, louder gurgle persuaded him to change his mind. A hot milky drink might help him to unwind, and if he made himself a sandwich, too, it would at least kill half an hour, bring dawn a little closer.

He crept out of bed and tiptoed to the door, opening it as softly as he could. It was a relief to reach the kitchen and be able to stretch his limbs, which felt stiff and cramped from the strain of lying still. He switched on the light, its neon glare hurting his eyes after the murky gloom of the bedroom. He never felt at ease in Juliet's flat. Its smugly decorous ambience seemed to hold him in disdain, especially now, when he was naked and unwashed. His clothes were in the bedroom, so he wrapped himself in a king-sized towel, borrowed from the bathroom. Some king, he reflected wryly as he caught sight of himself in the mirror, his shell-pink swaddlings topped by stubbly chin and unkempt hair. Clutching the slipping towel, he stole back to the kitchen to see what he could find to eat. Making a humble sandwich was clearly going to tax his ingenuity. There appeared to be no bread, not even Juliet's usual diet brand, and certainly no butter. Fat was evidently enemy number one, since everything he lighted on was labelled low in fat: milk, yogurt, salad-dressing, even Ovaltine. Well, at least he could make a hot drink: no-fat milk with low-fat Ovaltine, and sweetened with sugarless sugar. There were no biscuits to accompany it, but perhaps Juliet wouldn't begrudge him a bowl of Special K – the only permitted cereal (for slimmers, naturally). He ate some from the packet, dry, unwilling to make further inroads on the morning's milk supply.

The morning! He had totally forgotten that in a matter of a few short hours they would be sitting down to breakfast here –

together, yet apart; the spectre of last night still overshadowing everything. How could they make conversation, or behave in any normal fashion, as if nothing untoward had happened? He put away the cereal, turned off the gas under the pan of barely warm milk. Only now was he beginning to realize that the memory of what he'd done could never be erased. He would be compelled to live with the knowledge that he – a rational, liberal, decent sort of man (or so he'd thought, naïvely) – could actually use force against a woman; treat her like a punchbag or a scapegoat, to work off his own anger.

He slunk into the sitting-room and stood leaning against the bureau, staring at the neat array of stationery and file-cards. Almost without thinking, he reached for a cigarette. He lit it gratefully, trying to fix his attention only on the minutiae of smoking: his hand, his mouth, the ashtray, the all-absorbing business of inhaling and exhaling. Yet his mind refused to stop its anxious circling, especially when it dawned on him, with a sense of hopeless failure, that he was back to where he'd been two months ago: a smoker, with a mistress. All his efforts to renounce the two transgressions had proved completely fruitless. In fact, he and Juliet were now bonded more inextricably than ever. His very violence had convinced her that this new intense relationship couldn't possibly founder, as their previous one had done. How could he admit to her that what she regarded as his overwhelming passion was really vengeful fury, and directed against a long-dead pederast? That would be another sort of violence, and one she *wouldn't* forgive.

He drifted to the window and stood looking out at the well-tended lawns and flowerbeds. If only he had his own private gardener to hack away the undergrowth which choked him, cut down his rotten branches. Not only had the last two months proved sterile, but the new crises which had arisen had revealed a harrowing past.

'*But that's your problem, Daniel, isn't it? You can't leave anything behind – not the past, not your pain and suffering as a child.*'

The healer's voice was so distinct, he spun round from the window to confront him. No one there. Yet he had no more imagined the voice than the one in Leicester Square; each word unmistakable.

'Leave me alone!' he implored, not knowing where to direct his own voice – inside, outside, up or down. 'All you've done is make things worse, so for God's sake go away.'

31

DANIEL SQUEEZED HIMSELF into the one free patch of grass between the close-packed bodies lying on the bank. He glanced surreptitiously at his immediate neighbours: a lank-haired student strumming a guitar, and two lovers rubbing sun-tan oil into each other's naked backs. The fragrant scent of the oil mingled agreeably with the smell of fruit from their picnic-basket – some exotic foreign fruit he didn't recognize. He had the feeling once again of being on holiday abroad, this time at a beach resort. The beach itself would have to be imagined, since there was no sand, only grass, but the water and the swimmers, the sunbathers and lifeguard were all here before his eyes.

A group of teenage girls pranced self-consciously along the jetty which led into the water and started pushing each other off, their exaggerated shrieks alarming a pair of moorhens, which had been perching on a buoy. As the birds skittered away, the largest girl, in a striking black bikini, grabbed the buoy herself and tried to do a handstand on it, to the wild cheers of her friends. Daniel watched them larking around in the murky grey-brown water, their hair like seaweed, streaming out in long dark strands. Then his eyes strayed back to the couple on his right. The woman was topless and had now turned over on her back, exposing her voluptuous breasts, which were made still more conspicuous by their glistening sheen of oil. Her partner was immersed in the *Sunday Sport* (its pages splodged with grease from his hands) and seemed more engrossed in its full-frontal photographs than in her flesh-and-blood attractions.

Daniel unfolded his own *Observer*, but reading wasn't easy. The girls were still shouting and splashing, when suddenly a punk lad in his twenties dashed along the jetty completely palely naked, and caused a minor sensation by diving into the pool. The

373

lifeguard and another man struck out in pursuit and, when he ignored their remonstrations, removed him bodily. There were also further distractions from the bank. The guitarist had begun to sing in a soft and rather mournful voice, perhaps trying to evoke some sense of Latin melancholy. Daniel found it quite extraordinary to think that he was less than a dozen miles from home. No one played guitars on Wandsworth Common, or sunbathed topless, or tried to swim stark naked. North Londoners were clearly more uninhibited. In fact, Juliet had told him that she had actually seen a couple making love in public on this very stretch of grass.

It was Juliet who had persuaded him of the delights of Hampstead Heath, suggesting that he come and relax here by the Mixed Bathing Pond, or watch people flying kites on Parliament Hill. *She* was due at her mother's for a spell of Sunday duty, which apparently she couldn't cancel without causing deep offence. Daniel blessed the mother's tetchiness, since it afforded him a chance to think things out on his own before he met Juliet again at five. He was definitely feeling better than he had done in the early hours, though he attributed his lighter mood partly to champagne. Instead of an ascetic breakfast at the flat, they had gone out for an indulgent brunch: Buck's Fizz and coddled eggs, with chilled mangos as an appetizer and *pain au chocolat* to follow. He had ignored the mangos and concentrated on the Fizz; each successive mouthful helping to put things in proportion. Afterwards, they had returned to the flat to make love – and with the emphasis on love this time. At first he'd had to struggle with his conscience, though his usual guilt about Penny had been diluted by the champagne. He had also feared he wouldn't get an erection (as punishment for last night), but his fears proved quite unfounded. Both guilt and fear had dissipated in the tangled heat of the bed, and, despite his mounting excitement, he had made a special point of being as gentle and considerate as he'd been rough and relentless before – a recompense and peace-offering to Juliet.

She had responded not just physically – though he had never known her so abandoned – but with her own gesture of forgiveness: inviting him to accompany her to Paris. She was going there in three days' time, to attend an international conference on Third World education. It was too late to register him as well, but he could share her hotel room, and if he flew out with her on Wednesday, they could spend the evenings together and the whole of next weekend. The invitation had thrown him into a quandary, and he had found it quite impossible to say either yes or no. He still hadn't come to a decision – and was hardly likely to, distracted as he was by the squeals and giggles of those frolicking Lolitas and the strains of the Spanish Romanza.

Awkwardly, he got up from the grass and picked his way between the sun-worshippers, then walked on past the changing-huts in the direction of Parliament Hill. It would be easier to think up there, and the sense of height and space might help resolve the conflicts in his mind. If only Juliet's destination wasn't Paris (with all its traitorous memories of Penny and Pippa), and yet Paris was his favourite city, and one he hadn't visited for years. Ever since he'd met her, he'd been hoping – vainly – to go away with Juliet, but now he had the perfect opportunity. No one need even know. He would be back on Sunday evening and could return to Wales on the Monday; the official story being that he had merely spent two weeks at home. After all, it was Penny who had urged him not to hurry back to the camp, so she could hardly blame him if he took her at her word.

He slowed his pace, as if in direct response to her advice, strolling along between thickly wooded hedgerows overgrown with ivy. All the foliage looked luxuriant and lush; even weeds and stinging-nettles in their green and thrusting prime. Squirrels darted across the grass, their coiled tails forming question-marks; birds chattered overhead, and a pair of tortoiseshell butterflies were courting in the sun. Although still hot, the air was no longer humid, and the trees provided welcome shade. He was beginning to feel elated just by imagining next weekend: he and Juliet walking by the moonlit Seine, or revisiting his favourite haunts, or making love again – again – as passionately as they had this morning. He couldn't stop thinking about her body; savouring things he had half-forgotten in the impoverished weeks without her: the way her nipples tautened when he kissed the nape of her neck; the strange strangled noises she made when she was on the point of coming; screwing up her face – and toes – then letting go of everything with one fierce cry of '*Daniel!*' That '*Daniel!*' always thrilled him. It was so different from her usual cool composure;

seemed to fuse them in her climax; make his name a fanfare.

He was so deeply under her spell, he had hardly noticed his surroundings, and was surprised to see that the path had opened out into a wide expanse of green, sloping steeply upwards. This must be Kite Hill. The springy turf made the going easy, and he went striding up the incline, dodging out of the way of two large, boisterous labradors chasing each other downhill. They were followed by their owners – eccentric-looking twenty-somethings in matching fringed suede jerkins; the man's long hair was bleached blond, while hers was cropped above her ears and dyed an inky black. Daniel watched them saunter arm in arm. When he'd walked on the common yesterday, everyone had been alone, whereas here families or couples appeared to be the norm. He too could be a couple again – with Juliet in Paris – no longer odd man out (shunned for his lack of a womb), or a mere appendage to his wife, resented by Corinna. He could also pay JB back for his terrifying intrusion in the middle of last night by showing him that he *could* leave things behind – leave his wife and daughter behind, and the whole nonsense of the camp; leave his petty scruples behind, his futile bouts of guilt.

He reached the top of the hill and stood looking down on London spread below: grey roofs and stark white tower-blocks; church-spires dwarfing distant Docklands cranes; glints of lazy river meandering between swathes of trees in every shade from coppery red to the palest yellow-green. The whole was capped with puffs of cloud, like blobs of cream squirted from a giant aerosol by some cosmic pastrycook. Vying with the clouds, brightly coloured kites kicked and bobbed in the wind, straining against their strings and pursued at every twist and turn by their faithful looping tails. He, too, longed to soar that high, to cut all strings and float away to Paris – Juliet beside him, wild scarlet to his blue.

Instead, he stretched out on the grass, still mesmerized by the view. Children were racketing all around him, dogs yelping in excitement, but the noise was somehow exhilarating rather than annoying. He lit a cigarette and sat watching the blue kite perform a series of impressive stunts: somersaulting, spiralling, swooping down, then up again. He blew out a perfect smoke-ring, glad to see that he hadn't lost the knack. Smoking no longer seemed so heinous. Juliet had told him that even Sigmund Freud had found it impossible to quit, so at least he was in eminent company.

As the noisiest of the dogs ceased its frenzied barking, he caught a snatch of music drifting up from the other side of the hill: the plink-plunk sound of a steel band, faint but unmistakable. Spurred by curiosity, he scrambled to his feet and hurried downhill to investigate. He had always had a sneaking fondness for steel bands – not shared by Juliet, alas, but certainly by the enthusiastic crowd who had gathered by the bandstand and were clapping, stomping, swaying to the beat. The carnival mood was heightened by the brightly coloured costumes of the players: emerald satin shirts and patterned waistcoats in vibrant green and purple. As they launched into a Beatles tune, they were cheered on by the audience, who started linking arms and dancing on the grass, some kicking off their shoes and jigging around barefoot. A high-spirited West Indian boy even clambered up on the bandstand and wove his way between the players, doing a comic conga-for-one.

Daniel's feet were soon tapping to the rhythm, and when he finally left the bandstand, he found he was still marching in time to 'Sergeant Pepper'. The path led him past a café, and then a bowling green and tennis courts. Wherever he looked, people were enjoying themselves: tucking in to tea and cakes, rolling balls along velvety greens, darting to and fro returning powerful serves, or simply soaking up the sun. It was time he, too, relaxed and allowed himself some pleasure in life; learned that fun was not a dirty word, to be atoned for with a storm of self-reproach. *That* was the message he would extract from JB's words – not more guilt, but less – a break with his past habit of punishing himself for every small transgression. He *would* go to Paris with Juliet, and he'd bloody well enjoy it; relish every minute with her; make love night and morning – even in the lunch-hour if she could escape the conference then.

He already felt aroused, remembering her as she'd been this morning: avid and responsive, even uncharacteristically flushed; the bed itself expressing their abandon – duvet humped and tumbled, pillows on the floor. The enticing pictures stopped him in his tracks. Instinctively, he turned round and set off back the way he'd come, in the direction of her flat. Whatever happened, he didn't want her arriving home to find he wasn't there. He must get in well before her, buy some wine en route and chill it in the fridge, so that they could drink to his decision; drink to the new, hedonistic Daniel. Perhaps he'd play the true romantic and buy her flowers as well – sensuous red roses to match his sensuous mood.

The idyllic summer's day did indeed seem to be fostering romance. Even in the car-park he found a couple locked in an embrace; the pimply but impassioned youth kissing his under-age girlfriend in full view of all and sundry.

He drove out of the exit and took the road which skirted the Heath. A flock of wood-pigeons suddenly exploded from a clump of trees and flapped across the road, startled by the backfiring of a car. For a disorientating moment his vision was obscured, then one of the panicked birds slammed straight into his windscreen with a heavy, sickening thud. Glancing in his mirror, he saw the helpless body spinning over and over and over before it hit the tarmac. He jammed on the brakes and jumped out. The bird lay floundering in the gutter, while he stood watching impotently, praying for it to die. The thought of having to put it out of its misery was utterly repellent. The topaz eyes were still open, and fixed on him unnervingly. He knelt down by the kerb, ignoring the hoots of passing motorists angered by the obstruction of his car. The bird continued to gaze at him, clinging to its feeble spark of life. Torn between pity and annoyance, he scooped it from the gutter, feeling the faint heartbeat flickering through his hands. What now? Did he stay with it till it died, or leave it to suffer alone – perhaps right on through the night?

He decided on a third course: fetched his jacket from the car and wrapped it firmly round the bird, to prevent it from injuring itself any further. Then he placed the bundle on the passenger seat and drove to Woodleigh Chase. He parked outside the wrought-iron gates and opened the car door, but remained sitting there, immobile, eyes flicking from the drab stunned bird to the ostentatious building. Juliet wouldn't welcome a dying wood-pigeon messing up her flat. He shut the door again. He wasn't going to Juliet's – he wasn't even going home. He couldn't explain, not even to himself, why he was suddenly so certain of what he had to do; he simply knew he had no choice.

He drove swiftly down the street, turned left, then left again and into the Finchley Road, heading for the North Circular and eventually the motorway. There wasn't time to collect his stuff from Wandsworth, or phone Juliet and embark on a long argument.

However fanciful it might sound, he had a deep unerring conviction that he was being summoned back to Wales. He was needed there – at once.

32

DANIEL RAN TOWARDS the tents, still propelled by the adrenalin which had kept him roaring down the M4 at eighty miles an hour, in his dramatic dash from London. Even after the motorway, when the roads had narrowed and he'd been slowed by zigzag bends, he'd continued to feel that he was speeding; his mind and body so revved up, it had proved impossible to relax. Yet now he'd actually arrived, he was beginning to wonder if he had fabricated the crisis. The camp looked just the same – in fact, remarkably serene in the perfect summer's evening; no sign of any disturbance, nor anything out of the ordinary. Lazy smoke was curling from a fire, and the usual reassuring things were littered on the grass: sturdy saucepans, bright enamel mugs, Tim's sweater with the soldiers on, a box of purple plums. The only unfamiliar sight was a smart new camper-van parked beside the field (and shaming the other scruffier vehicles). Some well-heeled new-comers, presumably, who had come in search of a cure, but had no intention of roughing it.

A minute later he spotted them: an attractive girl in her twenties and two slightly older men, standing by the Big Tepee with Dylan, Gerard, Pat and Megan, all talking volubly. The taller man held a mobile phone, which looked incongruous in these primitive surroundings. Penny and Pippa were nowhere to be seen, nor Corinna, Claire or Happy. Were they busy with some female rite, or doing something more mundane like preparing supper in the tepee? He decided to check his own tent first, unwilling to join the noisy group, who were so involved in their discussion they hadn't even noticed him.

He crawled inside and was greeted by a cry from Penny – almost a howl of pain and relief. She rushed towards him, clutched him in a fierce embrace.

'Daniel, thank God you're here! I thought you'd never come.'

'What d'you mean?'

'Well, I left the message hours ago.'

'What message?'

'Oh, Daniel, don't be stupid. The message about *Rick* – on the answerphone. Three messages, in fact.'

He stared at her pale face and swollen eyes. He had not been home since Saturday afternoon, but he could hardly tell her that. 'Rick?' he prompted, still completely mystified.

'But I explained it all on the phone. Did the dratted thing cut out?'

He gave a noncommittal grunt; watched in horror as tears streamed down her face.

'He's . . . he's . . .' She was struggling to get the words out; tried again, her voice distorted, harsh. 'He . . . he drowned.'

'*What?*'

'This morning – in that lake you're so fond of. It's been absolutely terrible. You just can't imagine, Daniel! And these reporters got on to the story. Of course, to them it was the most fantastic scoop. They were practically drooling over it. God, I'd like to kill them!' She clenched her fists, tears giving way to anger. 'We didn't *know* they were reporters, or we'd have sent them packing straight away. They pretended they'd come for healing, you see, but . . .'

'Penny, wait, for Christ's sake! Never mind the reporters. I must know what's happened to Rick. Are you telling me he's . . . he's . . .' Now he was the one finding it difficult to speak. '. . . *dead*?' he whispered, the word knelling through the tent.

'No.' She shook her head, then nodded. 'Well, maybe now he is. No one knows for certain. They rushed him off to hospital and he's all wired up to drips and things.'

Daniel sank down in despair. He could see the life-support machine with its incessant whines and bleeps; its battery of hardware; Rick's restless fidgety body unnaturally still. He concealed his face from Penny. He too was drowning in a tidal wave of rage: fury at the treacherous lake which he'd regarded as a sanctuary; fury at so hideous a disaster; fury with himself for being in bed with Juliet through all this grief and horror. And what of

381

Claire? What must *she* be feeling as she waited by the hospital bed, not knowing whether her only child would survive?

'Claire's with him, I assume?' His voice was still unsteady, each word requiring effort.

'Yes. And Happy and Corinna. And Stephen, of course.' She pronounced the healer's name with indignant emphasis, almost as if blaming him for the tragedy. '*I* stayed here with Pippa. She's in the most appalling state. Well, I told you that on the phone. You did *get* the messages, didn't you, Daniel? Well, yes, of course you must have done, or you wouldn't have come back.'

Relieved that she didn't pursue the matter further, he drew her down beside him on the groundsheet. 'Pippa?' he repeated, already feeling a sense of foreboding.

'I've never seen her so distraught. Of course it *was* a ghastly shock, so you'd expect her to be upset. But not as bad as this. I just can't understand it. I mean, she detested Rick – we know that – yet she's completely gone to pieces.'

'Where *is* she?'

'In the cottage on the hill – you know, where you were sleeping the first week. She went up there to be alone. We've all been trying to comfort her and talk to her, but she just doesn't want to know. I tried again a few minutes ago, but she told me to go away. I thought I'd leave her for a little while, and then go up with Pat, perhaps, or . . .'

'*I'll* go.'

'No, don't, darling – please.' She put a restraining hand on his arm. 'You'll only make things worse.'

Rebuked, he sat in silence, staring at Pippa's stained and muddy sandals. He was recalling JB's words once more, about the 'someone' who was threatening her. Only a few hours ago he had betrayed her mother yet again; proving just how far he was from being a decent sort of father. And he'd betrayed Claire, too, in a way. If he hadn't left the camp for his own self-serving reasons, he might have prevented the drowning. After all, *he* was the one who spent most time with Rick, and he certainly would have warned him about the dangers of the lake – the way it shelved so unexpectedly; the unnerving depth of the water.

He turned back to Penny, sounding tetchy in his impatience for more details. 'Look, how the hell did it happen? Can't Rick swim, or was he on his own, or what?'

'No, he went with Andrew. They were both very hot and sticky and wanted to cool off. And he *told* us he could swim. But then he's used to a tiddly public baths, not a lake which is goodness knows how deep. He got into difficulties almost straight away. Andrew saw him struggling and rushed to the rescue. But he said Rick started panicking, and kept thrashing about and hitting him, and swallowing loads more water. Apparently he all but drowned them both. You can imagine how Anita feels.'

Daniel nodded grimly, though his thoughts were more with the healer. Rick had been brought here, most unwillingly, because he was suffering from mere stomach pains. And now he was fighting for his life. How did JB cope with that? He longed to question Penny further, but she seemed close to tears again; biting her lip, fiddling with her hair, even gnawing at her thumbnail in a way that reminded him, unbearably, of Rick.

'I've been so worried, Daniel, about what we ought to do. I suppose the obvious solution now you're here is to drive straight home and take Pippa to see Dr Steadman. Maybe he could prescribe something to get her over the shock. But it seems awfully callous just to disappear when Claire's in such a state, and we don't even know if Rick will . . . will make it. Thank God we're able to phone! That's the only good thing about those unspeakable reporters – they've got a portable phone. Mind you, it's not very reliable out here in the wilds, but at least we've managed to keep in touch with the hospital.'

'Look, who *are* these bloody reporters?'

'Bloody's the right word. I've never known such ghouls! Someone drowns or dies, and it's meat and drink to them.'

'But how did they find out about it? Surely no one would start gabbling to the press?'

'No, they were here already – on the spot. Conveniently!'

'What d'you mean? What for?'

'Oh, Daniel, there's so much you still don't know. How long have you been gone? It feels like an eternity.'

'Let me see – eight days.'

'It must be more than that!'

He counted on his fingers. He, too, could hardly believe that only a week had elapsed. It was something to do with Juliet. Once back in her affections (and her bed), it felt as if he'd been with her for months.

'Well, a few days after you left – the Thursday, I think it was – this man turned up and started snooping around. We didn't know at the time, but he was a freelance journalist who lives in Cwmystwyth. He was alerted by the local Friends of the Earth, who'd carried out a secret test on the stream which runs through here. They found it was full of gunge from the mine – not just tainted, but downright poisonous. There was lead in it and cadmium – which is lethal for the kidneys – and even sulphide of arsenic! I just can't tell you, Daniel, how furious I was – furious with Stephen most of all. Except I refuse to call him Stephen now. It's an insult to my father.'

Daniel was astonished by her vehemence. 'But, Penny, why blame *him*? He can't have known, surely?'

'Well, he bloody well should have done! Apparently it's common knowledge round here that those mines are a source of really damaging pollution. The toxins from the tunnels get washed into the watercourses and all the fish start dying, or the rivers running red. Okay, perhaps we should have thought ourselves, but then we're strangers to the area, whereas *he* lives on the spot. I mean, fancy luring all those sick people here – some of them seriously ill – and then exposing them to a danger like that. And he was actually making salves and things from the mud right near the tunnel-openings. As the reporters said themselves, it's bad enough drinking the poisons in the water, without slapping them on your skin as well. Pippa was forever rubbing ointments into that wretched Bernard's leg, so God knows what harm it's done her – or the poor dog, for that matter. And we're *all* at risk just by having camped here. Anyway, it's ruined any notion of community. So much for sisterhood! Everyone's at each other's throats and taking sides, either for or against the healer.' She gave a derisive snort. 'Some healer! Corinna won't even *speak* to me because I said it was his fault, and at least he should have thought to check before he set up camp here. She and Happy are like a pair of spaniels, still fawning on him and licking his hand and refusing to hear a word against their master.'

'I can't understand you, Penny. Okay, the pollution thing's

appalling, and thank heavens it's been brought to light. But I just don't believe the healer could have known. It goes entirely against his ethos – unless he's a madman or a hypocrite. And that's not likely either. Hell! Last time we discussed the man, you seemed to think he was another Jesus Christ. And, anyway, what about the miracles? You were so convinced about those.'

'I'm not convinced of anything – not now. I mean, when you come to think of it, there were so many different risks. That ghastly lake, to start with, and those poor old crocks like Doris, forced to live rough in terrible conditions. And even Dylan, who's still here, but no better at all – *worse*, if anything. And the awful weather we've had – rain and storms and lightning . . .'

Daniel glanced up through the tent-flaps at the expanse of deep blue sky. The sun was still serenely bright and he could hear some bird or other carolling its carefree song. He wondered for an instant if Penny had dreamt the whole disaster – or invented it, to punish him for Juliet; for his resolve this afternoon to become a ruthless hedonist.

'Of course, the reporters lapped it up – the whole business of us living in a New Age hippie commune, as they will insist on calling it, and the drama of the storm, and the healing sessions and wonder-cures. It'll be splashed all over the national press tomorrow. The local freelance chap sold the story to the *Daily Express*. I suppose it does make marvellous headlines – the miracle-worker who poisons his patients!'

She reached out for an apple, bit into it aggressively, then put it down, as if she had already lost all appetite. 'Anyway, these two Fleet Street hacks arrived – Dave the photographer and Zoe the reporter. Except of course we didn't know that. Dave passed himself off as a teacher, and said he was especially keen on geology and wildlife, so he'd brought his camera with him. Well, he snapped away quite merrily without rousing our suspicions. And we also swallowed his story that Zoe was his girlfriend and suffering from ME. Actually, she's as tough as old boots, but no one smelt a rat until the point where Rick was carried down the hillside on a makeshift stretcher-thing. He looked quite dreadful – sort of limp and bluish-pale, and lying so horribly still you'd have thought he was dead already.' Her voice began to falter again, but she regained control; continued with real bitterness.

'You'll hardly credit this, Daniel, but in the midst of all the commotion, Dave got out his camera and started taking photographs! I mean, everyone else was absolutely devastated – in tears and everything, but at least we were trying to help. And that bloody Dave just stands there, fussing with his light-meter! Andrew went berserk. He actually yanked the camera away and flung it on the ground. That did it! Dave launched himself on Andrew, and while the two of them were fighting tooth and nail, Zoe suddenly announced that they were *press*, and that Andrew ought to welcome Dave, not clobber him. God! She sounded like some missionary, come to root out evil. She said the healer was a total fraud who had deliberately deceived us all, so she and Dave intended to expose him . . .'

'But what about *Rick*?' Daniel interrupted, less concerned with public exposés than with his own private photographs: Rick's nondescript brown hair flopping into his eyes; his dirty bitten fingernails; the threadbare jeans, patched with bits from Claire's old paisley dressing-gown; his gruesome bone-collection. He picked up Penny's discarded apple, as if it needed comforting, sat cradling it in his hands, wishing he could concentrate. She was answering his question and he wasn't even listening.

'The ironic thing was that it was actually Dave and Zoe who took Rick to the hospital. They probably only offered because they wanted to be in at the kill. But it still seemed the best idea. I mean, that camper-van is really big and comfortable, and it's got a proper bed in the back. And there was room for Claire and Corinna and . . . and . . . everyone.'

He noticed how she'd avoided using JB's name. Indeed, he no longer had a name. She refused to call him Stephen, and he hardly merited the term 'healer' in the circumstances. Even his own 'JB' seemed crassly inappropriate since the trauma of the drowning. Rick had called him the Mega-Wanker, he remembered with affection and distress. They had laughed about it together, plotted joint rebellion over a bag of Creamline toffees.

'Anyway,' said Penny, thrusting a distracted hand through her hair, 'they were just driving off when Pippa started shaking – I mean, really shaking, as if she had a high fever. I insisted she lie down, but . . .'

'I've got to *see* her, Penny! We can't just leave her on her own when she's so dreadfully upset.'

Penny gave a despairing shrug. 'It won't do any good. I've been trying to get through to her all day. She wouldn't even let me sit with her, though I promised not to say a word, if that's what she preferred.'

'Well, I feel I ought to try, at least. And if she still refuses to talk, I'll walk on up the hill and get some air. There's so much to take in, I'm feeling a bit strange.'

Penny hugged him suddenly. 'I'm sorry, darling. Here I am, ranting on, and forgetting what a shock it is for *you*. You were closer to Rick than any of us.'

Yes, I was, he thought, registering the grimness of the past tense. If Rick didn't pull through, then part of himself would die as well – his skinny restless child-self. He dragged himself to his feet. 'I won't be long. Okay?'

She nodded. 'I'll stay here and wait for you. I can't face the thought of supper. I feel absolutely wrung out. And everything's so awkward with those reporters hanging around.'

'Why the hell are they still here?'

'Well, Zoe came sneaking back once she'd phoned her story through. And Dave's still at the hospital. Apparently he almost broke his neck trying to get the photos on the next fast train to London. But now they're safely with the *Express*, I expect he's hovering by the bedside, camera poised to record Rick's dying breath.'

'Penny, *don't*!'

'Well, they make me sick, the pair of them. I mean, Zoe's got a bloody cheek daring to show her face up here again. I suppose she's after another story – "Feuds Tear Healing Camp Apart".' She jabbed her foot against the canvas, the tent shuddering in protest. 'She arrived with the freelance journalist – the one who came originally about the water pollution thing. And they brought another photographer – a creepy little man called Boyd.' She broke off for a moment, chewed her thumb again. She seemed to have caught the habit, unconsciously, from Rick. 'What depresses me the most, Daniel, is the way the others have let themselves be conned, especially Pat and Megan. It's as if they *want* their pictures plastered all over the papers. They probably think they'll be paid

387

a big fat fee. Well, perhaps they will. Good luck to them!'

Daniel squeezed her hand sympathetically, though he couldn't really understand her venom. She seemed more distressed about the media-hacks than about the actual drowning. Was it because they'd used deception to infiltrate the camp, or more to do with the unpalatable fact that they'd knocked her idol from his pedestal? She had put such trust in Stephen – her all-wise, all-powerful father-figure – but now he'd been revealed as highly irresponsible, if not an out and out fraud. He had also failed to do anything for Pippa, who would be leaving here more disturbed than when she'd arrived.

He slipped out of the tent and looked warily around. The group outside the tepee had disappeared, thank God. He had no wish to be grilled by journalists, or approached by rival factions in the camp and asked to give his verdict pro or anti JB.

He slunk the long way round the field, keeping in the shelter of the bushes, then sprinted up the hill, only slowing down when he was safely out of sight. He stopped to inspect the stream, which looked as clear and sparkling as ever. Could it really be polluted? He drank a mouthful from his hands, as if defying it to poison him. It tasted fresh and clean. He splashed some on his face, hoping it would clear his head, wash the dark stains from his mind. The images were harrowing: Rick's gangling body too long for its stretcher; Dave's camera nosing into close-up; Claire's magenta glasses, their glittery glamour subverted by her tears. And Pippa, shaking uncontrollably. What in God's name could he *say* to Pippa, to ensure he wasn't dismissed, like all the rest?

He trudged on up the hill, resenting the beauty of the country-side as it basked in the evening sun; the sky a boastful gold, the clouds haloed and luxurious. All nature was affirming life: a whirr of swifts swooping across the stream; the usual sheep still munch-ing placidly; the grass itself a vibrant green. As he approached the ruined cottage he was aware how apprehensive he felt, not only on account of Pippa, but because of his own memories of the place. He steeled himself to walk up to it; peered in through the empty window-frame. He could see nothing but a stretch of stony floor, bleak and uninviting. Perhaps she'd gone, but where?

'Pippa,' he called softly. 'It's Daniel. I'm back.'

He was answered only by the noises all around him: the

388

rapturous stream tumbling down the hillside, two hoarse-voiced crows flapping from a thorn-tree, the orchestra of insects in the grass.

He stepped softly through the doorless door, relieved to see Pippa's blaze of hair – the only splash of colour in the gloom of the interior. She was standing with her back to him, leaning against the wall; face pressed against the stone, arms hanging limply by her sides. Her total stillness so unnerved him, his words faltered into nothing, and all he managed was to stutter out her name. She made not the slightest response; stood motionless, unhearing, as if she were part of the wall itself.

He took another step towards her, the stones scrunching under his feet. 'Listen, darling . . . Penny told me how upset you are. The whole thing's just so awful, I still can't take it in.' Tentatively he reached out his hand, let it brush her shoulder.

'Don't *touch* me!'

He recoiled as if he'd been scalded. He had never heard such fury in her voice. Penny was right – pointless trying to talk to her when she was in such a hostile mood. He retreated through the doorway, shading his eyes against the brilliance of the sunset. The sun was already sinking, birds flying home to roost. It would be dark in another hour or so – terrifying for her to stay out here alone, with the eerie shadows, that chilling sense of isolation he remembered all too well.

He turned back, cleared his throat, uncertain what to say. Even if he simply warned her about the dark, it might provoke another violent reaction, and any attempt at dialogue seemed guaranteed to fail. If Penny couldn't get through to her, what chance had he, for heaven's sake? Emotional encounters had never been his strong point, and his own grief on this occasion made him still more inept. But maybe he could build on that, admit how shocked he felt.

'I . . . I think I do know how you feel, darling. It's hit me really hard as well – especially the fact that Rick was . . .'

She suddenly exploded into life, wheeling round to face him, both fists clenched. 'Don't *say* his name! I don't want to hear it, ever!'

'But surely . . . I mean, wouldn't it be better . . . ?' He was so appalled by her appearance, he hardly knew what he was saying. Her clothes were bedraggled, her eyes puffy and inflamed; her whole face distorted from crying; red marks on her forehead from the imprint of the stones. Instinctively, he moved towards her, put his arms around her.

'Get off, get off! I *hate* you! And it's all your fault anyway.'

She blundered past him and through the door, stumbling over the tussocky grass, running headlong down the hill. He dashed in pursuit, frightened for her safety. She wasn't looking where she was going and might fall and hurt herself. He managed to catch up with her, grabbed her by the arm, steered her to a low and crumbling wall – another relic of the mine.

'Okay, you hate me, Pippa, and everything's my fault.' He was out of breath, his voice laboured and staccato. 'But you've got to tell me *why*, and what I've done. We can't go on like this. We've just got to sort it out. So let's sit down here, the two of us, and have a proper talk.'

She began to sob hysterically; her head pressed right down on her knees, so that he couldn't see her face. The few sheep grazing near them shied away in fear. The wild noise she was making seemed to startle the whole countryside; her outburst like a hand-grenade flung into the tranquil evening and blitzing it apart. He let her cry, one arm around her shoulders, as if to stop her breaking up, as these walls had broken up, these once-sturdy cottages. Bit by bit she quietened, if only through exhaustion and the sheer effort of such grief. Then he realized she was trying to speak, and strained to hear the words through her painful, strangled gasps. He was relieved when she sat up, at last, though her face was so blotched and swollen it alarmed him just to look at it.

'I . . . I *killed* him, don't you see?'

'Killed who?' he asked, confused.

'Rick, of course.' She punched the wall in frustration, as if maddened by his stupidity.

'What d'you mean, killed Rick?' He had a sudden horrific image of her pushing the boy under, holding him down until he . . . No. Unthinkable. And anyway Andrew would have seen her do it, or Penny known that she was there. He wiped her eyes with his handkerchief, as he had done when she was small. 'What are you trying to tell me, Pippa? I thought Rick went swimming with Andrew.'

'He did.'

390

'But you were there as well, you mean?'

She didn't answer, just grabbed his handkerchief and scoured her face with it.

'Pippa, I've got to get this straight. Were you anywhere near that lake when the accident happened?' He kept his tone deliberately calm. One of them must retain control.

She tried to pull away from him, but he kept hold of her arm. 'You haven't answered my question.'

'You don't understand! No one understands.'

'But how *can* we understand, when you won't explain or talk to us?'

She struggled against his restraining hand, then sat back on the wall, weary and defeated. There was silence for a while. The evening, too, seemed tired; its former verve now flagging; the gold and scarlet in the sky fading into a duller pinkish-grey. Daniel shut his eyes. He hadn't slept at all last night. Memories of Juliet began to seep back into his mind: erotic, traitorous images threatening to engulf him. Then, suddenly, he was aware of Pippa tensing, and became instantly alert. She was about to speak again.

'There's this . . . boy at school,' she began, her voice so low he could barely make it out.

'Yes?' he said encouragingly. She seemed to have changed the subject, but he must persuade her to continue, whatever she was saying.

'He's called . . . Rick.'

'Rick?'

'Yes.'

Another silence.

'Don't you think that's odd?'

'How d'you mean?'

'Well, most Richards aren't called Rick.'

'Aren't they?' He tried to keep the impatience from his voice. They were going even further off the subject. If Pippa *was* involved in some way in the drowning, perhaps she couldn't cope with the guilt, and was simply trying to divert him.

'No,' she insisted, 'they're not. In fact there are only two Richards in the whole of our year, and they're both called Richard, never Rick or Rich. There *is* a Rich in year seven, and a Ricky who's just left, but the only Rick is the one I'm talking about – and *your* Rick, here. Well, I think that's sort of . . . weird. Don't you?'

'Frankly, darling, no.' He was still wincing from the impact of 'his' Rick. 'I mean, Rick's a pretty ordinary name – not like Zachary or Silas or something. Anyway,' he prompted, shading his eyes to watch the last glints of the sun, 'what about him?'

She swallowed. 'He . . . he said he'd kill me if I . . .'

'He said *what*?' His grip tightened on her arm. Perhaps he hadn't heard right.

'Don't interrupt. Please. This is very . . . difficult. You see, I promised I'd never tell. He made me swear this oath. And he said he'd kill me if I broke it – push me on to the railway line just as a train was coming. And I knew he really meant it.' She peered nervously over her shoulder, as if expecting retribution even here. 'It got harder and harder, having to be so careful about what I said – you know, in case I let out something by mistake. I had to stop and think before I said anything to anyone, which was an awful sort of strain. So, in the end, it seemed safest not to speak at all. But that was hard as well. Especially as he just wouldn't leave me alone. I began to really hate him – so much, I wanted to kill *him*.' She put both hands across her mouth, appalled by the admission; continued speaking through her fingers, indistinctly.

'Then when we got here, this *other* Rick was . . . waiting for me. It was like the Rick at school had sent him to spy on me, or prove I'd never get away from him. Oh, I know they're nothing like each other. Rick's sixteen and he's *huge* – not just tall, but fat. He's got a sort of flabby face and these great big hands and feet. And he writes stuff on his arm in biro – you know, swear-words and threats of what he plans to do. And he rolls up his sleeve and flashes it at me, laughing in this horrid sneery way – though not if any teachers are around. He's all smarmy with the teachers, especially Miss O'Donovan. Anyway, he made me do these . . . these awful things. Like steal money from your wallet so he could buy cigarettes. And he kept asking me if you and Mum had any drink at home. And when I finally said yes, he told me to bring it in my school-bag and meet him outside Smith's. So I smuggled a bottle of whisky from the sideboard, but I was terrified you'd notice it had gone.'

She glanced at him, still fearing disapproval, but went rushing on again in an urgent panicked voice, not even pausing for breath. 'And he always took my dinner-money, so I couldn't have any lunch. He'd just say "*mine*", and hold his hand out. And he took my watch – the one you gave me for Christmas. You can't have forgotten that. You were ever so cross because I said I'd lost it. And then I lost my trainers, and you told me off for being careless. Well, that was Rick as well. And if ever I stood up to him, or tried to stop him taking things, he'd remind me of the railway line – describe what it would feel like to be electrocuted on the rails, then be run over by a train going at ninety miles an hour.'

'But Pippa, this . . . this is monstrous!' Daniel's cry of outrage was submerged in her next words. She was still reeling off her story, too fast for him to interrupt. The dam had finally burst, and all the things she had kept locked away inside were pouring, flooding out.

'Emma was the only one who knew. Well, she didn't know exactly, but she kept seeing Rick sneak up to me, so she asked me what was going on. At first she thought I fancied him.' Pippa screwed up her face in disgust. 'And because she was my best friend, Rick threatened her as well. He said he knew this Brixton gang and they'd beat her up on her way home from school, if she dared to open her mouth. Emma was so scared, she wouldn't go round with me any more. So I was always on my own. And then he started following me home. That was really frightening because he . . .'

'I'll *kill* the boy!' Daniel exploded. He gripped the wall, struggling to regain control. He would be no help to Pippa if he diverted his own guilty conscience into wild attacks on Rick. 'But we *asked* if you were being bullied,' he said, voice brusque from rage and shame. 'You must remember, surely. And we asked the Head the same thing. *And* Miss O'Donovan. Why ever didn't you *tell* someone?'

'How could I?' she yelled, her own fury surging up again. 'You haven't heard a single thing I've said! I've just *told* you, haven't I? Rick threatened to kill me if I said a word to anyone. But now your Rick has died instead. And it was me who killed him, because I wanted to kill the other Rick – Rick Scarth, he's called.' She shuddered at the name. 'I've never hated anyone before, but I hated *him*. I actually prayed for him to die. And he did die. But he was the wrong one, wasn't he? Except I hated your Rick, too, just because of his name. And because I couldn't get away from him – not even here, not even in the holidays. It brought it all back again – the awful things he'd made me do – other things I haven't even dared tell you yet. And the hate itself. Hate's horrible. It changes you. And I hated *you*, as well, because you sent me to the school. And because you hadn't the faintest idea of what was going on. I felt you *ought* to see. That if you cared about me, you *would* see. But you were always so busy with your work and stuff. And when we came here to the camp, I hated you even more. You kept sucking up to Rick and trying to get me to like him too. And the way you collected all those revolting bones. That was almost the worst thing of all. Rick said if I told on him, *I'd* end up as bones. And then he drew a coffin, and wrote my name on it.'

'Oh, Pippa, I . . . I'm . . .' He had no words. There *were* none. He longed to put his arms around her, to comfort her, commiserate, tell her how outraged he felt, how bitterly ashamed, but she had rebuffed him once already. She *hated* him – her father – and with reason. He was aghast at his own blindness and stupidity, wounded by her accusations, yet unable to deny them. It *had* been him who'd sent her to the school, championing it against Penny's reservations. He'd been more concerned about his daughter's academic prowess than about her happiness. Even during the last few months, when she was patently distressed, he had still nagged about her homework, pressured her to work hard, to meet *his* expectations. And yes, he was so busy with his own affairs, so preoccupied with petty problems, he hadn't seen the major problem overshadowing her life. Both he and Penny had remained in total ignorance of her weeks and weeks of torment. But there was less excuse for him, especially since his visit to Greystone Court, where he'd been forced to confront the trauma of his past which had led to his own self-imposed silence as a boy. Yet when Pippa had stopped speaking for a very similar reason, he'd failed to recognize the parallel. And how ironic that he had blamed his parents for their crass insensitivity, when he was every bit as culpable himself. It was like Sayers all over again. He had condemned him as a brute, then assaulted Juliet with much the same brutality.

Juliet! He gave a stifled exclamation as it dawned on him that Pippa didn't know about her, knew nothing about his affair. The 'someone' who was threatening her was not *him*, as he'd assumed, but a school bully called Rick Scarth.

'Don't *cry*!' said Pippa, breaking off her torrent of words to stare in consternation at his tears.

'I . . . I'm not.'

She pressed the damp and crumpled handkerchief into his hands, then tried awkwardly to put her arms around him. 'Oh, please don't cry! I can't bear it. I *don't* hate you, honestly. Not now – not any more. I'm just so glad I've told you. I couldn't go on any longer keeping it all to myself.'

He held her tight against him, hardly knowing who was comforting whom. Around them, dusk was falling; the sharp lines blurring between hill and sky, child and parent, innocence and guilt.

'I'm so desperately sorry, Pippa. It *was* my fault – you're right.'

'No, it wasn't. I only said that because I was so upset. Because I thought I'd killed Rick, and I wanted to blame *you*, instead.'

He shook her almost roughly. 'Rick *isn't* dead! Let's get that straight. He may pull through. They can do fantastic things in intensive care.' Suddenly, he remembered the injured woodpigeon, which had accompanied him on his headlong drive to Wales. It had lain passive on the seat beside him until a few miles past the border, when it started threshing around, clearly struggling to escape. He had pulled up in a lay-by and unwrapped it from the creased and smelly jacket, then walked with it to a gateway and held it out at arm's length, willing it to fly. It stood unsteadily a moment, its feet scrabbling on his palm, then, with a flurry of grey feathers, it launched itself from his hands. At first it dipped and floundered, as if it had lost the power of flight, then slowly seemed to gather strength, rising higher and higher until it wheeled away towards the distant hills.

He was about to tell Pippa the story, but decided it was too complicated, not to mention facile. There was no connection between bird and boy, and despite his optimistic assertion about Rick not being dead, he had no proof of that whatever. If Rick *had* drowned, then it was up to him to help Pippa cope, not offer her false comfort in the form of happy endings.

'Listen, darling, even if the news is . . . bad, you've got to understand that you're not to blame in any way at all. It was an accident – pure chance. Like the fact they were both called Rick.'

'But I'm still scared Rick Scarth will get me. What if he finds out that I've told you?'

'How could he? And anyway, I've no intention of letting you go back there. We'll find you a much nicer school – a smaller one – just girls, if you prefer. *You* can choose it this time.'

She hurled herself upon him, hugging him so fiercely he was almost knocked off balance. The intensity of that hug was proof how much she hated the place – as much as he had hated Greystone Court.

'I can really truly leave? You promise?'

'I promise. We'll go home tomorrow and start looking at prospectuses. And as for Scarth, I'll go and see Mrs Whittaker and insist that he's expelled.'

'*No!*' She drew away from him, shrank back against the wall.

'But he must be punished, darling. We can't let him get away with it.'

She didn't answer, just grazed her nails along the stone with a fretful rasping sound.

'He sounds really dangerous, Pippa, making threats like that. It's horrendous, inexcusable. After all, we've got to think of the other children. *You'll* be out of harm's way, but he's bound to pick on someone else.'

'I know, but . . .'

'But what?'

She continued scrabbling with her nails, dislodging shale and stones. 'Emma knows his father. She says he's horrid, too, and terribly cruel to Rick. He's even . . . No – I'm not allowed to tell you. I promised Emma I wouldn't.'

'All right, so he's had a rough time himself. But I still think we have a duty to . . .' His proposal petered out. He had just recalled the healer's words about the 'someone' who was threatening Pippa – '*someone with his own problems, who is suffering in his turn.*' So JB had been right – once more. But how could he have known about the sufferings of some vile young thug in Wandsworth, unless he possessed mysterious powers? And he, the rational Daniel Hughson, didn't believe in mysterious powers. He sat in silence, utterly confused. Where in God's name did his duty lie? To ensure this unspeakable bully was hauled up before the authorities and punished really severely, or to heed Pippa's plea for mercy, and prevent violence seeding violence in a never-ending chain? His mind felt far too small for all the emotions seething through it – vindictiveness and pity, anger and compassion, and an overriding fear that he might choose wrongly again. He and Pippa were sitting alone on a remote deserted hillside, yet more and more wan figures seemed to be clustering around them, arguing their case: Rick Scarth fighting his father; Rick Harris fighting for life; his parents seeking to justify themselves; even Sayers pleading some piteous past suffering. How did he resolve it all, how help Pippa best, without incurring still more guilt?

'*I led you to the lake myself. You needed to drown your fear, wash away your pain and grief from the past.*'

He rose slowly to his feet. He didn't believe in disembodied voices, any more than in irrational powers. Yet the voice was unmistakable – the healer's intonation, exactly as in London. So why hadn't Pippa reacted, or so much as raised her head?

'Pippa,' he said urgently, taking both her hands. 'Let's . . . let's go up to the lake.'

'The lake! No fear! I couldn't bear to go anywhere near it.'

'It'll be all right. I know.'

'But Rick almost drowned there, Daniel! It's the most beastly hateful place.'

'No. It's not. It needn't be.'

'And anyway, it's getting dark. We won't be able to see a thing.'

'There's a moon. And we'll get torches. I'll go back now and fetch them, tell Penny we're all right. No, you stay here. I shan't be long.' If she accompanied him to the tent, Penny would forbid her to go out again; would insist on her going straight to bed after such a hideous day. And as for his plan to take Pippa to the lake, he knew she'd refuse point-blank; regard it as reckless in the extreme. But there were more important things than sleep, or even safety.

'You won't be frightened, will you, darling, if I leave you for ten minutes? The camp's only just down there. See the lights?'

She nodded. 'I'll be okay, don't worry. But I still don't understand why we're going to the lake. What *for*?'

'Just trust me,' he pleaded. 'I know you've no reason to, but trust me anyway. And don't move from here. You promise?'

She shrugged. 'All right.'

He ran downhill towards the tents. The light was nearly gone, but he could make out just enough to see his way. Smoke was rising from Rainbow Lodge, and a buzz of earnest voices, but he raced on past and into Penny's tent. She looked pale and strained, her voice snappish as he crouched beside her.

'Whatever happened? You've been gone for simply ages! I've spent the whole day worrying – first Rick, then Pippa, and now you.'

'I'm all right.'

'And Pippa?'

'She's lots better now. I've managed to get her to talk.'

'Really, Daniel?' She sat up expectantly. 'What did she say? And where *is* she? You didn't leave her in that dreadful spooky cottage, did you?'

'No. She's waiting for me up the hill. I'm going back there now.'

'I'll come too.' She scrambled to her feet, started buttoning up her jacket.

'No, better not.'

'What for? I want to see her. And aren't you going to tell me what she said?'

'Later. There's a tremendous amount to tell, Penny. We can talk all night, if you want. But first I need a little longer on my own with her.'

'But why? Can't it wait till the morning? It's dark outside and she must be dead on her feet. For goodness sake let's bring her back and let her get some rest.'

'No, it must be now. I can't explain, but trust me.' That phrase again. Why *should* they bloody trust him, when he hadn't earned their trust? A lot of things would have to change, he realized – not just Pippa's school. He unrolled the double sleeping-bag, plumped up both the pillows. '*You* go to bed. You sound dead tired as well.'

'I am. Absolutely whacked. It's the worry more than anything.'

'There's been no more news of Rick, I take it?'

'It's still touch and go, I'm afraid. Zoe phoned the hospital half an hour ago.'

'Well, whatever the news, I think we ought to leave tomorrow. For Pippa's sake. She needs some peace and quiet. We *all* do, come to that. Let's go home and start again.'

'What d'you mean, start again?'

'I love you,' he said. It seemed as good an answer as any.

'Do you, Daniel? Really?'

'Why, have you been doubting it?'

'Yes,' she said impassively. 'I have.'

'I'm sorry.'

'Don't be.'

He seized her hand, kept hold of it. 'But I *am*! More sorry than you'll ever know.'

'What for?'

'Oh . . .' He paused. 'Everything and nothing.'

She climbed into the sleeping-bag, watched him zip it up. 'You're sounding really weird tonight.'

'It's rather a weird night.' He slipped the second pillow under her head, smoothed the rumpled sleeping-bag. 'Shall we kiss and make up, as Pippa used to say?'

She smiled. 'She hasn't said that for yonks.'

'Well, she hasn't let us kiss her for yonks.'

'No.' She let out a long frustrated sigh.

'Don't worry. She will.'

'You sure?'

'I'm sure.'

He leaned down and kissed her on the mouth. For one dis-quieting moment he smelt Juliet's seductive scent. He forced her out, made the kiss much gentler. Penny smelt of nettle tea and woodsmoke. 'I love you,' he repeated.

She didn't reply, didn't say 'I love you too.' She will, he thought, repeating to himself the same phrase he had used about Pippa. She *must*, he added desperately, suddenly realizing how presumptuous it was to expect unquestioning love from a wife, a daughter – anyone.

He backed away, began collecting up the things he needed: two sets of clothes, two warm and windproof anoraks, the torches, and a towel. 'I won't be long,' he reassured her, ducking out of the tent.

'Take care,' she shouted after him. 'And do please look after Pippa.'

'Yes,' he said. 'Of course.'

33

DANIEL STOOD AT THE WATER'S EDGE, beneath an immense
and daunting sky. The moon looked pocked and spongy; the
stars, in contrast, were sharp-edged glittering steel. All the familiar
night-noises seemed frozen in the silence like fossils in dark stone;
the only movement the flicker of pale moonlight on the black jet
of the lake. A second moon lay drowned there, trembling in the
trembling water. Pippa was trembling too; her hand sweaty in his
cool one, her teeth chattering, despite the warm night air. For
her, this place was evil, connected only with death. Somehow he
had to change that perception; make her understand that they had
to go deep down – beyond death and pain and evil, so that they
could emerge on the other side.

He squatted on the sand beside her, his face on a level with
hers. 'Pippa,' he said softly. 'We're going to wade into the water
and let it close above our heads. Just for a split second. That's all
it needs, so you musn't be afraid.'

She wrenched her hand away, all but spat out her retort. 'You're
mad!'

'Yes,' he said, slowly straightening up. 'But that's why we need
to do it – to leave the madness behind.'

'You mean, dr . . . drown like . . . like Rick?' Her face was
ashen in the moonlight, and her indignant voice had dwindled to
a stutter.

'No!' He took her hand again and clasped his other hand around
it, as if to provide a double shield. 'Not drown, but *live*, survive.'

'But why . . . why do we have to go into the water?'

'I . . . I don't know.' His certainty began to waver. *Was* he mad
– not in the healer's positive sense of seeing things he would be
blind to otherwise, but so hopelessly confused he was endangering
two more lives? Rick's limp body floated to the surface of his

mind: bluish-pale, deathly still, as Penny had described it. But that was part of the expiation. It was because Rick had almost drowned here that they, too, must go under. 'It's . . . difficult to explain. I just feel it's . . . right. And expected of us, somehow.' He was groping for the appropriate words, although she wouldn't understand them – sacrifice and ritual, total immersion.

'But suppose we *do* drown?' Pippa refused to meet his eyes. She kept fiddling with the switch on her torch, clicking it on and off, sending out panicked flashes of morse code. 'Andrew said the water's terribly deep. And it goes down all of a sudden, so you're out of your depth before you even realize.'

'No, it's not like that just here. This is the shallowest part. It's only a gentle slope, so we can wade in step by step. And I'll keep hold of you all the time. And if at any moment you want to stop, we'll turn back straight away, I promise.'

'But it's freezing cold, the water.'

'Yes,' he said. 'It *is* cold, but . . .' But what? There *were* no buts, no commonsense arguments. What he planned to do was foolhardy, ridiculous – and desperately important. 'Pippa, *please*. Do trust me. I'll look after you, I swear.' He could tell she didn't believe him, and why should she, when he had failed her up till now? But if they did this thing together, they would be bonded by it, changed.

They appeared to have reached stalemate. Pippa had turned her back, become only a shape in the darkness. Far away, a bird cried – one shrill call, then silence again. The moon and stars seemed to be retreating, obscured by swirls of mist; the lake growing blacker and more sinister as the night deepened around them.

He sat down on the shelf of rock where he had laid their anoraks; coaxed her to sit beside him. 'Listen, Pippa, this will probably sound far-fetched, but our going into the water may be a way of . . . of . . . saving Rick.'

She looked at him with total incredulity – even a touch of pity. He was forcing her to contend with a crazed father, on top of all the other horrors. Wouldn't it be kinder to forget the whole idea, turn back to safety, sanity? And yet he seemed held there by some external force, overpowering his own will. An age ago, he and the healer had sat in this same spot, and JB had talked about death. It seemed uncanny now, in light of what had happened. He could still recall the words: life was a whole series of deaths, but also a series of births, and you could be born into the present, which was a sort of resurrection. Whether it was true or false – or fatuous – a child of just thirteen couldn't be expected to make sense of it. He placed the palm of his hand on the smooth and solid surface of the rock, as if to ground himself, convince himself. JB had also told him that he'd been cured of his own sickness by what he'd described as a violent shock. Wasn't that what he was seeking himself – healing by ordeal? But JB had been discredited, and anyway, had he any right to inflict such a shock on Pippa, when she'd been traumatized enough? All that might result from it was that they'd both get chilled to the bone and wringing wet.

'Rick's probably dead already,' Pippa blurted out, her voice bitter and almost accusing.

'He could be, yes.'

'And even if he's not, how can we possibly save him by wading into the lake ourselves?'

He shook his head. He had reached the limits of language. 'Okay,' he said abruptly. 'Forget it. Let's go back. We'll tell Mum we went for a bracing walk and we're ready for a nice hot cup of tea.' Now *he* sounded bitter; the petulant thirteen-year-old who had failed to get his way. He snatched up their change of clothes, bundled them under his arm. They would no longer be required.

'No, wait.'

Wearily he sat down on the rock again, switching off his flash-light to save the batteries. The faint beam from Pippa's smaller torch cast a pool of sallow light. All other colour was extinguished – her radiant hair reduced to grey, as if the tragedy had aged her. He linked his hands together, pressing each finger hard into the knuckle; chafing one thumb with the other. He found it helped to focus on small tangible things: to trace the sore patch beneath his fingernail, or the callus on his palm. The silence seemed so endless, he wondered if they'd still be here at dawn; sitting dumb and motionless as the first streaks of light prised apart the dark crust of the sky.

'Okay, I'll *try*.'

He was startled when she spoke – her words grudgingly defiant, as if she was furious with herself for having changed her mind.

'But you're not to talk,' she ordered him. 'It's more scary when you talk.'

'All right. Hold my hand.' He kept his own voice calm; tried to reassure her through his firm protective hand-clasp. 'We'll just dip our feet in first, to get the feel of the water.'

'But what about our clothes?'

'We'll leave those on – well, all except our shoes and socks.' He helped her unlace her trainers; pulled off each sock in turn – the bumble-bee socks, he noticed, retrieved from her beloved dog. It, too, had died, in a way, though only since the loss of Rick had he fully understood her misery.

He removed his own shoes; the sand clammy-cool under his bare feet. Then he put his arm round her shoulder, drew her close against his side.

'All right?'

'Mm.'

They stepped from pale firm sand into dark and shifting water. She moved with him, unresisting, as if his intensity, his certainty – perhaps his very madness – had finally silenced her objections. Her first violent shudder of cold reverberated through his own body as they took a second step. The water was like a padlock snapped around their legs – cold and shock at once. Though neither said a word. They had left their torches on the shore and had only the wan stare of the moon to guide them, the remote unheeding stars. They were advancing with great caution, as if fearful of being sucked into the thick black slimy mud. There was no knowing what they might tread on; only a frightening sense of stepping into void. He was acutely aware of each part of his body as the cold steel manacles crept up, from ankle to calf to knee. His trouser-legs flapped dankly around his legs, and her jeans must feel the same – waterlogged and leaden. He kept a constant eye on her, experiencing every sensation twice over: *her* reaction and his. As the water reached her groin she let out a muffled gasp, and he registered the pain himself, a stabbing and relentless pain inching up her stomach. His taut grip on her arm must be hurting her as well, but it was life support, intensive care.

They continued in tense silence. Nothing existed any longer save the stretch of water in front of them – its density, its danger – and the black lid of the sky. The silence was a second lake:

vast, engulfing, infinite, and resenting their intrusion. They were churning up the moonlight as they walked; disturbing the dark shadows of the bleak surrounding hills. Time had been suspended, or changed to timeless time; a sense of night perpetual, without boundaries or dawn. It felt late – yet very early – as if life and colour, bird and beast had not yet been created, only darkness and immensity; the blind deaf world still waiting for its spark.

Pippa was clinging to him so tightly they had become one shape, one being – a strange amorphous creature with a single grotesque shadow. He was too numb to feel his individual limbs, but his mind had sharpened and all his senses were heightened, so that he could smell and taste the darkness; seemed to hear his silent footfalls on the soft bed of the lake.

He looked anxiously at Pippa again. The water was lapping at her chest, yet her face was set in a resolute expression and she had uttered no word of complaint.

'I think I'd better pick you up, Pippa, then you needn't put your head under – not if you don't want to.'

She gave the briefest nod. He lifted her awkwardly into his arms, so that her head was higher than his, well out of the water. It was more difficult to walk now. Her body restricted his view, blocked out the light of the moon. Though ironically it was not her bulk which impeded him, but his once lightweight summer clothes: the saturated trousers dragging at his legs; his shirtsleeves obscenely bloated, as if the flesh beneath had swollen. The cold had become a voracious mouth snapping at his chest and stomach, but still not satisfied; the black teeth eating into him, gnawing at his spine. Then, suddenly, the ground shelved steeply and he was floundering shoulder-deep. Pippa gave a cry, which involuntarily he echoed as icy water closed around his neck. It was impossible to stand now. The water was swirling about his legs, lifting his feet off the bottom, compelling him to float.

'Pippa . . .' he spluttered, trying to warn her that he was going to duck under, but the force of the water defeated him, mangling his words into meaningless gasps.

She appeared to understand, however, without the need for words. He felt her arms tighten round his neck; clasped her more securely in response. Then he shut his eyes and took a deep breath in. A rush of icy blackness surged past his lips and lashes; pounded in his ears, deadening all other sound. He continued plummeting down – deeper than it was possible to go, to the bottom of a bottomless lake. And yet still he went on down; back through the decades until he touched his childhood, felt it flinch with pain. He fought the pain, lungs bursting with the effort, chest constricted, heart hammering in fear. He had lost all sense of direction; lost his sight and speech. A blindfold sealed his eyes, a black rock stopped his mouth, and tight iron bands prevented him from breathing. And still darkness succeeded darkness, until, suddenly, he had left the pain behind; passed beyond a barrier where there was neither hate nor fear, and where all resistance was futile. He surrendered to the darkness, accepted it, embraced it; let himself be powerless: submerged, negated, drowned.

'*Daniel!* Come back.'

A voice was summoning him. He climbed towards the sound, gasping and struggling into life: a puny infant being born into the present. The voice rang out again, frightened but insistent, and much closer to him now.

'You were down so long! I was terrified. I thought you must have drowned.' Pippa was clutching on to his hair, pulling at his shirt-collar – the midwife tugging him wet and slimy into existence. He wanted to respond, to tell her that he *had* drowned, but he needed every shred of strength just to fight for his next breath. There was a fierce pain in his chest, and his stinging eyes had reduced his vision to a grey and flickering blur. He kept shaking his head and blinking, until Pippa's face jolted into focus. Water streamed from her hair, tiny droplets glistened on her lashes, and she was snatching gulps of air with the same urgency as he was. So she, too, had gone under. Or had he dragged her with him? Either way, they had both been down together; had both returned.

He positioned her more firmly in his arms and began to wade back slowly towards the shore, his clothes moulding themselves to his body, cumbersome and clammy as he laboured through the water beneath the cold breath of the sky.

All at once he stopped. There seemed to be a figure standing on the shore – a familiar figure, watching him – though it was so shadowy and blurred, it could be just a spur of rock silhouetted in the moonlight. Then suddenly, inexplicably, he felt flooding through his own body the motion of the wood-pigeon as it soared into the sky – uplifting and reviving him, as if he too had been released. He stood completely still, overwhelmed by the violence of the feelings: an exhilarating uprush of hope and reassurance.

'What's wrong?' asked Pippa, prodding his shoulder anxiously. 'Why have we stopped? What are you looking at?'

'N . . . nothing.'

The figure was already less distinct. Perhaps he'd only imagined it – a mere trick of the light, which he had clothed with flesh, with meaning. He set Pippa on her feet again. The water was barely knee-deep; no longer any hazard. She was looking at him fearfully, as if he might suggest some new preposterous exploit. He took her hand, chastened by its icy coldness. *Was* he just deluded: a blind and even dangerous man who had harmed all those around him, including an innocent bird?

Or had the healer come here to tell him Rick was saved?

He made himself wade on, eyes fixed obsessively on the shore. Only the moonlight now – shifting, insubstantial, confusing all certainties, rippling lake and sand alike. And the triumphant wings of the wood-pigeon still shocking through his body.